"What are they?"
said Philip

DAWN

Authorized Edition

DAWN

BY

H. RIDER HAGGARD

WITH FRONTISPIECE

P. F. COLLIER & SON
NEW YORK

9

" Our natures languish incomplete,
Something obtuse in this our star
Shackles the spirit's winged feet,
But a glory moves us from afar,
And we know that we are strong and fleet."

DAWN.

CHAPTER I.

"You lie; you always were a liar, and you always will be a liar. You told my father how I spent the money."

"Well, and what if I did? I had to look after myself, I suppose. You forget that I am only here on sufferance, whilst you are the son of the house. It does not matter to you, but he would have turned me out of doors," whined George.

"Oh, curse your fine words! It's you who forget, you swab. Ay, it's you who forget that you asked me to take the money to the gambling-tent, and made me promise that you should have half of what we won, but that I should play for both. What, are you beginning to remember now—is it coming back to you after a whole month? I am going to quicken your memory up presently, I can tell you; I have got a good deal to pay off, I'm thinking. I know what you are at; you want to play cuckoo, to turn 'Cousin Philip' out that 'Cousin George' may fill the nest. You know the old man's soft points, and you keep working him up against me. You think that you would like the old place when he's gone—ay, and I dare say that you will get it before you have done, but I mean to have my penn'orth out of you now, at any rate," and, brushing the tears of anger that stood in his brown eyes away with the back of his hand, the speaker proceeded to square up to George in a most determined way.

Now Philip, with his broad shoulders and his firm-knit frame, would, even at eighteen, have been no mean antagonist for a full-grown man; much more, then, did he look formidable to the lanky, overgrown stripling crouching against the corner of the wall that prevented his further retreat.

"Philip, you're not going to strike me, are you, when you know you are so much stronger?"

"Yes, I am, though; if I can't match you with my tongue, at any rate I will use my fists. Look out."

"Oh, Philip, don't! I'll tell your father."

"Tell him! why, of course you will, I know that; but you shall have something to lie about this time," and he advanced to the attack with a grim determination not pleasant for his cousin to behold.

Finding that there was no escape, George turned upon him with so shrill a curse that it even frightened from his leafy perch in the oak above the tame turtle-dove, intensely preoccupied as he was in cooing to a new-found mate. He did more than curse; he fought like a cornered rat, and with as much chance as the rat with a trained fox-terrier. In a few seconds his head was as snugly tucked away in the chancery of his cousin's arm as ever any property was in the court of that name, and, to speak truth, it seemed quite possible that when it emerged from its retreat it would, like the property, be much dilapidated and extensively bled.

Let us not dwell upon the scene; for George it was a very painful one, so painful that he never quite forgot it. His nose, too, was never so straight again. It was soon over, though to one of the parties the time went with unnatural slowness.

"Well, I think you've had about enough for once," soliloquized Philip, as he critically surveyed the writhing mass on the ground before him; and he looked a very handsome lad as he said it.

His curly black hair hung in waving confusion over his forehead, and flung changing lights and shadows into the depths of his brown eyes, whilst his massive and somewhat heavy features were touched into a more active life by the light of that pleasing excitement which animates nine men out of every ten of the Anglo-Saxon race when they are engaged in killing or hurting some other living creature. The face, too, had a certain dignity about it, a little of the dignity of justice; it was the face of one who feels that, if his action has been precipitate and severe, it has at any rate been virtuous. The full but clear-cut lips also had their own expression on them, half serious, half comical; humor, contempt, and even pity were blended in it. Altogether Philip Caresfoot's appearance in the moment of boyish vengeance was pleasing and not uninteresting.

Presently, however, something of the same change passed over his face that we see in the sky when a cloud passes over the sun; the light faded out of it. It was astonishing to note how dull and heavy—ay, more, how bad it made him look all in a breath.

"There will be a pretty business about this," he murmured, and then, administering a sharp kick to the prostrate and groaning form on the ground before him, he said: "Now, then, get up; I'm not going to touch you again. Perhaps, though, you won't be in quite such a hurry to tell lies about me another time, though I suppose that one must always expect a certain amount of lying from a half-bred beggar like you. Like mother, like son, you know."

This last sentence was accompanied by a bitter laugh, and produced a decided effect on the grovelling George, who slowly raised himself upon his hands, and, lifting his head, looked his cousin full in the face.

It was not the ghastly appearance of his mangled and blood-soaked countenance that made Philip recoil so sharply from the sight of his own handiwork—he had fought too often at school to be chicken-hearted about a little bloodshed; and, besides, he knew that his cousin was only knocked about, not really injured—but rather the intense and almost devilish malignity of the expression that hovered on the blurred features and in the half-closed eyes. But no attempt was made by George to translate the look into words, and indeed Philip felt that it was untranslatable. He also felt dimly that the hate and malice with which he was regarded by the individual at his feet was of a more concentrated and enduring character than most men have power to originate. In the lurid light of that one glance he was able, though he was not very clever, to pierce the darkest recesses of his cousin's heart, and to see his inmost thought, no longer through a veil, but face to face. And what he saw was sufficient to make the blood leave his ruddy cheek, and to fix his eyes into an expression of fear.

Next second George dropped his head onto the ground again, and began to moan in an ostentatious manner, possibly in order to attract some one whose footsteps could be plainly heard proceeding slowly down a shrubbery-path on the other side of the yard wall. At any rate, that was the effect produced; for next moment, before Philip could think of escape, had he wished to escape, a door in the wall was opened, and a gentleman, pausing on the threshold, surveyed the whole scene, with the assistance of a gold-mounted eye-glass, with some evident surprise and little apparent satisfaction.

The old gentleman, for he was old, made so pretty a picture, framed as he was in the arched doorway, and set off by a natural background of varying shades of green, that his general appearance is worth sketching as he stood. To begin with, he was dressed in the fashion of the commencement of this century, and, as has been said, old, though it was difficult to say how old. Indeed, so vigorous and comparatively youthful was his bearing that he was generally taken to be considerably under seventy, but, as a matter of fact, he was but a few years short of eighty. He was extremely tall, over six feet, and stood upright as a lifeguardsman; indeed, his height and stately carriage would alone have made him a remarkable-looking man, had there been nothing else unusual about him; but, as it happened, his features were as uncommon as his person. They were clear-cut and cast in a noble mould. The nose was large and aquiline; the chin, like his son Philip's, square and determined; but it was his eyes that gave a painful fascination to his countenance. They were steely blue, and glittered under the pent-house of his thick eyebrows, that, in striking contrast to the snow-white of his hair, were black in hue, as tempered steel glitters in a curtained room. It was those eyes, in conjunction with sundry little peculiarities of temper, that had earned for the old man the title of "Devil Caresfoot," a sobriquet in which he took peculiar pride. So pleased was he with it, indeed, that he caused it to be engraved in solid oak letters an inch long upon the frame of a life-sized and lifelike portrait of himself that hung over the staircase in the house.

"I am determined," he would say to his son, "to be known to my posterity as I was known to my contemporaries. The picture represents my person not inaccurately; from the nickname my descendants will be able to gather what the knaves and fools with whom I lived thought of my character. Ah! boy, I am wearing out; people will soon be staring at that portrait and wondering if it was like me. In a very few years I shall no longer be 'devil,' but 'devilled,'" and he would chuckle at his grim and ill-omened joke.

Philip felt his father's eyes playing upon him, and shrunk from them. His face had, at the mere thought of the consequences of his chastisement of his cousin, lost the beauty and animation that had clothed it a minute before; now it grew leaden and hard, the good died away from it altogether, and, instead of a young god bright with vengeance, there was nothing but a sullen youth with dull and frightened eyes. To his son, as to most people who came under his influence, "Devil" Caresfoot was a grave reality.

Presently the picture in the doorway opened its mouth and spoke in a singularly measured, gentle voice.

"You will forgive me, Philip, for interrupting your *tête-à-tête*, but may I ask what is the meaning of this?"

Philip returned no answer.

"Since your cousin is not in a communicative mood, George, perhaps you will inform me why you are lying on your face and groaning in that unpleasant and aggressive manner?"

George lifted his blood-stained face from the stones, and, looking at his uncle, groaned louder than ever.

"May I ask you, Philip, if George has fallen down and hurt himself, or if there has been an—an—altercation between you?"

Here George himself got up, and, before Philip could make any reply, addressed himself to his uncle.

"Sir," he said, "I will answer for Philip; there *has* been an altercation, and he in the scuffle knocked me down, and I confess," here he put his hand up to his battered face, "that I am suffering a good deal, but what I want to say is, that I beg you will not blame Philip. He thought that I had wronged him, and, though I am quite innocent, and could easily have cleared myself had he given me a chance, I must admit that appearances are to a certain extent against me—"

"He lies!" broke in Philip, sullenly.

"You will wonder, sir," went on the blood-stained George, "how I allowed myself to be drawn into such a brutal affair, and one so discreditable to your house. I can only say that I am very sorry,"—which indeed he was,—"and that I should never have taken any notice of his words—knowing how he would regret them on reflection—had he not in an unguarded moment allowed himself to taunt me with my birth. Uncle, you know the misfortune of my father's marriage, and that she was not his equal in birth, but you know, too, that she was my mother and I love her memory though I never saw her, and I could not bear to hear her spoken of like that, and I struck him. I hope that both you and he will forgive me; I cannot say any more."

"He lies again; he cannot speak the truth."

"Philip, will you allow me to point out," remarked his father, in his blandest voice, "that the continued repetition of the very ugly word 'lie' is neither narrative nor argument? Perhaps you will be so kind as to tell me your side of this story; you know I always wish to be perfectly impartial."

"He lied to you this morning about the money. It's true enough that I gambled away the ten pounds at Roxham fair, instead of paying it into the bank as you told me, but he persuaded me to it, and he was to have shared the profits if we won. I was a blackguard, and he was a bigger blackguard; why should I have all the blame and have that fellow continually shoved down my throat as a saint? And so I thrashed him, and that is all about it."

"Sir, I am sorry to contradict Philip, but indeed he is in error; the recollection of what took place has escaped him. I could, if necessary, bring forward evidence—Mr. Bellamy—"

"There is no need, George, for you to continue," and then, fixing his glittering eye on Philip—"It is very melancholy for me, having only one son, to know him to be such a brute, such a bearer of false witness, such an impostor as you are. Do you know that I have just seen Mr. Bellamy, the head clerk of the bank, and inquired if he knew anything of what happened about that ten pounds, and do you know what he told me?"

"No, I don't, and I don't want to."

"But I really must beg your attention: he told me that the day following the fair your cousin George came to the bank with ten pounds, and told him how you had spent the ten pounds I gave you to pay in, and that he brought the money, his own savings, to replace what you had gambled away; and Bellamy added that, under all the circumstances, he did not feel justified in placing it to my credit. What have you to say to that?"

"What have I to say? I have to say that I don't believe a word of it. If George had meant to do me a good turn he would have paid the money in and said nothing to Bellamy about it. Why won't you trust me a little more, father? I tell you that you are turning me into a scoundrel. I am being twisted up into a net of lies till I am obliged to lie myself to keep clear of ruin. I know what this sneak is at; he wants to work you into cutting me out of the property which should be mine by right. He knows your weaknesses—"

"My weaknesses, sir—my weaknesses!" thundered his father, striking his gold-headed cane onto the stones; "what do you mean by that?"

"Hush, uncle, he meant nothing," broke in George.

"Meant nothing! Then for an idle speech it is one that may cost him dear. Look you here, Philip Caresfoot, I know very well that our family has been quite as remarkable for its vices as its virtues, but for the last two hundred and fifty years we have been gentlemen, and you are not a gentleman; we have not been thieves, and you have proved yourself a thief; we have spoken the truth, and you are, what you are so fond of calling your cousin, who is worth two of you, a liar. Now listen. However imperious I may have grown in my old age, I can still respect the man who thwarts me, even though I hate him; but I despise the man who deceives me as I despise you, my son Philip—and I tell you this, and I beg you to lay it to heart, that if ever again I find that you have deceived me, by Heaven I will disinherit you in favor of—*oh, oh!*" and the old man fell back against the gray wall, pressing his hands to his breast and with the cold perspiration starting onto his pallid countenance.

Both the lads sprang forward, but before they reached him he had recovered himself.

"It is nothing," he said, in his ordinary gentle voice, "a trifling indisposition. I wish you both good-morning, and beg you to bear my words in mind."

When he was fairly gone, George came up to his cousin and laid his hand upon his arm.

"Why do you insist upon quarrelling with me, Philip? It always ends like this; you always get the worst of it."

But Philip's only reply was to shake him roughly off and to vanish through the door towards the lake. George regarded his departing form with a peculiar smile, which was rendered even more peculiar by the distortion of his swollen features.

CHAPTER II.

It is difficult to imagine any study that would prove more fascinating in itself, or more instructive in its issues, than the examination of the leading characteristics of individual families as displayed through a series of generations. But it is a subject that from its very nature is more or less unapproachable, since it is but little that we know even of our immediate ancestors. Occasionally in glancing at the cracking squares of canvas, many of which cannot even boast a name, but which alone remain to speak of the real and active life, the joys and griefs, the sins and virtues that centred in the originals of those hard daubs and of ourselves, we may light upon a face that about six generations since was the counterpart of the little boy upon our shoulder, or the daughter standing at our side. In the same way, too, partly through tradition and partly by other means, we are sometimes able to trace in ourselves and in our children the strong development of characteristics that distinguished the race centuries ago.

If local tradition and such records of their individual lives as remained are worthy of any faith, it is beyond a doubt that the Caresfoots of Bratham Abbey had handed down their own hard and peculiar cast of character from father to son unaffected in the main by the continual introduction of alien blood on the side of the mother.

The history of the Caresfoot family had nothing remarkable about it. They had been yeomen at Bratham from time immemorial, perhaps ever since the village had become a geographical fact; but it was on the dissolution of the monasteries that they first became of any importance in the county. Bratham Abbey, which had shared the common fate, was granted by Henry VIII. to a certain courtier, Sir Charles Varry by name. For two years the owner never came near his new possession, but one day he appeared in the village, and riding to the house of Farmer Caresfoot, which was its most respectable tenement, he begged him to show him the Abbey house and the lands attached. It was a dark November afternoon, and by the time the farmer and his wearied guest had crossed the soaked lands and reached the great gray house, the damps and shadows of the night had begun to curtain it and to render its appearance, forsaken as it was, inexpressibly dreary and lonesome.

"Damp here, my friend, is it not?" said Sir Charles, with a shudder, looking towards the lake, into which the rain was splashing.

"You are right, it be."

"And lonely, too, now that the old monks have gone."

"Ay, but they do say that the house be mostly full of the spirits of the dead," and the yeoman sank his voice to an awed whisper.

Sir Charles crossed himself and muttered, "I can well believe it," and then, addressing his companion—

"You do not know of any man who would buy an abbey with all its rights and franchises, do you, friend?"

"Not rightly, sir; the land is so poor it hath no heart in it; it doth scarce repay the tillage, and what the house is you may see. The curse of the monks is on it. But still, sir, if you have a mind to be rid of the place, I have a little laid by and a natural love for the land, having been bred on it, and taken the color of my mind and my stubby growth therefrom, and I will give you—" and this astutest of all the Caresfoots whispered a very small sum into Sir Charles's ear.

"Your price is very small, good friend; it doth almost vanish into nothing; and methinks the land that reared you cannot be so unkind as you would have me think. The monks did not love bad land, but yet, if thou hast it in the gold, I will take it; it will pay off a debt or two, and I care not for the burden of the land."

And so Farmer Caresfoot became the lawful owner of Bratham Abbey with its two advowsons, its royal franchises of treasure trove and deodand, and more than a thousand acres of the best land in Marlshire.

The same astuteness that had enabled this wise progenitor to acquire the estate enabled his descendants to stick tightly to it, and though, like other families, they had at times met with reverses, they never lost their grip on the Abbey property. During the course of the first half of the nineteenth century the land increased largely in value, and its acreage was considerably added to by the father of the present owner, a man of frugal mind, but with the family mania for the collection of all sorts of plate strongly developed. But it was Philip's father, "Devil" Caresfoot, who had, during his fifty years' tenure of the property, raised the family to its present opulent condition, firstly, by a strict attention to business and the large accumulations resulting from his practice of always living upon half his income; and secondly, by his marriage late in middle life with Miss Bland, the heiress of the neighboring Isleworth estates, that stretched over some two thousand acres of land.

This lady, who was Philip's mother, did not live long to enjoy her wealth and station. Her husband never spoke a rough word to her, and yet it is no exaggeration to say that she died of fear of him. The marriage had been one of convenience, not of affection; indeed poor Anna Bland had secretly admired the curate at Isleworth, and hated Mr. Caresfoot and his glittering eye. But she married him for all that, to feel that till she died that glance was always playing round her like a rapier in the hands of a skilled fencer. And very soon she did die, Mr. Caresfoot receiving her last words and wishes with the same exquisite and unmoved politeness that he had extended to every remark she had made to him in the course of their married life. Having satisfactorily eyed Mrs. Caresfoot off into a better world, her husband gave up all idea of further matrimonial ventures, and set himself to heap up riches. But a little before his wife's death, and just after his son's birth, an event had occurred in the family that had disturbed him not a little.

His father had left two sons, himself and a brother many years his junior. Now this brother was very dear to Mr. Caresfoot; his affection for him was the one weak point in his armor; nor was it rendered any the less sincere, but rather the more touching, by the fact that its object was little better than half-witted. It is therefore easy to imagine his distress and anger when he heard that a woman who had till shortly before been kitchen-maid at the Abbey House, and was now living in the village, had been confined of a son which she fixed upon his brother, whose wife she declared herself to be. Investigation only brought out the truth of the story; his weak-minded brother had been entrapped into a glaring *mésalliance.*

But Mr. Caresfoot proved himself equal to the occasion. So soon as his "sister-in-law," as it pleased him to call her sardonically, had sufficiently recovered, he called upon her. What took place at the visit never transpired, but next day Mrs. E. Caresfoot left her native place never to return, the child remaining with the father, or rather with the uncle. That boy was George. At the time when this story opens both his parents were dead: his father from illness resulting from entire failure of brain power, the mother from drink.

Whether it was that he considered that the circumstance of the lad's birth entitled him to peculiar consideration, or that he transferred to him the affection he bore his father, the result was that his nephew was quite as dear if not even dearer to Mr. Caresfoot than his own son. Not, however, that he allowed his preference to be apparent, save in the negative way that he was blind to faults in George that he was sufficiently quick to note in Philip. To observers this partiality seemed the more strange when they thought upon Philip's bonny face and form, and then noted how the weak-brained father and coarse-blooded mother had left their mark in George's thick lips, small, restless eyes, pallid complexion, and loose-jointed form.

When Philip shook off his cousin's grasp and vanished towards the lake, he did so with bitter wrath and hatred in his heart, for he saw but too clearly that he had deeply injured himself in his father's estimation, and, what was more, he felt that so much as he had sunk his side of the balance, by so much he had raised up that of George. He was inculpated; a Bellamy came upon the scene to save George, and, what was worse, an untruthful Bellamy; he was the aggressor, and George the meek in spirit with the soft answer that turneth away wrath. It was intolerable; he hated his father, he hated George. There was no justice in the world, and he had not wit to play rogue with such a one as his cousin. Appearances were always against him; he hated everybody.

And then he began to think that there was in the very next parish somebody whom he did not hate, but who, on the contrary, interested him, and was always ready to listen to his troubles, and he also became aware of the fact that whilst his mind had been thinking his legs had been walking, and that he was very near the abode of that person—almost at its gates, in short. He paused and looked at his watch; it had stopped at half-past eleven, the one blow that George had succeeded in planting upon him having landed on it, to the great detriment of both the watch and the striker's knuckles; but the sun told him that it was about half-past twelve, not too early to call. So he opened the gate, and, advancing up an avenue of old beeches to a square, red-brick house of the time of Queen Anne, boldly rang the bell.

Was Miss Lee at home? Yes, Miss Lee was in the green-house; perhaps Mr. Philip would step into the garden, which Mr. Philip did accordingly.

"How do you do, Philip? I'm delighted to see you; you've just come in time to help in the slaughter."

"Slaughter, slaughter of what—a pig?"

"No, green fly. I'm going to kill thousands."

"You cruel girl!"

"I dare say it is cruel, but I don't care. Grumps always said that I had no heart, and, so far as green fly are concerned, Grumps was certainly right. Now, just look at this lily. It is an auratum. I gave three-and-six (out of my own money) for that bulb last autumn, and now the bloom is not worth twopence, all through green fly. If I were a man I declare I should swear. Please swear for me, Philip. Go outside and do it, so that I mayn't have it on my conscience. But now for vengeance. Oh, I say, I forgot, you know, I suppose. I ought to be looking very sorry—"

"Why, what's the matter? Any one dead?"

"Oh, no, so much better than that. *It's got Grumps.*"

"Got her, what has got her? What is 'it'?"

"Why, Chancery, of course. I always call Chancery 'it.' I wouldn't take its name in vain for worlds. I am too much afraid. I might be made to 'show a cause why,' and then be locked up for contempt, which frequently happens after you have tried to 'show a cause.' That is what has happened to Grumps. She is now showing a cause; shortly she will be locked up. When she comes out, if she ever does come out, I think that she will avoid wards in Chancery in future; she will have too much sympathy with them, and too much practical experience of their position."

"But what on earth do you mean, Maria?" What has happened to Miss Gregson?" (*anglicè* Grumps.)

"Well, you remember one of my guardians, or rather his wife, got 'it' to appoint her my chaperon, but my other guardian wanted to appoint somebody else, and, after taking eighteen months to do it, he has moved the court to show that Grumps is not a 'fit and proper person.' The idea of calling Grumps improper. She nearly fainted at it, and swore that, whether she lived through it or whether she didn't, she would never come within a mile of me or any other ward if she could help it, not even the ward of an hospital. I told her to be careful, or she would be 'committing contempt,' which frightened her so that she hardly spoke again till she left yesterday. Poor Grumps! I expect she is on bread and water now; but if she makes herself half as disagreeable to the Vice-Chancellor as she did to me, I don't believe that they will keep her long. She'll wear the jailers out; she will wear the walls out; she will wear 'it' down to the bone; and then they will let her loose upon the world again. Why, there is the bell for lunch, and not a single green fly the less! Never mind, I will do for them to-morrow. How it would add to her sufferings in her lonely cell if she could see us going to a *tête-à-tête* lunch! Come on, Philip, come quick, or the cutlets will get cold, and I hate cold cutlets." And off she tripped, followed by the laughing Philip, who, by the way, was now looking quite handsome again.

Maria Lee was not very pretty at her then age—just eighteen—but she was a perfect specimen of a young English country girl; fresh as a rose, and sound as a bell, and endowed besides with a quick wit and a ready sympathy. She was essentially one of that class of Englishwomen who make the English upper middle class what it is—one of the finest and soundest in the world. Philip, following her into the house, thought that she was charming; nor, being a Caresfoot, and therefore having a considerable eye to the main chance, did the fact of her being the heiress to fifteen hundred a year in land detract from her charms.

The cutlets were excellent, and Maria ate three, and was very comical about the departed Grumps; indeed, anybody not acquainted with the circumstances would have gathered that that excellent lady was to be shortly put to the question. Philip was not quite so merry; he was oppressed both by recollections of what had happened and apprehensions of what might happen.

"What is the matter, Philip?" she asked, when they had left the table to sit under the trees on the lawn. "I can see that something is the matter. Tell me all about it, Philip."

And Philip told her what had happened that morning, laying bare all his heart-aches, and not even concealing his evil deeds. When he had done, she pondered awhile, tapping her little foot upon the turf.

"Philip," she said at last, in quite a changed voice, "I do not think that you are being well treated. I do not think that your cousin means kindly by you, but—but I do not think that you have behaved rightly either. I don't like that about the ten pounds; and I think that you should not have touched George; he is not so strong as you. Please try to do as your father—dear me, I am sure I don't wonder that you are afraid of him; I am—tells you, and regain his affection, and make it up with George; and, if you get into any more troubles, come and tell me about them before you do anything foolish; for though, according to Grumps, I am silly enough, two heads are better than one."

The tears stood in the lad's brown eyes as he listened to her. He gulped them down, however, and said:

"You are awfully kind to me; you are the only friend I have. Sometimes I think that you are an angel."

"Nonsense, Philip. If 'it' heard you talk like that, you would join Grumps. Don't let me hear any more such stuff;" but, though she spoke sharply, somehow she did not look displeased.

"I must be off," he said at length. "I promised to go with my father to see a new building on Reynold's farm. I have only twenty minutes to get home;" and rising they went into the house through a French window opening onto the lawn.

In the dining-room he turned, and, after a moment's hesitation, stuttered out:

"Maria, don't be angry with me, but may I give you a kiss?"

She blushed vividly.

"How dare you suggest such a thing?—but—but as Grumps has gone, and there is no new Grumps to refer to, and therefore I can only consult my own wishes, perhaps if you really wish to, Philip, why, Philip, you may."

And he did.

When he was gone she leaned her head against the cold marble mantel-piece.

"I do love him," she murmured, "yes, that I do."

CHAPTER III.

Philip was not very fond of taking walks with his father, since he found that in nine cases out of ten they afforded opportunities for inculcation of facts of the driest description with reference to estate management, or to the narration by his parent of little histories of which his conduct upon some recent occasion would adorn the moral. On this particular occasion the prospect was particularly unpleasant, for his father would, he was well aware, overflow with awful politeness; indeed, after the scene of the morning, it could not be otherwise. Oh, how much rather would he have spent that lovely afternoon with Maria Lee! Dear Maria, he would go and see her again the very next day.

When he arrived, some ten minutes after time in the antler-hung hall of the Abbey House, he found his father standing, watch in hand, exactly under the big clock, as though he was determined to make a note by double entry of every passing second.

"When I asked you to walk with me this afternoon, Philip, I, if my memory does not deceive me, was careful to say that I had no wish to interfere with any prior engagement. I was aware how little interest, compared with your cousin George, you take in the estate, and I had no wish to impose an uncongenial task. But, as you kindly volunteered to accompany me, I regret that you did not find it convenient to be punctual to the time you fixed. I have now waited for you for seventeen minutes, and let me tell you that at my time of life I cannot afford to lose seventeen minutes. May I ask what has delayed you?"

This long speech had given Philip the opportunity of recovering the breath that he had lost in running home. He replied promptly:

"I have been lunching with Miss Lee."

"Oh, indeed! Then I no longer wonder that you kept me waiting; and I must say that in this particular I commend your taste. Miss Lee is a young lady of good family, good manners, and means. If her estate went with this property it would complete as pretty a five thousand acres of mixed soil as there is in the county. Those are beautiful old meadows of hers, beautiful. Perhaps—" but here the old man checked himself.

On leaving the house they had passed together down a walk called the tunnel walk, on account of the arching boughs of the lime-trees that interlaced themselves overhead. At the end of this avenue, and on the borders of the lake, there stood an enormous but still growing oak, known as Caresfoot's Staff. It was the old squire's favorite tree, and the best-topped piece of timber for many miles round.

"I wonder," said Philip, by way of making a little pleasant conversation, "why that tree was called Caresfoot's Staff."

"Your ignorance astonishes me, Philip; but I suppose that there are some people who can live for years in a place and yet imbibe nothing of its traditions. Perhaps you know that the monks were driven out of these ruins by Henry VIII. Well, on the spot where that tree now stands there grew a still greater oak, a giant tree; its trunk measured sixteen loads of timber; which had, as tradition said, been planted by the first prior of the Abbey when England was still Saxon. The night the monks left a great gale raged over England. It was in October, when the trees were still full of leaf, and its fiercest gust tore the great oak from its roothold, and flung it into the lake. Look! do you see that rise in the sand, there, by the edge of the deep pool, in the eight-foot water? That is where it is supposed to lie. Well, the whole country-side said that it was a sign that the monks had gone forever from Bratham Abbey, and the country-side was right. But when your ancestor, old yeoman Caresfoot, bought this place and came to live here, in a year when there was a great black frost that set the waters of the lake like one of the new-fangled roads, he asked his neighbors, ay and his laboring folk, to come and dine with him and drink to the success of his purchase. It was a proud day for him, and when dinner was done and they were all mellow with strong ale, he bade them step down to the borders of the lake, as he would have them be witness to a ceremony. When they reached the spot they saw a curious sight, for there on a strong dray, and dragged by Farmer Caresfoot's six best horses, was an oak of fifty years' growth coming across the ice, earth, roots and all.

"On that spot where it now stands there had been a great hole, ten feet deep by fourteen square, dug to receive it, and into that hole Caresfoot Staff was tilted and levered off the dray. And when it had been planted, and the frozen earth well trodden in, your grandfather in the ninth degree brought his guests back to the old banqueting-hall, and made a speech which, as it was the first and last he ever made, was long remembered in the country-side. It was, put into modern English, something like this:

"'Neighbors,—Prior's Oak has gone into the water, and folks said that it was for a sign that the monks would never come back to Bratham, and that it was the Lord's wind that put it there. And, neighbors, as ye know, the broad Bratham lands and the fat marshes down by the brook passed by king's grant to a man that knew not clay from loam, or layer from pasturage, and from him they passed by the Lord's will to me, as I have asked you here to-day to celebrate. And now, neighbors, I have had a mind, and though it seem to you but a childish thing, yet I have a mind, and have set myself to fulfil it. When I was yet a little lad, and drove the swine out to feed on the hill yonder, when the acorns had fallen, afore Farmer Gyrton's father had gracious leave from the feoffees to put up the fence that doth now so sorely vex us, I found one day a great acorn, as big as a dow's egg, and of a rich and wondrous brown, and this acorn I bore home and planted in kind earth in the corner of my dad's garden, thinking that it would grow, and that one day I would hew its growth and use it for a staff. Now that was fifty long years ago, lads, and there where grew Prior's Oak, there, neighbors, I have set my Staff to-day. The monks have told us how in Israel every man planted his fig and his vine. For the fig I know not rightly what that is; but as for the vine, I will plant no creeping, clinging vine, but a hearty English oak, that, if they do but give it good room to breathe in, and save their heirloom from the axe, shall cast shade and throw acorns, and burst into leaf in the spring and grow naked in the winter, when ten generations of our children, and our children's children, shall have mixed their dust with ours yonder in the graveyard. And now, neighbors, I have talked too long, though I am better at doing than talking; but ye will even forgive me, for I will not talk to you again, though on this the great day of my life I was minded to speak. But I will bid you every man pledge a health to Caresfoot's Staff, and ask a prayer that, so long as it shall push its leaves, so long may the race of my loins be here to sit beneath its shade, and even mayhap when the corn is ripe and the moon is up, and their hearts grow soft towards the past, to talk with kinsman or with sweetheart of the old man who stuck it in this kindly soil.'"

The old squire's face grew tender as he told this legend of the forgotten dead, and Philip's young imagination summoned up the strange old-world scene of the crowd of rustics gathered in the snow and frost round this very tree.

"Philip," said his father, suddenly, "you will hold the yeoman's Staff one day; be like it of an oaken English heart, and you will defy wind and weather as it has done, and as your forebears have done. Come, we must go on."

"By the way, Philip," he continued, after a while, "you will remember what I said to you this morning—I hope that you will remember it, though I spoke in anger—never try to deceive me again, or you will regret it. And now I have something to say to you. I wish you to go to college and receive an education that will fit you to hold the position you must in the course of Nature one day fill in the county. The Oxford term begins in a few days, and you have for some years been entered at Magdalen College. I do not expect you to be a scholar, but I do expect you to brush off your rough ways and your local ideas, and to learn to become such a person both in your conduct and your mind as a gentleman of your station should be."

"Is George to go to college too?"

"No; I have spoken to him on the subject, and he does not wish it. He says very wisely that, with his small prospects, he would rather spend the time in learning how to earn his living. So he is going to be articled to the Roxham lawyers, Foster & Son, or rather Foster & Bellamy, for young Bellamy, who is a lawyer by profession, came here this morning, not to speak about you, but on a message from the firm to say that he is now a junior partner, and that they will be very happy to take George as articled clerk. He is a hard-working, shrewd young man, and it will be a great advantage to George to have his advice and example before him."

Philip assented, and went on in silence, reflecting on the curious change in his immediate prospects that this walk had brought to light. He was much rejoiced at the prospect of losing sight of George for a while, and was sufficiently intelligent to appreciate the advantages, social and mental, that the University would offer him; but it struck him that there were two things which he did not like about the scheme. The first of these was, that while he was pursuing his academical studies, George would practically be left on the spot—for Roxham was only six miles off—to put in motion any schemes he might have devised; and Philip was sure that he had devised schemes. And the second, that Oxford was a long way from Maria Lee. However, he kept his objections to himself. In due course they reached the buildings they had set out to examine, and the old squire, having settled what was to be done, and what was to be left undone, with characteristic promptitude and shrewdness, they turned homewards.

In passing through the shrubberies, on their way back to the house, they suddenly came upon a stolid-looking lad of about fifteen, emerging from a side-walk with a nest full of young blackbirds in his hand. Now, if there was one thing in this world more calculated than another to rouse the most objectionable traits of the old squire's character into rapid action, it was the discovery of boys, and more especially bird-nesting boys, in his plantations. In the first place, he hated trespassers; and in the second, it was one of his simple pleasures to walk in the early morning and listen to the singing of the birds that swarmed around. Accordingly, at the obnoxious sight he stopped suddenly, and, drawing himself up to his full height, addressed the trembling youth in his sweetest voice.

"Your name is, I believe—Brady—Jim Brady—correct me if I am wrong—and you have come here, you—you—young—villain—to steal my birds."

The frightened boy walked slowly backwards, followed by the old man with his fiery eyes fixed upon his face, till at last concussion against the trunk of a great tree prevented further retreat. Here he stood for about thirty seconds, writhing under the glance that seemed to pierce him through and through, till at last he could stand it no longer, but flung himself on the ground, roaring:

"Oh! don't ee, squire; don't ee now look at me with that 'ere eye. Take and thrash me, squire, but don't ee fix me so! I hayn't had no more nor twenty this year, and a nest of spinxes, and Tom Smith he's had fifty-two and a young owl. Oh! oh!"

Enraged beyond measure at this last piece of information, Mr. Caresfoot took his victim at his word, and, ceasing his ocular experiments, laid into the less honorable portion of his form with the gold headed Malacca cane in a way that astonished the prostrate Jim, though he was afterwards heard to declare that the squire's cane "warn't not nothing compared with the squire's eye, which wore a hot coal, it wore, and frizzled your innards as sich."

When Jim Brady had departed, never to return again, and the

old man had recovered his usual suavity of manner, he remarked to his son:

"There is some curious property in the human eye; a property that is, I believe, very much developed in my own. Did you observe the effect of my glance upon that boy? I was trying an experiment on him. I remember it was always the same with your poor mother. She could never bear me to look at her."

Philip made no reply, but he thought that, if she had been the object of experiments of that nature, it was not very wonderful.

Shortly after their return home he received a note from Miss Lee. It ran thus:

"My dear Philip: What *do* you think? Just after you had gone away, I got by the mid-day post, which Jones (the butcher) brought from Roxham, several letters, amongst them one from Grumps and one from Uncle Tom. Grumps has shown a cause. Why? 'It' said that she was not an improper person; but, for all that, she is so angry with Uncle Tom that she will not come back, but has accepted an offer to go to Canada as companion to a lady; so farewell Grumps.

"Now for Uncle Tom. 'It' suggested that I should live with some of my relations till I came of age, and pay them four hundred a year, which I think a good deal. I am sure it can't cost four hundred a year to feed me, though I have such an appetite. I had no idea they were so fond of me before; they all want me to come and live with them, except Aunt Chambers, who, you know, lives in Jersey. Uncle Tom says in his letter that he shall be glad if his daughters can have the advantage of my example, and of studying my polished manners (just fancy *my* polished manners! and I know, because little Tom, who is a brick, told me, that only last year he heard his father tell Emily—that's the eldest—that I was a dowdy, snub-nosed, ill-mannered miss, but that she must keep in with me and flatter me up). No, I will not live with Uncle Tom, and I will tell 'it' so. If I must leave my home, I will go to Aunt Chambers at Jersey. Jersey is a beautiful place for flowers, and one learns French there without the trouble of learning it; and I like Aunt Chambers, and she has no children, and nothing but the memory of a dear departed. But I don't like leaving home, and feel very much inclined to cry. *Hang* the Court of Chancery, and Uncle Tom and his interference too!—*there!* I suppose you can't find time to come over to-morrow morning to see me off? Good-by, dear Philip.

"Your affectionate friend,

"Maria Lee."

Philip did manage to find time next morning, and came back looking very disconsolate.

CHAPTER IV.

PHILIP went to college in due course, and George departed to learn his business as a lawyer at Roxham, but it will not be necessary for us to enter into the details of their respective careers during this period of their lives.

At college Philip did fairly well, and, being a Caresfoot, did not run into debt. He was, as his great bodily strength gave promise of, a first-class athlete, and for two years stroked the Magdalen boat. Nor did he altogether neglect his books, but his reading was of a desultory and out-of-the-way order, and much directed towards the investigation of mythical subjects. Fairly well liked amongst the men with whom he mixed, he could hardly be called popular; his temperament was too uncertain for that. At times he was the gayest of the gay, and then when the fit took him he would be plunged into a state of gloomy depression that might last for days. His companions, to whom his mystical studies were a favorite jest, were wont to assert that on these occasions he was preparing for a visit from his familiar, but the joke was one that he never could be prevailed upon to appreciate. The fact of the matter was that these fits of gloom were constitutional with him, and very possibly had their origin in the state of his mother's mind before his birth, when her whole thoughts were colored by her morbid and fanciful terror of her husband, and her frantic anxiety to conciliate him.

During the three years that he spent at college, Philip saw but little of George, since, when he happened to be down at Bratham, which was not often, for he spent most of his vacations abroad, George avoided coming there as much as possible. Indeed, there was a tacit agreement between the two young men that they would see as little of each other as might be convenient. But, though he did not see much of him himself, Philip was none the less aware that George's influence over his father was, if anything, on the increase. The old squire's letters were full of him and of the admirable way in which he managed the estate, for it was now practically in his hands. Indeed, to his surprise and somewhat to his disgust, he found that George began to be spoken of indifferently with himself as the "young squire." Long before his college days had come to an end Philip had determined that he would do his best, as soon as opportunity offered, to reduce his cousin to his proper place, not by the violent means to which he had resorted in other days, but rather by showing himself to be equally capable, equally assiduous, and equally respectful and affectionate.

At last the day came when he was to bid farewell to Oxford for good, and in due course he found himself in a second-class railway carriage—thinking it useless to waste money, he always went second—and bound for Roxham.

Just before the train left the platform at Paddington, Philip was agreeably surprised out of his meditations by the entry into his carriage of an extremely elegant and stately young lady, a foreigner as he judged from her strong accent when she addressed the porter. With the innate gallantry of twenty-one, he immediately laid himself out to make the acquaintance of one possessed of such proud, yet melting blue eyes, such lovely hair, and a figure that would not have disgraced Diana; and, with this view, set himself to render her such little services as one fellow-traveller can offer to another. They were accepted reservedly at first, then gratefully, and before long the reserve broke down entirely, and this very handsome pair dropped into a conversation as animated as the lady's broken English would allow. The lady told him that her name was Hilda von Holtzhausen, that she was of a German family, and had come to England to enter a family as companion, in order to obtain a perfect knowledge of the English language. She had already been to France and acquired French; when she knew English, then she had been promised a place as schoolmistress under government in her own country. Her father and mother were dead, and she had no brothers or sisters, and very few friends.

Where was she going to? She was going to a place called Roxham; here it was written on the ticket. She was going to be companion to a dear young lady, very rich, like all the English, whom she had met when she had travelled with her French family to Jersey—a Miss Lee.

"You don't say so!" said Philip. "Has she come back to Rewtham?"

"What! do you, then, know her?"

"Yes—that is, I used to three years ago. I live in the next parish."

"Ah! then perhaps you are the gentleman of whom I have heard heard her to speak, Mr. Car-es-foot, whom she did seem to appear to love; is not that the word?—to be very fond, you know."

Philip laughed, blushed, and acknowledged his identity with the gentleman whom Miss Lee "did seem to appear to love."

"Oh! I am glad; then we shall be friends, and see each other often—shall we not?"

He declared unreservedly that she should see him very often.

From Fräulein von Holtzhausen Philip gathered in the course of their journey a good many particulars about Miss Lee. It appeared that, having attained her majority, she was coming back to live at her old home at Rewtham, whither she had tried to persuade her Aunt Chambers to accompany her, but without success, that lady being too much attached to Jersey to leave it. During the course of a long stay on the island the two girls had become fast friends, and the friendship had culminated in an offer being made by Maria Lee to Fräulein von Holtzhausen to come and live with her as companion, a proposal that exactly suited the latter.

The mention of Miss Lee's name had awakened pleasant recollections in Philip's mind—recollections that, at any other time, might have tended towards the sentimental; but, when under fire from the blue eyes of this stately foreigner, it was impossible for him to feel sentimental about anybody save herself. "The journey is over all too soon," was the secret thought of each as they stepped on to the Roxham platform. Before they had finally said good-by, however, a young lady with a dainty figure, in a shady hat and pink and white dress, came running along the platform.

"Hilda, Hilda, here I am! How do you do, dear? Welcome home," and she was about to seal her welcome with a kiss, when her eye fell upon Philip standing by.

"Oh, Philip!" she cried with a blush, "don't you know me? Have I changed much? I should have known you anywhere; and I am glad to see you, awfully glad (excuse the slang, but it is such a relief to be able to say 'awful' without being pulled up by Aunt Chambers). Just think, it is three years since we met. Do you remember Grumps? How do I look? Do you think you will like me as much as you used to?"

"I think that you are looking the same dear girl that you always used to look, only you have grown very pretty, and it is not possible that I shall like you more than I used to."

"I think they must teach you to pay compliments at Oxford, Philip," she answered, flushing with pleasure, "but it is all rubbish for you to say that I am pretty, because I know I am not"—and then, confidentially, glancing round to see that there was nobody within hearing (Hilda was engaged with a porter in looking after her things): "Just look at my nose, and you will soon change your mind. It's broader, and flatter, and snubbier than ever. I consider that I have got a bone to pick with Providence about that nose. Ah! here comes Hilda. Isn't she lovely! There's beauty for you if you like. She hasn't got a nose. Come and show us to the carriage. You will come and lunch with us to-morrow, won't you? I am so glad to get back to the old house again; and I mean to have such a garden! 'Life is short, and joys are fleeting,' as Aunt Chambers always says, so I mean to make the best of it whilst it lasts. I saw your father yesterday. He is a dear old man, though he has such awful eyes. I never felt so happy in my life as I do now. Good-by. One o'clock." And she was gone, leaving Philip with something to think about.

Philip's reception at home was cordial and reassuring. He found his father considerably aged in appearance, but as handsome and upright as ever, and to all appearance heartily glad to see him.

"I am glad to see you back, my boy," he said. "You come to take your proper place. If you look at me, you will see that you won't have long to wait before you take mine. I can't last much longer, Philip, I feel that. Eighty-two is a good age to have reached. I have had my time, and put the property in order, and now I suppose I must make room. I went with the clerk, old Jakes, and marked out my grave yesterday. There's a nice little spot the other side of the stone that they say marks where old yeoman Caresfoot, who planted Caresfoot's Staff, laid his bones, and that's where I wish to be put, in his good company. Don't forget that when the time comes, Philip. There's room for another if you care to keep it for yourself, but perhaps you will prefer the vault."

"You must not talk of dying yet, father. You will live many years yet."

"No, Philip; perhaps one, perhaps two, not more than two; perhaps a month, perhaps not a day. My life hangs on a thread now." And he pointed to his heart. "It may snap any day, if it gets a strain. By the way, Philip, you see that cupboard? Open it! Now, you see that stoppered bottle with the red label? Good. Well now, if you ever see me taken with an attack of the heart (I have had once since you were away, you know, and it nearly carried me off), you run for that as hard as you can go, and give it me to drink, half at a time. It is a tremendous restorative of some sort, and old Caley says that, if I do not take it when the next attack comes, there'll be an end of 'Devil Caresfoot';" and he rapped his cane energetically on the oak floor.

"And so, Philip, I want you to go about and make yourself thoroughly acquainted with the property, so that you may be able to take things over when I die without any hitch. I hope that you will be careful and do well by the land. Remember that a big property like this is a sacred trust."

"And now there are two more things that I will take this opportunity to say a word to you about. First, I see that you and your cousin George don't get on well, and it grieves me. You have always had a false idea of George, always, and thought that he was underhand. Nothing could be more mistaken than such a notion. George is a most estimable young man, and my dear brother's only son. I wish you would try to remember that, Philip—blood is thicker than water, you know—and you will be the only two Caresfoots left when I am gone. Now, perhaps you may think that I intend enriching George at your expense, but that is not so. Take this key and open the top drawer of that secretaire, and give me that bundle. This is my will. If you care to look over it, and can understand it—which is more than I can—you will see that everything is left to you, with the exception of that outlying farm at Holston, those three Essex farms that I bought two years ago, and twelve thousand pounds in cash. Of course, as you know, the Abbey House, and the lands immediately round, are entailed—it has always been the custom to entail them for many generations. There, put it back. And now the last thing is, I want you to get married, Philip. I should like to see a grandchild in the house before I die. I want you to marry Maria Lee. I like the girl. She comes of a good old Marlshire stock—our family married into hers in the year 1703. Besides, her property would put yours into a ring fence. She is a sharp girl too, and quite pretty enough for a wife. I hope you will think it over, Philip."

"Yes, father; but perhaps she will not have me. I am going to lunch there to-morrow."

"I don't think you need be afraid, Philip; but I won't keep you any longer. Shake hands, my boy. You'll perhaps think of your old father kindly when you come to stand in his shoes. I hope you will, Philip. We have had many a quarrel, and sometimes I have been wrong, but I have always wished to do my duty by you, my boy. Don't forget to make the best of your time at lunch to-morrow."

Philip went out of his father's study considerably touched by the kindness and consideration with which he had been treated, and not a little relieved to find his position with reference to his succession to the estate so much better than he had anticipated, and his cousin George's so much worse.

"That red-haired fox has plotted in vain," he thought, with secret exultation. And then he set himself to consider the desirability of falling in with his father's wishes as regarded marriage. Of Maria he was, as the reader is aware, very fond; indeed, a few years before he had been in love with her, or something very like it; he knew too that she would make him a very good wife, and the match was one that in every way commended itself to his common sense and his interests. Yes, he would certainly take his father's advice. But every time he said this to himself—and he said it pretty often that evening—there would arise before his mind's eye a vision of the sweet blue eyes of Miss Lee's stately companion. What eyes they were, to be sure! It made Philip's blood run warm and quick merely to think of them; indeed, he could almost find it in his heart to wish that Hilda was Maria and Maria in Hilda's shoes.

What between thoughts of the young lady he had set himself to marry, and of the young lady he did not mean to marry, but whose eyes he admired, Philip did not sleep so well as usual that night.

CHAPTER V.

Philip did not neglect to go to luncheon at Rewtham House, and a very pleasant luncheon it was; indeed, it would have been difficult for him to have said which he found the pleasantest—Maria's cheerful chatter and flattering preference, or Hilda's sweet and gracious presence.

After luncheon, at Maria's invitation he gave Fräulein von Holtzhausen her first lesson in writing in English characters; and to speak truth he found the task of guiding her fair hand through the mysteries of the English alphabet a by no means uncongenial occupation. When he came away his admiration of Hilda's blue eyes was more pronounced than ever; but, on the other hand, so was his conviction that he would be very foolish if he allowed it to interfere with his intention of making Maria Lee his wife.

He who would drive two women thus in double harness must needs have a light hand and a ready lash, and it is certainly to the credit of Philip's cleverness that he managed so well as he did. For as time went on he discovered his position to be this: Both Hilda and Maria were in love with him, the former deeply and silently, the latter openly and ostensibly. Now, however gratifying this fact might be to his pride, it was in some ways a thorny discovery, since he dared not visibly pay his attentions to either. For his part he returned Hilda von Holtzhausen's devotion to a degree that surprised himself; his passion for her burnt him like a fire, utterly searing away the traces of his former affection for Maria Lee. Under these circumstances, most young men of twenty-one would have thrown prudence to the winds and acknowledged, either by acts or words, the object of their love; but not so Philip, who even at that age was by no means deficient in the characteristic caution of the Caresfoot family. He saw clearly that his father would never consent to his marriage with Hilda, nor, to speak truth, did he himself at all like the idea of losing Miss Lee and her estates.

On the other hand, he knew Hilda's proud and jealous mind. She was no melting beauty who would sigh and submit to an affront, but, for all her gracious ways, at heart a haughty woman, who, if she reigned at all, would reign like Alexander, unrivalled and alone. That she was well aware of her friend's tendresse for Philip the latter very shortly guessed; indeed, as he suspected, Maria was in the habit of confiding to her all her hopes and fears connected with himself, a suspicion that made him very careful in his remarks to that young lady.

The early summer passed away whilst Philip was still thinking over his position, and the face of the country was blushing with all the glory of July, when one afternoon he found himself, as he did pretty frequently, in the shady drawing-room at Miss Lee's. As he entered, the sound of voices told him that there were other visitors beside himself, and, as soon as his eyes had grown accustomed to the light, he saw his cousin George, together with his partner Mr. Bellamy, and a lady with whom he was not acquainted.

George had improved in appearance somewhat since we last saw him meeting with severe treatment at his cousin's hands. The face had filled up a little, with the result that the nose did not look so hooked, nor the thick lips so coarse and sensual. The hair, however, was as red as ever, and as for the small, light-blue eyes, they twinkled with the added sharpness and lustre that four years of such experience of the shady side of humanity as can be gathered in a lawyer's office, is able to give to the student of men and manners.

So soon as Philip had said how-do-you-do to Maria and Hilda, giving to each a gentle pressure of the hand, George greeted him with warmth.

"How are you, Philip? Delighted to see you. How is my uncle? Bellamy saw him this morning, and thought that he did not look well."

"I certainly did think, Mr. Philip," said the gentleman alluded to, a very young-looking, apple-faced little man, with a timid manner, who stood in the background nervously rubbing his dry hands together—"I certainly did think that the squire looked aged when I saw him this morning."

"Well, you see, Mr. Bellamy, eighty-two is a good age, is it not?" said Philip, cheerfully.

"Yes, Mr. Philip, a good age, a very good age, for the *next heir*," and Mr. Bellamy chuckled softly somewhere down in his throat, and retreated a little.

"He is getting facetious," broke in George; "that marriage has done that for him. By the way, Philip, do you know Mrs. Bellamy? she has only been down here a fortnight, you know. What, no! Then you have a pleasure to come" (raising his voice a little so that it might be heard at the other end of the room), "a very clever woman, and as handsome as she is clever."

"Indeed! I must ask you to introduce me presently, Mr. Bellamy. I only recently heard that you were married."

Mr. Bellamy blushed and twisted and was about to speak, when George cut in again.

"No, I dare say you didn't; sly dog, Bellamy; do you know what he did? I introduced him to a lady when we were up in town together last Christmas. I was dreadfully hard hit myself, I can assure you, and as soon as my back was turned he went and cut me out of the water—and turned my adored into Mrs. Bellamy."

"What are you taking my name in vain about, Mr. Caresfoot?" said a rich, low voice behind them.

"Bless me, Anne, how softly you move! You quite startled me." said little Mr. Bellamy, putting on his spectacles in an agitated manner.

"My dear, a wife, like an embodied conscience, should always be at her husband's shoulder, especially when he does not know it."

Bellamy made no reply, but looked as though the sentiment was one of which he did not approve; meantime the lady repeated her question to George, and the two fell into a bantering conversation. Philip, having dropped back a little, had an opportunity of carefully observing Mrs. Bellamy, an occupation not without interest, for she was certainly worthy of notice.

About twenty years of age, and of medium height, her figure was so finely proportioned and so roomily made that it gave her the appearance of being taller than she really was. The head was set squarely on the shoulders, the hair was cut short, and clustered in ringlets over the low, broad brow; while the clearly-carved Egyptian features and square chin gave the whole face a curious expression of resoluteness and power. The eyes were heavily-lidded and grayish-green in hue, with enormously large dark pupils that had a strange habit of expanding and contracting without apparent reason.

Gazing at her, Philip was at a loss to know whether this woman so bizarrely beautiful fascinated or repelled him; indeed, neither then nor at any future time did he succeed in deciding the question. Whilst he was still contemplating, and wondering how Bellamy of all people in the world had managed to marry such a woman, and what previous acquaintance George had had with her, he saw the lady whisper something to his cousin, who at once turned and introduced him.

"Philip," he said, "let me introduce you to the most charming lady of my acquaintance, Mrs. Bellamy."

Philip bowed and expressed himself delighted, whilst the lady courtesied with a mixture of grace and dignity that became her infinitely well.

"Your cousin has often spoken to me of you, Mr. Caresfoot, but he never told me—" here she hesitated, and broke off.

"What did he never tell you, Mrs. Bellamy? Nothing to my disadvantage, I hope."

"On the contrary, if you wish to know," she said, in that tone of flattering frankness which is sometimes so charming in a woman's mouth, "he never told me that you were young and handsome. I fancied you forty at least."

"I should dearly like to tell you, Mrs. Bellamy, what my cousin George never told *me;* but I won't, for fear I should make Bellamy jealous.

"Jealousy, Mr. Caresfoot, is a luxury that *my* husband is not allowed to indulge in; it is very well for lovers, but what is a compliment in a lover becomes an impertinence in a husband. But if I keep you here much longer, I shall be drawing the enmity of Miss Lee, and—yes, of Fräulein von Holtzhausen, too, onto my devoted head, and, as that is the only sort of jealousy I have any fear of, or indeed any respect for, being as it is the expression of the natural abhorrence of one woman for another, I had rather avoid it."

Philip followed the direction of her sleepy eyes, and saw that both Miss Lee and Hilda appeared to be put out. The former was talking absently to Mr. Bellamy, and glancing continually in the direction of that gentleman's wife. The latter, too, whilst appearing to listen to some compliment from George, was gazing at Mrs. Bellamy, with a curious look of dislike and apprehension on her face.

"You see what I mean ; Fräulein von Holtzhausen actually looks as though she were afraid of me. Can you fancy any one being afraid of me, except my husband, of course?—for as you know, when a woman is talking of men, her husband is *always* excepted. Come, we must be going; but, Mr. Caresfoot, bend a little nearer; if you will accept it from such a stranger, I want to give you a bit of advice—make your choice pretty soon, or you will lose them both."

"What do you mean—how do you know—"

"I mean nothing at all, or just as much as you like, and for the rest I use my eyes. Come, let us join the others."

A few minutes later Hilda put down her work, and, declaring that she felt hot, threw open the French window and went out into the garden, whither, on some pretext or other, Philip followed her.

"What a lovely woman that is!" said Mrs. Bellamy, with enthusiasm, to Miss Lee, so soon as Philip was out of earshot. "Her *tout ensemble* positively kills one. I feel plain and dowdy as a milkmaid alongside of a Court-beauty when I am in the room with her. Don't you, Miss Lee?"

"Oh, I don't know, I never thought about it, but of course she is lovely and I'm plain, so there is no possibility of a comparison between us."

"Well, I think you rate yourself rather low, if you will allow me to say so; but most women would but 'poorly satisfy the sight' of a man when she was present. I know that I should not care to trust my admirer (if I had one), however devoted he might be, for one single day in her company; would you?"

"I really don't know: what *do* you mean?"

"Mean, Miss Lee, why I mean nothing at all; what should I mean, except that beauty is a magnet which attracts all men; it serves them for a standard of morality and a test of right and wrong. Men are different from women. If a man is faithful to one of us, it is only because no other woman of sufficient charm has come between him and us. You can never trust a man."

"What dreadful ideas you have!"

"Do you think so? I hope not. I only speak what I have observed. Take the case of Fräulein von Holtzhausen, for instance. Did you not notice that whilst she was in the room the eyes of the three gentlemen were all fixed upon her, and as soon as she leaves it one of them follows her, as the others would have done had they not been forestalled? One cannot blame them; they are simply following a natural law. Any other man would do the same where such a charming person is concerned."

"I certainly did not notice it; indeed, to speak the truth, I thought that they were more occupied with you—"

"With me! why, my dear Miss Lee, *I* don't set up for being good-looking. What a strange idea! But I dare say you are right, it is only one of my theories, based upon my own casual observations; and, after all, men are not a very interesting subject, are they? Let's talk of something more exciting—dresses, for instance."

But poor Maria was too uncomfortable and disturbed to talk of anything else, so she collapsed into silence, and shortly after Mr. and Mrs. Bellamy and George made their adieux.

Meanwhile Philip and Hilda had been walking leisurely down the shrubberies adjoining the house.

"Why have you come out?" she asked in German—a language he understood well.

"To walk with you. Why do you speak to me in German?"

"Because it is my pleasure to do so, and I never asked you to walk with me. You are wanted in the drawing-room; you had better go back."

"No, I won't go, Hilda; that is, not until you have promised me something."

"Do not call me Hilda, if you please. I am the Fräulein von Holtzhausen. What is it you want me to promise?"

"I want you to meet me this evening at nine o'clock in the summer-house."

"I think, Mr. Caresfoot, that you are forgetting a little what is due to me, to yourself, and—to Miss Lee."

"What do you mean by due to Miss Lee?"

"Simply that she is in love with you, and that you have encouraged her in her affection; you need not contradict me; she tells me all about it."

"Nonsense, Hilda; if you will meet me to-night, I will explain everything; there is no need for you to be jealous."

She swept round upon him, tossing her head, and stamping her dainty foot upon the gravel.

"Mr. Caresfoot," she said, "once and for all I am not jealous, and I will not meet you; I have too much respect for myself, and too little for you," and she was gone.

Philip's face, as he stood looking after her, was not pleasant to see; it was very hard and angry.

"Jealous, is she? I will give her something to be jealous for, the proud minx;" and in his vexation he knocked off the head of a carnation with his stick.

"Philip, what *are* you doing? Those are my pet Australian carnations; at least, I think they are Australian. How can you destroy them like that?"

"All right, Maria; I was only plucking one for you. Won't you put it in your dress? Where are the others?"

"They have all gone. Come in, it is so hot out there; and tell me what you think of Mrs. Bellamy."

"I think that she is very handsome and very clever. I wonder where Bellamy picked her up."

"I don't know; I wish he hadn't picked her up at all. I don't like her; she says unpleasant things; and, though I have only seen her three times, she seems to know all about me and everybody else. I am not very quick; but do you know just now I thought that she was insinuating that you were in love with Hilda; that's not true, is it, Philip? Don't think me forward if I ask you if that is true, and if I say that, if it is, it is better that I should know it. I shan't be angry, Philip;" and the girl stood before him to await his answer, one hand pressed against her bosom to still the beating of her heart, whilst with the other she screened her blushing brow.

And Philip too stood face to face with her sweet self, with conscience, and with opportunity. "Now," whispered conscience, "is the time, before very much harm is done; now is the acceptable time to tell her all about it, and, whilst forbidding her love, to enlist her sympathy and friendship. It will be wrong to encourage her affection; when you ardently love another woman, you cannot palter any more." "Now," whispered opportunity, shouldering conscience aside, "is the time to secure her, her love, and her possessions, and to reward Hilda for her pride. Do not sacrifice yourself to an infatuation; do not tell her about Hilda—it would only breed jealousies; you can settle with her afterwards. Take the goods the gods provide you."

All this and more passed through his mind; and he had made his choice long before the rich blood that mantled in the lady's cheek had sunk back to the true breast from whence it came.

Oh, instant of time born to color all eternity to thine own hue, for this man thou hast come and gone! Oh, fleeting moment, bearing desolation or healing on thy wings, how the angels, in whose charge lie the souls of men, must tremble and turn pale, as they mark thy flight through the circumstances of a man's existence, and thence taking thy secrets with thee away to add thy fateful store to the records of his past!

He took her hand, the hand that was pressed upon her bosom.

"Maria," he said, "you should not get such ideas into your head. I admire Hilda very much, and that is all. Why, dear, I have always looked upon myself as half engaged to you—that is, so far as I am concerned; and I have only been waiting till circumstances would allow me to do so, to ask you if you think me worth marrying."

For a while she made no reply, but only blushed the more; at last she looked up a little.

"You have made me very happy, Philip." That was all she said.

"I am very glad, dear, that you can find anything in me to like; but if you do care for me, and think me worth waiting for, I am going to ask something of your affection; I am going to ask you to trust me as well as to love me. I do not, for reasons that I will not enter into, but which I beg you to believe are perfectly straightforward, wish anything to be said of our engagement at present, not even to your friend Hilda. Do you trust me sufficiently to agree to that?"

"Philip, I trust you as much as I love you, and for years I have loved you with all my heart. And now, dear, please go; I want to think."

In the hall a servant gave him a note; it was from Hilda, and ran thus:

"I have changed my mind. I will meet you in the summer-house this evening. I have something to say to you."

Philip whistled as he read it.

"Devilish awkward," he thought to himself; "if I am going to marry Maria, she must leave this. But I cannot bear to part with her. I love her! I love her!"

CHAPTER VI.

It was some time before Philip could make up his mind whether or no he would attend his tryst with Hilda. In the first place, he felt that it was an unsafe proceeding generally, inasmuch as moonlight meetings with so lovely a person might, should they come to the knowledge of Miss Lee, be open to misconstruction; and particularly because, should she show the least tenderness towards him, he knew in his heart that he could not trust himself, however much he might be engaged in another direction. At twenty-one the affections cannot be outraged with impunity, but have an awkward way of asserting themselves, ties of honor notwithstanding.

But as a rule, when in our hearts we wish to do anything, that thing must be bad indeed if we cannot find a satisfactory excuse for doing it; and so it was with Philip. Now, thought he to himself, would be his opportunity to inform Hilda of his relations with Maria Lee, and to put an end to his flirtation with her; for, ostensibly at any rate, it was nothing more than a very serious flirtation —that is to say, though there had been words of love, and even on her part a passionate avowal of affection, wrung in an unguarded moment from the depths of her proud heart, there had been no formal engagement. It was a thing that must be done, and now was the time to do it. And so he made up his mind to go.

But when, that night, he found himself sitting in the appointed place, and waiting for the coming of the woman he was about to discard, but whom he loved with all the intensity of his fierce nature, he began to view the matter in other lights, and to feel his resolution oozing from him. Whether it was the silence of the place that told upon his nerves, strained as they were with expectation,—for silence, and more especially silence by night, is a great unveiler of realities,—or the dread of bitter words, or the prescience of the sharp pang of parting—for he knew enough of Hilda to know that, what he had to say once said, she would trouble him no more—whether it was these things, or whatever it was that affected him, he grew most unaccountably anxious and depressed. Moreover, in this congenial condition of the atmosphere of his mind, all its darker and hidden characteristics sprang into a vigorous growth. Superstitions and presentiments crowded in upon him. He peopled his surroundings with the shades of intangible deeds that yet awaited doing, and grew afraid of his own thoughts. He would have fled from the spot, but he could not fly; he could only watch the flicker of the moonlight upon the peaceful pool beside him, and—wait.

At last she came with quick and anxious steps, and, though but a few minutes before he had dreaded her coming, he now welcomed it eagerly. For our feelings, of whatever sort, when directed towards each other, are so superficial as compared with the intensity of our fears when we are terrified by calamity, or the presence, real or fancied, of the unknown, that in any moment of emergency, more especially if it be of a mental kind, we are apt to welcome our worst enemy as a drowning man welcomes a spar.

"At last," he said, with a sigh of relief. "How late you are!"

"I could not get away. There were some people to dinner;" and then, in a softened voice, "How pale you look! Are you ill?"

"No, only a little tired."

After this there was silence, and the pair stood facing one another, each occupied with their own thoughts, and each dreading to put them into words. Once Philip made a beginning of speech, but his voice failed him; the beating of his heart seemed to choke his utterance.

At length she leaned, as though for support, against the trunk of a pine-tree, in the boughs of which the night-breeze was whispering, and spoke in a cold clear voice.

"You asked me to meet you here to-night. Have you anything to say to me? No, do not speak; perhaps I had better speak first. I have something to say to you, and what I have to say may influence whatever is in your mind. Listen; you remember what passed between us nearly a month ago, when I was so weak as to let you see how much I loved you?"

Philip bowed his head in assent.

"Very good. I have come here to-night, not to give you any lover's meeting, but to tell you that no such words must be spoken again, and that I am about to make it impossible that they should be spoken either by you or by me. I am going away from here, *never*, I hope, to return."

"Going away!" he gasped. "When?"

Here was the very thing he hoped for coming to pass, and yet the words that should have been so full of comfort fell upon him cold as ice, and struck him into misery.

"When! why, to-morrow morning. A relation of mine is ill in Germany, the only one I have. I never saw him, and care nothing for him, but it will give me a pretext; and, once gone, I shall not return. I have told Maria that I must go. She cried about it, poor girl."

At these words, all recollection of his purpose passed out of Philip's mind; all he realized was that, unless he could alter her determination, he was about to lose the woman he so passionately adored, and whose haughty pride was to him in itself more charming than all poor Maria's gentle love.

"Hilda, do not go," he said, seizing her hand, which she immediately withdrew; "do not leave me. You know how I love you."

"And why should I not leave you, even supposing it to be true that you do love me? To my cost I love you, and am I any longer to endure the daily humiliation of seeing myself, the poor German companion who has nothing but her beauty, put aside in favor of another whom I also love? You say you love me, and bid me stay; now, tell me what is your purpose towards me? Do you intend to try to take advantage of my infatuation to make me your mistress? It is, I am told, a common thing for such proposals to be made to women in my position, whom it would be folly for wealthy gentlemen to marry. If so, abandon that idea; for I tell you, Philip, that I would rather die than so disgrace my ancient name to gratify myself I know you money-loving English do not think very much of race unless the bearers of the name are rich; but we do; and, although you would think it a *mésalliance* to marry me, I, on the other hand, should not be proud of an alliance with you. Why, Philip, my ancestors were princes of royal blood when yours still herded the swine in these woods. I can show more than thirty quarterings upon my shield, each the mark of a noble house, and I will not be the first to put a bar sinister across them. Now, I have spoken plainly, indelicately perhaps, and there is only one more word to be said between us, and that word is *good-by*," and she held out her hand.

He did not seem to see it; indeed, he had scarcely heard the latter part of what she said. Presently he lifted his face, and it bore traces of a dreadful inward struggle. It was deadly pale, and great black rings had painted themselves beneath the troubled eyes.

"Hilda," he said, hoarsely, "don't go; I cannot bear to let you go. I will marry you."

"Think of what you are saying, Philip, and do not be rash. I do not wish to entrap you into marriage. You love money. Remember that Maria, with all her possessions, asks nothing better than to become your wife, and that I have absolutely nothing but my name and my good looks. Look at me," and she stepped out into a patch of moonlight that found its way between the trees, and, drawing the filmy shawl she wore from her head and bare neck and bosom, stood before him in all the brightness of her beauty, shaded as it was, and made more lovely by the shadows of the night.

"Examine me very carefully," she went on, with bitter sarcasm, "look into my features and study my form and carriage, or you may be disappointed with your bargain, and complain that you have not got your money's worth. Remember, too, that an accident, an illness, and at the best the passage of a few years, may quite spoil my value as a beautiful woman, and reflect, before I take you at your word."

Philip had sat or rather crouched himself down upon the log of a tree that lay outside the summer-house, and covered his face with his hand, as though her loveliness was more than he could bear to look upon. Now, however, he raised his eyes and let them dwell upon her scornful features.

"I had rather," he said slowly—"I had rather lose my life than lose you; I love you so that I would buy you at the price even of my honor. When will you marry me?"

"What, have you made up your mind so quickly? Are you sure? Then,"—and here she changed her whole tone and bearing, and passionately stretched out her arms towards him,—"my dearest Philip, my life, my love, I will marry you when you will."

"To-morrow?"

"To-morrow, if you like!"

"You must promise me something first."

"What is it?"

"That you will keep the marriage a complete secret, and bear another name until my father's death. If you do not, he will most probably disinherit me."

"I do not like your terms, Philip. I do not like secret marriages; but you are giving up much to marry me, so I suppose I must give up something to marry you."

"You solemnly promise that nothing shall induce you to reveal that you are my wife until I give you permission to do so?"

"I promise—that is, provided you do not force me to in self-defence."

Philip laughed.

"You need not fear that," he said. "But how shall we arrange about getting married?"

"I can meet you in London."

"Very well. I will go up early to-morrow, and get a license, and then on Wednesday I can meet you, and we can be married."

"As you will, Philip; where shall I meet you?"

He gave her an address which she carefully noted down.

"Now," she said, "you must go, it is late. Yes, you may kiss me now. There, that will do, now go." In another minute he was gone.

"I have won the game," she mused; "poor Maria. I am sorry for her, but perhaps hers is the better part. She will get over it, but mine is a sad fate; I love passionately, madly, but I do not trust the man I love. Why should our marriage be so secret? He cannot be entangled with Maria, or she would have told me." And she stretched out her arms towards the path by which he had left her, and cried aloud, in the native tongue that sounded so soft upon her lips, "Oh, my heart's darling! if I could only trust you as well as I love you, it is a happy woman that I should be to-night."

CHAPTER VII.

Nothing occurred to interfere with the plan of action decided on by Hilda and Philip; no misadventure came to mock them, dashing the Tantalus cup of joy to earth before their eyes. On the contrary, within forty-eight hours of the conversation recorded in the last chapter, they were as completely and irrevocably man and wife as a special license and the curate of a city church, assisted by the clerk and the pew-opener, could make them.

Then followed a brief period of such delirium as turned the London lodgings, dingy and stuffy as they were in the height of the hot summer, into an earthly paradise, a garden of Eden, into which, alas! the serpent had no need to seek an entrance. But, as was natural, when the first glory of realized happiness was beginning to grow faint on their horizon, the young couple turned themselves to consider their position, and found in it, mutually and severally, many things that did not please them. For Philip, indeed, it was full of anxieties, for he had many complications to deal with. First there was his secret engagement to Maria Lee, of which, be it remembered, his wife was totally ignorant, and which was in itself a sufficiently awkward affair for a married man to have upon his hands. Then there was the paramount need of keeping his marriage with Hilda as secret as the dead, to say nothing of the necessity of his living, for the most part, away from his wife. Indeed, his only consolation was that he had plenty of money on which to support her, inasmuch as his father had, from the date of his leaving Oxford, made him an allowance of one thousand a year.

Hilda had begun to discover that she was not without her troubles. For one thing, her husband's fits of moodiness and fretful anxiety troubled her, and led her, possessed as she was with a more than ordinary share of womanly shrewdness, to suspect that he was hiding something from her. But what chiefly vexed her proud nature was the necessity of concealment, and all its attendant petty falsehoods and subterfuges. It was not pleasant for Hilda Caresfoot to have to pass as Mrs. Roberts, and to be careful not to show herself in public places in the daytime, where there was a possibility of her being seen by any one who might recognize in her striking figure the lady who had lived with Miss Lee in Marlshire. It was not pleasant to her to be obliged to reply to Maria Lee's affectionate letters, full as they were of entreaty for her return, by epistles that had to be forwarded to a country town in a remote district of Germany to be posted, and which were in themselves full of lies that, however white they might have seemed under all the circumstances, she felt in her conscience to be very black indeed. In short, there was in their union none of that sense of finality and of security that is, under ordinary circumstances, the distinguishing mark of marriage in this country; it partook rather of the nature of an illicit connection.

At the end of a fortnight of wedded bliss all these little things had begun to make themselves felt, and in truth they were but the commencement of evils. For, one afternoon, Philip, for the first time since his wedding, tore himself away from his wife's side, and paid a visit to a club to which he had been recently elected. Here he found no less than three letters from his father, the first requesting his return, the second commanding it in exceptionally polite language, and the third—which, written in mingled anxiety and anger, had just arrived—coolly announcing his parent's intention, should he not hear of him by return, of setting detective officers to work to discover his whereabouts. From this letter it appeared, indeed, that his cousin George had already been despatched to London to look for him, and on reference to the hall porter he discovered that a gentleman answering to his description had already inquired for him several times.

Cursing his own folly in not having kept up some communication with his father, he made the best of his way back to his lodgings, to find Hilda waiting for him somewhat disconsolately.

"I am glad you have come back, love," she said, drawing him towards her till his dark curls mingled with her own fair locks, and kissing him upon the forehead. "I have missed you dreadfully. I don't understand how I can have lived all these years without you."

"I am afraid, dear, you will have to live without me for a while now; listen," and he read her the letters he had just received.

She listened attentively till he had finished.

"What are you going to do?" she asked, with some anxiety in her voice.

"Do? Why of course I must go home at once."

"And what am I to do?"

"Well, I don't know; I suppose that you must stop here."

"That will be pleasant for me, will it not?"

"No, dear, it will be pleasant neither for you nor me; but what can I do? You know the man my father is to deal with; if I stop here in defiance of his wishes, especially as he has been anxious about me, there is no knowing what might not happen. Remember, Hilda, that we have to deal with George, whose whole life is devoted to secret endeavors to supplant me. If I were to give him such an opportunity as I should by stopping away now, I should deserve all I got, or rather all I did not get."

Hilda sighed and acquiesced; had she been a softer-minded woman she would have wept and relieved her feelings, but she was not soft-minded. And so, before the post went out, he wrote an affectionate letter to his father, expressing his sorrow at the latter's anxiety and at his own negligence in not having written to him, the fact of the matter being, he said, that he had been taken up with visiting some of his Oxford friends and had not till that afternoon been near his club to look for letters. He would, however, he added, return on the morrow, and make his apologies in person.

This letter he handed to his wife to read.

"Do you think that will do ?" he asked, when she had finished.

"Oh, yes!" she replied, with a touch of her old sarcasm, "it is a masterpiece of falsehood."

Philip looked very angry, and fumed and fretted; but he made no reply, and on the following morning he departed to Bratham Abbey.

"Ah, Philip, Philip!" said his father, under the mellow influence of his fourth glass of port, on the night of his arrival. "I know well enough what kept you up in town. Well, well, I don't complain; young men will be young men; but don't let these affairs interfere with the business of life. Remember Maria Lee, my boy; you have serious interests in that direction, interests that must not be trifled with, interests that I have a right to expect you will *not* trifle with."

His son made no reply, but sipped his wine in silence, aching at his heart for his absent bride, and wondering what his father would say did he really know what had "kept him in town."

After this, matters went on smoothly enough for a month or more; since, fortunately for Philip, the great Maria Lee question—a question that the more he considered it the more thorny did it appear—was for the moment shelved by the absence of that young lady on a visit to her aunt in the Isle of Wight. Twice during that month he managed, on different pretexts, to get up to London and visit his wife, whom he found as patient as was possible under the circumstances, but anything but happy. Indeed, on the second occasion, she urged on him strongly the ignominy of her position, and even begged him to make a clean breast of it to his father, offering to undertake the task herself. He refused equally warmly, and some sharp words ensued, to be, however, quickly followed by a reconciliation.

On his return from this second visit, Philip found a note signed "affectionately yours, Maria Lee," waiting for him, which announced that young lady's return, and begged him to come over to lunch on the following day.

He went—indeed, he had no alternative but to go; and again fortune favored him in the person of a diffident young lady who was stopping with Maria, and who never left her side all that afternoon, much to the disgust of the latter and the relief of Philip. One thing, however, he was not spared, and that was the perusal of Hilda's last letter to her friend, written apparently from Germany, and giving a lively description of the writer's daily life and the state of her uncle's health, which, she said, precluded all possibility of her return. Alas! he already knew its every line too well; for, as Hilda refused to undertake the task, he had but a week before drafted it himself. But Philip was growing hardened in deception, and found it possible to read it from end to end, and speculate upon its contents with Maria without blush or hesitation.

But he could not always expect to find Miss Lee in the custody of such an obtuse friend; and, needless to say, it became a matter of very serious importance to him to know how he should treat her. It occurred to him that his safest course might be to throw himself upon her generosity and make a clean breast of it; but when it came to the point he was too weak thus to expose his shameful conduct to the woman whose heart he had won, and to whom he was bound by every tie of honor that a gentleman holds sacred.

He thought of the scornful wonder with which she would listen to his tale, and preferred to take the risk of greater disaster in the future to the certainty of present shame. In the end, he contrived to establish a species of confidential intimacy with Maria, which, whilst it somewhat mystified the poor girl, was not without its charm, inasmuch as it tended to transform the every-day Philip into a hero of romance.

But in the main Maria was ill-suited to play heroine to her wooer's hero. Herself as open as the daylight, it was quite incomprehensible to her why their relationship should be kept such a dark and mysterious secret, or why, if her lover gave her a kiss, it should be done with as many precautions as though he were about to commit a murder.

She was a very modest maiden, and in her heart believed it a wonderful thing that Philip should have fallen in love with her—a thing to be very proud of; and she felt it hard that she should be denied the gratification of openly acknowledging her lover, and showing him off to her friends, after the fashion that is so delightful to the female mind.

But, though this consciousness of the deprivation of a lawful joy set up a certain feeling of irritation in her mind, she did not allow it to override her entire trust in and love for Philip. Whatever he did was no doubt wise and right; but, for all that, on several occasions she took an opportunity to make him acquainted with her views of the matter, and to ask him questions that he found it increasingly difficult to answer.

In this way, by the exercise of ceaseless diplomacy, and with the assistance of a great deal of falsehood of the most artistic nature, Philip managed to tide over the next six months; but at the end of that time the position was very far from improved. Hilda was chafing more and more at the ignominy of her position; Maria was daily growing more and more impatient to have their engagement made public; and last, but by no means least, his father was almost daily at him on the subject of Miss Lee, till at length he succeeded in wringing from him the confession that there existed some sort of understanding between Maria and himself.

Now, the old squire was a shrewd man of the world, and was not therefore slow to guess that what prevented this understanding from being openly acknowledged as an engagement was some entanglement on his son's part. Indeed, it had recently become clear to him that London had developed strange attractions for Philip. That this entanglement could be marriage was, however, an idea that never entered into his head: he had too good an opinion of his son's common-sense to believe it possible that he would deliberately jeopardize his inheritance by marrying without his permission. But Philip's reticence and obstinacy annoyed him excessively. "Devil" Caresfoot was not a man accustomed to be thwarted; indeed, he had never been thwarted in his life, and he did not mean to be now. He had set his heart upon this marriage, and it would have to be a good reason indeed that could turn him from his purpose.

Accordingly, having extracted the above information, he said no more to Philip, but proceeded to lay his own plans.

That very afternoon he commenced to put them into action. At three o'clock he ordered the carriage and pair, a vehicle that was rarely used, giving special directions that the coachman should see that his wig was properly curled. An ill-curled wig had before now been known to produce a very bad effect upon Mr. Caresfoot's nerves, and also upon its wearer's future prospects in life.

At three precisely the heavy open carriage, swung upon C. springs and drawn by two huge grays, drew up in front of the hall-door, and the squire, who was as usual dressed in the old-fashioned knee-breeches, and carried in his hand his gold-headed cane, stepped solemnly into it, and seated himself exactly in the middle of the back seat, not leaning back, as is the fashion of our degenerate days, but holding himself bolt upright. Any more imposing sight than this old gentleman presented thus seated, and moving at a stately pace through the village street, it is impossible to conceive; but it so oppressed the very children that fear at the spectacle (which was an unwonted one, for the squire had not thus driven abroad in state for some years) overcame their curiosity, and at his approach they incontinently fled.

So soon as the carriage had passed through the drive-gates of the Abbey, the squire ordered the coachman to drive to Rewtham House, whither in due course he safely arrived.

He was ushered into the drawing-room, whilst a servant went in search of Miss Lee, whom she found walking in the garden.

"A gentleman to see you, miss."

"I am not at home. Who is it?"

"Mr. Caresfoot, miss!"

"Oh, why didn't you say so before?" and taking it for granted that Philip had paid her an unexpected visit, she started off for the house at a run.

"Why, Philip," she exclaimed, as she swung open the door, "this *is* good of you—oh—oh!" for at that moment Mr. Caresfoot senior appeared from behind the back of the door where he had been standing by the fireplace, and made his most imposing bow.

"That, my dear Maria, was the first time that I have heard myself called Philip for many a long year, and I fear that that was by accident; neither the name nor the blush were meant for me; now, were they?"

"I thought," replied Maria, who was still overwhelmed with confusion, "I thought that it was Philip, your son, you know; he has not been here for so long."

"With such a welcome waiting him, it is indeed wonderful that he can keep away;" and the old squire bowed again with such courtly grace as to drive what little self-possession remained to poor Maria after her flying entry entirely out of her head.

"And now, my dear," went on her visitor, fixing his piercing eyes upon her face, "with your permission, we will sit down and have a little talk together. Won't you take off your hat?"

Maria took off her hat as suggested, and sat down meekly, full under fire of the glowing eyes that had produced such curious effects upon subjects so dissimilar as the late Mrs. Caresfoot and Jim Brady. She could, however, think of nothing appropriate to say.

"My dear," the old gentleman continued presently, "the subject upon which I have taken upon myself to speak to you is one very nearly affecting your happiness and also of a delicate nature. My excuse for alluding to it must be that you are the child of my old friend—ah! we were great friends fifty years ago, my dear—and that I have myself a near interest in the matter. Do you understand me?"

"No, not quite."

"Well then, forgive an old man, who has no time to waste, if he comes to the point. I mean I have come to ask you, Maria, if any understanding or engagement exists between Philip and yourself?"

The eyes were full upon her now, and she felt that they were drawing her secret from her as a corkscrew does a cork. At last it came out with a pop.

"Yes, we are engaged."

"Thank you, my dear. How long have you been engaged?"

"About eight months."

"And why has the affair been kept so secret?"

"I don't know; Philip wished it. He told me not to tell any one. I suppose that I should not by rights have told you."

"Make yourself easy, my dear. Philip has already told me that there was an understanding between you; I only wanted to hear the confirmation of such good news from your own lips. Young men are great coxcombs, my dear, and apt to fancy things where ladies are concerned. I am rejoiced to hear that there is no mistake on his part."

"I am so glad that you are pleased," she said shyly.

"Pleased, my dear!" said the old gentleman, rising and walking up and down the room in his excitement, "pleased is not the word for it. I am more rejoiced than if some one had left me another estate. Look here, Maria, I had set my heart upon this thing coming to pass; I have thought of it for years. I loved your father, and you are like your father, girl; ay, I love you too, because you are a generous, honest woman, and will bring a good strain of blood into a family that wants generosity—ay, and I sometimes think wants honesty too. And then your land runs into ours, and, as I can't buy it, I am glad that it should come in by marriage. I have always wanted to see the Abbey, Isleworth, and Rewtham estates in a ring fence before I die. Come and give me a kiss, my dear."

Maria did as she was bid.

"I will try to be a good daughter to you," she said, "if I marry Philip; but," and here her voice trembled a little, "I want to make you understand that, though this engagement exists, I have sometimes thought of late that perhaps he wanted to break it off, and—"

"Break it off?" almost shouted the old man, his eyes flashing.

"Break it off; by God, the day he plays fast and loose with you, that day I leave the property to his cousin George;—there, there, I frightened you, I beg your pardon; but in his own interest, Maria, I advise you to hold him fast to his word. To change the subject, your news has freshened me up so much that I mean to have a little company; will you come and dine with me next Thursday?"

"I shall be very glad, Mr. Caresfoot."

"Thank you; and perhaps till then you will not, unless he happens to ask you, mention the subject of our conversation to Philip. I want to have a talk with him first."

Maria assented, and the squire took his leave with the same magnificence of mien that had marked his arrival.

CHAPTER VIII.

THAT evening his father astonished Philip by telling him that he intended to give a dinner-party on that day week.

"You see, Philip," he said, with a grim smile, "I have only got a year or so at the most before me, and I wish to see a little of my neighbors before I go. I have not had much society of late years. I mean to do the thing well while I am about it, and ask everybody in the neighborhood. How many can dine with comfort in the old banqueting-hall, do you suppose?"

"About five-and-forty, I should think."

"Five-and-forty! I remember that we sat down sixty to dinner when I came of age, but then we were a little crowded; so we will limit the number to fifty."

"Are you going to have fifty people to dinner?" asked Philip, aghast.

"Certainly; I shall ask you to come and help me to write the invitations presently. I have prepared a list; and will you kindly send over to Bell at Roxham? I wish to speak to him; he must bring his men over to do up the old hall a bit; and, by the way, write to Gunter's and order a man-cook to be here on Tuesday, and to bring with him materials for the best dinner for fifty people that he can supply. I will see after the wine myself; we will finish off that wonderful port my grandfather laid down. Now, bustle about, my lad, we have no time to lose; we must get all the notes out to-day."

Philip started to execute his orders, pretty well convinced in his own mind that his father was taking leave of his senses. Who ever heard of a dinner being given to fifty people before, especially in a house where such rare entertainments had always been of a traditionally select and solemn nature? The expense, too, reflected Philip, would be large; a man of his father's age had, in his opinion, no right to make such ducks-and-drakes of money that was so near to belonging to somebody else. But one thing was clear: his father had set his mind upon it, and when once that was the case, to try to thwart him was more than Philip dared.

When the notes of invitation arrived at their respective destinations, great was the excitement in the neighborhood of Bratham Abbey. Curiosity was rampant on the point, and the refusals were few and far between.

At length the eventful evening arrived, and with it the expected guests, amongst whom the old squire, in his dress of a past generation—resplendent in diamond buckles, frilled shirt-front, and silk stockings—was, with his snow-white hair and stately bearing, himself by far the most striking figure.

Standing near the door of the large drawing-room, he received his guests as they arrived with an air that would have done credit to an ambassador; but when Miss Lee entered, Philip noticed with a prophetic shudder that, in lieu of the accustomed bow, he gave her a kiss. He also noticed, for he was an observant man, that the gathered company was pervaded by a curious air of expectation. They were nearly all of them people who had been neighbors of the Caresfoot family for years—in many instances for generations—and as intimate with its members as the high-stomached stiffness of English country-life will allow. They therefore were well acquainted with the family history and peculiarities; but it was clear from their faces that their knowledge was of no help to them now, and that they were totally in the dark as to why they were all gathered together in this unwonted fashion.

At length, to the relief of all, the last of the chosen fifty guests put in an appearance, and dinner was announced. Everybody made his way to his allotted partner, and awaited the signal to move forward, when a fresh piquancy was added to the proceedings by an unexpected incident—in which Maria Lee played a principal part. Maria was sitting in a corner of the drawing-room, wondering if Philip was going to take her in to dinner, and why he had not been to see her lately, when suddenly she became aware that all the room was looking at her, and on raising her eyes she perceived the cause. For there, close upon her, and advancing with majestic step and outstretched arm, was old Mr. Caresfoot, possessed by the evident intention of taking her down in the full face of all the married ladies and people of title present. She prayed that the floor might open and swallow her; indeed, of the two, she would have preferred that way of going down to dinner. But it did not, so there was no alternative left to her but to accept the proffered arm, and to pass, with as much dignity as she could muster in such a trying moment, in front of the intensely interested company—from which she could hear an involuntary murmur of surprise—through the wide-flung doors, down the great oak staircase loaded with exotics, thence along a passage carpeted with crimson cloth, and through double doors of oak that were flung open at their approach, into the banqueting-hall. On its threshold not only she, but almost every member of the company who passed in behind them, uttered an exclamation of surprise; and indeed the sight before them amply justified it.

The hall was a chamber of noble proportions, sixty feet in length by thirty wide. It was very lofty, and the dark chestnut beams of the beautiful arched roof were thrown into strong relief by the light of many candles. The walls were panelled to the roof with oak that had become almost black in the course of centuries, here and there relieved by portraits and shining suits of armor.

Down the centre of the room ran a long wide table, whereon, and on a huge sidèboard, was spread the whole of the Caresfoot plate, which, catching the light of the suspended candles, threw it back in dazzling gleams till the beholder was positively bewildered with the brilliancy of the sight.

"Oh, how beautiful!" said Maria, in astonishment.

"Yes," answered the old gentleman, as he took his seat at the head of the table, placing Maria on his right, "the plate is very fine, it has taken two hundred years to get together; but my father did more in that way than all of us put together, he spent ten thousand pounds on plate during his lifetime; that gold service on the sideboard belonged to him. I have only spent two. Mind, my love," he added in a low voice, "when it comes into your keeping that it is preserved intact; but I don't recommend you to add to it, there is too much already for a simple country gentleman's family."

Maria blushed and was silent.

The dinner, which was served on a most magnificent scale, wore itself away, as all big county-dinners do, in bursts of sedate but not profoundly interesting conversation. Indeed, had it not been for the novelty of the sight, Maria would have been rather bored, the squire's stately compliments notwithstanding. As it was, she felt inclined to envy the party at the other end, amongst whom, looking down the long vista of sparkling glass and silver, she could now and again catch sight of Philip's face beaming with animation, and even in the pauses of conversation hear the echo of his distant laughter.

"What good spirits he is in!" she thought to herself.

And, indeed, Philip was, or appeared to be, in excellent spirits. His handsome face, that of late had been so gloomy, was lit up with laughter, and he contrived by his witty talk to keep those round him in continual merriment.

"Philip seems very happy, doesn't he," said George, *sotto voce* to Mrs. Bellamy, who was sitting next to him.

"You must be a very bad judge of the face as an index to the mind if you think that he is happy. I have been watching him all dinner, and I draw a very different conclusion."

"Why, look how he is laughing."

"Have you never seen a man laugh to hide his misery; never mind his lips, watch his eyes: they are dilated with fear, see how he keeps glancing towards his father and Miss Lee. There, did you see him start? Believe me he is not happy, and unless I am mistaken he will be even less so before the night is over. We are not all asked here for nothing."

"I hope not, I hope not; if so we shall have to act upon our information, eh! But, to change the subject, you look lovely to-night."

"Of course I do; I *am* lovely; I wish I could return the compliment, but conscientiously I can't. Did you ever see such plate? Look at that centre-piece."

"It is wonderful," said George. "I never saw it all out before. I wonder," he added, with a sigh, "if I shall ever have the fingering of it."

"Yes," she said, with a strange look of her large eyes, "if you continue to be guided by me, you shall. I tell you so, and I *never* make mistakes. Hush, something is going to happen. What is it?"

The dinner had come to an end, and in accordance with the old-fashioned custom the cloth had been removed, leaving bare an ancient table of polished oak nearly forty feet in length, and composed of slabs of timber a good two inches thick.

When the wine had been handed round, the old squire motioned to the servants to leave the room, and then, having first whispered something in the ear of Miss Lee that caused her to turn very red, he slowly rose to his feet in the midst of a dead silence.

"Look at your cousin's face," whispered Mrs. Bellamy. George looked; it was ghastly pale, and the black eyes were gleaming like polished jet against white paper.

"Friends and neighbors, amongst whom or among whose fathers I have lived for so many years," began the speaker, whose voice, soft as it was, filled the great hall with ease, "it was, if tradition does not lie, in this very room and at this very table that the only Caresfoot who ever made an after-dinner speech of his own accord, delivered himself of his burden. That man was my ancestor in the eighth degree, old yeoman Caresfoot, and the occasion of his speech was to him a very important one, being the day on which he planted Caresfoot's Staff, the great oak by the water yonder, to mark the founding of a house of country gentry. Some centuries have elapsed since my forefather stood where I stand, most like with his hand upon this board as mine is now, and addressed a company not so fine or so well dressed, but perhaps—I mean no disrespect—on the whole, as good at heart as that before me now. Yes, the sapling oak has grown into the biggest tree in the country-side 'twixt then and now. It seems, therefore, to be fit that on what is to me as great a day as the planting of that oak was to my yeoman forefather, that I, like him, should gather my friends and neighbors round me under the same ancient roof that I may, like him, make them the partakers of my joy.

"None of you sitting at this board to-day can look upon the old man who now asks your attention, without realizing what he himself has already learned: namely, that his day is over. Now, life is hard to quit. When a man grows old, the terrors of the unknown land loom just as large and terrible as they did to his youthful imagination, larger perhaps. But it is a fact that must be faced, a hard, inevitable fact. And age, realizing this, looks round it for consolations, and finds only two: first, that as its interests and affections *here* fade and fall away, in just that same proportion do they grow and gather *there* upon the further shore; and secondly that, after Nature's eternal fashion, the youth and vigor of a new generation is waiting to replace the wornout decrepitude of that which sinks into oblivion. My life is done; it cannot be long before the churchyard claims its own, but I live again in my son; and take such cold comfort as I may from that idea of family, and of long-continued and assured succession, that has so largely helped to make this country what she is.

"But you will wonder what can be the particular purpose for which I have bidden you here to-night. Be assured that it was not to ask you to listen to gloomy sermons on the, to others, not very interesting fact of my approaching end, but rather for a joyful and a definite reason. One wish I have long had, it is—that before I go, I may see my son's child, the little Caresfoot that is to fill my place in future years, prattling about my knees. But this I shall never see. What I have to announce to you, however, is the first step towards it, my son's engagement to Miss Lee, the young lady on my right."

"Look at his face," whispered Mrs. Bellamy to her neighbor, during the murmur of applause that followed this announcement. "Look quick."

Philip had put his hands down upon his chair as though to raise himself up, and an expression of such mingled rage and terror swept across his features as, once seen, could not easily be forgotten. But so quickly did it pass that perhaps Mrs. Bellamy, who was watching, was the only one in all that company to observe it. In another moment he was smiling and bowing his acknowledgments to whispered and telegraphed congratulations.

"You all know Miss Lee," went on the old squire, "as you knew her father and mother before her; she is a sound shoot from an honest stock, a girl after my own heart, a girl that I love, and that all who come under her influence will love, and this engagement is to me the most joyful news that I have heard for many a year. May God, ay, and man too, so deal with my son as he deals with Maria Lee!

"And now I have done; I have already kept you too long. With your consent, we will have no more speeches, no returning of thanks; we will spare Philip his blushes. But before I sit down I will bid you all farewell, for I am in my eighty-third year, and I feel that I shall never see very many of your faces again. I wish that I had been a better neighbor to you all, as there are many other things I wish, now that is too late to fulfil them; but I still hope that some of you will now and again find a kind thought for the old man whom among yourselves you talk of as 'Devil Caresfoot.' Believe me, my friends, there is truth in the old proverb:

the devil is not always as black as he is painted. I give you my toast—My son Philip and his affianced wife, Maria Lee."

The whole company rose, actuated by a common impulse, and drank the health standing; and such was the pathos of the old squire's speech, that there were eyes among those present that were not free from tears. Then the ladies retired, amongst them poor Maria, who was naturally upset at the unexpected, and, in some ways, unwelcome notoriety thus given to herself.

In the drawing-room, she was so overwhelmed with congratulations, that at last, feeling that she could not face a fresh edition from the male portion of the gathering, she ordered her carriage, and quietly slipped away home, to think over the matters at her leisure.

Philip, too, came in for his share of honors down below, and acknowledged them as best he might, for he had not the moral courage to repudiate the position. He felt that his father had forced his hand completely, and that there was nothing to be done, and sank into the outward calmness of despair. But if his companions could have seen the whirlpool of hatred, terror and, fury that raged within his breast as he sat and chatted, and sipped his great-grandfather's port, they would have been justifiably astonished.

At length the banquet, for it was nothing less, came to an end, and having bowed their farewell to the last departing guest, the old man and his son were left alone together in the deserted drawing-room. Philip was seated by a table, his face buried in his hand, while his father was standing by the dying fire, tapping his eye-glass nervously on the mantel-piece. It was he who broke the somewhat ominous silence.

"Well, Philip, how did you like my speech?"

Thus addressed, the son lifted his face from his hand; it was white as a sheet.

"By what authority," he asked, in a harsh whisper, "did you announce me as engaged to Miss Lee?"

"By my own, Philip. I had it from both your lips that you were engaged. I did not choose that it should remain a secret any longer."

"You had no right to make that speech. I will not marry Miss Lee; understand once for all, I will *not* marry her."

In speaking thus, Philip had nerved himself to bear one of those dreadful outbursts of fury that had earned his father his title; but, to his astonishment, none such came. The steely eyes glinted a little as he answered in his most polite manner, and that was all.

"Your position, Philip, then is that you are engaged, very publicly engaged, to a girl whom you have no intention of marrying—a very disgraceful position; mine is that I have, with every possible solemnity, announced a marriage that will not come off—a very ridiculous position. Very good, my dear Philip; please yourself. I cannot force you into a distasteful marriage. But you must not suppose that you can thus thwart me with impunity. Allow me to show you the alternative. I see you are tired, but I shall not detain you long. Take that easy-chair. This house and the land round it, also the plate, which is very valuable, but cannot be sold —by the way, see that it is safely locked up before you go to bed— are strictly entailed, and must, of course, pass to you. The value of the entailed land is about £1000 a year, or a little less in bad times; of the unentailed, a clear £4000; of my personal property about £900. Should you persist in your refusal to marry Miss Lee, or should the marriage in any way fall through, except from circumstances entirely beyond your control, I must, to use your own admirably emphatic language, ask you to 'understand, once and for all,' that, where your name appears in my will with reference to the unentailed and personal property, it will be erased, and that of your cousin George substituted. Please yourself, Philip, please yourself; it is a matter of entire indifference to me. I am very fond of George, and shall be glad to do him a good turn if you force me to it, though it is a pity to split up the property. But probably you will like to take a week to consider whether you prefer to stick to the girl you have got hold of up in town there—oh, yes! I know there is some one—and abandon the property, or marry Miss Lee and retain the property—a very pretty problem for an amorous young man to consider. There, I won't keep you up any longer. Good-night, Philip; good-night. Just see to the plate, will you? Remember, you have a personal interest in that; I can't leave it away."

Philip rose without a word and left the room, but when he was gone it was his father's turn to hide his face in his hands.

"Oh, God!" he groaned aloud, "to think that all my plans should come to such an end as this; to think that I am as powerless to prevent their collapse as a child is to support a falling tree; that the only power left me is the power of vengeance—vengeance on my own son. I have lived too long, and the dregs of life are bitter.

CHAPTER IX.

Poor Hilda found life in her London lodging anything but cheerful, and frequently begged Philip to allow her to settle somewhere in the country. This, however, he refused to do on two grounds: in the first place, because few country villages would be so convenient for him to get at as London; and in the second, because he declared that the great city was the safest hiding-place in the world.

And so Hilda continued perforce to live her lonesome existence, that was only cheered by her husband's short and uncertain visits. Friends she had none, nor did she dare to make any. The only person whose conversation she could rely on to relieve the tedium of the long weeks was her landlady, Mrs. Jacobs, the widow of a cheesemonger, who had ruined a fine business by his drinking and other vicious propensities, and out of a good property had only left his wife the leasehold of a house in Lincoln's Inn Fields, which, fortunately for her, had been settled upon her at her marriage. Like most people who have seen better days—not but what she was now very comfortably off—she delighted in talking of her misfortunes, and of the perfidiousness of man; and in Hilda, who had, poor girl, nothing else to listen to, she found a most attentive audience. As was only natural where such a charming person and such a good listener were concerned, honest Mrs. Jacobs soon grew fond of her interesting lodger, about whose husband's circumstances and history she soon wove many an imaginary tale; for, needless to say, her most pertinent inquiries failed to extract much information from Hilda. One of her favorite fictions was that her lodger was the victim of her handsome husband, who had in some way beguiled her from her home beyond the seas, in order to keep her in solitary confinement and out of the reach of a hated rival. Another, that he kept her thus that he might have greater liberty for his own actions.

In course of time these ideas took such possession of her mind that she grew to believe in them, and, when speaking of Hilda to any of her other lodgers, would shake her head and talk of her mysteriously as a "lamb" and a "victim."

As for that lady herself, whilst far from suspecting her good landlady's gloomy surmises, she certainly fell more and more a prey to depression and anxieties, and occasionally even to suspicion, to all of which evils she grew increasingly liable as she drew nearer to an event that was no longer very distant. She could not but notice a change in Philip's manner on the rare occasions when he was able to visit her, of which the most marked developments were fits of silence and irritability. A certain reticence also, that became more and more noticeable as time went on, led her to feel that there was an invisible something growing up between them—a something that the pride she possessed in such a striking degree forbade her to attempt to pierce, but which was none the less galling to her on that account. Very shortly before the events narrated in the last chapter she had taken the occasion of a visit from Philip to complain somewhat bitterly of her position, begging him to tell her when there was any prospect of her being allowed to take her rightful place—a question her husband was quite unable to answer satisfactorily. Seeing that there was nothing to be got out of him, with womanly tact she changed the subject, and asked after Maria Lee (for whom she entertained a genuine affection)—when he last saw her, how she was looking, if there was any prospect of her getting married, and other questions of the same sort—the result of which was to evoke a most violent, and to her inexplicable, fit of irritability on the part of her husband. Something of a scene ensued, which was finally terminated about five o'clock in the afternoon by Philip's abrupt departure to catch his train.

Shortly afterwards Mrs. Jacobs, coming up to bring some tea, found Hilda indulging in tears that she had been too proud to shed before her husband; and, having had an extended personal experience of such matters, rightly guessed that there had been a conjugal tiff, the blame of which, needless to say, she fixed upon the departed Philip.

"Lor, Mrs. Roberts" (as Hilda was called), she said, "don't take on like that; they're all brutes, that's what they are; if only you could have seen my Samuel, who's dead and gone these ten years and buried in a private grave at Kensal Cemetery—though he didn't leave anything to pay for it except three dozen and five of brandy—he was a beauty, poor dear, he was; your husband ain't nothing to him."

"My husband, let me tell you, Mrs. Jacobs, is not a brute at all," sobbed Hilda, with dignity.

"Ah, Mrs. Roberts, that is just what I used to say of Samuel, but he was the biggest brute in the three kingdoms, for all that; but if you ask me, meaning no offence, I call a man a brute as only comes to see his lawful wife about twice a month, let alone making an angel cry."

"Mr. Roberts has his reasons, Mrs. Jacobs; you must not talk of him like that."

"Ah, so my Samuel used to say when he stopped away from home for three nights at a time, till I followed him and found out his 'Reason,' and a mighty pretty 'Reason' she was too, all paint and feathers, the hussy, and eyes as big as a teacup. They all have their reasons, but they never tell 'em. But come and put on your things and go out a bit, there's a dear; it is a beautiful warm evening. You feel tired—oh, never mind that; it is necessary for people as is in an interesting way to take exercise. I well remembers—"

Here Hilda, however, cut the subject short, and deprived herself of Mrs. Jacobs's reminiscences by going to put on her things.

It was a bright warm evening, and she found the air so pleasant that, after strolling round Lincoln's Inn Fields, she thought she would extend her walk a little, and struck past Lincoln's Inn Hall into New Square, and then made her way to the archway opposite to where the New Law Courts now stand. Under this archway a legal bookseller has built his nest, and behind windows of broad plate-glass were ranged specimens of his seductive wares, baits on which to catch students avaricious of legal knowledge as they pass on their way to Chambers or Hall. Now, at this window a young man was standing at the moment that Hilda entered the archway, his eyes fixed upon a pamphlet on the laws of succession. That young man was George Caresfoot, who was considering whether it would be worth his while to buy the pamphlet in order to see if he would be entitled to anything if his uncle should happen to die intestate, as he sometimes feared might be the case. He had come up to town on business connected with his firm, and was now waiting till it was time to begin an evening of what he understood as pleasure; for George was a very gay young man.

He was, however, also a very sharp one, so sharp that he even noticed shadows, especially when, as in this case, the shadow was clearly defined and flung, life-sized, on the dark background of the books before him. He watched it for a moment, and as its owner, with an absent air, slowly passed from the bright sunlight into the shade of the arch, it struck the astute George that there was something familiar about this particular and by no means unpleasing shadow. Waiting till it had vanished and the footsteps gone past him, he turned round and at a glance recognized Hilda von Holtzhausen, Miss Lee's beautiful companion, who was supposed to have departed into the more distant parts of Germany. George's eyes twinkled, and a whole host of ideas rushed into his really able mind.

"Caught at last, for a sovereign," he muttered.

Meanwhile Hilda walked slowly on into Chancery Lane, then turned to the left till she came into Holborn, and thence made her way round by another route back to Lincoln's Inn Fields. Needless to say, George followed at a respectful distance. His first impulse had been to go up and speak to her, but he resisted the inclination.

On the doorstep of the house where Hilda lodged stood her landlady, giving a piece of her mind to a butcher-boy both as regarded his master's meat and his personal qualities. She paused for breath just as Hilda passed up the steps, and, turning, said something that made the latter laugh. The butcher-boy took the opportunity of beating a rapid retreat, leaving Mrs. Jacobs crowing after him from her own doorstep. As soon as Hilda had gone into the house, George saw his opportunity. Advancing politely towards Mrs. Jacobs, he asked her if she was the landlady of the house, and, when she had answered in the affirmative, he made inquiries about apartments.

"Thank you, sir," said Mrs. Jacobs, "but I do not let rooms to single gentlemen."

"You take too much for granted, ma'am. I am married."

She looked at him doubtfully. "I suppose, sir, you would have no objection to giving a reference."

"A dozen, if you like, ma'am; but shall we look at the rooms?"

Mrs. Jacobs assented, and they made their way upstairs, George keeping in front. On the first-floor he saw a pair of lady's shoes on a mat outside the door, and guessed to whom they belonged.

"Are these the rooms?" he said, laying his hand upon the door-handle.

"No, sir, no, they are Mrs. Roberts's; next floor, please, sir."

"Mrs. Roberts?—I suppose the very handsome young lady I saw come into the house. No offence, ma'am; but a man's bound to be cereful where he brings his wife. I suppose she's all right."

"Lord, yes, poor dear!" answered Mrs. Jacobs, in indignation; "why, they came here straight from St. Jude's, Battersea, the day they were married; a runaway match, I fancy."

"That's all right; she looked charming. I hope her husband is worthy of her," remarked George, as he gazed round Mrs. Jacobs's rooms.

"Well, as to that, he's handsome enough, for them as likes those black men; but I don't like people as only comes to visit their lawful wives about twice a month. But," suddenly checking herself, "it isn't any affair of mine."

"No, indeed, very reprehensible: I am, as a married man, entirely of your mind. These are charming rooms, ma'am, charming. I shall certainly take them if my wife approves; I will let you know by to-morrow's post—Jacobs, yes, I have it down. Good evening, ma'am," and he was gone.

Instead of going out that evening as he had intended, George sat in the smoking-room of his hotel and thought. He also wrote a letter which he addressed to Mrs. Bellamy.

Next morning, taking a cab, he drove to St. Jude's, Battersea, and inspected the register.

Presently he asked for a certified copy of the following entry: "August 1, 1856. Philip Caresfoot, bachelor, gentleman, to Hilda von Holtzhausen, spinster (by license). Signed, J. Few, curate; as witness, Fred. Natt, Eliza Chambers."

That evening Hilda received an anonymous letter, written in a round clerk's hand, that had been posted in the City. It was addressed to Mr. Roberts, and its contents ran thus:

"A sincere friend warns Mrs. Philip Caresfoot that her husband is deceiving her, and has become entangled with a young lady of her acquaintance. *Burn this; wait and watch!*"

The letter fell from her hands as though it had stung her.

"Mrs. Jacobs was right," she said aloud, with a bitter laugh, "men always have a 'reason.' Oh, let him beware!" And she threw back her beautiful head, and the great blue eyes sparkled like those of a snake about to strike. The sword of jealousy, that she had hitherto repelled with the shield of a woman's trust in the man she loves, had entered into her soul, and, could Philip have seen her under these new circumstances, he would have realized that he had indeed good reason to "beware." "No wonder," she went on, "no wonder that he finds her name irritating upon my lips; no doubt to him it is a desecration. Oh, oh!" And she flung herself on her face, and wept tears of jealous rage.

"Well," said George to Mrs. Bellamy, as they drove home together after the great dinner-party (do not be shocked, my reader, Bellamy was *on the box*), "well, how shall we strike? Shall I go to the old man to-morrow, and show him my certified copy? There is no time to lose. He might die any day."

"No; we must act through Mrs. Philip."

"Why?"

"It is more scientific, and it will be more amusing."

"Poor thing! it will be a blow to her. Don't you like her?"

"No."

"Why not?"

"Because she did not trust me, and because she eclipses me. Therefore I am glad of an opportunity of destroying her."

"You are a very ruthless woman."

"When I have an end in view, I march straight to it; I do not vacillate—that is all. But never mind me; here we are near home. Go to town by the first train to-morrow morning and post another letter announcing what has happened here. Then come back and wait."

"Ay," reflected George, "that is a wonderful woman—a woman it is good to have some hold over."

We left Hilda stretched on her face sobbing. But the fit did not last long. She rose, and flung open the window; she seemed stifled for want of air. Then she sat down to think what she should do. Vanish and leave no trace? No; not yet. Appear and claim her place? No; not yet. The time was not ripe for choice between these two extremes. Upbraid Philip with his faithlessness? No; not without proofs. What did that hateful letter say? "Wait and watch;" yes, that was what she would do. But she could not wait here; she felt as though she must go somewhere, get some change of scene, or she should break down. She had heard Mrs. Jacobs speak of a village not more than two hours from London that a convalescent lodger of hers had visited and found charming. She would go there for a week, and watch the spring cast her mantle over the earth, and listen to the laughter of the brooks, and try to forget her burning love and jealousy, and just for that one week be happy as she was when, as a little girl, she roamed all day through the woods of her native Germany. Alas! she forgot that it is the heart and not the scene that makes happiness.

That evening she wrote a note to her husband, saying that she felt that change of air was necessary for her, and that she was going out of London for a few days, to some quiet place, from whence she would write to him. He must not, however, expect many letters, as she wanted complete rest.

On the following morning she went; and, if the sweet spring air did not bring peace to her mind, at any rate it to a very great extent set her up in strength. She wrote but one letter during her absence, and that was to say that she should be back in London by midday on the first of May. This letter reached Philip on the morning of the great dinner-party, and was either accidentally or on purpose sent without the writer's address. On the morning of the first of May—that is, two days after the dinner-party, which was given on the twenty-ninth of April—Hilda rose early, and commenced to pack her things with the assistance of a stout servant-girl, who did all the odd jobs and a great deal of the work in the old-fashioned farmhouse in which she was staying. Presently the cowboy came whistling up the little garden, bright with crocuses and tulips, that lay in front of the house, and knocked at the front door.

"Lawks!" said the stout girl, in accents of deep surprise, as she drew her head in from the open lattice; "Jim's got a letter."

"Perhaps it is for me," suggested Hilda, a little nervously; she had grown nervous about the post of late. "Will you go and see?"

The letter was for her, in the handwriting of Mrs. Jacobs. She opened it; it contained another addressed in a character the sight of which made her feel sick and faint. She could not trust herself to read it in the presence of the girl.

"Sally," she said, "I feel rather faint; I shall lie down a little. I will ring for you presently."

Sally retired, and she opened her letter.

Fifteen minutes after the girl received her summons. She found Hilda very pale, and with a curious look upon her face.

"I hope you're better, mum," she said, for she was a kind-hearted girl.

"Better—ah, yes! thank you, Sally; I am cured, quite cured; but please be quick with the things, for I shall leave by the nine-o'clock train."

CHAPTER X.

The night of the dinner-party was a nearly sleepless one for Philip, although his father had so considerately regretted his wearied appearance; he could do nothing but walk, walk, walk, like some unquiet ghost, up and down his great, oak-panelled bedroom, till, about dawn, his legs gave way beneath him; and think, think, think, till his mind recoiled, confused and helpless, from the dead wall of its objects. And out of all this walking and thinking there emerged, after an hour of stupor that it would be a misnomer to call sleep, two fixed results. The first of these was that he hated his father as a lost soul must hate its torturing demon, blindly, madly, impotently hated him; and the second, that he could no longer delay taking his wife into his confidence. Then he remembered the letter he had received from her on the previous morning. He got it, and saw that it bore no address, merely stating that she would be in London by midday on the first of May, that was on the morrow. Till then it was clear he must wait, and he was not sorry for the reprieve. His was not a pleasant story for a husband to have to tell.

Fortunately for Philip, there was an engagement of long standing for this day, the thirtieth of April, to go, in conjunction with other persons, to effect a valuation of the fallows, etc., of a large tenant who was going out at Michaelmas. This prevented any call being made upon him to go and see Maria Lee, as, after the events of the previous evening, it might have been expected he would. He started early on this business, and did not return till late, so he saw nothing of his father that day.

On the morning of the first of May he breakfasted about half-pass eight, and then, without seeing his father, drove to Roxham to catch a train that got him up to London about twenty minutes to twelve. As he steamed slowly into Paddington Station, another train steamed out, and had he been careful to examine the occupants of the first-class carriages as they passed him in a slow procession, he might have seen something that would have interested him; but he was, not unnaturally, too much occupied with his own thoughts to allow of the indulgence of an idle curiosity. On the arrival of his train, he took a cab and drove without delay to the house in Lincoln's Inn Fields, and asked for Mrs. Roberts.

"She isn't back yet, sir," was Mrs. Jacobs's reply. "I got this note from her this morning to say that she would be here by twelve, but it's twenty past now, so I suppose that she has missed the train or changed her mind; but there will be another in at three, so perhaps you had best wait for that, sir."

Philip was put out by this contretemps, but at the same time he was relieved to find that he had a space to breathe in before the inevitable and dreadful moment of exposure and infamy, for he had grown afraid of his wife.

Three o'clock came in due course, but no Hilda. Philip was seriously disturbed; but there was now no train by which she could arrive that day, so he was forced to the conclusion that she had postponed her departure. There were now two things to be done, one to follow her down to where she was staying—for he had ascertained her address from Mrs. Jacobs; the other, to return home and come back on the morrow. For reasons which appeared to him imperative, but which need not be entered into here, he decided on the latter course; so, leaving a note for his wife, he drove, in a very bad temper, to Paddington in time to çatch the five-o'clock train to Roxham.

Let us now return to the Abbey House, where, whilst Philip was cooling his heels in Lincoln's Inn Fields, a rather curious scene was in progress.

At one o'clock, old Mr. Caresfoot, as was his rule, sat down to lunch, which, frugal as it was, so far as he was concerned, was yet served with some old-fashioned ceremony by a butler and a footman. Just as the meal was coming to an end, a fly, with some luggage on it, drove up to the hall-door. The footman went to open it.

"Simmons," said the squire to the old butler, "look out and tell me who that is."

Simmons did as he was bid, and replied:

"I don't rightly know, squire; but it's a lady, and she be wonderful tall."

Just then the footman returned, and said that a lady, who would not give her name, wished to speek to him in private.

"Are you sure the lady did not mean Mr. Philip?"

"No, sir; she asked for Mr. Philip first, and when I told her that he was out, she asked for you, sir. I have shown her into the study."

"Humph! at any rate, she has come off a journey, and must be hungry. Set another place and ask her in here."

In another moment there was the rustle of a silk dress, and a lady, arrayed in a long cloak and with a thick veil on, was shown into the room. Mr. Caresfoot, rising with that courteous air for which he was remarkable, bowed and begged her to be seated, and then motioned to the servants to leave the room.

"Madam, I am told that you wish to speak to me; might I ask whom I have the honor of addressing?"

She, with a rapid motion, removed her hat and veil, and exposed her sternly beautiful face to his inquiring gaze.

"Do you not know me, Mr. Caresfoot?" she said, in her foreign accent.

"Surely, yes, you are the young lady who lived with Maria—Miss von Holtzhausen."

"That *was* my name; it is now Hilda Caresfoot. I am your son Philip's wife."

As this astounding news broke upon his ears, her hearer's face became a shifting study. Incredulity, wonder, fury, all swept across it, and then in a single second it seemed to freeze. Next moment he spoke with overpowering politeness.

"So, madam; then I have to congratulate myself on the possession of a very lovely daughter-in-law."

A silence ensued that they were both too moved to break; at last, the old man said, in an altered tone:

"We have much to talk of, and you must be tired. Take off your cloak, and eat whilst I think."

She obeyed him, and he saw that not only was she his son's wife, but that she must before long present the world with an heir to the name of Caresfoot. This made him think the more; but meanwhile he continued to attend to her wants. She ate little, but calmly.

"That woman has nerve," said he to himself.

Then he rang the bell, and bade Simmons wait till he had written a note.

"Send James to Roxham at once with this. Take this lady's things off the fly, and put them in the red bedroom. By the way, I am at home to nobody except Mr. Bellany;" and then, turning to Hilda, "Now, if you will come into my study, we will continue our chat," and he offered her his arm. "Here we are secure from interruption," he said, with a ghost of a smile. "Take this chair. Now, forgive my impertinence, but I must ask you if I am to understand that you are my son's *legal* wife?"

She flushed a little as she answered:

"Sir, I am. I have been careful to bring the proof; here it is;" and she took from a little hand-bag a certified copy of the register of her marriage, and gave it to him. He examined it carefully through his gold eye-glass, and handed it back.

"Perfectly in order. Hum! some eight months since, I see. May I ask why I am now for the first time favored with a sight of this interesting document—in short, why you come down, like an angel from the clouds, and reveal yourself at the present moment?"

"I have come," she answered, "because of these." And she handed him two letters. "I have come to ascertain if they are true; if my husband is a doubly-perjured or a basely-slandered man."

He read the two anonymous letters. With the contents of the first we are acquainted; the second merely told of the public announcement of Philip's engagement.

"Speak," she said, with desperate energy, the calm of her face breaking up like ice before a rush of waters. "You must know everything; tell me my fate!"

"Girl, these villainous letters are in every particular true. You have married in my son the biggest scoundrel in the county. I can only say that I grieve for you."

She listened in silence; then rising from her chair, said, with a gesture infinitely tragic in its simplicity:

"Then it is finished; before God and man I renounce him. Listen," she went on, turning to her father-in-law: "I loved your son; he won my heart; but, though he said he loved me, I suspected him of playing fast and loose with me, on the one hand, and with my friend, Maria Lee, on the other. So I determined to go away, and told him so. Then it was that he offered to marry me at once if I would change my purpose. I loved him, and I consented—yes, because I loved him so, I consented to even more. I agreed to pass by a false name, and to enter on a course of trickery in order to keep the marriage secret from you. You see what it has led to. I, a Von Holtzhausen, and the last of my name, stand here a by-word and a scorn; my story will be found amusing at every dinner-table in the country-side, and my shame will even cling to my unborn child. This is the return he has made me for my sacrifice of self-respect, and for consenting to marry him at all; to outrage my love and make me a public mockery."

"We have been accustomed," broke in the old squire, his pride somewhat nettled, "to consider our own a good family to marry into. You do not seem to share that view."

"Good; yes, there is plenty of your money for those who care for it; but, sir, as I told your son, it is not a *family*. He did me no honor in marrying me, though I was nothing but a German companion, with no dower but her beauty. I"—and here she flung her head back with an air of ineffable pride—"did him the honor. My ancestors, sir, were princes when his were plough-boys."

"Well, well," answered the old squire, testily, "ten generations of country gentry, and the Lord only knows how many more of stout yeomen before them, is a good enough descent for us; but I like your pride, and I am glad that you spring from an ancient race. You have been shamefully treated, Hilda—is not your name Hilda?—but there are others, more free from blame than you are, who have been treated worse."

"Ah, Maria! Then she knows nothing?"

"Yes, there is Maria and myself. But never mind that. Philip will, I suppose, be back in a few hours—oh, yes! he will be back," and his eyes glinted unpleasantly; "and what shall you do then? what course do you intend to take?"

"I intend to claim my rights, to force him to acknowledge me here where he suffered his engagement to another woman to be proclaimed, and then I intend to leave him. He has killed my respect; I will not live with him again. I can earn my living in Germany. I have done with him; but, sir, do not you be hard upon him. It is a matter between me and him. Let him not suffer on my account."

"My dear, pray confine yourself to your own affairs, and leave me to settle mine. There shall be no harshness; nobody shall suffer more than they deserve. There, don't break down; go and rest, for there are painful scenes before you."

He rang the bell, and sent for the housekeeper. She came presently—a pleasant-looking woman of about thirty years of age, with a comely face and honest eyes.

"This lady, Pigott," said the old squire, addressing her, "is Mrs. Philip Caresfoot, and you will be so kind as to treat her with all respect. Don't open your eyes, but attend to me. For the present, you had best put her in the red room, and attend to her yourself. Do you understand?"

"Oh, yes, sir, I understand," Pigott replied, courtesying. "Will you be pleased to come along with me, ma'am?"

Hilda rose and took Pigott's arm. Excitement and fatigue had worn her out. Before she went, however, she turned, and with tears in her eyes thanked the old man for his kindness to a friendless woman.

The hard eyes grew kindly as he stooped and kissed the broad, white brow, and said in his stately way:

"My dear, as yet I have shown you nothing but the courtesy due to a lady. Should I live, I hope to bestow on you the affection I owe to a much-wronged daughter. Good-by."

And thus they parted, little knowing where they should meet again.

"A woman I respect—well, English or German, the blood will tell"—he said, as soon as the door had closed. "Poor thing—poor Maria, too. The scoundrel!—ah! there it is again;" and he pressed his hand to his heart. "This business has upset me, and no wonder."

The pang passed, and, sitting down, he wrote a letter that evidently embarrassed him considerably, and addressed it to Miss Lee. This he put in the post-box, and then, going to a secretaire, he unlocked it, and taking out a document, he began to puzzle over it attentively.

Presently Simmons announced that Mr. Bellamy was waiting.

"Show him in at once," said the old man, briskly.

CHAPTER XI.

It was some minutes past seven that evening when the lawyer left, and he had not been gone a quarter of an hour before a hired gig drove up to the door containing Philip, who had got back from town in the worst of bad tempers, and, as no conveyance was waiting for him, had been forced to post over from Roxham. Apparently his father had been expecting his arrival, for the moment the servant opened the door, he appeared from his study, and addressed him in a tone that was as near to being jovial as he ever went.

"Hallo, Philip, back again, are you? Been up to town, I suppose, and driven over in the 'George' gig? That's lucky; I wanted to speak to you. Come in here, there's a good fellow, I want to speak to you."

"Why is he so infernally genial?" reflected Philip. "Timeo Danaos et dona ferentes;" then aloud, "All right, father; but if it is all the same to you, I should like to get some dinner first."

"Dinner! why, I have had none yet; I have been too busy. I shall not keep you long; we will dine together presently."

Philip was surprised, and glanced at him suspiciously. His habits were extremely regular; why had he had no dinner?

Meanwhile his father led the way into the study, muttering below his breath:

"One more chance—his last chance."

A wood fire was burning brightly on the hearth, for the evening was chilly, and some sherry and glasses stood upon the table.

"Take a glass of wine, Philip; I am going to have one; it is a good thing to begin a conversation on. What says the Psalmist: 'Wine that maketh glad the heart of man, and oil to make him a cheerful countenance'—a cheerful countenance! Ho, ho! my old limbs are tired; I am going to sit down—going to sit down."

He seated himself in a well-worn leather arm-chair by the side of the fire so that his back was towards the dying daylight. But the brightness of the flames threw the clear-cut features into strong relief against the gloom, and by it Philip could see that the withered cheeks were flushed. Somehow the whole strongly-defined scene made him feel uncanny and restless.

"Cold for the first of May, isn't it, lad? The world is very cold at eighty-two. Eighty-two: a great age, yet it seems but the other day that I used to sit in this very chair and dandle you upon my knee, and make this repeater strike for you. And yet that is twenty years since, and I have lived through four twenties and two years. A great age, a cold world!"

"Ain't you well?" asked his son, brusquely, but not unkindly.

"Well; ah, yes! thank you, Philip, I never felt better; my memory is so good; I can see things I have forgotten seventy years or more. Dear, dear, it was behind that book-case in a hole in the board that I used to hide my flint and steel which I used for making little fires at the foot of Caresfoot Staff. There is a mark on the bark now. I was mischievous as a little lad, and thought that the old tree would make a fine blaze. I was audacious, too, and delighted to hide the things in my father's study under the very nose of authority. Aye, and other memories come upon me as I think. It was here upon this very table that they stood my mother's coffin. I was standing where you are now when I wrenched open the half-fastened shell to kiss her once more before they screwed her down forever. I wonder would you do as much for me? I loved my mother, and that was fifty years ago. I wonder shall we meet again? That was on the first of May, a long-gone first of May. They threw branches of blackthorn bloom upon her coffin. Odd, very odd! But business, lad, business—what was it? ah! I know," and his manner changed in a second, and became hard and stern. "About Maria—have you come to a decision?"

Philip moved restlessly on his chair, poked the logs to a brighter blaze, and threw on a handful of pine chips from a basket by his side before he answered. Then he said:

"No, I have not."

"Your reluctance is very strange, Philip; I cannot understand it. I suppose that you are not already married, are you, Philip?"

There was a lurid calm about the old man's face as he asked this question that was very dreadful in its intensity. Under the shadow of his thick black eyebrows gleams of light glinted and flickered in the expanded pupils, as before the outburst of a tempest the forked lightning flickers in the belly of the cloud. His voice, too, was constrained and harsh.

Owing to the position of his father's head, Philip could not see this play of feature, but he heard the voice, and thought that it meant mischief. He had but a second to decide between confession and the lie that leaped to his lips. An inward conviction told him that his father was not long for this world—was it worth while to face his anger when matters might yet be kept dark till the end? The tone of the voice—ah! how he mistook its meaning—deceived him. It was not, he thought, possible that his father could know anything. Had he possessed a little more knowledge of the world, he might have judged differently.

"Married? no, indeed; what put that idea into your head?" and he laughed outright.

Presently he became aware that his father had risen and was approaching him. Another moment and a hand of iron was laid upon his shoulder, the awful eyes blazed into his face and seemed to pierce him through and through, and a voice that he could not have recognized hissed into his ear:

"You unutterable liar, you everlasting hound, your wife is at this moment in this house."

Philip sprang up with an exclamation of rage and cursed Hilda aloud.

"No," went on his father, standing before him, his tall frame swaying backwards and forwards with excitement; "no, do not curse her; she, like your other poor dupe, is an honest woman; on yourself be the damnation—you living fraud, you outcast from all honor, who have brought shame and reproach upon our honest name, on you be it; may every curse attend *you*, and may remorse torture *you*. Listen: you lied to me, you lied to your wife, trebly did you lie to the unfortunate girl you have deceived; but, if you will not speak it, for once hear the truth, and remember that you have to deal with one so relentless, that fools, mistaking justice for oppression, call him 'devil.' I, 'Devil Caresfoot,' tell you that I will disinherit you of every stick, stone, and stiver that the law allows me, and start you in the enjoyment of the rest with my bitterest curse. This I will do now whilst I am alive; when I am dead, by Heaven I will haunt you if I can!"

Here he stopped for want of breath, and stood for a moment in the full light of the cheery blaze, one hand raised above his head as though to strike, and presenting with his glittering eyes and working features so terrible a spectacle of rage that his son recoiled involuntarily before him.

But fury begets fury as love begets love, and in another second Philip felt his own wicked temper boil up within him. He clinched his teeth and stood firm.

"Do your worst," he said; "I hate you; I wish to God that you were dead."

Hardly had these dreadful words left his lips when a change came over the old man's face; it seemed to stiffen, and putting one hand to his heart he staggered back into his chair, pointing and making signs as he fell towards a little cupboard in the angle of the wall. His son at once guessed what had happened; his father had got one of the attacks of the heart to which he was subject, and was motioning to him to bring the medicine which he had before shown him, and which alone could save him in these seizures. Actuated by a common impulse of humanity, Philip for the moment forgot their quarrel, and stepped with all speed to fetch it. As it happened, there stood beneath this cupboard a table, and on this table lay the document which his father had been reading that afternoon before the arrival of Mr. Bellamy. It was his will, and, as is usual in the case of such deeds, the date was indorsed upon the back. All this Philip saw at a single glance, and he also saw that the will was dated some years back, and therefore one under which he would inherit; doubtless the same that his father had some months before offered to show him.

It flashed through his mind that his father had got it out in order to burn it; and this idea was followed by another that for a moment stilled his heart.

"*If he should die now he cannot destroy it!* If he does not take the medicine he *will* die."

Thought flies fast in moments of emergency. Philip, too, was a man of determined mind where his own interests were concerned, and his blood was heated and his reason blinded by fury and terror. He was not long in settling on his course of action. Taking the bottle from the cupboard, he poured out its contents into one of the wine-glasses that stood upon the table, and coming up to his father with it, addressed him. He knew that these attacks, although they were of a nature to cause intense pain, did not rob the sufferer of his senses. The old man, though he lay before him gasping with agony, was quite in a condition to understand him.

"Listen to me," he said, in a slow, distinct voice. "Just now you said that you would disinherit me. This medicine will save your life, and if I let it fall you will die, and there is no more in the house. Swear before God that you will not carry out your threat, and I will give it to you. Lift up your hand to show me that you swear."

Silence followed, only broken by the gasps of the dying man.

"If you will not swear, I will pour it out before your eyes."

Again there was silence; but this time the old man made an effort to rise and ring the bell.

His son threw him roughly back.

"For the last time," he said, in a hoarse whisper, "will you swear?"

A struggle passed over his father's face, now nearly black with pain; and presently from the distended lips, that did not seem to move, there burst a single word—destined to echo for ever in his son's ears—

"*Murderer!*"

It was his last. He sank back, groaned, and died; and at the same moment the flame from the pine-chips flickered itself away, and of a sudden the room grew nearly dark. Philip stood for a while aghast at his own handiwork, and watched the dull light glance on the dead white of his father's brow. He was benumbed by terror at what he had done, and in that awful second of realization would have given his own life to have it undone.

Presently, however, the instinct of self-preservation came to his aid. He lit a candle, and taking some of the medicine in the glass, smeared it over the dead man's chin and coat, and then broke the glass on the floor by his side—thus making it appear that he had died while attempting to swallow the medicine.

Next he raised a loud outcry, and violently rang the bell. In a minute the room was full of startled servants, one of whom was instantly despatched for Mr. Caley, the doctor. Meanwhile, after a vain attempt to restore animation, the study-table was cleared and the corpse laid on it, as its mother's had been on that day fifty years before.

Then came a dreadful hush, and the shadow of death came down upon the house and brooded over it. The men-servants moved to and fro with muffled feet, and the women wept, for in a way they had all loved the imperious old man, and the last change had come very suddenly. Philip's brain burned; he was consumed by the desire of action. Suddenly he bethought him of his wife upstairs: after what he had just passed through, no scene with her could disturb him—it would, he even felt, be welcome. He went up to the room where she was, and entered. It was evident that she had been told of what had happened, as both she and Pigott, who was undressing her—for she was wearied out—were weeping. She did not appear surprised at his appearance; the shock of the old man's death extinguished all surprise. It was he who broke the silence.

"He is dead," he said.

"Yes, I have heard."

"If you are at liberty for a few minutes, I wish to talk to you." he said savagely.

"I, too," she answered, "have something to say, but I am too weary and upset to say it now. I will see you to-morrow."

He turned and went without answering, and Pigott noticed that no kiss or word of endearment passed between them, and that the tone of their words was cold.

Soon after Philip got downstairs the doctor came. Philip met him in the hall and accompanied him into the study, where the body was. He made a rapid examination, more as a matter of form than anything else, for his first glance had told him that life was extinct.

"Quite dead," he said sorrowfully; "my old friend gone at last. One of a fine sort too; a just man for all his temper. They called him 'devil,' and he was fierce when he was younger, but if I never meet a worse devil than he was I shall do well. He was very kind to me once—very. How did he go?—in pain, I fear."

"We were talking together, when suddenly he was seized with the attack. I got the medicine as quick as I could and tried to get it down his throat, but he could not swallow, and in the hurry the glass was knocked by a jerk of his head right out of my hands. Next second he was dead."

"Very quick—quicker than I should have expected. Did he say anything?"

"No."

Now, just as Philip delivered himself of this last lie, a curious incident happened, or rather an incident that is apt to seem curious to a person who has just told a lie. The corpse distinctly moved its right hand—the same that had been clasped over the old man's head as he denounced his son.

"Good God!" said Philip, turning pale as death, "what's that?" and even the doctor started a little, and cast a keen look at the dead face.

"Nothing," he said. "I have seen that happen before when there had been considerable tension of the muscles before death; it is only their final slackening, that is all. Come, will you ring the bell? They had better come and take it upstairs."

This sad task had just been performed, and Mr. Caley was about to take his leave, when Pigott came down and whispered something into his ear that evidently caused him the most lively astonishment. Drawing Philip aside, he said:

"The housekeeper asks me to come up and see 'Mrs. Philip Caresfoot,' whom she thinks is going to be confined. Does she mean your wife?"

"Yes," answered Philip, sullenly, "she does. It is a long story, and I am too upset to tell it you now. It will soon be all over the country, I suppose."

The old doctor whistled, but judged it advisable not to put any more questions, when suddenly an idea seemed to strike him.

"You said you were talking to your father when the fit took him; was it about your marriage?"

"Yes."

"When did he first know of it?"

"To-day, I believe."

"Ah, thank you;" and he followed Pigott upstairs.

That night, exactly at twelve o'clock, another little lamp floated out on the waters of life: Angela was born.

CHAPTER XII.

WHEN the doctor had gone upstairs, Philip went into the dining-room to eat something, only to find that food was repugnant to him; he could scarcely swallow a mouthful. To some extent, however, he supplied its place by wine, of which he drank several glasses. Then, drawn by a strange fascination, he went back into the little study, and, remembering the will, bethought himself that it might be as well to secure it. In taking it off the table, however, a folded and much-erased sheet of manuscript was disclosed. Recognizing Bellamy's writing, he took it up and commenced to read the draft, for it was nothing else. Its substance was as follows.

The document began by stating that the testator's former will was declared null and void on account of the "treacherous and dishonorable conduct of his son Philip." It then, in brief but sweeping terms, bequeathed and devised to trustees, of whom Philip was not one, the unentailed property and personalty to be held by them: firstly, for the benefit of any *son* that might be born to the said disinherited Philip by *his wife Hilda*—the question of daughters being, probably by accident, passed over in silence—and failing such issue, then to the testator's nephew, George Caresfoot, absolutely, subject, however, to the following curious condition: Should the said George Caresfoot, *either by deed or gift or will*, attempt to reconvey the estate to his cousin Philip, or to descendants of the said Philip, then the gift over to the said George was to be of none effect, and the whole was to pass to some distant cousins of the testator's who lived in Scotland. Then followed several legacies and one charge on the estate to the extent of £1,000 a year payable to the *separate* use of the aforesaid Hilda Caresfoot for life, and reverting at death to the holder of the estate.

In plain English, Philip was, under this draft, totally disinherited, first in favor of his own male issue, by his wife Hilda, all mention of daughters being omitted, and failing such issue, in favor of his hated cousin George, who, as though to add insult to injury, was prohibited from willing the property back either to himself or his descendants, by whom the testator had probably understood the children of a second marriage.

Philip read the document over twice carefully.

"Phew!" he said, "that was touch and go. Thank heavens he had no time to carry out his kind intentions."

But presently a terrible thought struck him. He rang the bell hastily. It was answered by the footman, who, since he had an hour before helped to carry his poor master upstairs, had become quite demoralized. It was some time before Philip could get an answer to his question as to whether or no any one had been with his father that day while he was out. At last he succeeded in extracting a reply from the man that nobody had been except the young lady—"leastways, he begged pardon, Mrs. Caresfoot, as he was told she was."

"Never mind her," said Philip, feeling as though a load had been taken from his breast; "you are sure nobody else has been?"

"No sir, nobody; leastways he begged pardon, nobody except lawyer Bellamy and his clerk, who had been there all the afternoon writing with a black bag, and had sent for Simmons to be witnessed."

"You can go," said Philip, in a quiet voice. He saw it all now, he had let the old man die *after* he had executed the fresh will disinheriting him. He had let him die; he had effectually and beyond redemption cut his own throat. Doubtless, too, Bellamy had taken the new will with him; there was no chance of his being able to destroy it.

By degrees, however, his fit of brooding gave way to one of sullen fury against his wife, himself, but most of all against his dead father. Drunk with excitement, rage, and baffled avarice, he seized a candle and staggered up to the room where the corpse had been laid, launching imprecations as he went at his dead father's head. But when he came face to face with that dread Presence his passion died, and a cold sense of the awful quiet and omnipotence of death came upon him and chilled him into fear. In some indistinct way he realized how impotent is the chafing of the waters of Mortality against the iron-bound coasts of Death. To what purpose did he rail against that solemn quiet thing, that husk and mask of life which lay in unmoved mockery of his reviling?

His father was dead, and he, even he, had killed his father. He was his father's murderer. And then a terror of the reckoning that must one day be struck between that dead man's spirit and his own took possession of him, and a foreknowledge of the awful shadow under which he must henceforth live crept into his mind and froze the very marrow in his bones. He looked again at the face, and, to his excited imagination, it appeared to have assumed a sardonic smile. The curse of Cain fell upon him as he looked, and weighed him down; his hair rose, and the cold sweat poured from his forehead. At length he could bear it no longer, but, turning, fled out of the room and out of the house, far into the night.

When, haggard with mental and bodily exhaustion, he at length returned, it was after midnight. He found Dr. Caley waiting for him: he had just come from the sick-room and wore an anxious look upon his face.

"Your wife has been delivered of a fine girl," he said; "but I am bound to tell you that her condition is far from satisfactory. The case is a most complicated and dangerous one."

"A girl!" groaned Philip, mindful of the will. "Are you sure that it is a girl?"

"Of course I am sure," answered the doctor, testily.

"And Hilda ill—I don't understand."

"Look here, my good fellow, you are upset; take a glass of brandy and go to bed. Your wife does not wish to see you now, but, if necessary, I will send for you. Now, do as I tell you, or you will be down next. Your nerves are seriously shaken."

Philip did as he was bid, and, as soon as he had seen him off to his room, the doctor returned upstairs.

In the early morning he sent for two of his brother-practitioners, and they held a consultation, the upshot of which was that they had come to the conclusion nothing short of a miracle could save Hilda's life—a conclusion that she herself had arrived at some hours before.

"Doctor," she said, "I trust to you to let me know when the end is near. I wish my husband to be present when I die, but not before."

"Hush, my child—never talk of dying yet. Please God, you have many years of life before you."

She shook her golden head a little sadly.

"No, doctor, my sand has run out, and perhaps it is as well. Give me the child—why do you keep the child away from me? It is the messenger sent to call me to a happier world. Yes, she is an angel messenger. When I am gone, see that you call her 'Angela,' so that I may know by what name to greet her when the time comes."

During the course of the morning she expressed a strong desire to see Maria Lee, who was accordingly sent for.

It will be remembered that old Mr. Caresfoot had on the previous day, immediately after Hilda had left him, sat down and written to Maria Lee. In this note he told her the whole shameful truth, ending it with a few words of bitter humiliation and self-reproach that such a thing should have befallen her at the hands of one bearing his name. Over the agony of shame and grief thus let loose upon this unfortunate girl we will draw a veil. It is fortunate for the endurance of human reason that life does not hold many such hours as that through which she passed after the receipt of this letter. As was but natural, notwithstanding old Mr. Caresfoot's brief vindication of Hilda's conduct in his letter, Maria was filled with indignation at what to herself she called her treachery and deceit.

While she was yet full of these thoughts, a messenger came galloping over from Bratham Abbey, bringing a note from Dr. Caley that told her of her old friend's sudden death, and of Hilda's dangerous condition, and her desire to see her. The receipt of this news plunged her into a fresh access of grief, for she had grown fond of the old man; nor had the warm affection for Hilda that had found a place in her gentle heart been altogether wrenched away; and, now that she heard that her rival was face to face with that King of Terrors before whom all earthly love, hate, hope, and ambition must fall down and cease their troubling, it revived in all its force; nor did any thought of her own wrongs come to chill it.

Within half an hour she was at the door of the Abbey House, where the doctor met her, and, in answer to her eager question, told her that, humanly speaking, it was impossible her friend could live through another twenty-four hours, adding an injunction that she must not stay with her long.

She entered the sick-room with a heavy heart, and there from Hilda's dying lips she heard the story of her marriage and of Philip's perfidy. Their reconciliation was as a complete as her friend's failing voice and strength would allow. At length she tore herself away, and, turning at the door, took her last look at Hilda, who had raised herself upon her elbow, and was gazing at her retreating form with an earnestness that was very touching. The eyes, Maria felt, were taking their fill of what they looked upon for the last time in this world. Catching her tearful gaze, the dying woman smiled, and, lifting her hand, pointed upwards. Thus they parted.

But Maria could control herself no longer: her own blasted prospects, the loss of the man she loved, and the affecting scene through which she had just passed, all helped to break her down. Running downstairs into the dining-room, she threw herself on a sofa, and gave full passage to her grief. Presently she became aware that she was not alone. Philip stood before her, or rather, the wreck of him whom she knew as Philip. Indeed, it was hard to recognize in this scared man, with dishevelled hair, white and trembling lips, and eyes ringed round with black, the bold, handsome youth whom she had loved. The sight of him stayed her sorrow, and a sense of her bitter injuries rushed in upon her.

"What do you want with me?" she asked.

"Want! I want forgiveness. I am crushed, Maria, crushed—quite crushed," and he put his hands to his face and sobbed.

She answered him with the quiet dignity that good women can command in moments of emergency—dignity of a very different stamp from Hilda's haughty pride, but perhaps as impressive in its way.

"You ask forgiveness of me, and say that you are crushed. Has it occurred to you that, without fault of my own, except the fault of trusting you as entirely as I loved you, I too am crushed? Do you know that you have wantonly, or to gain selfish ends, broken my heart, blighted my name, and driven me from my home, for I can live here no more? Do you understand that you have done me one of the greatest injuries one person can do to another? I say, do you know all this, Philip Caresfoot, and, knowing it, do you still ask me to forgive you? Do you think it possible that I *can* forgive?"

He had never heard her speak like this before, and did not remember that intense feeling is the mother of eloquence. He gazed at her for a moment in astonishment; then he dropped his face into his hands again and groaned, making no other answer. After waiting awhile, she went on—

"I am an insignificant creature, I know, and perhaps the mite of my happiness or misery makes little difference in the scale of things; but to me the gift of all my love was everything. I gave it to you, Philip—gave it without a doubt or murmur, gave it with both hands. I can never have it back to give again! How you have treated it you best know." Here she broke down a little, and then continued: "It may seem curious, but though my love has been so mistakenly given; though you to whom it was given have dealt so ill with it; yet I am anxious that on my side there should be no bitter memory, that, in looking back at all this in after years, you should never be able to dwell upon any harsh or unkind word of mine. It is on that account, and also because I feel that it is not for me to judge you, and that you have already much to bear, that I do as you ask me, and say, 'Philip, from my heart I forgive you, as I trust that the Almighty may forgive me.'"

He flung himself upon his knees before her, and tried to take her hand. "You do not know how you have humbled me," he groaned.

She gazed at him with pity.

"I am sorry," she said; "I did not wish to humble you. I have one word more to say, and then I must go. I have just bid my last earthly farewell to—your wife. My farewell to you must be as complete as that, as complete as though the grave had already swallowed one of us. We have done with each other for ever. I do not think that I shall come back here. In my waking moments your name shall never willingly pass my lips again. I will say it for the last time now. *Philip, Philip, Philip*, whom I chose to love out of all the world, I pray God that he will take me, or deaden the edge of what I suffer, and that He may never let my feet cross your path or my eyes fall upon your face again."

In another second she had passed out of the room and out of his life.

That night, or rather just before dawn on the following morning, Hilda, knowing that her end was very near, sent for her husband.

"Go quickly, doctor," she said. "I shall die at dawn."

The doctor found him seated in the same spot where Maria Lee had left him.

"What, more misery!" he said, when he had told his errand. "I cannot bear it. There is a curse upon me—death and wickedness, misery and death!"

"You must come if you wish to see your wife alive."

"I will come;" and he rose and followed him.

A sad sight awaited him. The moment of the gray dawn was drawing near, and, by his wife's request, a window had been unshuttered, that her dimmed eyes might once more look upon the light. On the great bed in the centre of the room lay Hilda, whose life was now quickly draining from her, and by her side was placed the sleeping infant. She was raised and supported on either side by pillows, and her unbound golden hair fell around her shoulders, inclosing her face as in a frame. Her pallid countenance seemed touched with an awful beauty that had not belonged to it in life, whilst in her eyes was that dread and prescient gaze which sometimes come to those who are about to solve death's mystery.

By the side of the bed knelt Mr. Fraser, the clergyman of the parish, repeating in an earnest tone the prayers for the dying, whilst the sad-faced attendants moved with muffled tread backwards and forwards from the ring of light around the bed into the dark shadows that lay beyond.

When Philip came, the clergyman ceased praying, and drew back into the further part of the room, as did Pigott and the nurse, the former taking the baby with her.

Hilda motioned to him to come close to her. He came, and bent over and kissed her, and she, with an effort, threw one ivory arm around his neck, and smiled sweetly. After about a minute, during which she was apparently collecting her thoughts, she spoke in a low voice, and in her native tongue.

"I have not sent for you before, Philip, for two reasons—first, because I wished to spare you pain; and next, in order that I might have time to rid my mind of angry thoughts against you. They are all gone now—gone with every other earthly interest; but I *was* angry with you, Philip. And now listen to me—for I have not much time—and do not forget my words in future years, when the story of my life will seem but as a shadow that once fell upon your path. Change your ways, Philip dear; abandon deceit, atone for the past; if you can, make your peace with Maria Lee, and marry her—ah! it is a pity that you did not do that at first, and leave me to go my ways—and, above all, humble your heart before the Power that I am about to face. I love you, dear, and, notwithstanding all, I am thankful to have been your wife. Please God, we shall meet again."

She paused awhile, and then spoke in English. To the astonishment of all in the room, her voice was strong and clear, and she uttered her words with an energy that, under the circumstances, seemed almost awful.

"Tell her to bring the child."

There was no need for Philip to repeat what she said, for Pigott heard her, and at once came forward with the baby, which she laid beside her.

The dying woman placed her hand upon its tiny head, and, turning her eyes upwards with the rapt expression of one who sees a vision, said:

"May the power of God be about you to protect you, my motherless babe, may angels guard you, and make you as they are; and may the heavy curse and everlasting doom of the Almighty fall upon those who would bring evil upon you."

She paused, and then addressed her husband.

"Philip, you have heard my words; in your charge I leave the child, see that you never betray my trust."

Then, turning to Pigott, she said in a fainter voice:

"Thank you for your kindness to me. You have a good face; if you can, stop with my child, and give her your love and care. And now, may God have mercy on my soul!"

Then came a minute's silence, broken only by the stifled sobs of those who stood around, till a ray of light from the rising sun struggled through the gray mist of the morning, and, touching the heads of mother and child, illumined them as with a glory. It passed as quickly as it came, drawing away with it the mother's life. Suddenly, as it faded, she spread out her arms, sighed, and smiled. When the doctor reached the bed, her story was told: she had fallen asleep.

Death had been very gentle with her.

CHAPTER XIII.

Go, my reader, if the day is dull, and you feel inclined to moralize—for whatever may be said to the contrary, there are less useful occupations—and look at your village churchyard. What do you see before you? A plot of inclosed ground backed by a gray old church, a number of tombstones more or less decrepit, and a great quantity of little oblong mounds covered with rank grass. If you have any imagination, any power of thought, you will see more than that. First, with the instinctive selfishness of human nature, you will recognize your own future habitation; perhaps your eye will mark the identical spot where the body you love must lie through all seasons and weathers, through the slow centuries that will flit so fast for you, till the crash of doom. It is good that you should think of that, although it makes you shudder. The English churchyard takes the place of the Egyptian mummy at the feast, or the slave in the Roman conqueror's car—it mocks your vigor, and whispers of the end of beauty and strength.

Probably you need some such reminder. But if, giving to the inevitable the sigh that is its due, you pursue the vein of thought, it may further occur to you that the plot before you is in a sense a summary of the aspirations of humanity. It marks the realization of human hopes, it is the crown of human ambitions, the grave of human failures. Here, too, is the end of the man, and here the birthplace of the angel or the demon. It is his sure inheritance, one that he never solicits and never squanders; and, last, it is the only certain resting-place of sleepless, tired mortality.

Here it was that they brought Hilda and the old squire, and laid them side by side against the coffin of yeoman Caresfoot, whose fancy it had been to be buried in stone, and then, piling primroses and blackthorn blooms upon their graves, left them to their chilly sleep. Farewell to them; they have passed to where as yet we may not follow. Violent old man and proud and lovely woman, rest in peace, if peace be the portion of you both!

To return to the living. The news of the sudden decease of old Mr. Caresfoot; of the discovery of Philip's secret marriage and the death of his wife; of the terms of the old man's will, under which, Hilda being dead, and having only left a daughter behind her, George inherited all the unentailed portion of the property, with the curious provision that he was never to leave it back to Philip or his children; of the sudden departure of Miss Lee, and of many other things, that were some of them true and some of them false, following as they did upon the heels of the great dinner-party, and the announcement made thereat, threw the country-side into a state of indescribable ferment. When this settled down, it left a strong and permanent residuum of public indignation and contempt directed against Philip, the more cordially, perhaps, because he was no longer a rich man. People very rarely express contempt or indignation against a rich man who happens to be their neighbor in the country, whatever he may have done. They keep their virtue for those who are impoverished, or for their unfortunate relations. But for Philip it was felt that there was no excuse and no forgiveness; he had lost both his character and his money, and must therefore be cut, and from that day forward he was cut accordingly.

As for Philip himself, he was fortunately, as yet, ignorant of the kind intentions of his friends and neighbors, who had been so fond of him a week ago. He had enough upon his shoulders without that—for he had spoken no lie when he told Maria Lee that he was crushed by the dreadful and repeated blows that had fallen upon him, blows that had robbed him of everything that made life worth living, and given him in return nothing but an infant who could not inherit, and who was therefore only an incumbrance.

Who is it that says, "After all, let a bad man take what pains he may to push it down, a human soul is an awful, ghostly, unique possession for a bad man to have"? During the time that had elapsed between the death and burial of his father and wife, Philip had become thoroughly acquainted with the truth of this remark.

Do what he would, he could never for a single hour shake himself free from the recollection of his father's death; whenever he shut his eyes, his uneasy mind continually conjured up the whole scene with uncanny distinctness; the gloomy room, the contorted face of the dying man, the red flicker of the firelight on the wall—all these things were burnt deep into the tablets of his memory. More and more did he recognize the fact that, even should he live long enough to bury the events of that hour beneath the débris of many years, the lapse of time would be insufficient to bring forgetfulness, and the recognition brought with it moral helplessness. He had, too, sufficient religious feeling to make him uneasy as to his future fate, and possessed a certain amount of imagination, which was at this time all directed toward that awful day when he and his dead father must settle their final accounts. Already, in the quiet nights, he would wake with a start, thinking that the inevitable time had come. Superstitious fears also would seize him with their clammy fingers, and he would shake and tremble at the fancied step of ghostly feet, and his blood would curdle in his veins as his mind hearkened to voices that were for ever still.

And, worst of all, what had been done, and could never be undone, had been done in vain. These deadly torments must be endured, whilst the object for which they had been incurred had utterly escaped him. He had sold himself to the powers of evil for a price, and that price had not been paid. But the bond was good for all that.

And so he would brood, hour after hour, till he felt himself drawing near to madness. Sometimes by a strong effort he would succeed in tearing his mind away from the subject, but then its place was instantly filled by a proud form with reproachful eyes, and he would feel that there, too, death had put it out of his power to make atonement. Of those whom he had wronged Maria Lee alone survived, and she had left him in sorrow, more bitter than any anger. Truly, Philip Caresfoot was in melancholy case. Somewhere he had read that the wages of sin is death, but surely what he felt surpassed the bitterness of death. His evil-doing had not prospered with him. The snare he had set for his father had fallen back upon himself, and he was a crushed and ruined man.

It affords a curious insight into his character to reflect that all these piled-up calamities, all this wreck and sudden death, did not bring him penitent on his knees before the Maker he had outraged. The crimes he had committed, especially if unsuccessful, or the sorrows that had fallen upon him, would have sufficed to reduce nine-tenths of ordinary men to a condition of humble supplication. For, generally speaking, irreligion, or rather forgetfulness of God, is a plant of no deep growth in the human heart, since its roots are turned by the rock of that innate knowledge of a higher Power that forms the foundation of every soul, and on which we are glad enough to set our feet when the storms of trouble and emergency threaten to destroy us. But with Philip this was not so. He never thought of repentance. His was not the nature to fall down and say, "Lord, I have sinned, take Thou my burden from me." Indeed, he was not so much sorry for the past as fearful for the future. It was not grief for wrong-doing that wrung his heart and broke his spirit, but rather his natural sorrow at losing the only creature he had ever deeply loved, chagrin at the shame of his position and the failure of his hopes, and the icy fingers of superstitious fears.

The crisis had come and passed: he had sinned against his Father in heaven and his father on earth, and he did not sorrow for his sin; his wife had left him, murmuring with her dying lips exhortations to repentance, and he did not soften; shame and loss had fallen upon him, and he did not turn to God. But his pride had broken, all that remained to him of strength was his wickedness; the flood that had swept over him had purged away not the evil but the good, from the evil it only took its courage. Henceforth, if he sins at all, his will be no bold and hazardous villainy which, while it excites horror, can almost compel respect, but rather the low and sordid crime, the safe and treacherous iniquity.

Ajax no longer defies the lightning—he mutters curses on it beneath his breath.

On the evening of the double funeral—which Philip did not feel equal to attending, and at which George, in a most egregious hat-band and with many sobs and tears, officiated as chief mourner—Mr. Fraser thought it would be a kind act on his part to go and offer such consolation to the bereaved man as lay within his power, if indeed he would accept it. Somewhat contrary to his expectation, he was, on arrival at the Abbey House, asked in without delay.

"I am glad to see a human face," said Philip to the clergyman, as he entered the room; "this loneliness is intolerable. I am as much alone as though I lay stark in the churchyard like my poor wife."

Mr. Fraser did not answer him immediately, so taken up was he in noticing the wonderful changes a week had wrought in his appearance. Not only did his countenance bear traces of the illness and exhaustion that might not unnaturally be expected in such a case of bereavement, but it faithfully reflected the change that had taken place in his mental attitude. His eyes had lost the frank boldness that had made them very pleasing to some people; they looked scared; the mouth too was rendered conspicuous by the absence of the firm lines that once gave it character; indeed, the man's whole appearance was pitiful and almost abject.

"I am afraid," he said at length in a tone of gentle compassion, "that you must have suffered a great deal, Caresfoot."

"Suffered! I have suffered the tortures of the damned! I still suffer them, I shall always suffer them."

"I do not wish," said the clergyman, with a little hesitation, "to appear officious or to make a mockery of your grief by telling you that it is for your good; but I should fail in my duty if I did not point out to you that He who strikes the blow has the power to heal the wound, and that very often such things are for our ultimate benefit, either in this world or the next. Carry your troubles to Him, my dear fellow, acknowledge His hand, and, if you know in your heart of any way in which you have sinned, offer Him your hearty repentance; do this, and you will not be deserted. Your life, that now seems to you nothing but ashes, may yet be both a happy and a useful one."

Philip smiled bitterly as he answered:

"You talk to me of repentance—how can I repent when Providence has treated me so cruelly, robbing me at a single blow of my wife and my fortune? I know that I did wrong in concealing my marriage, but I was driven to it by fear of my father. Ah! if you had seen him as I saw him, you would have known that they were right to call him 'Devil Caresfoot.'" He checked himself, and then went on. "He forced me into the engagement with Miss Lee, and announced it without my consent. Now I am ruined—everything is taken from me."

"You have your little daughter, and all the entailed estate—at least, so I am told."

"My little daughter!—I never want to see her face; she killed her mother. If it had been a boy, it would have been different, for then, at any rate, that accursed George would not have got my birthright. My little daughter, indeed! don't enumerate her among my earthly blessings."

"It is rather sad to hear you talk like that of your child; but, at any rate, you are not left in want. You have one of the finest old places in the county, and a thousand a year, which to most men would be riches."

"And which to me," answered Philip, "is beggary. I should have had six, and I have got one. But look you here, Fraser, I swear before God—"

"Hush! I cannot listen to such talk."

"Well, then, before anything you like, that, while I live, I will never rest one single moment until I get my own back again. It may seem impossible, but I will find a way. For instance," he added, as a thought struck him, "strangely enough, the will does not forbid me to buy the lands back. If I can get them no other way, I will buy them—do you hear?—I will buy them. I *must* have them again before I die."

"How will you get the money?"

"The money? I will save it, make it, steal it, get it somehow. Oh! do not be afraid; I will get the money. It will take a few years, but I will get it somehow. It is not the want of a few thousands that will stop a determined man."

"And suppose your cousin won't sell."

"I will find a way to make him sell—some bribe, something. There, there," and his enthusiasm and eagerness vanished in a moment, and the broken look came back upon his face. "It's all nonsense; I am talking impossibilities—a little weak in my mind, I suppose. Forget it, there's a good fellow; say nothing about it. And so you buried them? Ah, me! ah, me! And George did chief mourner. I suppose he blubbered freely; he always could blubber freely when he liked. I remember how he used to take folks in as a lad, and then laugh at them; that's why they called him 'Crocodile' at school. Well, he's my master now, and I'm his very humble servant; perhaps one day it will be the other way up again. What, must you go? If you knew how fearfully lonely I am, you would not go. My nerves have quite gone, and I fancy all sorts of things. I can think of nothing but those two graves out there in the dark. Have they sodded them over? Tell them to sod them over. It was kind of you to come to see me. You mustn't pay any attention to my talk; I am not quite myself. Good-night."

Mr. Fraser was an extremely unsuspicious man, but somehow, as he picked his way to the vicarage to eat his solitary chop, he felt a doubt rising in his mind as to whether, his disclaimer notwithstanding, Philip had not sincerely meant all he said.

"He is shockingly changed," he mused, "and I am not sure that it is a change for the better. Poor fellow, he has a great deal to bear, and should be kindly judged. It is all so painful that I must try to divert my mind. Mrs. Brown, will you bring me a little chocolate-colored book, that you will see on the table in my study, when you come back with the potatoes? It has Plato—P-l-a-t-o—printed on the back."

CHAPTER XIV.

THE jubilation of George at the turn events had taken may perhaps be more easily imagined than described. There is generally one weak point about all artful schemes to keep other people out of their rights; they break down over some unforeseen detail, or through the neglect of some trivial and obvious precaution. But this was one of the glorious instances to the contrary that prove the rule. Nothing had broken down, everything had prospered as a holy cause always should, and does—in theory. The stars in their courses had fought for Sisera, everything had succeeded beyond expectation, nothing had failed. In the gratitude of his heart, George would willingly have given a thousand pounds towards the establishment of a training-school for anonymous letter-writers, or the erection of a statue to Hilda Caresfoot, whose outraged pride and womanly jealousy had done him such yeoman service.

Speaking seriously, he had great cause for rejoicing. Instead of a comparatively slender younger son's portion, he had stepped into a fine and unincumbered property of over five thousand a year, and that in the heyday of his youth, when in the full possession of all his capacities for enjoyment, which were large indeed. Henceforth everything that money could buy would be his, including the respect and flattery of his poorer neighbors. An added flavor, too, was given to the overflowing cup of his good fortune by the fact that it had been wrenched from the hands of the cousin whom he hated, and on whom he had from a boy sworn to be avenged. Poor Philip! bankrupt in honor and broken in fortune, he could afford to pity him now, to pity him ostentatiously and in public. He was open-handed with his pity, was George. Nor did he lack a sympathizer in these delicious moments of unexpected triumph.

"Did I not tell you," said Mrs. Bellamy, in her full, rich tones, on the afternoon of the reading of the will—"did I not tell you that, if you would consent to be guided by me, I would pull you through, and have I not pulled you through? Never misdoubt my judgment again, my dear George; it is infinitely sounder than your own."

"You did, Anne, you certainly did; you are a charming woman, and as clever as you are charming."

"Compliments are all very well, and I am sure I appreciate yours"—and she gave a little courtesy—"at their proper value; but I must remind you, George, that I have done my part of the bargain, and that now you must do yours."

"Oh! that's all right; Bellamy shall have the agency and two hundred a year with it, and, to show you that I have not forgotten you, perhaps you will accept this in memorial of our joint achievement;" and he drew from his pocket and opened a case containing a superb set of sapphires.

Mrs. Bellamy had all a beautiful woman's love for jewels, and especially adored sapphires.

"Oh!" she said, clasping her hands, "thank you, George; they are perfectly lovely."

"Perhaps," he replied, politely; "but not half so lovely as their wearer. I wonder," he added, with a little laugh, "what the old boy would say, if he could know that a thousand pounds of his personalty have gone by anticipation to buy a necklace for Anne Bellamy."

To this remark she made no reply, being apparently absorbed in her own thoughts. At last she spoke.

"I don't want to seem ungracious, George, but these"—and she touched the jewels—"were not the reward I expected: I want the letters you promised me back."

"My dear Anne, you are under a mistake; I never promised you the letters; I said that, under the circumstances, I might possibly restore them—a very different thing from promising."

Mrs. Bellamy flushed a little, and the great pupils of her sleepy eyes contracted till she looked quite dangerous.

"Then I must have strangely misunderstood you," she said.

"What do you want the letters for? Can't you trust me with them?"

"Don't you think, George, that if you had passed through something very terrible, you would like to have all the mementoes of that dark time destroyed? Those letters are the record of my terrible time; nothing remains of it but those written lines. I want to burn them, to stamp them into powder, to obliterate them as I have obliterated all the past. Whilst they exist I can never feel safe. Supposing you were to turn traitor to me and let those letters fall into the hands of others, supposing that you lost them, I should be a ruined woman. I speak frankly, you see; I fully appreciate my danger, principally because I know that the more intimate a man and woman have been, the more chance there is of their becoming bitter enemies. George, give me those letters; do not overcloud my future with the shadows of the past."

"You talk as well as you do everything else, Anne; you are really a very remarkable woman. But, curiously enough, those letters, the existence of which is so obnoxious to you, are to me a source of great interest. You know that I love to study character —curious occupation for a young man, isn't it?—but I do. Well, in my small experience, I have never yet, either in fiction or in real life, come across such a fascinating display as is reflected in those letters. There I can, and often do, trace in minutest detail the agony of a strong mind, can see the barriers of what people call religion, early training, self-respect, and other curiosities which we we name virtues, bursting away one by one under pressure, like the water-tight bulkheads they put in passenger steamers, till at length the work is done; the moral ship sinks, and the writer stands revealed what you are, my dear Anne, the loveliest, the cleverest, and the most utterly unscrupulous woman in the three kingdoms."

She rose very quietly, but quite white with passion, and answered in her low voice:

"Whatever I am you made me, and *you* are a devil, George Caresfoot, or you would not take pleasure in the tortures you inflicted before you destroyed. But, don't go too far, or you may regret it. Am I a woman to be played with? I think that you have trained me too well."

He laughed a little uneasily.

"There, you see; *grattez le Russe*, etc., and out comes the true character. Look at your face in the glass; it is magnificent, but not pleasant; rather dangerous, indeed. Why, Anne, do be reasonable; if I gave you those letters, I should never be able to sleep in peace. For the sake of my own safety I dare not abandon the whip-hand I have of you. Remember, you could, if you chose, say some unpleasant things about me, and I don't want that any more than you do just now. But, you see, whilst I hold in my power what would, if necessary, effectually ruin you, and probably Bellamy too—for this county society is absurdly prejudiced—I have little cause for fear. Perhaps in the future you may be able to render me some service for which you shall have the letters—who knows? You see I am perfectly frank with you, for the simple reason that I know that it is useless to try to conceal my thoughts from a person of your penetration."

"Well, well, perhaps you are right; it is difficult to trust oneself, much more any one else. At any rate," she said, with a bitter smile, "you have given me Bellamy, a start in society, and a sapphire necklace. In twenty years I hope, if the fates are kind, to have lost Bellamy on the road—he is really unendurable—to rule society, and to have as many sapphire necklaces and other fine things as I care for. In enumerating my qualities, you omitted one—ambition."

"With your looks, your determination, and your brains, there is nothing that you will not be able to do if you set your mind to it, and don't make an enemy of your devoted friend."

And thus the conversation ended.

Now little Mr. Bellamy had, after much anxious thought, just about this time come to a bold determination—namely, to assert his marital authority over Mrs. Bellamy. Indeed, his self-pride was much injured by the treatment he received at his wife's hands, for it seemed to him that he was utterly ignored in his own house. In fact, it would not be too much to say that he *was* an entire nonentity. He had married Mrs. Bellamy for love, or rather from fascination, though she had nothing in the world—married her in a fortnight from the time that George had first introduced him. When he had walked out of church with his beautiful bride, he had thought himself the luckiest man in London, whereas now he could not but feel that matrimony had not fulfilled his expectations. In the first place, Love's young dream—he was barely thirty—came to a rude awakening, for, once married, it was impossible—though he had, in common with the majority of little men, a tolerably good opinion of himself—but that he should perceive that his wife did not care one brass farthing about him. To his soft advances she was as cold as a marble statue, the lovely eyes never grew tender for him. Indeed, he found that she was worse than a statue, for statues cannot indulge in bitter mockery and contemptuous comments, and Mrs. Bellamy could, and, what is more, frequently did.

"It is very well," reflected her husband, "to marry the loveliest woman in the county, but I don't see the use of it if she treats one like a dog."

At last this state of affairs had grown intolerable, and, meditating in the solitude of his office, Mr. Bellamy resolved to assert himself once for all, and set matters on a proper footing, and Mrs. Bellamy in her place. But it is one thing for husbands of the Bellamy stamp to form high-stomached resolutions, and another for them to put those resolutions into active and visible operation on wives of the Mrs. Bellamy stamp. Indeed, had it not been for a little incident about to be detailed, it is doubtful if Mr. Bellamy would have ever come to the scratch at all.

When George had gone, Mrs. Bellamy sat down in by no means the sweetest of tempers to think. But thinking, in this instance, proved an unprofitable occupation, and she gave it up in order to admire the sapphire necklace that lay upon her knee. At that moment her husband entered the room, but she took no notice, merely going on examining the stones. After moving about a little, as though to attract attention, the gentleman spoke.

"I have managed to get home to lunch, my dear."

"Indeed."

"Well, you might take a little notice of me."

"Why? Is there anything remarkable about you this morning?"

"No, there is not; but, remarkable or not, a man who has been fool enough"—Mr. Bellamy laid great emphasis on the word "fool" —"to get married has a right to expect when he comes into his own house that he will have a little notice taken of him, and not be as completely overlooked as—as though he were a tub of butter in a grocer's shop;" and he puffed out his chest, rubbed his hands, and looked defiant.

The lady laid her head back on the chair, and laughed with exquisite enjoyment.

"Really, my dear John, you will kill me," she said at length.

"May I ask," he replied, looking as though there was nothing in the world that he would like better, "what you are laughing at?"

"Your slightly vulgar but happy simile; it is easy to see where you draw your inspiration from. If you had only said butterine, inferior butter, you know, the counterfeit article, it would have been perfect."

Her husband gave a glance at his tubby little figure in the glass.

"Am I to understand that you refer to me as 'butterine,' Mrs. Bellamy?"

"Oh! certainly yes, if you like; but, butter or not, you will melt if you lose your temper so."

"I have not lost my temper, madam; I am perfectly cool," he replied, positively gasping with fury. Here his eye fell upon the necklace. "What necklace is that? Who gave you that necklace? I demand to know."

"You *demand* to know! Be careful what you say, please. Mr. George Caresfoot gave me the necklace. It cost a thousand pounds. Are you satisfied?"

"No, I am not satisfied; I will not have that cursed George Caresfoot continually here. I will send him back his necklace. I will assert my rights as an Englishman and a spouse, I will—"

"You will sit down and listen to me."

The tone of the voice checked his absurd linguistic and physical capers, and caused him to look at his wife. She was standing and pointing to a chair. Her face was calm and immovable, only her eyes appeared to expand and contract with startling rapidity. One glance was enough for Bellamy. He felt frightened, and sat down in the indicated chair.

"That's right," she said, pleasantly; "now we can have a cosey chat. John, you are a lawyer, and therefore, I suppose, more or less a man of the world. Now, *as* a lawyer and a man of the world I ask you to look at me and then at yourself, and say if you think it likely or even possible that I married you for love. To be frank, I did nothing of the sort; I married you because you were the person most suited to my purpose. If you will only understand that, it will save us both a great deal of trouble. As for your talk about asserting yourself and exerting your authority, it is simple nonsense.

You are very well in your way, my dear John, and a fair attorney; but do you suppose for one moment that you are capable of matching yourself against me? If so, you make a shocking mistake. Be advised, and do not try the experiment. But don't think that the bargain is all my side—it is not. If you will behave yourself properly, and be guided by my advice, I will make you one of the richest and most powerful man in the county. If you will not, I shall shake myself free of you as soon as I am strong enough. Rise I must and will, and if you will not rise with me, I will rise alone. As regards your complaints of my not caring about you, the world is wide, my dear John; console yourself elsewhere. I shall not be jealous. And now I think I have explained everything. It is so much more satisfactory to have a clear understanding. Come, shall we go to lunch?"

But Bellamy wanted no lunch that day.

"After all," he soliloquized to himself between the pangs of a racking headache brought on by his outburst of temper, "time sometimes brings its revenges, and, if it does, you may look out, Mrs. Bellamy."

CHAPTER XV.

It is perhaps time that the reader should know a little of the ancient house and locality where many of the personages of whose history these pages treat, lived and moved and had their being.

The Abbey House, so called, was in reality that part of the monastery which had been devoted to the use of successive generations of priors. It was, like the ruins that lay to its rear, entirely built of gray masonry, rendered grayer still by the lichens that fed upon its walls, which were of exceeding strength and thickness. It was a long, irregular building, and roofed with old and narrow tiles, which from red had, in the course of ages, faded to sober russet. The banqueting-hall was a separate building at its northern end, and connected with the main dwelling by a covered way. The aspect of the house was westerly, and the front windows looked on to an expanse of park-like land, heavily timbered with oaks of large size, some of them pollards that might have pushed their first leaves in the time of William the Conqueror. In spring their vivid green was diversified by the reddish brown of a double line of noble walnut-trees, a full half mile in length, marking the track of the carriage-drive that led to the Roxham high-road.

Behind the house lay the walled garden, celebrated in the time of the monks as being a fortnight earlier than any other in the neighborhood. Skirting the southern wall of this garden, which was a little less than a hundred paces long, the visitor reached the scattered ruins of the old monastery that had for generations served as a stone quarry to the surrounding villages, but of which enough was left, including a magnificent gateway, to show how great had been its former extent. Passing on through these, he would come to an inclosure that marked the boundaries of the old graveyard, now turned to agricultural uses, and then to the church itself, a building with a very fine tower, but possessing no particular interest, if we except some exceedingly good brasses and a colossal figure of a monk cut out of the solid heart of an oak, and supposed to be the effigy of a prior of the abbey who died in the time of Edward I. Below the church again, and about one hundred and fifty paces from it, was the vicarage, a comparatively modern building, possessing no architectural attraction, and evidently reared out of the remains of the monastery.

At the south end of the Abbey House itself lay a small grass plot and pleasure-garden fringed with shrubberies, and adorned with two fine cedar-trees. One of these trees was at its farther extremity, and under it there ran a path cut through the dense shrubbery. This path, which was edged with limes and called the "Tunnel Walk," led to the lake, and debouched in the little glade where stood Caresfoot Staff. The lake itself was a fine piece of water, partly natural and partly constructed by the monks, measuring a full mile round, and from fifty to two hundred yards in width. It was in the shape of a man's shoe, the heel facing west like the house, but projecting beyond it, the narrow part representing the hollow of the instep, being exactly opposite to it, and the sole swelling out in an easterly direction.

Bratham Abbey was altogether a fine old place, but the most remarkable thing about it was its air of antiquity and the solemnity of its peace. It did not, indeed, strike the spirit with that religious awe which is apt to fall upon us as we gaze along the vaulted aisles of great cathedrals, but it appealed perhaps with equal strength to the softer and more reflective side of our nature. For generation after generation that house had been the home of men like ourselves; they had passed and were forgotten, but it remained, the sole witness of the stories of their lives. Hands of which the very bones had long since crumbled into dust had planted those old oaks and walnuts, that still donned their green robes in summer, and shed them in the autumn, to stand great skeletons through the winter months, awaiting the resurrection of the spring.

There lay upon the place and its surroundings a burden of dead lives, intangible, but none the less real. The air was thick with memories, as suggestive as the gray dust in a vault. Even in the summer, in the full burst of nature revelling in her strength, the place was sad. But in the winter, when the wind came howling through the groaning trees, and drove the gray scud across an ashy sky, when the birds were dumb, and there were no cattle on the sodden lawn, its isolated melancholy was a palpable thing.

That hoary house might have been a gateway of the dim land we call the Past, looking down in stony sorrow on the follies of those who so soon must cross its portals, and, to the wise who could hear the lesson, pregnant with echoes of the warning voices of many generations.

Here it was that Angela grew up to womanhood.

Some nine and a half years had passed from the date of the events described in the foregoing pages, when one evening Mr. Fraser bethought him that he had been indoors all day, and proposed reading till late that night, and that therefore he had better take some exercise.

A tall and somewhat nervous-looking man, with dark eyes, a sensitive mouth, and that peculiar stoop and pallor of complexion which those devoted to much study almost invariably acquire, he had "student" written on his face. His history was a sufficiently common one. He possessed academical abilities of a very high order, and had in his youth distinguished himself greatly at college, both as a classical and a mathematical scholar. When quite young, he was appointed, through the influence of a relation, to his present living, where the income was good and the population very small indeed. Freed from all necessity for exertion, he shut himself up with his books, having his little round of parish work for relaxation, and never sought to emerge from the quiet of his aimless studies to struggle for fame and place in the laborious world. Mr. Fraser was what people call an able man thrown away. If they had known his shy, sensitive nature a little better, they would have understood that he was infinitely more suited for the solitary and peaceful lot in life which he had chosen than to become a unit in the turbulent and greedy crowd that is struggling through all the ages up the slippery steps of the temple of that greatest of our gods—Success.

There are many such men; probably you, my reader, know one or two. With infinite labor they store up honey from the fields of knowledge, collect endless data from the statistics of science, pile up their calculations against the very stars; and all to no end. As a rule, they do not write books; they gather the learning for the learning's sake, and for the very love of it rejoice to count their labor lost. And thus they go on from year to year, until the golden bowl is broken and the pitcher broken at the fountain, and the gathered knowledge sinks, or appears to sink, back to whence it came. Alas, that one generation cannot hand on its wisdom and experience—more especially its experience—to another in its perfect form! If it could, we men should soon become as gods.

It was a mild evening in the latter end of October when Mr. Fraser started on his walk. The moon was up in the heavens as he, an hour later, made his way from the side of the lake, where he had been wandering, back to the churchyard through which he had to pass to reach the vicarage. Just before he came to the gate, however, he was surprised, in such a solitary spot, to see a slight figure leaning against the wall opposite the place where lay the mortal remains of the old squire and his daughter-in-law, Hilda. He stood still and watched; the figure appeared to be gazing steadily at the graves. Presently it turned and saw him, and he recognized the great gray eyes and golden hair of little Angela Caresfoot.

"Angela, my dear, what are you doing here at this time of night?" he asked, in some surprise.

She blushed a little as she shook hands rather awkwardly with him.

"Don't be angry with me," she said in a deprecatory voice; "but I was so lonely this evening that I came here for company."

"Came here for company! What do you mean?"

She hung her head.

"Come," he said, "tell me what you mean."

"I don't quite know myself. How can I tell you?"

He looked more puzzled than ever, and she observed it and went on:

"I will try to tell you, but you must not be cross like Pigott when she cannot understand me. Sometimes I feel ever so much alone, as though I was looking for something and could not find it, and then I come and stand here and look at my mother's grave, and I get company and am not lonely any more. That is all I know; I cannot tell you any more. Do you think me silly? Pigott does."

"I think you are a very strange child. Are you not afraid to come here alone at night?"

"Afraid—oh, no! Nobody comes here; the people in the village dare not come here after dark, because they say that the ruins are full of spirits. Jakes told me that. But I must be stupid; I cannot see them, and I want so very much to see them. I hope it is not wrong, but I told my father so the other day, and he turned white and was angry with Pigott for giving me such ideas; but you know Pigott did not give them to me at all. I am not afraid to come; I like it, it is so quiet, and, if one listens enough in the quiet, I always think one may hear something that other people do not hear."

"Do you hear anything, then?"

"Yes, I hear things, but I cannot understand them. Listen to the wind in the branches of that tree, the chestnut, off which the leaf is falling now. It says something, if only I could catch it."

"Yes, child, yes, you are right in a way; all Nature tells the same eternal tale, if our ears were not stopped to its voices," he answered, with a sigh; indeed, the child's talk had struck a vein of thought familiar to his own mind, and, what is more, it deeply interested him; there was a quaint, far-off wisdom in it.

"It is pleasant to-night, is it not, Mr. Fraser?" said the little maid, "though everything is dying. The things die softly without any pain this year; last year they were all killed in the rain and wind. Look at that cloud floating across the moon, is it not beautiful? I wonder what it is the shadow of; I think all the clouds are shadows of something up in heaven."

"And when there are no clouds?"

"Oh! then heaven is quite still and happy."

"But heaven is always happy."

"Is it? I don't understand how it can be always happy if *we* go there. There must be so many to be sorry for."

Mr. Fraser mused a little: that last remark was difficult to answer. He looked at the fleecy cloud, and, falling into her humor, said:

"I think your cloud is the shadow of an eagle carrying a lamb to its little ones."

"And I think," she answered confidently, "that it is the shadow of an angel carrying a baby home."

Again he was silenced; the idea was infinitely more poetical than his own.

"This," he reflected, "is a child of a curious mental calibre."

Before he could pursue the thought further, she broke in upon it in quite a different strain.

"Have you seen Jack and Jill? They *are* jolly."

"Who are Jack and Jill?"

"Why, my ravens, of course. I got them out of the old tree with a hole in it at the end of the lake."

"The tree at the end of the lake! Why, the hole where the ravens nest is fifty feet up. Who got them for you?"

"I got them myself. Sam—you know Sam—was afraid to go up. He said he should fall, and that the old birds would peck his eyes. So I went by myself one morning quite early, with a bag tied round my neck, and got up. It was hard work, and I nearly tumbled once; but I got on the bough beneath the hole at last. It shook very much; it is so rotten, you have no idea. There were three little ones in the nest, all with great mouths. I took two, and left one for the old birds. When I was nearly down again, the old birds found me out, and flew at me, and beat my head with their wings, and pecked—oh, they did peck! Look here," and she showed him a scar on her hand; "that's where they pecked. But I stuck to my bag, and got down at last, and I'm glad I did, for we are great friends now; and I am sure the cross old birds would be quite pleased if they knew how nicely I am educating their young ones, and how their manners have improved. But I say, Mr. Fraser, don't tell Pigott; she cannot climb trees, and does not like to see me do it. She does not know I went after them myself."

Mr. Fraser laughed.

"I won't tell her, Angela, my dear; but you must be careful—you might tumble and kill yourself."

"I don't think I shall, Mr. Fraser, unless I am meant to. God looks after me as much when I am up a tree as when I am upon the ground."

Once more he had nothing to say; he could not venture to disturb her faith.

"I will walk home with you, my dear. Tell me, Angela, would you like to learn?"

"Learn!—learn what?"

"Books, and the languages that other nations, nations that have passed away, used to talk, and how to calculate numbers and distances."

"Yes, I should like to learn very much; but who will teach me?

I have learnt all Pigott knows two years ago, and since then I have been trying to learn about the trees and flowers and stars; but I look and watch, and can't understand."

"Ah! my dear, contact with Nature is the highest education; but the mind that would appreciate her wonders must have a foundation of knowledge to work upon. The uneducated man is rarely sensitive to the thousand beauties and marvels of the fields around him and the skies above him. But, if you like, I will teach you, Angela. I am practically an idle man, and it will give me great pleasure; but you must promise to work and do what I tell you."

"Oh, how good you are! Of course I will work. When am I to begin?"

"I don't know—to-morrow, if you like; but I must speak to your father first."

Her face fell a little at the mention of her father's name, but presently she said, quietly:

"My father, he will not care if I learn or not. I hardly ever see my father; he does not like me. I see nobody but Pigott and you and old Jakes, and Sam sometimes. You need not ask my father; he will never miss me whilst I am learning. Ask Pigott."

At that moment Pigott herself hove in view, in a great flurry.

"Oh, here you are Miss Angela! Where have you been to, you naughty girl? At some of your star-gazing tricks again. I'll be bound, frightening the life out of a body. It's just too bad of you, Miss Angela."

The little girl looked at her with a peculiarly winning smile, and took her very solid hands between her own tiny palms.

"Don't be cross, Pigott, dear," she said. "I didn't mean to frighten you. I couldn't help going—I couldn't indeed; and then I stopped talking to Mr. Fraser."

"There, there, I should just like to know who can be cross with you when you put on those ways. Are your feet wet? Ah! I thought so. Run on in and take them off."

"Won't that be just a litttle difficult?" and she was gone with a merry laugh.

"There, sir, that's just like her, catching a body up like and twisting what she says, till you don't know which is head and which is heels. I'll be bound you found her down yonder;" and she nodded towards the churchyard.

"Yes."

Pigott drew a little nearer, and spoke in a low voice.

"'Tis my belief, sir, that that child sees *things;* she is just the oddest child I ever saw. There's nothing she likes better than to slip out of a night, and to go to that there beastly churchyard, saving your presence, for 'company,' as she calls it—nice sort of company, indeed. And it is just the same way with storms. You remember that dreadful gale a month ago, the one that took down the North Grove and blew the spire off Rewtham Church. Well, just when it was at its worst, and I was a-sitting and praying that the roof might keep over our heads, I look round for Angela, and can't see her. 'Some of your tricks again,' thinks I to myself; and just then up comes Mrs. Jakes to say that Sam had seen little missy creeping down the tunnel walk. I was that scared that I ran down, got hold of Sam, for Jakes said he wouldn't go out with all them trees a-flying about in the air like straws—no, not for a thousand pounds, and off we set after her." Here Pigott paused to groan at the recollection of that walk.

"Well," said Mr. Fraser, who was rather interested—everything about this queer child interested him; "where did you find her?"

"Well, sir, you know where the old wall runs out into the water, below Caresfoot's Staff there? Well, at the end of it there's a post sunk in, with a ring in it to tie boats to. Now, would you believe it? out there at the end of the wall, and tied to the ring by a scarf passed round her middle, was that dreadful child. She was standing there, her back against the post, right in the teeth of the gale, with the spray dashing over her, her arms stretched out before her, her hat gone, her long hair standing out behind straight as an iron bar, and her eyes flashing as though they were on fire, and all the while there were the great trees crashing down all round in a way enough to make a body sick with fright. We got her back safe, thank God; but how long we shall keep her, I'm sure I don't know. Now she is drowning herself in the lake, for she takes to the water like a duck, and now breaking her neck off trees, and now going to ghosts in the churchyard for company. Its wearing me to the bone—that's what it is."

Mr. Fraser smiled, for, to tell the truth, Pigott's bones were pretty comfortably covered.

"Come," he said, "you would not part with her for all her wicked deeds, would you?"

"Part with her," answered Pigott, in hot indignation, "part with my little beauty! I would rather part with my head. The love, there never was another like her, nor never will be, with her sweet ways; and, if I know anything about girls, she'll be the beauty of England, she will. She's made for a beautiful woman; and look at them eyes and forehead and hair—where did you ever see the like? And as for her queer ways, what can you expect from a child as has got a great empty mind and nothing to put in it, and no one to talk to but a common woman like me, and a father"—here she dropped her voice—"as is a miser, and hates the sight of his own flesh and blood?"

"Hush! you should not say such things, Pigott! Now I will tell you something; I am going on to ask your master to allow me to educate Angela."

"I'm right glad to hear it, sir. She's sharp enough to learn anything, and it's kind of you to teach her. If you can make her mind like what her body will be if she lives, somebody will be a lucky man one of these days. Good-night, sir, and many thanks for bringing missy home."

Next day Angela began her education.

CHAPTER XVI.

READER, we are about to see Angela again, and to see a good deal of her; but you must be prepared for a change in her personal appearance, for the curtain has been down for ten years since last you met the child whose odd propensities excited Pigott's wonder and indignation and Mr. Fraser's interest; and ten years, as we all know, can work many changes in the history of the world and individuals. In ten years some have been swept clean off the board, and their places taken by others; a few have grown richer, many poorer, some of us sadder, some wiser, and all of us ten years older. Now, this was exactly what happened to little Angela—that is, the Angela we knew as little, and ten years make curious differences between the slim child of nine and a half and the woman of nearly twenty.

When we last saw her, Angela was about to commence her education. Let us re-introduce ourselves on the memorable evening when, after ten years of study, Mr. Fraser, a master by no means easily pleased, expressed himself unable to teach her any more.

It is Christmas Eve. Drip, drop, drip, falls the rain from the leafless boughs onto the sodden earth. The apology for daylight that had been doing its dull duty for the last few hours is slowly effacing itself, and the gale is celebrating the fact, and showing its joy at the closing-in of the melancholy night by howling its loudest through the trees, and flogging the flying scud it has brought with it from the sea, till it whirls across the sky like a succession of ghostly racehorses.

This is outside the vicarage; let us look within. In a well-worn arm-chair in the comfortable study, near to a table covered with books, and holding some loose sheets of foolscap in his hand, sits Mr. Fraser. His hair is a little grayer than when he began Angela's education, about as gray as rather accommodating hair will get at the age of fifty-three; otherwise his general appearance is much the same, and his face as refined and gentlemanlike as ever. Presently he lays down the sheets of paper which he has been studying attentively, and says:

"Your solution is perfectly sound, Angela; but you have arrived at it in a characteristic fashion, and by your own road. Not but what your method has some merits—for one thing, it is more concise than my own; but, on the other hand, it shows feminine weakness. It is not possible to follow every step from your premises to your conclusion, correct as it is."

"Ah!" says a low voice, with a happy ripple in it, the owner of which is busy with some tea-things out of range of the ring of light thrown by the double reading-lamp, "you often blame me for jumping to conclusions; but what does it matter, provided they are right? The whole secret is that I used the equivalent algebraic formula, but suppressed the working in order to puzzle you," and the voice laughed sweetly.

"That is not worthy of a mathematician," said Mr. Fraser, with some irritation; "it is nothing but a trick, a *tour de force*."

"The solution is correct, you say?"

"Quite."

"Then I maintain that it is perfectly mathematical; the object of mathematics is to arrive at the truth."

"*Vox, et prœterea nihil.* Come out of that corner, my dear. I hate arguing with a person I cannot see. But there, there, what is the use of arguing at all? The fact is, Angela, you are a first-class mathematician, and I am only second-class. I am obliged to stick to the old tracks; you cut a Roman road of your own. Great masters are entitled to do that. That algebraic formula never occurred to me when I worked the problem out, and it took me two days to do."

"You are trying to make me vain. You forget that whatever I know, which is just enough to show me how much I have to learn, I have learnt from you. As for being your superior in mathematics, I don't think that, as a clergyman, you should make such a statement. Here is your tea." And the owner of the voice came forward into the ring of light.

She was tall beyond the ordinary height of woman, and possessed unusual beauty of form, that the tight-fitting gray dress she wore was well calculated to display. Her complexion, which was of dazzling fairness, was set off by the darkness of the lashes that curled over the deep gray eyes. The face itself was rounded and very lovely, and surmounted by an ample forehead, whilst her hair, which was twisted into a massive knot, was of a tinge of chestnut gold, and marked with deep-set ripples. The charm of her face, however, did not, as is so often the case, begin and end with its physical attractions. There was more, much more, in it than that. But how is it possible to describe on paper a presence at once so full of grace and dignity, of the soft loveliness of woman, and a higher and more spiritual beauty? There hangs in the Louvre a picture by Raphael which represents a saint passing with light steps over the prostrate form of a dragon. There is in that heaven-inspired face, the equal of which has been rarely, if ever, put on canvas, a blending of earthly beauty and of the calm, awe-compelling spirit-gaze—that gaze, that holy dignity which can only come to such as are in truth and in deed "pure in heart"—that will give to those who know it a better idea of what Angela was like than any written description.

At times, but, ah, how rarely! we may have seen some such look as that she wore on the faces of those around us. It may be brought by a great sorrow, or be the companion of an overwhelming joy. It may announce the consummation of some sublime self-sacrifice, or convey the swift assurance of an everlasting love. It is to be found alike on the features of the happy mother as she kisses her new-born babe, and on the pallid countenance of the saint sinking to his rest. The sharp moment that brings us nearer God, and goes nigh to piercing the veil that hides His presence, is the occasion that calls it into being. It is a beauty born of the murmuring sound of the harps of heaven; it is the light of the eternal lamp gleaming faintly through its earthly casket.

This spirit-look, before which all wickedness must feel ashamed, had found a home in Angela's gray eyes. There was a strange nobility about her. Whether it dwelt in the stately form, or on the broad brow, or in the large glance of the deep eyes, it is not possible to say; but it was certainly a part of herself as self-evident as her face or features. She might well have been the inspiration of the lines that run—

"Truth in her might, belovèd,
 Grand in her sway;
Truth with her eyes, belovèd,
 Clearer than day;
Holy and pure, belovèd,
 Spotless and free;
Is there one thing, belovèd,
 Fairer than thee?"

Mr. Fraser absently set down the tea that Angela was giving him when we took the liberty to describe her personal appearance.

"Now, Angela, read a little."

"What shall I read?"

"Oh! anything you like; please yourself."

Thus enjoined, she went to a bookshelf, and, taking down two volumes, handed one to Mr. Fraser, and then, opening her copy at haphazard, announced the page to her companion, and, sitting down, began to read.

What sound is this, now soft and melodious as the sweep of a summer gale over a southern sea, and now again like to the distant stamp and rush and break of the wave of battle? What can it be but the roll of those magnificent hexameters with which Homer charms a listening world. And rarely have English lips given them with a juster cadence.

"Stop, my dear, shut up your book; you are as good a Greek scholar as I can make you. Shut up your book for the last time. Your education, my dear Angela, is satisfactorily completed. I have succeeded with you—"

"Completed, Mr. Fraser!" said Angela, open-eyed. "Do you mean to say that I am to stop now just as I have begun to learn?"

"My dear, you have learnt everything that I can teach you, and, besides, I am going away the day after to-morrow."

"Going away!" and then and there, without the slightest warning, Angela—who, for all her beauty and learning, very much resembled the rest of her sex—burst into tears.

"Come, come, Angela," said Mr. Fraser, in a voice meant to be gruff, but only succeeded in being husky, for, oddly enough, it is trying even to a clergyman on the wrong side of middle-age to be wept over by a lovely woman; "don't be nonsensical; I am only going for a few months."

At this intelligence she pulled up a little.

"Oh," she said, between her sobs, "how you frightened me! How could you be so cruel! Where are you going to?"

"I am going for a long trip in southern Europe. Do you know that I have scarcely been away from this place for twenty years? So I mean to celebrate the conclusion of our studies by taking a holiday."

"I wish you would take me with you."

Mr. Fraser colored slightly, and his eye brightened. He sighed as he answered:

"I am afraid, my dear, that it would be impossible."

Something warned Angela not to pursue the subject.

"Now, Angela, I believe that it is usual, on the occasions of the severance of a scholastic connection, to deliver something in the nature of a farewell oration. Well, I am not going to do that, but I want you to listen to a few words."

She did not answer, but, drawing a stool to the corner of the fireplace, she wiped her eyes and sat down almost at his feet, clasping her knees with her hands, and gazing rather sadly into the fire.

"You have, dear Angela," he began, "been educated in a somewhat unusual way, with the result that, after ten years of steady work that has been always interesting, though sometimes arduous, you have acquired information denied to the vast majority of your sex, whilst at the same time you could be put to the blush in many things by a school-girl of fifteen. For instance, though I firmly believe that you could at the present moment take a double first at the University, your knowledge of English literature is almost nil, and your history of the weakest. All a woman's ordinary accomplishments, such as drawing, playing, singing, have of necessity been to a great extent neglected, since I was not able to teach them to you myself, and you have had to be guided solely by books and the light of Nature in giving to them such time as you could spare.

"Your mind, on the other hand, has been daily saturated with the noblest thoughts of the intellectual giants of two thousand years ago, and would in that respect be as much in place in a well educated Grecian maiden living before the time of Christ as in an English girl of the nineteenth century.

"I have educated you thus, Angela, partly by accident and partly by design. You will remember when you began to come here some ten years since—you were a little thing then—and I had offered to give you some teaching, because you interested me, and I saw that you were running wild in mind and body. But when I had undertaken the task, I was somewhat puzzled how to carry it out. It is one thing to offer to educate a little girl, and another to do it. Not knowing where to begin, I fell back upon the Latin grammar, where I had begun myself, and so by degrees you slid into the curriculum of a classical and mathematical education. Then, after a year or two, I perceived your power of work and your great natural ability, and I formed a design. I said to myself, 'I will see how far a woman cultivated under favorable conditions can go. I will patiently teach the girl till the literature of Greece and Rome becomes as familiar to her as her mother-tongue, till figures and symbols hide no mysteries from her, till she can read the heavens like a book. I will teach her mind to follow the secret ways of knowledge. I will train it till it can soar above its fellows like a falcon above sparrows.' Angela, my proud design, pursued steadily through many years, has been at length accomplished; your bright intellect has risen to the strain I have put upon it, and you are at this moment one of the best all-round scholars of my acquaintance."

She flushed to the eyes at this high praise, and was about to speak, but he stopped her with a motion of the hand, and went on:

"I have recognized in teaching you a fact but too little known, that a classical education, properly understood, is the foundation of all learning. There is little that is worth saying which has not already been beautifully said by the ancients, little that is worthy of meditation on which they have not already profoundly reflected, save, indeed, the one great subject of Christian meditation. This foundation, my dear Angela, you possess to an eminent degree. Henceforth you will need no assistance from me or any other man, for, to your trained mind, all ordinary knowledge will be easy to assimilate. You will receive in the course of a few days a parting present from myself in the shape of a box of carefully-chosen books on European literature and history. Devote yourself to the study of these, and of the German language, which was your mother's native tongue, for the next year, and then I shall consider that you are fairly finished, and then, too, my dear Angela, I shall expect to reap a full reward for my labors."

"What is it that you will expect of me?"

"I shall expect, Angela," and he rose from his chair and walked up and down the room in his excitement—"I shall expect to see you take your proper place in your generation. I shall say: 'Choose your own line, become a critical scholar, a practical mathematician, or—and perhaps that is what you are most suited for with your imaginative powers—a writer of fiction. For remember that fiction, properly understood and directed to worthy aims, is the noblest and most far-reaching, as it is also the most difficult of the arts.' In watching the success that will assuredly attend you in this or any other line, I shall be amply rewarded for my trouble."

Angela shook her head with a gesture of doubt, but he did not wait for her to answer.

"Well, my dear, I must not keep you any longer—it is quite dark and blowing a gale of wind—except to say one more word. Remember that all this is—indirectly perhaps, but still none the less truly—a means to an end. There are two educations, the education of the mind and the education of the soul; unless you minister to the latter, all the time and toil spent upon the former will prove of little purpose. The learning will, it is true, remain; but it will be as the quartz out of which the gold has been already crushed, or the dry husks of corn. It will be valueless and turn to no good use, will serve only to feed the swine of intellectual voluptuousness and infidelity. It is, believe me, the higher learning of the soul that gilds our earthly lore. The loftier object of all education is so to train the intellect that it may become competent to understand something, however little, of the nature of our God, and to the true Christian the real end of learning is the appreciation of His attributes as exemplified in His mysteries and earthly wonders. But perhaps that is a subject upon which you are as well fitted to discourse as I am, so I will not enter into it. 'Finis,' my dear, 'finis.'"

Angela's answer to this long oration was a simple one. She rose slowly from her low seat, and putting her hands upon Mr. Fraser's shoulders, kissed him on the forehead and said:

"How shall I ever learn to be grateful enough for all I owe you? What should I have been now but for you? How good and patient you have been to me!"

This embrace affected the clergyman strangely; he put his hand to his heart, and a troubled look came into his eyes. Thrusting her gently away from him, he sat down.

"Angela," he said presently, "go away now, dear, I am tired to-night; I shall see you at church to-morrow to say good-by."

And so she went homewards through the wind and storm, little knowing that she left her master to struggle with a tempest far more tremendous than that which raged around her.

As for him, as the door closed, he gave a sigh of relief.

"Pray God I have not put it off too long," he said to himself. "And now for to-morrow's sermon. Sleep for the young! laughter for the happy! work for old fools—work, work, work!"

And thus it was that Angela became a scholar.

CHAPTER XVII.

THE winter months passed away slowly for Angela, but not by any means unhappily. Though she was quite alone and missed Mr. Fraser sadly, she found considerable consolation in his present of books, and in the thought that she was getting a good hold of her new subjects of study. And then came the wonder of the spring with its rush of budding life, and who, least of all Angela, could be sad in spring-time? But nevertheless that spring marked an important change in our heroine, for it was during its sweet hours, when, having put her books aside, she would roam alone, or in company with her ravens, through the flower-starred woods around the lake, that a feeling of restlessness, amounting at times almost to dissatisfaction, took possession of her. Indeed, as the weeks crept on and she drew near the completion of her twentieth year, she realized with a sigh that she could no longer call herself a girl, and began to feel that he life was incomplete, that something was wanting in it. And this was what was wanting in Angela's life: she had, if we except her nurse, no one to love, and she had so much love to give!

Did she but guess it, the still recesses of her heart already tremble to the footfall of one now drawing near: out of the multitude of the lives around her, a life is marked to mingle with her own. She does not know it, but as the first reflection of the dawn strikes the unconscious sky and shadows the coming of its king, so the red flush that now so often springs unbidden to her brow tells of girlhood's twilight ended, and proclaims the advent of woman's life and love.

"Angela," called her father one day, as he heard her footsteps passing his study, "come in here; I want to speak to you."

His daughter stopped, and a look of blank astonishment spread itself over her face. She had not been called into that study for years. She entered, however, as bidden. Her father, who was seated at his writing-table, which was piled up with account-books, did not greatly differ in appearance from what he was when we last saw him twenty years ago. His frame had grown more massive, and acquired a slight stoop, but he was still a young, powerful-looking man, and certainly did not appear a day more than his age of forty-two. The eyes, however, so long as no one was looking at them, had contracted a concentrated stare, as though they were eternally gazing at some object in space, and this appearance was rendered the more marked by an apparently permanent puckering of the skin of the forehead. The moment, however, that they came under the fire of anybody else's optics, and, oddly enough, more particularly those of his own daughter, the stare vanished, and they grew shifty and uncertain to a curious degree.

Philip was employed in adding up something when his daughter entered, and motioned to her to sit down. She did so, and fixed her great gray eyes on him with some curiosity. The effect was remarkable; her father fidgeted, made a mistake in his calculations, glanced all round the room with his shifty eyes (ah, how changed from those bold black orbs with which Maria Lee fell in love four-and-twenty years ago!), and finally threw down his pen with an exclamation that would have shocked Angela had she understood it.

"How often, Angela, have I asked you not to stare me out of countenance! It is a most unladylike trick of yours."

She blushed painfully.

"I beg your pardon; I forgot. I will look out of the window."

"Don't be a fool; look like other people. But now I want to speak to you. In the first place, I find that the household expenditure for the last year was three hundred and fifty pounds. That is more than I can afford; it must not exceed three hundred this year."

"I will do my best to keep the expenses down, father; but I can assure you that there is no money wasted now."

Then came a pause, which, after humming and hawing a little, Philip was the first to break.

"Do you know that I saw your cousin George yesterday? He is back at last at Isleworth."

"Yes, Pigott told me that he had come. He has been away a long while."

"When did you last see him?"

"When I was about thirteen, I believe; before he lost the election, and went away."

"He has been down here several times since then. I wonder that you did not see him."

"I always disliked him, and kept out of his way."

"Gad, you can't dislike him more than I do; but I keep good friends with him for all that, and you must do the same. Now, look here, Angela, will you promise to keep a secret?"

"Yes, father, if you wish it."

"Well, then, I appear to be a poor man, don't I? And remember," he added, hastily, "that, with reference to household expenses, I am poor; but, as a matter of fact"—and here he sunk his voice, and glanced suspiciously round—"I am worth at this moment nearly one hundred and fifty thousand pounds in hard cash."

"That is six thousand pounds a year at four per cent," commented Angela, without a moment's hesitation. "Then I really think you might put a flue into the old greenhouse, and allow a shilling a week to Mrs. Jakes's mother."

"Curse Mrs. Jakes's mother! Nobody but a woman would have interrupted with such nonsense. Listen. You must have heard how I was disinherited on account of my marriage with your mother, and the Isleworth estates left to your cousin George, and how, with a refined ingenuity, he was forbidden to bequeath them back to me or to my children. But mark this, he is not forbidden to sell them to me; no doubt the old man never dreamt that I should have the money to buy them; but, you see, I have almost enough."

"How did you get so much money?"

"Get it! First, I took the gold plate my grandfather bought, and sold it. I had no right to do it, but I could not afford to have so much capital lying idle. It fetched nearly five thousand pounds. With this I speculated successfully. In two years I had eighteen thousand. The eighteen thousand I invested in a fourth share in a coal-mine, when money was scarce and coals cheap. Coals rose enormously just then, and in five years' time I sold my share to the co-holders for eighty-two thousand, in addition to twenty-one thousand received by way of interest. Since then I have not speculated, for fear my luck should desert me. I have simply allowed the money to accumulate on mortgage and other investments, and bided my time, for I have sworn to have those estates back before I die. It is for this cause that I have toiled, and thought, and screwed, and been cut by the whole neighborhood for twenty years; but now I think that, with your help, my time is coming."

"With *my* help. What is it that you wish me to do?"

"Listen," answered her father, nervously tapping his pencil on the account-book before him. "George is not very fond of Isleworth—in fact, he rather dislikes it; but, like all the Caresfoots, he does not care about parting with landed property, and, though we appear to be good friends, he hates me too much ever to consent, under ordinary circumstances, to sell it to me. It is to you I look to overcome that objection."

"I! How?"

"You are a woman and ask me how you should get the blind side of a man!"

"I do not in the least understand you."

Philip smiled incredulously.

"Then I suppose I must explain. If you ever take the trouble to look at yourself in the glass, you will probably see that Nature has been very kind to you in the matter of good looks; nor are you by any means deficient in brains. Your cousin George is very fond of a pretty woman, and, to be plain, what I want you to do is to make use of your advantages to get him under your thumb and persuade him into selling the property."

"Oh! father, how can you?" ejaculated Angela, in an agony of shame

"You idiot, I don't want you to marry him; I only want you to make a fool of him. Surely, being of the sex you are, you won't find *that* an uncongenial occupation."

Angela's blushes had given way to pallor now, and she answered with cold contempt:

"I don't think you quite understand what a girl feels—at least, what I feel, for I know no other girls. Perhaps it would be useless for me to try to explain. I had rather go blind than use my eyes for such a shameful purpose."

"Angela," said her father, with as much temper as he ever showed now, "let me tell you that you are a silly fool; you are more, you are an encumbrance. Your birth," he added, bitterly, "robbed me of your mother, and the fact of your being a girl deprived our branch of the family of their rights. Now that you have grown up, you prefer to gratify your whims rather than help me to realize the object of my life by a simple course of action that could do no one any harm. I never asked you to commit yourself in any way. Well, well, it is what I must expect. We have not seen much of each other heretofore, and perhaps the less we meet in the future the better."

"You have no right to talk to me so," she answered, with flashing eyes, "though I am your daughter, and it is cowardly to reproach me with my birth, my sex, and my dependence. Am I responsible for any of these things? But I will not burden you long. And as to what you wanted me to do, and think such a little of, I ask you, is it what my poor mother would have wished her daughter—"

Here Philip abruptly rose, and left the room and the house.

"She is as like her mother as possible," he mused, as soon as he was clear of the house. "It might have been Hilda herself, only she is twice as beautiful as Hilda was. I shall have another bad night after this, I know I shall. I must get rid of that girl somehow, I cannot bear her about me; she is a daily reminder of things I dare not remember, and whenever she stares at me with those great eyes of hers, I feel as though she were looking through me. I wonder if she knows the story of Maria Lee!"

And then dismissing, or trying to dismiss, the matter from his mind, he took his way across the fields to Isleworth Hall, a large white brick mansion in the Queen Anne style, about two miles distant from the Abbey, and, on arrival, asked for his cousin George, and was at once shown into that gentleman's presence.

Years had told upon George more than they had upon Philip, and, though there were no touches of gray in the flaming red of his hair, the bloodshot eyes, and the puckered crowsfeet beneath them, to say nothing of the slight but constant trembling of the hand, all showed that he was a man well on in middle-life, and who had lived every day of it. Time, too, had made the face more intensely unpleasant and vulgar-looking than ever. Such Caresfoot characteristics as it possessed were, year by year, giving place, in an increasingly greater degree, to the kitchen-maid strain introduced by the mother. In short, George Caresfoot did not even look a gentleman, whereas Philip certainly did.

"You don't seem very well, George. I am afraid that your travels have not agreed with you."

"My dear Philip," answered his cousin, in a languid and affected voice, "if you had lived the life that I have for the last twenty years, you would look a little knocked up. I have had some very good times; but the fact is, that I have been too prodigal of my strength, not thought enough about the future. It is a great mistake, and one of the worst results is that I am utterly *blasé* of everything; even *la belle passion* is played out for me. I haven't seen a woman I care twopence about for ten years."

"Ah! you should sell this place, and take a house in town; it would suit you much better."

"I can do that without selling the place. I don't intend to sell the place—in fact, nothing would induce me to do so. Some day I may marry, and want to transmit it to some future Caresfoot; but I confess I don't mean to do that just yet. Marry when you want a nurse, but never before; that's my maxim. Marriage is an excellent institution for parsons and fools, the two classes that Providence has created to populate the world; but a wise man should as soon think of walking into a spring-trap. Take your own case, for instance, my dear Philip ; look what marriage led to."

"At any rate," answered his cousin, bitterly, "it led to your advantage."

"Exactly ; and that is one of the reasons why I have such a respect for the institution in the abstract. It has been my personal benefactor, and I worship it accordingly—at a distance. By the way, talking of marriage reminds me of its legitimate fruits. Bellamy tells me that your daughter Angela (if I had a daughter, I should call her Diabola, it is more appropriate for a woman) has grown uncommonly handsome. Bring her to see me ; I adore beauty in all its forms, especially its female form. Is she really so handsome ?"

"I am no judge, but you will soon have an opportunity of forming an opinion—that is, I hope so. I propose coming with Angela to make a formal call on you to-morrow."

"Good. Tell my fair cousin that I shall be certain to be in, and be prepared, metaphorically, to fall at the feet of so much loveliness. By the way, that reminds me; you have heard of Bellamy's, or rather Mrs. Bellamy's, good fortune, I suppose ?"

"No."

"What—not ? Why, he is now Sir John Bellamy, knight."

"Indeed ! How is that ?"

"You remember the bye-election six months back ?"

"Oh, yes! I was actually badgered by Mrs. Bellamy into promising to vote, much against my personal convenience."

"Exactly. Well, just at the time old Prescott died, you may remember that Mr. Showers, the member of the Government, was unseated on petition from some borough or other, and came down here post haste to get re-elected. But he had Sir Percy Vivyan against him, and, as I know to my cost, this benighted county is not fond of those who preach the gospel of progress. Bellamy, who is a stout Radical, as you know—chiefly, I fancy, because there is more to be got out of that side of politics—got the job as Showers' agent. But, three days before, it became quite clear that his cause, cabinet minister or not, was hopeless. Then it was that Mrs.—I beg her pardon, Lady—Bellamy came to the fore. Just as Showers was thinking of withdrawing, she demanded a private interview with him. Next day she posted off to old Sir Percy, who is a perfect fool of the chivalrous school, and was desperately fond of her, and, *mirabile dictu*, that evening Sir Percy withdraws on the plea of ill-health, or some such rubbish, and Showers walks over. Within three months, Mr. Bellamy becomes Sir John Bellamy, nominally for his services as town-clerk of Roxham, and I hear that old Sir Percy is now perfectly rampant, and goes about cursing her ladyship up hill and down dale, and declaring that he has been shockingly taken-in. How our mutual friend worked the ropes is more than I can tell you, but she did work them, and to some purpose."

"She is an uncommonly handsome woman."

"Ah! yes, you're right there; she is A 1; but let us stroll out a little; it is a fine evening for the thirtieth of April. To-morrow will be the first of May, so it will—a day neither of us are likely to forget."

Philip winced at the allusion, but said nothing.

"By the way," George went on, "I am expecting a visitor, my ward, young Arthur Heigham, who is just back from India. He will be twenty-five in a few days, when he comes of age, and is coming down to settle up. The fact is, that ten thousand of his money is on that Jatley property, and both Bellamy and myself are anxious that it should stop there for the present, as if the mortgage were called in it might be awkward."

"Is he well off?"

"Comfortably; about a thousand a year; comes of an old family too. Bellamy and I knew his father, Captain Heigham, slightly, when we were in business. His wife, by the way, was a distant cousin of ours. They are both dead now; the captain was wiped out at Inkerman, and, for some unknown reason, left me the young gentleman's sole guardian and joint trustee with a London lawyer, a certain Mr. Borley. I have never seen him yet—my ward, I mean—he has always been at Eton, or Cambridge, or in India, or somewhere."

Here Philip began to manifest signs of considerable uneasiness, the cause of which was sufficiently apparent; for, whilst they were talking, a very large and savage-looking animal of the sheep-dog order had emerged from the house, and was following him up and down, growling in a low and ominous undertone, its nose being the while glued to his calves as they alternately presented themselves in his line of vision.

"Would you mind calling off this animal, George?" he said at length. "He does not look amiable."

"Oh! that's Snarleyow; don't mind him, he never bites unless you stop." Philip instinctively quickened his pace. "Isn't he a beauty? He's a pure-bred Thibet sheep-dog, and I will back him to fight against any animal of his own weight. He killed two dogs in one morning the other day, and pulled down a beggar-woman in the evening. You should have heard her holler."

At that moment, fortunately for Philip's calves, which were beginning to tingle with an unwholesome excitement, Mr. Snarleyow's attention was diverted by the approach of a dog-cart, and he left to enjoy the amusement of snapping and barking at the horse. The cart pulled up at the door, and out of it emerged a tall and extremely gentlemanly-looking young fellow, followed by a very large red bull-dog.

"Mr. Caresfoot, I believe," said the young gentleman to George, taking off his hat.

"Yes, Mr. Heigham, at your service. I am very glad to see you. My cousin, Mr. Philip Caresfoot."

CHAPTER XVIII.

"I MUST apologize for having brought Aleck, my dog, you know, with me," began Arthur Heigham; "but the fact was, that at the very last moment the man I was going to leave him with had to go away, and I had no time to find another place before the train left. I thought that, if you objected to dogs, he could easily be sent somewhere into the village. He is very good-tempered, though appearances are against him."

"Oh! he will be all right, I dare say," said George, rather sulkily; for, with the exception of Snarleyow, in whose fiendish temper he found something refreshing and congenial, he liked no dogs. "But you must be careful, or Snarleyow, *my* dog, will give him a hammering. Here, good dog, good dog," and he attempted to pat Aleck on the head, but the animal growled savagely, and avoided him.

"I never knew him do that before," ejaculated Arthur, in confusion, and heartily wishing Aleck somewhere else. "I suppose he has taken a dislike to you. Dogs do sometimes, you know."

Next second it struck him that this was one of those things that had better have been left unsaid, and he grew more uncomfortable than ever. But at this very moment the situation was rendered intensely lively by the approach of the redoubtable Snarleyow himself, who, having snapped at the horse's heels all the way to the stables, had on his return to the front of the house spotted Aleck from afar. He was now advancing on tiptoe in full order of battle, his wicked-looking teeth gleaming, and his coat and tail standing out like an angry bear's.

Arthur, already sufficiently put out about the dog question, thought it best to take no notice; and even when he distinctly heard George quietly "sah" on his dog as he passed him, he contented himself with giving Aleck a kick by way of a warning to behave himself, and entered into some desultory conversation with Philip. But presently a series of growls behind him announced that an encounter was imminent. Looking round, he perceived that Snarleyow was standing over the bull-dog, of which he was more than twice the size, and holding on to the skin of his neck with his long teeth; whilst George was looking on with scarcely suppressed amusement.

"I think, Mr. Caresfoot, that you had better call your dog off," said Arthur, good-temperedly. "Mine is a peaceable animal, but he is an awkward customer when he does fight."

"Oh! better let them settle it; they will be much better friends afterwards. Hold him, Snarleyow."

Thus encouraged, the big dog seized the other, and fairly lifted him off the ground, shaking him violently—a proceeding that had the effect of thoroughly rousing Aleck's temper. And then began a most Homeric combat. At first the bull-dog was dreadfully mauled; his antagonist's size, weight, and length of leg and jaw, to say nothing of the thick coat by which he was protected, all telling against him. But he took his punishment very quietly, never so much as uttering a growl, in strange contrast to the big dog's vociferous style of doing business. And at last patience was rewarded by his enemy's fore-paw finding its way into Aleck's powerful jaw, and remaining there till Snarleyow's attentions to the back of his neck forced him to shift his hold. From that time forward the sheep-dog had to fight on three legs, which he found demoralizing. But still he had the advantage, and it was not until any other dog of Aleck's size would have retreated half killed that the bull-dog's superior courage and stamina began to tell. Quite heedless of his injuries, and the blood that poured into his eyes, he slowly but surely drove the great sheep-dog, who by this time would have been glad to stop, back into an angle of the wall, and then suddenly pinned him by the throat. Down went Snarleyow on the top of the bull-dog, and rolled right over him, but when he staggered to his legs again, his throat was still in its cruel grip.

"Take your dog off!" shouted George, seeing that affairs had taken a turn he very little expected.

"I fear that is impossible," replied Arthur, politely, but looking anything but polite.

"If you don't get it off, I will shoot it."

"You will do nothing of the sort, Mr. Caresfoot; you set the dog on, and you must take the consequences. Ah! the affair is finished."

As he spoke, the choking Snarleyow, whose black tongue was protruding from his jaws, gave one last convulsive struggle, and ceased to breathe. Satisfied with this result, Aleck let go, and having sniffed contemptuously at his dead antagonist, returned to his master's side, and, sitting quietly down, began to lick such of his numerous wounds as he could reach.

George, when he realized that his favorite was dead, turned upon his guest in a perfect fury. His face looked like a devil's. But Arthur, acting with wonderful self-possession for so young a man, stopped him.

"Remember, Mr. Caresfoot, before you say anything that you may regret, that neither I nor my dog is to blame for what has happened. I am exceedingly sorry that your dog should have been killed, but it is your own fault. I am afraid, however, that, after what has happened, I shall be as unwelcome here as Aleck; so, if you will kindly order the cart for me again, I will move on. Our business can no doubt be finished off by letter."

George made no reply: it was evident that he could not trust himself to speak, but, turning sullenly on his heel, walked towards the house.

"Wait a bit, Mr. Heigham," said Philip, who had been watching the whole scene with secret delight. "You are perfectly in the right. I will go and try to bring my cousin to his senses. I am very thankful to your dog for killing that accursed brute."

He was away for about ten minutes, during which Arthur took Aleck to a fountain there was in the centre of a grass-plot in front of the house, and washed his many wounds, none of which, however, were, thanks to the looseness of his hide, very serious. Just as he had finished that operation, a gardener arrived with a wheelbarrow to fetch away the deceased Snarleyow.

"Lord, sir," he said to Arthur, "I am glad to have the job of tucking up this here brute. He bit my missus last week, and killed a whole clutch of early ducks. I seed the row through the bushes. That 'ere dog of yours, sir, he did fight in proper style; I should like to have a dog like he."

Just then the re-arrival of Philip put a stop to the conversation. Drawing Arthur aside, he told him that George begged to apologize for what had occurred, and hoped that he would not think of going away.

"But," added Philip, with a little laugh, "I don't pretend that he has taken a fancy to you, and, if I were you, I should cut my visit short."

"That is exactly my view of the case. I will leave to-morrow evening."

Philip made no further remarks for a few moments. He was evidently thinking. Presently he said,

"I see you have a fishing-rod amongst your things; if you find the time hang heavy on your hands to-morrow, or wish to keep out of the way, you had better come over to Bratham Lake and fish. There are some very large carp and perch there, and pike too, for the matter of that, but they are out of season."

Arthur thanked him, and said that he should probably come, and, having received instructions as to the road, they parted, Arthur to go and shut up Aleck in an outhouse pointed out to him by his friend the gardener, and thence to dress for a dinner that he looked forward to with dread, and Philip to make his way home. As he passed up through the little flower-garden at the Abbey House, he came across his daughter, picking the blight from her shooting rose-trees.

"Angela," he said, "I am sorry if I offended your prejudices this afternoon. Don't let us say anything more about it; but I want you to come and pay a formal call with me at Isleworth to-morrow. It will only be civil that you should do so."

"I never paid a call in my life," she answered, doubtfully, "and I don't want to call on my cousin George."

"Oh! very well," and he began to move on. She stopped him.

"I will go, if you like."

"At three o'clock, then. Oh! by the way, don't be surprised if you see a young gentleman fishing here to-morrow."

Angela reflected to herself that she had never yet seen a young gentleman to speak to in her life, and then asked, with undisguised interest, who he was.

"Well, he is a sort of connection of your own, through the Prestons, who are cousins of ours, if any of them are left. His mother was a Preston, and his name is Arthur Preston Heigham. George told me something about him just now, and, on thinking it over, I remember the whole story. He is an orphan, and George's ward."

"What is he like?" asked Angela, ingenuously.

"Really I don't know; rather tall, I think—a gentlemanly fellow. It really is a relief to speak to a gentleman again. There has been a nice disturbance at Isleworth," and then he told his daughter the history of the great dog-fight.

"I should think Mr. Heigham was perfectly in the right, and I should like to see his dog," was her comment on the occurrence.

As Arthur dressed himself for dinner that evening he came to the conclusion that he disliked his host more than any man he ever saw, and, to say the truth, he descended into the dining-room with considerable misgivings. Just as he entered, the opposite door opened, and Sir John Bellamy was announced. On seeing him, George emerged from the sulky silence into which he was plunged, and advanced to meet him.

"Hullo, Bellamy! I must congratulate you upon your accession to rank."

"Thank you, Caresfoot, thank you," replied Mr. Bellamy, who, with the exception that he had grown a size larger, and boasted a bald patch on the top of his head that gave him something of the appearance of a jolly little monk, looked very much the same as when we last saw him as a newly-married man.

"A kind Providence," he went on, rubbing his dry hands, and glancing nervously under the chairs, "has put this honor into my hands."

"A Providence in petticoats, you mean," broke in George.

"Possibly, my dear Caresfoot; but I do not see him. Is it possible that he is lurking yonder, behind the sofa?"

"Who on earth do you mean?"

"I mean that exceedingly fine dog of yours, Snarleyow. Snarleyow, where are you? Excuse me for taking precautions, but last time he put his head under my chair and bit me severely, as I dare say you remember."

Arthur groaned at hearing the subject thus brought forward.

"Mr. Heigham's dog killed Snarleyow this afternoon," said George, in a savage voice.

At this intelligence, Sir John's face became wreathed in smiles.

"I am deeply delighted—I mean grieved—to hear it. Poor Snarleyow! he was a charming dog; and to think that such a fate should have overtaken him, when it was only last week that he did the same kind office for Anne's spaniel. Poor Snarleyow! you should really have him stuffed. But, my dear Caresfoot, you have not yet introduced me to the hero of the evening, Mr. Heigham. Mr. Heigham, I am delighted to make your acquaintance," and he shook hands with Arthur with gentle enthusiasm, as though he were the last scion of a race that he had known and loved for generations.

Presently dinner was announced, and the three sat down at a small round table in the centre of the big dining-room, on which was placed a shaded lamp. It was not a cheerful dinner. George, having said grace, relapsed into moody silence, eating and drinking with gusto but in moderation, and savoring every sip of wine and morsel of food as though he regretted its departure. He was not free from gluttony, but he was a judicious glutton. For his part, Arthur found a certain fascination in watching his guardian's red head as he bobbed up and down opposite to him, and speculating on the thickness of each individual hair that contributed to give it such a spiky effect. What had his mother been like, he wondered, that she had started him in life with such an entirely detestable countenance? Meanwhile he was replying in monosyllables to Sir John's gentle babblings, till at last even that gentleman's flow of conversation ran dry, and Arthur was left free to contemplate the head in solemn silence. As soon as the cloth had been cleared away, George suggested that they had better get to work. Arthur assented, and Sir John, smiling with much sweetness, remarked profoundly that business was one of the ills of life, and must be attended to.

"At any rate, it is an ill that has agreed uncommonly well with you," growled George, as, rising from the table, he went to a solid iron safe that stood in the corner of the room, and, unlocking it with a small key that he took from his pocket, extracted a bundle of documents.

"That is an excellent deed-box of yours, Caresfoot," said Sir John, carelessly.

"Yes; that lock would not be very easy to pick. It is made on my own design."

"But don't you find that small parcels such as private letters are apt to get lost in it? It is so big."

"Oh, no; there is a separate compartment for them. Now, Mr. Heigham." And then, with the able and benign assistance of Sir John, he proceeded to utterly confuse and mystify Arthur, till stocks, preference-shares, consols, and mortgages were all whirling in his bewildered brain. Having satisfactorily reduced him to this condition, he suddenly sprang upon him the proposal he had in view with reference to the Jotley mortgage, pointing out to him that it was an excellent investment, and strongly advising him, "as a friend," to leave the money upon the land. Arthur hesitated a little, more from natural caution than anything he could urge to the contrary, and George, noticing it, said:

"It is only right that, before you come to any decision, you should see the map of the estate, and a copy of the deed. I have both in the next room, if you care to come and look at them."

Arthur assented, and they went off together; Sir John, whose eyes appeared to-be a little heavy under the influence of the port, presuming that he was not wanted. But, no sooner had the door closed, than the worthy knight proved himself very wide-awake. Indeed, he commenced a singular course of action. Advancing on tiptoe to the safe in the corner of the room, he closely inspected it through his eye-glasses. Then he cautiously tried the lid of an artfully contrived subdivision.

"Um!" he muttered, half aloud, "that's where they are; I wish I had ten minutes."

Next he returned swiftly to the table, and, taking a piece of the soft bread which he was eating instead of biscuit with his wine, he rapidly kneaded it into dough, and, going to the safe, divided the material into two portions. One portion he carefully pressed upon the key-hole of the subdivision, and then, extracting the key of the safe itself, took a very fair impress of its wards on the other. This done, he carefully put the pieces of dough in his breast-pocket, in such a way that they were not likely to be crushed, and, with a smile of satisfaction, returned to his chair, helped himself to a glass of port, and dozed off.

"Hullo, Bellamy, gone to sleep! Wake up, man. We have settled this business about the mortgage. Will you write to Mr. Borley, and convey Mr. Heigham's decision? And perhaps"—addressing Arthur—"you will do the same on your own account."

"Certainly I will write, Caresfoot; and now I think that I must be off. Her ladyship does not like having to sit up for me."

George laughed in a peculiarly insulting way.

"I don't think she would care much, Bellamy, if you stayed away all night. But look here, tell her I want to see her to-morrow; don't forget."

Sir John bit his knightly lip, but answered, smiling, that he would remember, and begging George not to ring, as his trap was at the hall-door, and the servant waiting, he bade an affectionate good-night to Arthur, to whom he expressed a hope that they would soon meet again, and let himself out of the room. But, as soon as the door was closed, he went through another performance exceedingly inappropriate in a knight. Turning round, his smug face red with anger, he pirouetted on his toes, and shook his fist violently in the direction of the door.

"You scoundrel!" he said between his teeth, "you have made a fool of me for twenty years, and I have been obliged to grin and bear it; but I will be even with you yet, and her too, more especially her."

So soon as Sir John had left, Arthur told his host that, if the morning was fine, he proposed to go and fish in Bratham Lake, and that he also proposed to take his departure by the last train on the following evening. To these propositions George offered no objection—indeed, they were distinctly agreeable to him, as lessening the time he would be forced to spend in the society of a guest he cordially detested, for such was the feeling that he had conceived towards Arthur.

Then they parted for the night; but, before he left the room,

George went to lock up the safe that was still open in the corner. Struck by some thought, he unlocked the separate compartment with a key that hung on his watch-chain, and extracted therefrom a thick and neatly-folded packet of letters. Drawing out one or two, he glanced through them and replaced them.

"Oh! Lady Anne, Lady Anne," he said to himself as he closed the case, "you are up in the world now, and you aspire to rule the county society, and have both the wealth and the wit to do it; but you must not kick over the traces, or I shall be forced to suppress you, Lady Anne, though you are the wife of a Brummagem knight, and I think that it is time you had a little reminder. You are growing a touch too independent."

CHAPTER XIX.

Arthur's sleep was oppressed that night by horrible nightmares of fighting dogs, whereof the largest and most ferocious was fitted with George's red head, the effect of which, screwed, without any eye to the fitness of things, to the body of the deceased Snarleyow, struck him as peculiarly disagreeable. He himself was armed with a gun, and whilst he was still arguing with Sir John Bellamy the nice point whether, should he execute that particular animal, as he felt a carnal longing to do, it would be manslaughter or dog-slaughter, he found himself wide awake.

It was very early in the morning of the first of May, and, contrary to the usual experience of the inhabitants of these islands, the sky gave promise of a particularly fine day, just the day for fishing. He did not feel sleepy, and, had he done so, he had had enough of his doggy dreams; so he got up, dressed, and taking his fishing-rod, let himself out of the house as he had been instructed to do on the previous evening, and, releasing Aleck from his outhouse, proceeded towards Bratham Lake.

And about this time Angela woke up too, for she always rose early, and ran to the window to see what sort of a day she had got for her birthday. Seeing it to be so fine, she threw open the old lattice, at which her pet raven Jack was already tapping to be admitted, and let the sweet air play upon her face and neck, and thought what a wonderful thing it was to be twenty years old. And then, kneeling by the window, she said her prayers after her own fashion, thanking God who had spared her to see this day, and praying Him to show her what to do with her life, and, if it was His will, to make it a little less lonely. Then she rose and dressed herself, feeling that now that she had done with her teens, she was in every respect a woman grown—indeed, quite old. And in honor of the event, she chose out of her scanty store of dresses, all of them made by Pigott and herself, her very prettiest, the one she had had for Sunday wear last summer, a tight-fitting robe of white stuff, with soft little frills round the neck and wrists. Next she put on a pair of stout boots calculated to keep out the morning dew, and started off.

Now all this had taken a good time, nearly an hour, perhaps; for, being her birthday, and there having been some mention of a young gentleman who might possibly come to fish, she had plaited up her shining hair with extra care, a very laborious business when your hair hangs down to your knees.

Meanwhile our other early riser, Arthur, had made his way first to the foot of the lake and then along the little path that skirted its area till he came to Caresfoot Staff. Having sufficiently admired that majestic oak, for he was a great lover of timber, he proceeded to investigate the surrounding water with the eye of a true fisherman. A few yards farther up there jutted into the water that fragment of wall on which stood the post, now quite rotten, to which Angela had bound herself on the day of the great storm. At his feet, too, the foundations of another wall ran out for some distance into the lake, being, doubtless, the underpinning of an ancient boat-house, but this did not rise out of the water, but stopped within six inches of the surface. Between these two walls lay a very deep pool.

"Just the place for a heavy fish," reflected Arthur, and, even as he thought it, he saw a five-pound carp rise nearly to the surface, in order to clear the obstruction of the wall, and sink silently into the depths.

Retiring carefully to one of two quaintly carven stone blocks placed at the foot of the oak-tree, on which, doubtless, many a monk had sat in meditation, he set himself to get his fishing-gear together. Presently, however, struck by the beauty of the spot and its quiet, only broken by the songs of many nesting birds, he stopped a while look around him. Above his head the branches of the great oak, now clothing themselves with the most vivid green, formed a dome-like roof, beneath the shade of which grew the softest moss, starred here and there with primroses and violets. Outside the circle of its shadow the brushwood of mingled hazel and ash-stubs rose thick and high, ringing-in the little spot as with a wall, except where its depths were pierced by the passage of a long green lane of limes that, unlike the shrubberies, appeared to be kept in careful order, and of which the arching boughs formed a perfect leafy tunnel. Before him lay the lake where the long morning lights quivered and danced, as its calm was now and again ruffled by a gentle breeze. The whole scene had a lovely and peaceful look, and, gazing on it, Arthur fell into a reverie.

Sitting thus dreamily, his face looked at its best, its expression of gentle thoughtfulness giving it an attraction beyond what it was entitled to, judged purely from a sculptor's point of view. It was an intellectual face, a face that gave signs of great mental possibilities, but for all that a little weak about the mouth. The brow indicated some degree of power, and the mouth and eyes no small capacities for affection and all sorts of human sympathy and kindness. These last, in varying lights, could change as often as the English climate; their groundwork, however, was blue, and they were honest and bonny. In short, a man in looking at Arthur Heigham at the age of twenty-four would have reflected that, even among English gentlemen, he was remarkable for his gentleman-like appearance, and a "fellow one would like to know;" a girl would have dubbed him "nice-looking;" and a middle-aged woman —and most women do not really understand the immense difference between men until they are getting on that way—would have recognized in him a young man by no means uninteresting, and one who might, according to the circumstances of his life, develop into anything or—nothing in particular.

Presently, drawn by some unguessed attraction, Arthur took his eyes off an industrious water-hen, who was building a nest in a hurried way, as though she were not quite sure of his intentions, and perceived a large raven standing on one leg on the grass, about three yards from him, and peering at him comically out of one eye. This was odd. But his glance did not stop at the raven, for a yard or two beyond it he caught sight of a white skirt, and his eyes, travelling upwards, saw first a rounded waist, and then a bust and pair of shoulders such as few women can boast, and at last, another pair of eyes; and he then and there fell utterly and irretrievably in love.

"Good heavens!" he said, aloud—poor fellow, he did not mean to say it, it was wrung from the depth of his heart—"good heavens, how lovely she is!"

Let the reader imagine the dreadful confusion produced in that other pair of eyes at the open expression of such a sentiment, and the vivid blush that stained the fair face in which they were set, if he can. But somehow they did not grow angry—perhaps it was not in the nature of the most sternly repressive young lady to grow angry at a compliment which, however marked, was so evidently genuine and unpremeditated. In another moment Arthur bethought him of what he had said, and it was his turn to blush. He recovered himself pretty well, however. Rising from his stone seat, he took off his hat, and said, humbly,

"I beg your pardon, but you startled me so, and really for a moment I thought that you were the spirit of the place, or," he added, gracefully, pointing to a branch of half-opened hawthorn bloom she held in her hand, "the original Queen of the May."

Angela blushed again. The compliment was only implied this time; she had therefore no possible pretext for getting angry.

For a moment she dropped the sweet eyes that looked as though they were fresh from reading the truths of heaven before his gaze of unmistakable admiration, and stood confused; and, as she stood, it struck Arthur that there was something more than mere beauty of form and feature about her—an indescribable something, a glory of innocence, a reflection of God's own light that tinged the worship her loveliness commanded with a touch of reverential awe.

"The angels must look like that," he thought. But he had no time to think any more, for next moment she had gathered up her courage in both her hands, and was speaking to him in a soft voice, of which the tones went ringing on through all the changes of his life.

"My father told me that he had asked you to come and fish, but I did not expect to meet you so early. I—I fear that I am disturbing you," and she made as though she would be going.

Arthur felt that this was a contingency to be prevented at all hazards.

"You are Miss Caresfoot," he said, hurriedly, "are you not?"

"Yes—I am Angela; I need not ask your name, my father told it me. You are Mr. Arthur Heigham."

"Yes. And do you know that we are cousins?" This was a slight exaggeration, but he was glad to advance any plea to her confidence that occurred to him.

"Yes; my father said something about our being related. I have no relations except my cousin George, and I am very glad to make the acquaintance of one," and she held out her hand to him in a winning way.

He took it almost reverently.

"You cannot," he said with much sincerity, "be more glad than I am. I, too, am without relations. Till lately I had my mother, but she died last year."

"Were you very fond of her?" she asked, softly.

He nodded in reply, and, feeling instinctively that she was on delicate ground, Angela pursued the conversation no farther.

Meanwhile Aleck had awoke from a comfortable sleep in which he was indulging on the other stone seat, and, coming forward, sniffed at Angela and wagged his tail in approval—a liberty that was instantly resented by the big raven, who had now been joined by another not quite so large. Advancing boldly, it pecked him sharply on the tail—a proceeding that caused Master Aleck to jump round as quickly as his maimed condition would allow him, only to receive a still harder peck from its companion-bird; indeed, it was not until Angela intervened with the bough of hawthorn that they would cease from their attack.

"They are such jealous creatures," she explained; "they always follow me about, and fly at every dog that comes near me. Poor dog! that is the one, I suppose, who killed Snarleyow. My father told me all about it."

"Yes, it is easy to see that," said Arthur, laughing, and pointing to Aleck, who, indeed, was in lamentable case, having one eye entirely closed, a large strip of plaster on his head, and all the rest of his body more or less marked with bites. "It is an uncommonly awkward business for me, and your cousin will not forgive it in a hurry, I fancy; but it really was not poor Aleck's fault—he is gentle as a lamb, if only he is let alone."

"He has a very honest face, though his nose does look as though it were broken," she said, and, stooping down, she patted the dog.

"But I must be going into breakfast," she went on, presently. "It is eight o'clock; the sun always strikes that bough at eight in spring," and she pointed to a dead limb, half hidden by the budding foliage of the oak.

"You must observe closely to have noticed that, but I do not think that the sun is quite on it yet. I do not like to lose my new-found relations in such a hurry," he added, with a somewhat forced smile, "and I am to go away from here this evening."

The intelligence was evidently very little satisfactory to Angela, nor did she attempt to conceal her concern.

"I am very sorry to hear that," she said. "I hoped you were going to stay for some time."

"And so I might have, had it not been for that brute Aleck; but he has put a long sojourn with your cousin and the ghost of Snarleyow out of the question; so I suppose I must go by the six-twenty train. At any rate," he added, more brightly, as a thought struck him, "I must go from Isleworth."

She did not appear to see the drift of the last part of his remark, but answered,

"I am going with my father to call at Isleworth at three this afternoon, so perhaps we shall meet again there; but now, before I go in, I will show you a better place than this to fish, a little higher up, where Jakes, our gardener, always sets his night-lines."

Arthur assented, as he would have been glad to assent to anything likely to prolong the interview, and they walked off slowly together, talking as cheerfully as a sense that the conversation must soon come to an end would allow. The spot was reached all too soon, and Angela with evident reluctance, for she was not accustomed to conceal her feelings, said that she must now go.

"Why must you go so soon?"

"Well, to tell you the truth, to-day is my birthday—I am twenty to-day—and I know that Pigott, my old nurse, means to give me a little present at breakfast, and she will be dreadfully disappointed if I am late. She has been thinking a great deal about it, you see."

"May I wish you many, very many, happy returns of the day? and"—with a little hesitation—"may I also offer you a present, a very worthless one, I fear?"

"How can I—" stammered Angela, when he cut her short.

"Don't be afraid; it is nothing tangible, though it is something that you may not think worth accepting."

"What do you mean?" she said bluntly, for her interest was aroused.

"Don't be angry. My present is only the offer of myself as your sincere friend."

She blushed vividly as she answered,

"You are very kind. I have never had but one friend—Mr. Fraser; but, if you think you can like me enough, it will make me very happy to be your friend too." And in another second she was gone, with her ravens flying after her, to receive her present and a jobation from Pigott for being late, and to eat her breakfast with such appetite as an entirely new set of sensations can give.

In the garden she met her father, walking up and down before the house, and informed him that she had been talking to Mr. Heigham. He looked up with a curious expression of interest.

"Why did you not ask him in to breakfast?" he said.

"Because there is nothing to eat except bread and milk."

"Ah!—well, perhaps you were right. I will go down and speak to him. No; I forgot I shall see him this afternoon."

And Arthur, let those who disbelieve in love at first sight laugh if they will, sat down to think, trembling in every limb, utterly shaken by the inrush of a new and strong emotion. He had not come to the age of twenty-four without some experiences of the other sex, but never before had he known any such sensation as that which now overpowered him, never before had he fully realized what solitude meant as he did now that she had left him. In youth, when love does come, he comes as a strong man armed.

And so, steady and overwhelming all resistance, the full tide of a pure passion poured itself into his heart. There was no pretence or make-believe about it; the bolt that sped from Angela's gray eyes had gone straight home, and would remain an "ever-fixed mark" so long as life itself should last.

For only once in a lifetime does a man succumb after this fashion. To many, indeed, no such fortune—call it good or ill—will ever come, since the majority of men flirt or marry, indulge in "platonic friendships," or in a consistent course of admiration of their neighbors' wives, as fate or fancy leads them, and wear their time away without ever having known the meaning of such love as this. There is no fixed rule about it; the most unlikely, even the more sordid and contemptible of mankind, are liable to become the subjects of an enduring passion; only then it raises them; for though strong affection, especially if unrequited, sometimes wears and enervates the mind, its influence is, in the main, undoubtedly ennobling. But, though such affection is bounded by no rule, it is curious to observe how generally true are the old sayings which declare that a man's thoughts return to his first real love, as naturally and unconsciously as the needle, that has for a while been drawn aside by some overmastering influence, returns to its magnetic pole. The needle has wavered, but it has never shaken off its allegiance; that would be against nature, and is therefore impossible; and so it is with the heart. It is the eyes that he loved as a lad which he sees through the gathering darkness of his death-bed; it is a chance but that he will always adore the star which first came to share his loneliness in this shadowed world above all the shining multitudes in heaven.

And, though it is not every watcher who will find it, early or late, that star may rise for him, as it did for Arthur now. A man may meet a face which it is quite beyond his power to forget, and be touched of lips that print their kiss upon his very heart. Yes, the star may rise, to pursue its course, perhaps beyond the ken of his horizon, or only to set again before he has learnt to understand its beauty—rarely, very rarely, to shed its perfect light upon him for all his time of watching. The star may rise and set; the sweet lips whose touch still thrills him after so many years may lie to-day

"Beyond the graveyard's barren wall,"

or, worse still, have since been sold to some richer owner. But if once it has risen, if once those lips have met, the memory *must* remain; the Soul knows no forgetfulness, and, the little thread of life spun out, will it not claim its own? For the compact that it has sealed is holy among holy things; that love which it has given is of its own nature, and not of the body alone—it is inscrutable as death, and everlasting as the heavens.

Yes, the fiat has gone forth; for good or for evil, for comfort or for scorn, for the world and for eternity, he loves her! Henceforth that love, so lightly and yet so irredeemably given, will become the guiding spirit of his inner life, rough-hewing his destinies, directing his ends, and shooting its memories and hopes through the whole fabric of his being like an interwoven thread of gold. He may sin against it, but he can never forget it; other interests and ties may overlay it, but they cannot extinguish it; he may drown its fragrance in voluptuous scents, but, when these have satiated and become hateful, it will re-arise, pure and sweet as ever. Time or separation cannot destroy it—for it is immortal; use cannot stale it, pain can only sanctify it. It will be to him as a beacon-light to the sea-worn mariner that tells of home and peace upon the shore, as a rainbow-promise set upon his sky. It alone of all things pertaining to him will defy the attacks of the consuming years, and when, old and withered, he lays him down to die, it will at last present itself before its glazing eyes, an embodied joy, clad in shining robes, and breathing the airs of Paradise!

For such is love to those to whom it has been given to see him face to face.

CHAPTER XX.

ARTHUR did not do much fishing that morning; indeed, he never so much as got his line into the water—he simply sat there lost in dreams, and hoping in a vague way that Angela would come back again. But she did not come back, though it would be difficult to say what prevented her; for, had he but known it, she was for the space of a full hour sitting within a hundred yards of him, and occasionally peeping out to watch his mode of fishing with some curiosity. It was, she reflected, exceedingly unlike that practiced by Jakes. She, too, was wishing that he would detect her, and come to talk to her; but, amongst other new sensations, she was now the victim of a most unaccountable shyness, and could not make up her mind to reveal her whereabouts.

At last Arthur awoke from his long reverie, and remembered

with a sudden pang that he had had nothing to eat since the previous evening, and that he was consequently exceedingly hungry. He also discovered, on consulting his watch, that it was twelve o'clock, and, moreover, that he was quite stiff from sitting so long in the same position. So, sighing to think that such a vulgar necessity as that of obtaining food should force him to depart, he put up his unused fishing-rod and started for Isleworth, where he arrived just as the bell was ringing for lunch.

George received him with cold civility, and asked him what sport he had, to which he was forced to reply—none.

"Did you see anybody there?"

"Yes, I met Miss Caresfoot."

"Ah! trust a girl to trail out a man. What is she like? I remember her a raw-boned girl of fourteen with fine eyes."

"I think that she is the handsomest woman I ever saw," Arthur replied coldly.

"Ah!" said George, with a rude little laugh, "youth is always enthusiastic, especially when the object is of the dairy-maid cut."

There was something so intensely insolent in his host's way of talking that Arthur longed to throw a dish at him, but he restrained his feelings, and dropped the subject.

"Let me see: you are only just home from India, are you?" asked George, presently.

"I got back at the beginning of last month."

"And what were you doing there?"

"Travelling about and shooting."

"Did you get much sport?"

"No, I was rather unfortunate; but I and another fellow killed two tigers, and went after a rogue elephant; but he nearly killed us. I got some very good ibex-shooting in Cashmere, however."

"What do you intend to do with yourself now? Your education has been extravagantly expensive, especially the Cambridge part of it. Are you going to turn it to any account?"

"Yes. I am going to travel for another year, and then read for the Bar. There is no particular object in being called too young, and I wish to see something more of the world first."

"Ah! I see; idleness called by a fine name."

"Really I cannot agree with you," said Arthur, who was rapidly losing his temper.

"Of course you can't, but every man has a right to choose his own road to the dogs. Come," he added, with a smile of malice, as he noticed Arthur's rising color, "no need to get angry; you see I stand *in loco parentis*, and feel bound to express my opinion."

"I must congratulate you on the success with which you assume the character," answered Arthur, now thoroughly put out; "but, as everything I have done or mean to do is so distasteful to you, I think it is a pity that you did not give me the benefit of your advice a little sooner."

George's only answer was a laugh, and presently the two parted, detesting each other more cordially than ever.

At half-past three, when George was still away, for he had gone out with his bailiff immediately after lunch, Philip and his daughter were shown into the drawing-room, where we may be sure Arthur was awaiting them.

"Mr. Caresfoot is not back yet," said Arthur, "but I do not suppose that he will be long."

"Oh, he will be here soon," said Philip, "because I told him we were coming to call. What sort of sport did you have? What, none? I am very sorry. You must come and try again—ah! I forgot you are going away. By the way, Mr. Heigham, why should you go just yet? If you are fond of fishing, and have nothing better to do, come and put up at the Abbey House for a while; we are plain people, but there is plenty of room, and you shall have a hearty welcome. Would you care to come?"

It would have been amusing to any outsider to watch Angela's face as she heard this astounding proposition, for nobody had been invited inside her father's doors within her recollection. It assumed first of all a look of blank amazement, which was presently changed into one of absolute horror.

"Would he come, indeed?" reflected Arthur. "Would he step into Paradise? would he accept the humble offer of free quarters in the Garden of Eden?" Rapture beamed so visibly from every feature of his face that Philip saw it and smiled. Just as he was about to accept with enthusiasm, he caught sight of Angela's look of distress. It chilled him like the sudden shock of cold water; she did not wish him to come, he thought; she did not care for him. Obliged, however, to give an answer, he said,

"I shall be delighted if"—and here he bowed towards her—"Miss Caresfoot does not object."

"If, father," broke in Angela, with hesitation, "you could arrange that Mr. Heigham come to-morrow, not to-day, it would be more convenient. I must get a room ready."

"Ah! domestic details; I had overlooked them. I dare say you can manage that—eh, Heigham?"

"Oh, yes, easily, thank you."

As he said the words, the door was flung open, and "Lady Bellamy" was announced with the energy that a footman always devotes to the enunciation of a title, and next second a splendid creature, magnificently dressed, sailed into the room.

"Ah! how do you do, Mr. Caresfoot?" she said, in that low, rich voice that he remembered so well. "It is some time since we met; indeed, it quite brings back old times to see you, when we were all young people together."

"At any rate, Lady Bellamy, you show no signs of age; indeed, if you will permit me to say so, you look more beautiful than ever."

"Ah! Mr. Caresfoot, you have not forgotten how to be gallant; but let me tell you that it entirely depends upon what light I am in. If you saw me in the midst of one of those new-fangled electric illuminations, you would see that I do look old; but what can one expect at forty?" Here her glance fell upon Angela's face for the first time, and she absolutely started; the great pupils of her eyes expanded, and a dark frown spread itself for a moment over her countenance. Next second it was gone. "Is it possible that that beautiful girl is your daughter? But, remembering her mother, I need not ask. Look at her, Mr. Caresfoot, and then look at me, and say whether or not I look old. And who is the young man? Her lover, I suppose—at any rate, he looks like it; but please introduce me."

"Angela," said Philip, crossing to the window where they were talking, "let me introduce you to Lady Bellamy. Mr. Heigham—Lady Bellamy."

"I am delighted to make your acquaintance, Miss Caresfoot, though I think it is very generous of me to say so."

Angela looked puzzled.

"Indeed!" she said.

"What! do you not guess why it is generous? Then look at yourself in the glass, and you will see. I used to have some pretension to good looks, but I could never have stood beside you at the best of times, and now— Your mother, even when I was at my best, always *killed* me if I was in the same room with her, and you are even handsomer than your mother."

Angela blushed very much at this unqualified praise, and, putting it and the exclamation her appearance had that morning wrung from Arthur together, she suddenly came to the conclusion—for, odd as it may seem, she had never before taken the matter into serious consideration—that she must be very good-looking, a conclusion that made her feel extremely happy, she could not quite tell why.

It was whilst she was thus blushing, and looking her happiest and loveliest, that George, returning from his walk, chanced to look in at the window and see her, and, gradually drawn by the attraction of her beauty, his eyes fixed themselves intently upon her, and his coarse features grew instinct with a mixture of hungry wickedness and delighted astonishment. It was thus that Arthur and Lady Bellamy saw him. Philip, who was looking at a picture in the corner of the room, did not see him; nor, indeed, did Angela. The look was unmistakable, and once more the dark frown settled upon Lady Bellamy's brow, and the expanding pupils filled the heavy-lidded eyes. As for Arthur, it made him feel sick with unreasonable alarm.

Next minute George entered the room with a stupid smile upon his face, and looking as dazed as a bat that has suddenly been shown the sun. Angela's heaven-lit beauty had come upon his gross mind as a revelation; it fascinated him; he had lost his command over himself.

"Oh! here you are at last, George," said Lady Bellamy—it was always her habit to call him George. "We have all been like sheep without a shepherd, though I saw you keeping an eye on the flock, through the window."

George started. He did not know that he had been observed.

"I did not know that you were all here, or I would have been back sooner," he said, and then began to shake hands.

When he came to Angela, he favored her with a tender pressure of the fingers and an elaborate and high-flown speech of welcome, both of which were inexpressibly disagreeable to her. But here Lady Bellamy intervened, and skilfully forced him into a conversation with her, in which Philip joined.

"What does Lady Bellamy remind you of?" Angela asked Arthur, as soon as the hum of talk made it improbable that they would be overheard.

"Of an Egyptian sorceress, I think. Look at the low, broad, forehead, the curling hair, the full lips, and the inscrutable look of the face."

"To my mind she is an ideal of the Spirit of Power. I am very much afraid of her, and, as for him"—nodding towards George—"I dislike him even more than I was prepared to," and she gave a little shudder. "By the way, Mr. Heigham, you really must not be so rash as to accept my father's invitation."

"If you do not wish to see me, of course I will not," he answered, in a hurt and disappointed tone.

"Oh! it is not that, indeed; how could you think so, when only this morning we agreed to be friends?"

"Well, what is it, then?" he asked, blankly.

"Why, Mr. Heigham, the fact is that we—that is, my old nurse and I, for my father is irregular in his meals, and always takes them by himself—live so very plainly, and I am ashamed to ask you to share our mode of life. For instance, we have nothing but bread and milk for breakfast;" and the golden head sunk in some confusion before his amused gaze.

"Oh! is that all?" he said, cheerily. "I am very fond of bread and milk."

"And then," went on Angela with her confession, "we never drink wine, and I know that gentlemen do"

"I am a teetotaller, so that does not matter."

"Really?"

"Yes—really."

"But then, you know, my father shuts himself up all day, so that you will have nobody but myself to talk to."

"Oh, never mind"—encouragingly. "I am sure that we shall get on."

"Well, if, in spite of all this and a great deal more—oh! a very great deal that I have not time to tell you—you still care to come, I will do my best to amuse you. At any rate, we can read together; that will be something, if you don't find me too stupid. You must remember that I have only had a private education, and have never been to college like you. I shall be glad of the opportunity of rubbing up my classics a little; I have been neglecting them rather lately, and actually got into a mess over a passage in Aristophanes that I shall ask you to clear up."

This was enough for Arthur, whose knowledge of the classics was that of the ordinary University graduate; he turned the subject with remarkable promptitude.

"Tell me," he said, looking her straight in the face, "are you glad that I am coming?"

The gray eyes dropped a little before the boldness of his gaze, but she answered, unhesitatingly,

"Yes, for my own sake I am glad; but I fear that you will find it very dull."

"Come, Angela, we must be off; I want to be home by a quarter to six," said Philip just then.

She at once rose and shook hands with Arthur, murmuring, "Good-by till to-morrow morning," and then with Lady Bellamy.

George, meanwhile, with the most unwonted hospitality, was pressing her father to stay to dinner, and, when he declined, announced his intention of coming over to see him on the morrow. At last he got away, but not before Lady Bellamy had bid him a seemingly cordial adieu.

"You and your charming daughter must come and visit me at Rewtham House, when we get in. What, have you not heard that Sir John has bought it from poor Maria Lee's executors?"

Philip turned pale as death and hurried from the room.

"It is good," reflected Lady Bellamy, as she watched the effect of her shaft, "to let him know that I never forget."

But, even when her father had gone, the path was still blocked to Angela.

"What!" said George, who was, when in an amiable mood, that worst of all cads, a jocose cad, "are you going to play truant too, my pretty cousin? Then first you must pay the penalty—not a very heavy one, however." And he threw his long arm round her waist, and prepared to give her a cousinly embrace.

At first Angela, not being accustomed to little jokes of the sort, did not understand what his intentions were, but as soon as she did, being an extremely powerful young woman, she soon put a stop to them, shaking George away from her so sharply by a single swing of her lithe body, that, stumbling over a footstool in his rapid backward passage, he in a trice measured his length upon the floor. Seeing what she had done, Angela turned and fled after her father.

As for Arthur, the scene was too much for his risible nerves, and he fairly roared with laughter, whilst even Lady Bellamy went as near to it as she ever did.

George rose white with wrath.

"Mr. Heigham," he said, "I see nothing to laugh at in an accident."

"Don't you?" replied Arthur. "I do; it is just the most ludicrous accident that I ever saw."

George turned away, muttering something that it was perhaps as well his guest did not hear, and at once began to attack Lady Bellamy.

"My dear George," was her rejoinder, "let this little adventure teach you that it is not wise for middle-aged men to indulge in gallantries towards young ladies, and especially young ladies of thews and sinews. Good-night."

At the same moment the footman announced that the dog-cart which Arthur had ordered was waiting for him.

"Good-by, Mr. Heigham, good-by," said George, with angry sarcasm. "Within twenty-four hours you have killed my favorite dog, taken offence at my well-meant advice, and ridiculed my misfortune. If we should ever meet again, doubtless you will have further surprises in store for me;" and, without giving Arthur time to make any reply, he left the room.

CHAPTER XXI.

EARLY on the day following Arthur's departure from Isleworth, Lady Bellamy received a note from George requesting her, if convenient, to come and see him that morning, as he had something rather important to talk to her about.

"John," she said to her husband at breakfast, "do you want the brougham this morning?"

"No. Why?"

"Because I am going over to Isleworth."

"Hadn't you better take the luggage-cart too, and your luggage in it, and go and live there altogether? It would save trouble, sending backwards and forwards," suggested her husband, with severe sarcasm.

Lady Bellamy cut the top off an egg with a single clean stroke—all her movements were decisive—before she answered.

"I thought," she said, "that we had done with that sort of nonsense some years ago: are you going to begin it again?"

"Yes, Lady Bellamy, I am. I am not going to stand being bullied and jeered at by that damned scoundrel Caresfoot any more. I am not going to stand your eternal visits to him."

"You have stood them for twenty years; rather late in the day to object now, isn't it?" she remarked, coolly, beginning her egg.

"It is never too late to mend; it is not too late for you to stop quietly at home and do your duty by your husband."

"Most men would think that I had done my duty by him pretty well. Twenty years ago you were nobody, and had, comparatively speaking, nothing. Now you have a title and between three and four thousand a year. Who have you to thank for that? Certainly not yourself."

"Curse the title and the money! I had rather be a poor devil of an attorney with a large family, and five hundred a year to keep them on, than live the life I do between you and that vulgar beast Caresfoot. It's a dog's life, not a man's;" and poor Bellamy was so overcome at his real or imaginary wrongs that the tears actually rolled down his puffy little face.

His wife surveyed him with some amusement.

"I think," she said, "that you are a miserable creature."

"Perhaps I am, Anne; but I tell you what it is, even a miserable creature can be driven too far. It may perhaps be worth your while to be a little careful."

She cast one swift look at him, a look not without apprehension in it, for there was a ring about his voice that she did not like, but his appearance was so ludicrously wretched that it reassured her. She finished her egg, and then, slowly driving the spoon through the shell, she said,

"Don't threaten, John; it is a bad habit, and shows an un-Christian state of mind; besides, it might force me to cr-r-rush you, in self-defence, you know;" and, John and the egg-shell having finally collapsed together, Lady Bellamy ordered the brougham.

Having thus sufficiently scourged her husband, she departed in due course to visit her own taskmaster, little guessing what awaited her at his hands. After all, there is a deal of poetic justice in the world. Little Smith, fresh from his mother's apron-strings, is savagely beaten by the cock of the school, Jones, and to him Jones is an all-powerful, cruel devil, placed above all possibility of retribution. If, however, little Smith could see the omnipotent Jones being mentally ploughed and harrowed by his papa the clergyman, in celebration of the double event of his having missed a scholarship and taken too much sherry, it is probable that his wounded feelings would be greatly soothed. Nor does it stop there. Robinson, the squire of the parish, takes it out of the Reverend Jones, and speaks ill of him to the bishop, a Low Churchman, on the matter of vestments, and very shortly afterwards Sir Buster Brown, the Chairman of Quarter Sessions, expresses his opinion pretty freely of Robinson in his magisterial capacity, only in his turn to receive a most unexampled wigging from Her Majesty's judge, Baron Muddlebone, for not showing him that respect he was accustomed to receive from the High Sheriff of the county. And even over the august person of the judge himself there hangs the fear of the only thing that he cannot commit for contempt, public opinion. Justice! why, the world is full of it, only it is mostly built upon a foundation of wrong.

Lady Bellamy found George sitting in the dining-room beside the safe that had so greatly interested her husband. It was open, and he was reading a selection from the bundle of letters which the reader may remember having seen in his hands before.

"How do, Anne?" he said, without rising. "You look very handsome this morning. I never saw a woman wear better."

She vouchsafed no reply to his greeting, but turned as pale as death.

"What!" she said, huskily, pointing with her finger to the letters in his hand, "what are you doing with those letters?"

"Bravo, Anne; quite tragic. What a Lady Macbeth you would make! Come, quote, 'All the perfumes of Araby will not sweeten this little hand. Oh, oh, oh!' Go on."

"What are you doing with those letters?"

"Have you never broken a dog by showing him the whip, Anne? I have got something to ask of you, and I wish to get you into a generous frame of mind first. Listen now, I am going to read you a few extracts from a past that is so vividly recorded here."

She sank into a chair, hid her face in her hands, and groaned. George, whose own features betrayed a certain nervousness, took a yellow sheet of paper, and began to read.

"'Do you know how old I am to-day? Nineteen, and I have been married a year and a half. Ah! what a happy lass I was before I married; how they worshipped me in my old home! "Queen Anne," they always called me. Well, they are dead now, and pray God they sleep so sound that they can neither hear nor see. Yes, a year and a half—a year of happiness, half a year of hell; happiness whilst I did not know you, hell since I saw your face. What secret spring of wickedness did you touch in my heart? I never had a thought of wrong before you came. But when I first set eyes upon your face, I felt some strange change come over me: I recognized my evil destiny. How you discovered my fascination, how you led me on to evil, you best know. I am no coward, I do not wish to excuse myself, but sometimes I think that you have much to answer for, George. Hark, I hear my baby crying, my beautiful boy with his father's eyes. Do you know, I believe that the child has grown afraid of me: it beats at me with its tiny hands. I think that my very dog dislikes me now. They know me as I am; Nature tells them; everybody knows me except *him*. He will come in presently from visiting his sick and poor, and kiss me and call me his sweet wife, and I shall act the living lie. Oh! God, I cannot bear it much longer—'

"There is more of the same sort," remarked George, coolly. 'It affords a most interesting study of mental anatomy, but I have no time to read more of it. We will pass on to another."

Lady Bellamy did not move; she sat trembling a little, her face buried in her hands.

He took up a second letter, and began to read a marked passage.

"'The die is cast, I will come; I can no longer resist your influence; it grows stronger every day, and now it makes me a murderess, for the shock will kill him. And yet I am tired of the sameness and smallness of my life, my mind is too big to be cramped in such narrow fetters.'

"That extract is really very funny," said George, critically. "But don't look depressed, Anne, I am only going to trouble you with one more dated a year or so later. Listen:

"'I have several times seen the man you sent me; he is a fool and contemptible in appearance, and worst of all, shows signs of falling in love with me; but, if you wish it, I will go through the marriage ceremony with him, poor little dupe! You will not marry me yourself, and I would do more than that to keep near you; indeed, I have no choice, I *must* keep near you. I went to the Zoological Gardens the other day and saw a rattlesnake fed upon a live rabbit; the poor thing had ample room to run away in, but could not, it was fascinated, and sat still and screamed. At last the snake struck it, and I thought that its eyes looked like yours. I am as helpless as that poor animal, and you are much more cruel than the snake. And yet my mind is infinitely stronger than your own in every way. I cannot understand it. What is the source of your power over me? But I am quite reckless now, so what does it matter? I will do anything that does not put me within reach of the law. You know that my husband is dead. I *knew* that he would die; he expired with my name upon his lips. The child, too, I hear, died in a fit of croup; the nurse had gone out, and there was no one to look after it. Upon my word, I may well be reckless, for there is no forgiveness for such as you and I. As for little B——, as I think I told you, I will lead him on and marry him: at any rate, I will make his fortune for him: I *must* devote myself to something, and ambition is more absorbing than anything else—at least, I shall rise to something great. Good-night; I don't know which aches the most, my head or my heart.'

"Now that extract would be interesting reading to Bellamy, would it not?"

Here she suddenly sprang forward and snatched at the letter. But George was too quick for her; he flung it into the safe by his side, and swung the heavy lid to.

"No, no, my dear Anne, that property is too valuable to be parted with except for a consideration."

Her attempt frustrated, she dropped back into her chair.

"What are you torturing me for?" she asked, hoarsely. "Have you any object in dragging up the ghost of that dead past, or is it merely for amusement?"

"Did I not tell you that I had a favor to ask of you, and wished to get you into a proper frame of mind first?"

"A favor? You mean that you have some wickedness in hand that you are too great a coward to execute yourself. Out with it; I know you too well to be shocked."

"Oh, very well. You saw Angela Caresfoot, Philip's daughter, here yesterday?"

"Yes, I saw her."

"Very good. I mean to marry her, and you must manage it for me."

Lady Bellamy sat quite still, and made no answer.

"You will now," continued George, relieved to find that he had not provoked the outburst he had expected, "understand why I read you those extracts. I am thoroughly determined upon marrying that girl at whatever cost, and I see very clearly that I shall not be able to do so without your help. With your help the matter will be easy; for no obstacle, except the death of the girl herself, can prevail against your iron determination and unbounded fertility of resource."

"And if I refuse?"

"I must have read those extracts to very little purpose for you to talk about refusing. If you refuse, the pangs of conscience will overcome me, and I shall feel obliged to place these letters, and more especially those referring to himself, in the hands of your husband. Of course it will, for my own sake, be unpleasant to me to have to do so, but I can easily travel for a year or two till the talk has blown over. For you it will be different. Bellamy has no cause to love you now; judge what he will feel when he knows all the truth. He will scarcely keep the story to himself, and, even were he to do so, it could easily be set about in other ways, and in either case you will be a ruined woman, and all that you have toiled and schemed for for twenty years will be snatched from you in an instant. If, on the other hand, you do not refuse, and I cannot believe that you will, I will on my wedding-day burn these uncomfortable records before your eyes, or, if you prefer it, you shall burn them yourself."

"You have only seen this girl once; is it possible that you are in earnest in wishing to marry her?"

"Do you think that I should go through this scene by way of a joke? I never was so much in earnest in my life before. I am in love with her, I tell you, as much in love as though I had known her for years. What happened to you with reference to me has happened to me with reference to her, or something very like it, and marry her I must and will."

Lady Bellamy, as she heard these words, rose from her chair and flung herself on the ground before him, clasping his knees with her hands.

"Oh, George, George!" she cried, in a broken voice, "have some little pity; do not force me to do this unnatural thing. Is your heart a stone, or are you altogether a devil, that by such cruel threats you can drive me into becoming the instrument of my own shame? I know what I am, none better: but for whose sake did I become so? Surely, George, I have some claim on your compassion, if I have none on your love. Think again, George; and, if you will not give her up, choose some other means to compass this poor girl's ruin."

"Get up, Anne, and don't talk sentimental rubbish. Not but what," he added, with a sneer, "it is rather amusing to hear you pitying your successful rival."

She sprang to her feet, all the softness and entreaty gone from her face, which was instead now spread with her darkest and most vindictive look.

"*I* pity her!" she said. "I hate her. Look you, if I have to do this, my only consolation will be in knowing that what I do will drag my successor down below my own level. I suffer: she shall suffer more. I know you a fiend: she shall find a whole hell with you. She is purer and better than I have ever been: soon you shall make her worse than I have dreamt of being. Her purity shall be dishonored, her love betrayed, her life reduced to such chaos that she shall cease to believe even in her God, and in return for these things I will give her—*you*. Your new plaything shall pass through my mill, George Caresfoot, before ever she comes to yours; and on her I will repay with interest all that I have suffered at your hands;" and, exhausted with the fierceness of her own invective and the violence of conflicting passions, she sank back into her chair.

"Bravo, Anne! quite in your old style. I dare say that the young lady will require a little moulding, and she could not be in better hands; but mind, no tricks—I am not going to be cheated out of my bride."

"You need not fear, George; I shall not murder her. I do not believe in violence; it is the last resource of fools. If I did, you would not be alive now."

George laughed a little uneasily.

"Well, we are good friends again, so there is no need to talk of such things," he said. "The campaign will not be by any means an easy one—there are many obstacles in the way, and I don't think that my intended has taken a particular fancy to me. You will have to work for your letters, Anne; but first of all take a day or two to think it over, and make a plan of the campaign. And now good-by; I have got a bad headache, and am going to lie down."

She rose, and went without another word; but all necessity for setting about her shameful task was soon postponed by news that reached her the next morning, to the effect that George Caresfoot was seriously ill.

CHAPTER XXII.

The dog-cart that Arthur had hired to take him away belonged to an old-fashioned inn in the parish of Rewtham, situated about a mile from Rewtham House (which had just passed into the hands of the Bellamys), and two from Bratham Abbey, and thither Arthur had himself driven. His Jehu, known through all the country round as "Old Sam," was an ancient ostler, who had been in the service of the Rewtham "King's Head," man and boy, for over sixty years, and from him Arthur collected a good deal of inaccurate information about the Caresfoot family, including a garbled version of the death of Angela's mother and Philip's disinheritance.

After all, there are few more comfortable places than an inn; not a huge London hotel, where you are known as No. 48, and have to lock the door of your cell when you come out of it, and deliver up your key to the warder in the hall; but an old-fashioned country establishment where they cook your beefsteak exactly as you like it, and give you sound ale and a four-poster. At least, so thought Arthur, as he sat in the private parlor smoking his pipe and reflecting on the curious vicissitudes of existence. Now, here he was, with all the hopes and interests of his life utterly changed in a single space of six-and-twenty hours. Why, six-and-twenty hours ago, he had never met his respected guardian, nor Sir John and Lady Bellamy, nor Philip and his daughter. He could hardly believe that it was only that morning that he had first seen Angela. It seemed weeks ago, and, if time could have been measured on a new principle, by events and not by minutes, it would have been weeks. The wheel of life, he thought, revolves with a strange irregularity. For months and years it turns slowly and steadily under the even pressure of monotonous events. But, on some unexpected day, a tide comes rushing down the stream of being, and spins it round at speed; and then tears onward to the ocean called the Past, leaving its plaything to creak and turn, to turn and creak, or wrecked, perhaps, and useless.

Thinking thus, Arthur made his way to bed. The excitement of the day had wearied him, and for a while he slept soundly, but, as the fatigue of the body wore off, the activity of his mind asserted itself, and he began to dream vague, happy dreams of Angela, that by degrees took shape and form, till they stood out clear before the vision of his mind. He dreamt that he and Angela were journeying, two such happy travellers, through the green fields in summer, till by and by they came to the dark entrance of a wood, into which they plunged, fearing nothing. Thicker grew the overshadowing branches, and darker grew the path, and now they journeyed lover-wise, with their arms around each other. But, as they passed along, they came to a place where the paths forked, and here he stooped to kiss her. Already he could feel the thrill of her embrace, when she was swept from him by an unseen force, and carried down the path before them, leaving him rooted where he was. But still he could trace her progress as she went, wringing her hands in sorrow; and presently he saw the form of Lady Bellamy, robed as an Egyptian sorceress, and holding a letter in her hand, which she offered to Angela, whispering in her ear. She took it, and then in a second the letter turned to a great snake, with George's head, that threw its coils around her and struck at her with its fangs. Next, the darkness of night rushed down upon the scene, and out of the darkness came wild cries and mocking laughter, and the choking sounds of death. And his senses left him.

When sight and sense came back, he dreamt that he was still walking down a wooded lane, but the foliage of the overhanging trees was of a richer green. The air was sweet with the scent of unknown flowers, beautiful birds flitted around him, and from far-off came the murmur of the sea. And as he travelled, broken-hearted, a fair woman with a gentle voice stood by his side, and kissed and comforted him, till at length he grew weary of her kisses, and she left him, weeping, and he went on his way alone, seeking his lost Angela. And then at length the path took a sudden turn, and he stood on the shore of an illimitable ocean, over which brooded a strange light, as where

> "The quiet end of evening smiles
> Miles on miles."

And there, with the soft light lingering on her hair, and tears of gladness in her eyes, stood Angela, more lovely than before, her arms outstretched to greet him. And then the night closed in, and he awoke.

His eyes opened upon the solemn and beautiful hour of the first quickening of the dawn, and the thrill and softness that comes from contact with the things we meet in sleep was still upon him. He got up and flung open his lattice window. From the garden beneath rose the sweet scent of May flowers, very different from that of his dream which yet lingered in his nostrils, whilst from a neighboring lilac-bush streamed the rich melody of the nightingale. Presently it ceased before the broadening daylight, but in its stead, pure and clear and cold, arose the notes of the mavis, giving tuneful thanks and glory to its Maker. And, as he listened, a great calm stole upon his spirit, and kneeling down there by the open window, with the breath of spring upon his brow, and the voice of the happy birds within his ears, he prayed to the Almighty with all his heart that it might please Him in His wise mercy to verify his dream, inasmuch as he would be well content to suffer, if by suffering he might at last attain to such an unutterable joy. And rising from his knees, feeling better and stronger, he knew in some dim way that that undertaking must be blest which, in such a solemn hour of the heart, he did not fear to pray God to guide, to guard, and to consummate.

And on many an after-day, and in many another place, the book of his life would reopen at this well-conned page, and he would see the dim light in the faint, flushed sky, and hear the song of the thrush swelling upwards strong and sweet, and remember his prayer and the peace that fell upon his soul.

By ten o'clock that morning, Arthur, his dog, and his portmanteau had all arrived together in front of the Abbey House. Before his feet had touched the moss-grown gravel, the hall-door was flung open, and Angela appeared to welcome him, looking, as old Sam the ostler forcibly put it afterwards to his helper, "just like a hangel with the wings off." Jakes, too, emerged from the recesses of the garden, and asked Angela, in a tone of aggrieved sarcasm, as he edged his way suspiciously past Aleck, why the gentleman had not brought the "rampingest lion from the Zoologic Gardens" with him at once? Having thus expressed his feelings on the subject of bull-dogs, he shouldered the portmanteau, and made his way with it upstairs. Arthur followed him up the wide oak stairs, every one of which was squared out of a single log, stopping for a while on the landing, where the staircase turned, to gaze at the stern-faced picture that hung so that it looked through the large window facing it, right across the park and over the whole stretch of the Abbey lands, and to wonder at the deep-graved inscription of "Devil Caresfoot" set so conspicuously beneath.

His room was the largest upon the first landing, and the same in which Angela's mother had died. It had never been used from that hour to this, and, indeed, in a little recess or open space between a cupboard and the wall, there still stood two trestles, draped with rotten black cloth, that had originally been brought there to rest her coffin on, and which Angela had overlooked in getting the room ready.

This spacious but somewhat gloomy apartment was hung round with portraits of the Caresfoots of past ages, many of which bore a marked resemblance to Philip, but amongst whom he looked in vain for one in the slightest degree like Angela, whose handiwork he recognized in two large bowls of flowers placed upon the dark oak dressing-table.

Just as Jakes had finished unbuckling his portmanteau, a task that he had undertaken with some grumbling, and was departing in haste, lest he should be asked to do something else, Arthur caught sight of the trestles.

"What are those ?" he asked, cheerfully.

"Coffin-stools," was the abrupt reply.

"Coffin-stocls !" ejaculated Arthur, feeling that it was unpleasant to have little details connected with one's latter end brought thus abruptly into notice. "What the deuce are they doing here ?"

"Brought to put the last as slept in that 'ere bed on, and stood ever since."

"Don't you think," insinuated Arthur, gently, "that you had better take them away ?"

"Can't do so; they be part of the furniture, they be—stand there all handy for the next one, too, maybe you;" and he vanished with a sardonic grin.

Jakes did not submit to the indignities of unbuckling portmanteaus and having his legs sniffed at by bull dogs for nothing. Not by any means pleased by suggestions so unpleasant, Arthur took his way downstairs, determined to renew the coffin-stool question with his host. He found Angela waiting for him in the hall, and making friends with Aleck.

"Will you come in and see my father for a minute before we go out ?" she said.

Arthur assented, and she led the way into the study, where Philip always sat, the same room in which his father had died. He was sitting at a writing-table as usual, at work on farm accounts. Rising, he greeted Arthur civilly, taking, however, no notice of his daughter, although he had not seen her since the previous day.

"Well, Heigham, so you have made up your mind to brave these barbarous wilds, have you ? I am delighted to see you, but I must warn you that, beyond a pipe and a glass of grog in the evening, I have not much time to put at your disposal. We are rather a curious household. I don't know whether Angela has told you, but for one thing we do not take our meals together, so you will have to make your choice between the dining-room and the nursery, for my daughter is not out of the nursery yet;" and he gave a little laugh. "On the whole, perhaps you had better be relegated to the nursery; it will, at any rate, be more amusing to you than the society of a morose old fellow like myself. And, besides, I am very irregular in my habits. Angela, you are staring at me again; I should be so very much obliged if you would look the other way. I only hope, Heigham, that old Pigott won't talk your head off; she has got a dreadful tongue. Well, don't let me keep you any longer; it is a lovely day for the time of year. Try to amuse yourself somehow, and I hope for your sake that Angela will not occupy herself with you as she does with me, by staring as though she wished to examine your brains and backbone. Good-by for the present."

"What does he mean?" asked Arthur, as soon as they were fairly outside the door, "about your staring at him?"

"Mean!" answered poor Angela, who looked as though she were going to cry. "I wish I could tell you; all I know is that he cannot bear me to look at him—he is always complaining of it. That is why we do not take our meals together—at least, I believe it is. He detests my being near him. I am sure I don't know why; it makes me very unhappy. I cannot see anything different in my eyes from anydody else's, can you?" and she turned them, swimming as they were with tears of mortification, full upon Arthur.

He scrutinized their depths very closely, so closely indeed, that presently she turned them away again with a blush.

"Well," she said, "I am sure you have looked long enough. Are they different?"

"Very different," replied the oracle, with enthusiam.

"How?"

"Well, they—they are larger."

"Is that all?"

"And they are deeper."

"Deeper—that is nothing. I want to know if they produce any unpleasant effect upon you—different from other people's eyes, I mean?"

"Well, if you ask me, I am afraid that your eyes do produce a strange effect upon me, but I cannot say that it is an unpleasant one. But you did not look long enough for me to form a really sound opinion. Let us try again."

"No, I will not; and I do believe that you are laughing at me. I think that is very unkind;" and she marched on in silence.

"Don't be angry with me, or I shall be miserable. I really was not laughing at you; only, if you knew what wonderful eyes you have got, you would not ask such ridiculous questions about them. Your father must be a strange man to get such ideas. I am sure I should be delighted if you would look at me all day long. But tell me something more about your father: he interests me very much."

Angela felt the tell-tale blood rise to her face as he praised her eyes, and bit her lips with vexation; it seemed to her that she had suddenly caught an epidemic of blushing.

"I cannot tell you very much about my father, because I do not know much; his life is, to a great extent, a sealed book to me. But they say that once he was a very different man—when he was quite young, I mean. But all of a sudden his father—my grandfather, you know—whose picture is on the stairs, died, and within a day or two my mother died too; that was when I was born. After that he broke down, and became what he is now. For twenty years he has lived as he does now, poring all day over books of accounts, and very rarely seeing anybody, for he does all his business by letter, or nearly all of it, and he has no friends. There was some story about his being engaged to a lady who lived at Rewtham when he married my mother, which I dare say you have heard; but I don't know much about it. But, Mr. Heigham"—and here she dropped her voice—"there is one thing that I must warn you of: my father has strange fancies at times. He is dreadfully superstitious, and thinks that he has communications with beings from another world. I believe that it is all nonsense, but I tell you so that you may not be surprised at anything he says or does. He is not a happy man, Mr. Heigham."

"Apparently not. I cannot imagine any one being happy who is superstitious; it is the most dreadful bondage in the world."

"Where are your ravens to-day?" asked Arthur presently.

"I don't know; I have not seen very much of them for the last week or two. They have made a nest in one of the big trees at the back of the house, and I dare say that they are there, or perhaps they are hunting for their food—they always feed themselves. But I will soon tell you," and she whistled in a soft but penetrating note.

Next minute there was a swoop of wings, and the largest raven, after hovering over her for a minute, lit upon her shoulder, and rubbed his black head against her face.

"This is Jack, you see; I expect that Jill is busy sitting on her eggs. Fly away, Jack, and look after your wife." She clapped her hands, and the great bird, giving a reproachful croak, spread his wings, and was gone.

"You have a strange power over animals to make those birds so fond of you."

"Do you think so? It is only because I have, living as I do quite alone, had time to study all their ways, and make friends of them. Do you see that thrush there? I know him well; I fed him during the frost last winter. If you will stand back with the dog, you shall see."

Arthur hid himself behind a thick bush and watched. Angela whistled again, but in another note, with a curious result. Not only the thrush in question, but quite a dozen other birds of different sorts and sizes, came flying round her, some settling at her feet, and one, a little robin, actually perching itself upon her hat. Presently she dismissed them as she had done the raven, by clapping her hands, and came back to Arthur.

"In the winter-time," she said, "I could show you more curious things than that."

"I think that you are a witch," said Arthur, who was astounded at the sight.

She laughed as she answered,

"The only witchery that I use is kindness."

CHAPTER XXIII.

PIGOTT, Angela's old nurse, was by no means sorry to hear of Arthur's visit to the Abbey House, though, having in her youth been a servant in good houses, she was distressed at the nature of his reception. But, putting this aside, she thought it high time that her darling should see a young man or two, that she might "learn what the world was like." Pigott was no believer in female celibacy, and Angela's future was a frequent subject of meditation with her, for she knew very well that her present mode of life was scarcely suited either to her birth, her beauty, or her capabilities. Not that she ever, in her highest flights, imagined Angela as a great lady, or one of society's shining stars; she loved to picture her in some quiet, happy home, beloved by her husband, and surrounded by children as beautiful as herself. It was but a moderate ambition for one so peerlessly endowed, but she would have been glad to see it fulfilled. For of late years there had sprung up in nurse Pigott's mind an increasing dislike of her surroundings, which sometimes almost amounted to a feeling of horror. Philip she had always detested, with his preoccupied air and uncanny ways.

"There must," she would say, "be something wicked about a man as is afraid to have his own bonny daughter look him in the face, to say nothing of his being that mean as to grudge her the clothes on her back, and make her live worse nor a servant-girl."

Having, therefore, by a quiet peep through the curtains, ascertained that he was nice-looking and about the right age, Pigott confessed to herself that she was heartily glad of Arthur's arrival, and determined that, should she take to him on further acquaintance, he should find a warm ally in her in any advances he might choose to make on the fortress of Angela's affections.

"I do so hope that you don't mind dining at half-past twelve, and with my old nurse," Angela said, as they went together up the stairs to the room they used as a dining-room.

"Of course I don't—I like it, really I do."

Angela shook her head, and, looking but partially convinced, led the way down the passage, and into the room, where, to her astonishment, she perceived that the dinner-table was furnished with a more sumptuous meal than she had seen upon it for years, the fact being that Pigott had received orders from Philip which she did not know of, not to spare expense whilst Arthur was his guest.

"What waste!" reflected Angela, in whom the pressure of circumstances had developed an economical turn of mind, as she glanced at the unaccustomed jug of beer. "He said he was a teetotaller."

A loud "Hem!" from Pigott, arresting her attention, stopped all further consideration of the matter. That good lady, who, in honor of the occasion, was dressed in a black gown of a formidable character, and a many-ribboned cap, was standing up behind her chair waiting to be introduced to the visitor. Angela proceeded to go through the ceremony, which Pigott's straight-up-and-down attitude rendered rather trying.

"Nurse, this is the gentleman that my father has asked to stay with us. Mr. Heigham, let me introduce you to my old nurse Pigott."

Arthur bowed politely, whilst Pigott made two elaborate courtesies, retiring a step backwards after each, as though to make room for another. Her speech, too, carefully prepared for the occasion, is worthy of transcription.

"Hem!" she said, "this, sir, is a pleasure as I little expected, and I well knows that it is not what you or the likes is accustomed to, a-eating of dinners and teas with old women; which I hopes, sir, how as you will put up with it, seeing how as the habits of this house is what might, without mistake, be called peculiar, which I says without any offence to Miss Angela, 'cause though her bringing-up has been what I calls odd, she knows it as well as I do, which, indeed, is the only consolation I has to offer, being right sure, as indeed I am, how as any young gentleman as ever breathed would sit in a pool of water to dine along with Miss Angela, let alone an old nurse. I ain't such a fool as I may look; no need for you to go a-blushing of, Miss Angela. And now, sir, if you please, we will sit down, for fear lest the gravy should begin to grease;" and, utterly exhausted by the exuberance of her own verbosity, she plunged into her chair—an example which Arthur, bowing his acknowledgments of her opening address, was not slow to follow.

One of his first acts was, at Pigott's invitation, to help himself to a glass of beer, of which, to speak truth, he drank a good deal.

Angela watched the proceeding with interest.

"What," she asked presently, "is a teetotaller?"

The recollection of his statement of the previous day flashed into his mind. He was, however, equal to the occasion.

"A teetotaller," he replied, with gravity, "is a person who only drinks beer;" and Angela, the apparent discrepancy explained, retired satisfied.

That was a very pleasant dinner. What a thing it is to be young and in love! How it gilds the dull gingerbread of life; what new capacities of enjoyment it opens up in us, and, for the matter of that, of pain also; and oh! what stupendous fools it makes of us in everybody else's eyes except our own and, if we are lucky, those of our adored!

The afternoon and evening passed much as the morning had done. Angela took Arthur round the place, and showed him all the spots connected with her strange and lonely childhood, of which she told him many a curious story. In fact, before the day was over he knew all the history of her innocent life, and was struck with amazement at the variety and depth of her scholastic acquirements and the extraordinary power of her mind, which, combined with her simplicity and total ignorance of the ways of the world, produced an effect as charming as it was unusual. Needless to say that every hour he knew her, he fell more deeply in love with her.

At length, about eight o'clock, just as it was beginning to get dark, she suggested that he should go and sit a while with her father.

"And what are you going to do?" asked Arthur.

"Oh! I am going to read a little, and then go to bed; I always go to bed about nine;" and she held out her hand to say good night. He took it and said:

"Good-night, then; I wish it were to-morrow."

"Why?"

"Because then I should be saying, 'Good-morning, Angela,' instead of 'Good-night, Angela.' May I call you Angela? We seem to know each other so well, you see."

"Yes, of course," she laughed back; "everybody I know calls me Angela, so why shouldn't you?"

"And will you call me Arthur? Everybody I know calls me Arthur."

Angela hesitated, and Angela blushed, though why she hesitated and why she blushed was perhaps more than she could have exactly said.

"Y-e-s, I suppose so—that is, if you like it. It is a pretty name, Arthur. Good-night, Arthur!" and she was gone.

His companion gone, Arthur turned and entered the house. The study-door was open, so he went straight in. Philip, who was sitting and staring in an abstracted way at the empty fireplace with a light behind him, turned quickly round as he heard his footstep.

"Oh! it's you, is it, Heigham? I suppose Angela has gone upstairs; she goes to roost very early. I hope that she has not bored you, and that old Pigott hasn't talked your head off. I told you that we were an odd lot, you know; but if you find us odder than you bargained for, I should advise you to clear out."

"Thank you, I have spent a very happy day."

"Indeed, I am glad to hear it. You must be easily satisfied, have an Arcadian mind, and that sort of thing. Take some whiskey, and light your pipe."

Arthur did so; and presently Philip, in that tone of gentlemanly ease which above everything distinguished him from his cousin, led the conversation round to his guest's prospects and affairs, more especially his money affairs. Arthur answered him frankly enough, but this money talk had not the same charms for him that it had for his host. Indeed, a marked repugnance to everything that had to do with money was one of his characteristics; and, wearied out at length with pecuniary details and endless researches into the mysteries of investment, he took advantage of a pause to attempt to change the subject.

"Well," he said, "I am much obliged to you for your advice, for I am very ignorant myself, and hate anything to do with money. I go back to first principles, and believe that we should all be better without it."

"I always thought," answered Philip, with a semi-contemptuous smile, "that the desire of money, or, amongst savage races, its equivalent, shells or what not, was *the* first principle of human nature."

"Perhaps it is—I really don't know; but I heartily wish that it could be eliminated off the face of the earth."

"Forgive me," laughed Philip, "but that is the speech of a very young man. Why, eliminate money, and you take away the principal interest of life, and destroy the social fabric of the world. What is power but money, comfort?—money, social consideration?—money, ay, and love, and health, and happiness itself? Money, money, money. Tell me," he went on, rising, and addressing him with a curious earnestness, "what god is there more worthy of our adoration than Plutus, seeing that, if we worship him enough, he alone of the idols we set in high places will never fail us at need?"

"It is a worship that rarely brings lasting happiness with it. In our greed to collect the means of enjoyment, surely we lose the power to enjoy."

"Pshaw! that is the cant of fools, of those who do not know, of those who cannot feel. But I know and I feel, and I tell you that it is not so. The collection of those means is in itself a pleasure, because it gives a consciousness of power. Don't talk to me of Fate; that sovereign" (throwing the coin onto the table) "is Fate's own seal. You see me, for instance, apparently poor and helpless, a social pariah, one to be avoided, and even insulted, Good; before long these will right all that for me. I shall by their help be powerful and courted yet. Ay, believe me, Heigham, money is a living, moving force; leave it still, and it accumulates; expend it, and it gratifies every wish; save it, and that is best of all, and you hold in your hand a lever that will lift the world. I tell you that there is no height to which it cannot bring you, no gulf it will not bridge you."

"Except," soliloquized Arthur, "the cliffs of the Hereafter and —the grave."

His words produced a curious effect. Philip's eloquence broke off short, and for a moment a great fear crept into his eyes.

Silence ensued which neither of them seemed to care to break. Meanwhile the wind suddenly sprang up, and began to moan and sigh amongst the half-clad boughs of the trees outside—making, Arthur thought to himself, a very melancholy music. Presently Philip laid his hand upon his guest's arm, and he felt that it shook like an aspen leaf.

"Tell me," he said, in a hoarse whisper, "what do you see there?"

Arthur started, and followed the direction of his eyes to the bare wall opposite the window, at that end of the room through which the door was made.

"I see," he said, "some moving shadows."

"What do they resemble?"

"I don't know; nothing in particular. What are they?"

"What are they?" hissed Philip, whose face was livid with terror, "they are the shades of the dead sent here to torture me. Look, she goes to meet him; the old man is telling her. Now she will wring her hands."

"Nonsense, Mr. Caresfoot, nonsense," said Arthur, shaking himself together; "I see nothing of the sort. Why, it is only the shadows flung by the moonlight through the swinging boughs of that tree. Cut it down, and you will have no more writing upon your wall."

"Ah! of course you are right, Heigham, quite right," ejaculated his host, faintly, wiping the cold sweat from his brow; "it is nothing but the moonlight. How ridiculous of me! I suppose I am a little out of sorts—liver wrong. Give me some whiskey, there's a good fellow, and I'll drink damnation to all shadows and *the trees that throw them*. Ha, ha, ha!"

There was something so excessively uncanny about his host's manner, and his evident conviction of the origin of the wavering figures on the wall (which had now disappeared), that Arthur felt, had it not been for Angela, he would not be sorry to get clear of him and his shadows as soon as possible, for superstition, he knew, is as contagious as small-pox. When at length he reached his great bare bedchamber, not, by the way, a comfortable sort of place to sleep in after such an experience, it was only after some hours, in the excited state of his imagination, that, tired though he was, he could get the rest he needed.

CHAPTER XXIV.

NEXT morning, when they met at their eight-o'clock breakfast, Arthur noticed that Angela was distressed about something.

"There is bad news," she said, almost before he greeted her; "my cousin George is very ill with typhus fever."

"Indeed!" remarked Arthur, rather coolly.

"Well, I must say it does not appear to distress you very much."

"No, I can't say it does. To be honest, I detest your cousin, and I don't care if he is ill or not; there."

As she appeared to have no reply ready, the subject then dropped.

After breakfast Angela proposed that they should walk—for the day was again fine—to the top of a hill about a mile away, whence a view of the surrounding country could be obtained. He consented, and on the way told her of his curious experience with her father on the previous night. She listened attentively, and, when he had finished, shook her head.

"There is," she said, "something about my father that separates him from everybody else. His life never comes out into the sunlight of the passing day, it always gropes along in the shadow of some gloomy past. What the mystery is that envelops him I neither know nor care to inquire; but I am sure that there is one."

"How do you explain the shadows?"

"I believe your explanation is right; they are, under certain conditions of light, thrown by a tree that grows some distance off. I have seen something that looks like figures on that wall myself in full daylight. That he should interpret such a simple thing as he does shows a curious state of mind."

"You do not think, then," said Arthur, in order to draw her out, "that it is possible, after all, he was right, and that they were something from another place? The reality of his terror was almost enough to make one believe in them, I can tell you."

"No, I do not," answered Angela, after a minute's thought. "I have no doubt that the veil between ourselves and the unseen world is thinner than we think. I believe, too, that communication, and even warnings sometimes, under favorable conditions, or when the veil is worn thin by trouble or prayer, can pass from the other world to ourselves. But the very fact of my father's terror proves to me that his shadows are nothing of the sort, for it is hardly possible that spirits can be permitted to come to terrify us poor mortals; if they come at all, it is in love and gentleness, to comfort or to warn, and not to work upon our superstitions."

"You speak as though you knew all about it; you should join the new Ghost Society," he answered, irreverently, sitting himself down on a fallen tree, an example that she followed.

"I have thought about it sometimes, that is all, and, so far as I have read, I think that my belief is a common one, and what the Bible teaches us; but, if you will not think me foolish, I will tell you something that confirms me in it. You know that my mother died when I was born; well, it may seem strange to you, but I am convinced that she is sometimes very near me."

"Do you mean that you see or hear her?"

"No, I only feel her presence; more rarely now, I am sorry to say, as I grow older."

"How do you mean?"

"I can hardly explain what I mean, but sometimes—it may be at night, or when I am sitting alone in the daytime—a great calm comes upon me, and I am a changed woman. All my thoughts rise into a higher, purer air, and are, as it were, tinged with a reflected light; everything earthly seems to pass away from me, and I feel as though fetters had fallen from my soul, and I *know* that I am near my mother. Then everything passes, and I am left myself again."

"And what are the thoughts you have at these times?"

"Ah! I wish I could tell you; they pass away with her who

brought them, leaving nothing but a vague after-glow in my mind like that in the sky after the sun has set. But now look at the view; is it not beautiful in the sunlight? All the world seems to be rejoicing."

Angela was right; the view was charming. Below lay the thatched roofs of the little village of Bratham, and to the right the waters of the lake shone like silver in the glancing sunlight, whilst the gables of the old house, peeping out from amongst the budding foliage, looked very picturesque. The spring had cast her green garment over the land; from every copse rang out the melody of birds, and the gentle breeze was heavy with the scent of the unnumbered violets that starred the mossy carpet at their feet. In the fields where grew the wheat and clover, now springing into lusty life, the busy weeders were at work, and on the warm brown fallows the sower went forth to sow. From the early pastures beneath, where purled a little brook, there came a pleasant lowing of kine, well contented with the new grass, and a cheerful bleating of lambs, to whom as yet life was nothing but one long skip. It was a charming scene, and its influence sank deep into the gazers' hearts.

"It is depressing to think," said Arthur, rather sententiously, but really chiefly with the object of getting at his companion's views, "that all this cannot last, but is, as it were, like ourselves, under sentence of death."

"It rose and fell and fleeted
Upon earth's troubled sea,
A wave that swells to vanish
Into eternity.
Oh! mystery and wonder
Of wings that cannot fly,
Of ears that cannot hearken,
Of life that lives—to die!"

quoth Angela, by way of comment.

"Whose lines are those?" asked Arthur. "I don't know them."

"My own," she said shyly; "that is, they are a translation of a verse of a Greek ode I wrote for Mr. Fraser. I will say you the original, if you like; I think it is better than the translation, and I believe that it is fair Greek."

"Thank you, thank you, Miss Blue-stocking; I am quite satisfied with your English version. You positively alarm me, Angela. Most people are quite content if they can put a poem written in English into Greek; you reverse the process, and, having coolly given expression to your thoughts in Greek, condescend to translate them into your native tongue. I only wish you had been at Cambridge, or—what do they call the place?—Girton. It would have been a joke to see you come out double-first."

"Ah!" she broke in, blushing, "you are like Mr. Fraser, you overrate my acquirements. I am sorry to say I am not the perfect scholar you think me, and about most things I am shockingly ignorant. I should indeed be silly if, after ten years' patient work under such a scholar as Mr. Fraser, I did not know some classics and mathematics. Why, do you know, for the last three years that we worked together, we used as a rule to carry on our ordinary conversations during work in Latin and Greek, month and month about, sometimes with the funniest results. One never knows how little one does know of a dead language till one tries to talk it. Just try to speak in Latin for the next five minutes, and you will see."

"Thank you, I am not going to expose my ignorance for your amusement, Angela."

She laughed.

"No," she said, "it is you who wish to amuse yourself at my expense by trying to make me believe that I am a great scholar. But what I was going to say, before you attacked me about my fancied acquirements, was that, in my opinion, your remark about the whole world being under sentence of death was rather a morbid one."

"Why? It is obviously true."

"Yes, in a sense; but to my mind this scene speaks more of resurrection than of death. Look at the earth pushing up her flowers, and the dead trees breaking into beauty. There is no sign of death there, but rather of a renewed and glorified life."

"Yes, but there is still the awful *fact* of death to face; Nature herself has been temporarily dead before she blooms into beauty; she dies every autumn, to rise again in the same form every spring. But how do we know in what form *we* shall emerge from the chrysalis? As soon as a man begins to think at all, he stands face to face with this hideous problem, to the solution of which he knows himself to be drawing daily nearer. His position, I often think, is worse than that of a criminal under sentence, because the criminal is only being deprived of the enjoyment of a term, indefinite, indeed, but absolutely limited; but man at large does not know of what he is deprived, and what he must inherit in the æons that await him. It is the uncertainty of death that is its most dreadful part, and, with that hanging over our race, the wonder to me is not only that we, for the most part, put the subject entirely out of mind, but that we can ever think seriously of anything else."

"I remember," answered Angela, "once thinking very much in the same way, and I went to Mr. Fraser for advice. 'The Bible,' he said, 'will satisfy your doubts and fears, if only you will read it in a right spirit.' And indeed, more or less, it did. I cannot, of course, venture to advise you, but I pass his advice on; it is that of a very good man."

"Have you, then, no dread of death, or, rather, of what lies beyond it?"

She turned her eyes upon him with something of wonder in them.

"And why," she said, "should I, who am immortal, fear a change that I know has no power to harm me, that can, on the contrary, only bring me nearer to the purpose of my being? Certainly I shrink from death itself, as we all must, but of the dangers beyond I have no fear. Pleasant as this world is at times, there is something in us all that strives to rise above it, and, if I knew that I must die within this hour, I *believe* that I could meet my fate without a qualm. I am sure that when our trembling hands have drawn the veil from Death, we shall find His features, passionless indeed, but very beautiful."

Arthur looked at her with astonishment, wondering what manner of woman this could be who, in the first flush of youth and beauty, could face the great unknown without a tremor. When he spoke again, it was with something of envious bitterness.

"Ah! it is very well for you, whose life has been so pure and free from evil, but it is different for me, with all my consciousness of sins and imperfections. For me, and thousands like me, strive as we will, immortality has terrors as well as hopes. It is, and always will be, human to fear the future, for human nature never changes. You know the lines in 'Hamlet.' It is

> 'that the dread of something after death,
> The undiscovered country from whose bourn
> No traveller returns, puzzles the will
> And makes us rather bear those ills we have
> Than fly to others that we know not of.
> Thus conscience does make cowards of us all.'

They are true, and, while men last, they always will be true."

"Oh! Arthur," she answered, earnestly, and for the first time addressing him in conversation by his Christian name, "how limited your trust must be in the mercy of a Creator whose mercy is as wide as the ocean, that you can talk like that! You speak of me, too, as better than yourself—how am I better? I have my bad thoughts and do bad things as much as you, and, though they may not be the same, I am sure they are quite as black as yours, since everybody must be responsible according to their characters and temptations. I try, however, to trust in God to cover my sins, and believe that, if I do my best, He will forgive me, that is all. But I have no business to preach to you, who are older and wiser than I am."

"If," he broke in, laying his hand involuntarily upon her own, "you knew—although I have never spoken of them to any one before, and could not speak of them to anybody but yourself—how these things weigh upon my mind, you would not say that, but would try to teach me your faith."

"How can I teach you, Arthur, when I have so much to learn myself?" she answered, simply; and from that moment, though she did not know it as yet, she loved him.

This conversation—a very curious one, Arthur thought to himself afterwards, for two young people on a spring morning—having come to an end, nothing more was said for some while, and they took their way down the hill, varying the route in order to pass through the little hamlet of Bratham. Under a chestnut-tree that stood upon the village green, Arthur noticed, *not* a village blacksmith, but a small crowd, mostly composed of children, gathered round somebody. On going to see who it was, he discovered a battered-looking old man with an intellectual face, and the remnants of a gentlemanlike appearance, playing on the violin. A very few touches of his bow told Arthur, who knew something of music, that he was in the presence of a performer of no mean merit. Seeing the quality of his two auditors, and that they appreciated his performance, the player changed his music, and from a village jig passed to one of the more difficult opera airs, which he executed in brilliant fashion.

"Bravo!" cried Arthur, as the last notes thrilled and died away; "I see you understand how to play the fiddle."

"Yes, sir, and so I should, for I have played first violin at Her Majesty's Opera before now. Name what you like, and I will play it you. Or, if you like it better, you shall hear the water running in a brook, the wind passing through the trees, or the waves falling on the beach. Only say the word."

Arthur thought for a moment.

"It is a beautiful day; let us have a contrast—give us the music of a storm."

The old man considered a while.

"I understand; but you set a difficult subject even for me," and taking up his bow he made several attempts at beginning. "I can't do it," he said; "set something else."

"No, no, try again, that or nothing."

Again he started, and this time his genius took possession of him. The notes fell very softly at first, but with an ominous sound, then rose and wailed like the rising of the wind. Next the music came in gusts, the rain pattered, and the thunder roared, till at length the tempest seemed to spend its force and pass slowly away into the distance.

"There, sir, what do you say to that—have I fulfilled your expectations?"

"Write it down and it will be one of the finest pieces of violin music in the country."

"Write it down! The divine 'afflatus' is not to be caged, sir; it comes and goes. I could never write that music down."

Arthur felt in his pocket without answering, and found five shillings.

"If you will accept this?" he said.

"Thank you, sir, very much. I am gladder of five shillings now than I once was of as many pounds;" and he rose to go.

"A man of your talent should not be wandering about like this."

"I must earn a living somehow, for all Talleyrand's witticism to the contrary," was the curious answer.

"Have you no friends?"

"No, sir, this is my only friend; all the rest have deserted me," and he tapped his violin and was gone.

"Lord, sir," said a farmer, who was standing by, "he's gone to get drunk; he is the biggest old drunkard in the countryside, and yet they do say that he was a gentleman once, and the best fiddler in London; but he can't be depended on, so no one will hire him now."

"How sad!" said Angela, as they moved homewards.

"Yes, and what music that was; I never heard any with such imagination before. You have a turn that way, Angela; you should try to put it into words: it would make a poem."

"I complain, like the old man, that you set a difficult subject," she said; "but I will try, if you will promise not to laugh at the result."

"If you succeed on paper only half so well as he did on the violin, your verses will be worth listening to, and I certainly shall not laugh."

CHAPTER XXV.

On the day following the somewhat curious religious conversation between Arthur and Angela—a conversation which, begun on Arthur's part out of curiosity, had ended on both sides very much in earnest—the weather broke up and the grand old English climate reasserted its treacherous supremacy. From summer weather the inhabitants of the county of Marlshire suddenly found themselves plunged into a spell of cold that was by contrast almost arctic. Storms of sleet drove against the window-panes, and there was even a very damaging night-frost, while that dreadful scourge, which nobody in his senses except Kingsley *can* ever have liked, the east wind, literally pervaded the whole place, and went whistling through the surrounding trees and ruins in a way calculated to make even a Laplander shiver.

Under these cheerless circumstances, our pair of companions—for as yet they were, ostensibly at any rate, nothing more—gave up their out-door excursions and took to rambling over the disused rooms in the old house, and hunting up many a record, some of them valuable and curious enough, of long-forgotten Caresfoots, and even of the old priors before them; a splendidly-illuminated missal being amongst the latter prizes. When this amusement was exhausted, they sat together over the fire in the nursery, and Angela translated to him from her favorite classical authors, especially Homer, with an ease and fluency of expression that, to Arthur, was little short of miraculous. Or, when they got tired of that, he read to her from standard writers, which, elaborate as her education had been, in certain respects, she had scarcely yet even opened, notably Shakespeare and Milton. Needless to say, herself imbued with a strong poetic feeling, these immortal writers were a source of intense delight to her.

"How is it that Mr. Fraser never gave you Shakespeare to read?" asked Arthur one day, as he shut up the volume, having come to the end of "Hamlet."

"He said that I should be better able to appreciate it when my mind had been prepared to do so by the help of a classical and mathematical education, and that it would be 'a mistake to cloy my mental palate with sweets before I had learned to appreciate their flavors.'"

"There is some sense in that," remarked Arthur. "By the way, how are the verses you promised to write me getting on? Have you done them yet?"

"I have done something," she answered, modestly, "but I really do not think that they are worth producing. It is very tiresome of you to have remembered about them."

Arthur, however, by this time knew enough of Angela's abilities to be sure that her "something" would be something more or less worth hearing, and mildly insisted on their production, and then, to her confusion, on her reading them aloud. They ran as follows, and, whatever Angela's opinion of them may have been, the reader shall judge of them for himself:

A STORM ON THE STRINGS.

"The minstrel sat in his lonely room,
Its walls were bare, and the twilight gray
Fell and crept and gathered to gloom;
It came like the ghost of the dying day,
And the chords fell hushed and low.
Pianissimo!

"His arm was raised, and the violin
Quivered and shook with the strain it bore,
While the swelling forth of the sounds within
Rose with a sweetness unknown before,
And the chords fell soft and low.
Piano!

* * * * * *

"The first cold flap of the tempest's wings
Clashed with the silence before the storm,
The rain-drops pattered across the strings
As the gathering thunder-clouds took form—
Drip, drop, high and low.
Staccato!

"Heavily rolling the thunder roared,
Sudden and jagged the lightning played,
Faster and faster the rain-drops poured,
Sobbing and surging the tree-crests swayed,
Cracking and crashing above, below.
Crescendo!

"The wind tore howling across the wold,
And tangled his train in the groaning trees,
Wrapped the dense clouds in his mantle cold,
Then shivered and died in a wailing breeze,
Whistling and weeping high and low,
Sostenuto!

"A pale sun broke from the driving cloud,
And flashed in the rain-drops serenely cool;
At the touch of his finger the forest bowed,
As it shimmered and glanced in the ruffled pool,
While the rustling leaves soughed soft and low.
Gracioso!

* * * * * *

"It was only a dream on the throbbing strings,
An echo of Nature in fantasy wrought,
A breath of her breath and a touch of her wings
From a kingdom outspread in the regions of thought.
Below rolled the sound of the city's din,
And the fading day, as the night drew in,
Showed the quaint old face and the pointed chin,
And the arm that was raised o'er the violin,
As the old man whispered his hope's dead tale
To the friend who could comfort, though others might fail,
And the chords stole hushed and low.
Pianissimo!"

He stopped, and the sheet of paper fell from his hands.

"Well," she said, with all the eagerness of a new-born writer, "tell me, do you think them *very* bad?"

"Well, Angela, you know—"

"Ah! go on now; I am ready to be crushed. Pray don't spare my feelings."

"I was about to say that, thanks be to Providence, I am not a critic; but I think—"

"Oh! yes, let me hear what you think. You are speaking so slowly, in order to get time to invent something extra cutting. Well, I deserve it."

"Don't interrupt; I was going to say that I think the piece above the average of second-class poetry, and that a few of the lines touch the first-class standard. You have caught something of the 'divine afflatus' that the drunken old fellow said he could not cage. But I do not think that you will ever be popular as a writer of verses if you keep to that style; I doubt if there is a magazine in the kingdom that would take those lines unless they were by a known writer. They would return them marked, 'Good, but too vague for the general public.' Magazine editors don't like lines from 'a kingdom outspread in the regions of thought,' for, as they say, such poems are apt to excite vagueness in the brains of that dim entity, the 'general public.' What they do like are commonplace ideas, put in pretty language, and sweetened with sentimentality or emotional religious feelings, such as the thinking powers of their subscribers are competent to absorb without mental strain, and without leaving their accustomed channels. To be popular it is necessary to be commonplace, or at the least to describe the commonplace, to work in a well-worn groove, and not to startle—requirements which, unfortunately, simple as they seem, very few persons possess the art of acting up to. See what happens to the unfortunate novelist, for instance, who dares to break the unwritten law, and defraud his readers of the orthodox transformation scene of the reward of virtue and the discomfiture of vice; or to make his creation finish up in a way that, however well it may be suited to its tenor, or illustrate its more subtle meaning, is contrary to the 'general reader's' idea as to how it should end—badly, as it is called. He simply collapses, to rise no more, if he is new at the trade, and, if he is a known man, that book won't sell."

"You talk quite feelingly," said Angela, who was getting rather bored, and wanted, not unnaturally, to hear more about her own lines.

"Yes," replied Arthur, grimly; "I do. Once I was fool enough to write a book, but I must tell you that it is a painful subject with me. It never came out. Nobody would have it."

"Oh! Arthur, I am so sorry; I should like to read your book. But, as regards the verses, I am glad that you like them, and I really don't care what a hypothetical general public would say; I wrote them to please you, not the general public."

"Well, my dear, I am sure I am much obliged to you; I shall value them doubly, once for the giver's sake, and once for their own."

Angela blushed, but did not reprove the term of endearment which had slipped unawares from his lips. Poetry is a dangerous subject between two young people who at heart adore one another; it is apt to excite the brain, and bring about startling revelations.

The day following the reading of Angela's piece of poetry was rendered remarkable by two events, of which the first was that the weather suddenly turned a somersault, and became beautifully warm; and the second that news reached the Abbey House that, thanks chiefly to Lady Bellamy's devoted nursing—who, fearless of infection, had, to the great admiration of all her neighbors, volunteered her services when no nurse could be found to undertake the case—George was pronounced out of danger. This piece of news was peculiarly grateful to Philip, for, had his cousin died, the estates must have passed away for ever under the terms of his uncle's will; for he knew that George had made none. Angela, too, tried, like a good girl as she was, to lash herself into enthusiasm about it, though in her heart she went as near hating her cousin, since his attempted indignity towards herself, as her gentle nature would allow. Arthur alone was cynically indifferent; he hated George without any reservation whatsoever.

And after this there came for our pair of embryo lovers some ten or twelve such happy days (for there was no talk of Arthur's departure, Philip having on several occasions pointedly told him that the house was at his disposal for as long as he chose to remain in it). The sky was blue in those days, or only flecked with summer clouds, just as Arthur and Angela's perfect companionship was flecked and shaded with the deeper hues of dawning passion. Alas, the sky in this terrestrial clime is never *quite* blue!

But as yet nothing of love had passed between them, no kiss or word of endearment; only when hand touched hand a strange thrill had moved them both, and sent the warm blood to stain Angela's clear brow, like a wavering tint of sunlight thrown upon the marble features of some white Venus; only in each other's eyes they found a holy mystery. The spell was not yet fully at work, but the wand of earth's great enchanter had touched them, and they were changed. Angela is hardly the same girl she was when we met her a little more than a fortnight back. A nameless change has come over her face and manner; the merry smile, once so bright, has grown softer and more sweet, and the laughing light of her gray eyes has given place to a look of some such gratitude and wonder as that with which the traveller in lonely deserts gazes on the oasis of his perfect rest.

Many times Arthur had almost blurted out the truth to the woman he passionately adored, and every day so added to the suppressed fire of his love that at length he felt that he could not keep his secret to himself much longer. And yet he feared to tell it; better, he thought, to live happy, if in doubt, than to risk all his fortune on a single throw, for before his eyes there lay the black dread of failure, and then what would life be worth? Here with Angela he lived in a Garden of Eden that no forebodings, no anxieties, no fear of that partially scotched serpent George, could render wretched, so long as it was gladdened by the presence of her whom he hoped to make his Eve. But without, and around where she could not be, there was nothing but clouds and thistles and a black desolation that, even in imagination, he dared not face.

And Angela, gazing on veiled mysteries with wondering eyes, was she happy during those spring-tide days? Almost; but still there was in her heart a consciousness of effort, a sense of transformation and knowledge of the growth of hidden things. The bud bursting into the glory of the rose must, if there be feeling in a rose, undergo some such effort before it can make its beauty known; the butterfly but newly freed from the dull husk that hid its splendors, at first must feel the imperfect wings it stretches in the sun to be irksome to its unaccustomed sense. And so it was with Angela; she spread her half-grown wings in the sun of her new existence, and found them strange, not knowing as yet that they were shaped to bear her to the flower-crowned heights of love.

Hers was one of those rare natures in which the passion that we know by the generic term of love approached as near perfection as is possible in our human hearts. For there are many sorts and divisions of love, ranging from the affection, pure, steady, and divine, that is showered upon us from above, to the degrading madness of such a one as George Caresfoot. It is surely one of the saddest evidences of our poor humanity that, even among the purest of us, there are none who can altogether rid the whiteness of the love they have to offer of its earthy stain. Indeed, if we could so far conquer the promptings of our nature as to love with perfect purity, we should become like angels. But, just as white flowers are sometimes to be found on the blackest peak, so there do bloom in the world spirits as pure as they are rare—so free from evil, so closely shadowed by the Almighty wing, that they can almost reach to this perfection. Then the love they have to give is too refined, too holy and strong, to be understood of the mass of men: often it is squandered on some unequal and unanswering nature; sometimes it is wisely offered up to Him from whom it came.

We gaze upon an ice-bound river, and there is nothing to tell us that beneath that white cloak its current rushes to the ocean. But presently the spring comes, the prisoned waters burst their fetters, and we see a glad torrent sparkling in the sunlight. And so it was with our heroine's heart; the breath of Arthur's passion and the light of Arthur's eyes had beat upon it, and almost freed the river of its love. Already the listener might hear the ice-sheets crack and start; soon they will be gone, and her deep devotion will set as strong towards him as the tide of the torrent towards its receiving sea.

"Fine writing!" perhaps the reader will say; but surely none too fine to describe the most beautiful thing in this strange world, the irrevocable gift of a good woman's love!

However that may be, it will have served its purpose if it makes it clear that a crisis is at hand in the affairs of the heart of two of the central actors on this mimic stage.

CHAPTER XXVI.

One Saturday morning, when May was three parts gone, Philip announced his intention of going up to London till the Monday on business. He was a man who had long since become callous to appearances, and though Arthur, fearful lest spiteful things should be said of Angela, almost hinted that it would look odd, his host merely laughed, and said that he had little doubt but that his daughter was quite able to look after herself, even when such a fascinating young gentleman as himself was concerned. As a matter of fact, his object was to get rid of Angela by marrying her to this young Heigham, who had so opportunely tumbled down from the skies, and whom he rather liked than otherwise. This being the case, he rightly concluded that, the more the two were left together, the greater probability there was of his object being attained. Accordingly he left them together as much as possible.

It was on the evening of this Saturday that Arthur gathered up his courage and asked Angela to come and walk through the ruins with him. Angela hesitated a little; the shadow of something about to happen had fallen on her mind; but the extraordinary beauty of the evening, to say nothing of the prospect of his company, turned the scale in Arthur's favor.

It was one of those nights of which, if we are lucky, we get some five or six in the course of an English summer. The moon was at her full, and, the twilight ended, she filled the heavens with her light. Every twig and blade of grass showed out as clearly as in the day, but looked like frosted silver. The silence was intense, and so still was the air that the sharp shadows of the trees were motionless upon the grass, only growing with the growing hours. It was one of those nights that fill us with an indescribable emotion, bringing us into closer companionship with the unseen than ever does the garish, busy day. In such an hour, we can sometimes feel, or think that we can feel, other presences around us, and involuntarily we listen for the whisper of the wings and the half-forgotten voices of our beloved.

On this particular evening some such feeling was stirring in Angela's heart as with slow steps she led the way into the little village churchyard, a similar spot to that which is to be found in many a country parish, except that, the population being very small, there were but few recent graves. Most of the mounds had no head-stones to recall the names of the neglected dead, but here and there were dotted, discolored slabs, some sunk a foot or two into the soil, a few lying prone upon it, and the remainder thrown by the gradual subsidence of their supports into every variety of angle, as though they had been suddenly halted in the maddest whirl of a grotesque dance of death.

Picking her way through these, Angela stopped under an ancient yew, and, pointing to one of two shadowed mounds to which the moonlight scarcely struggled, said, in a low voice,

"That is my mother's grave."

It was a modest tenement enough, a little heap of close green turf, surrounded by a railing, and planted with sweet-williams and forget-me-nots. At its head was placed a white marble cross, on which Arthur could just distinguish the words "Hilda Caresfoot," and the date of death.

He was about to speak, but she stopped him with a gentle movement, and then, stepping forward to the head of the railing, she buried her face in her hands, and remained motionless. Arthur watched her with curiosity. What, he wondered, was passing in the mind of this strange and beautiful woman, who had grown up so sweet and pure amidst moral desolation, like a white lily blooming alone on the black African plains in winter? Suddenly she raised her head, and saw the inquiring look he bent upon her. She came towards him, and in that sweet, half-pleading voice which was one of her greatest charms she said:

"I fear you think me very foolish."

"Why should I think you foolish?"

"Because I have come here at night to stand before a half-forgotten grave."

"I do not think you foolish, indeed. I was only wondering what was passing in your mind."

Angela hung her head and made no answer, and the clock above them boomed out the hour, raising its sullen note in insolent defiance of the silence. What is it that is so solemn about the striking of the belfry-clock when one stands in a churchyard at night? Is it that the hour softens our natures, and makes them more amenable to semi-superstitious influences? Or is it that the thousand evidences of departed mortality which surround us, appealing with dumb force to natural fears, throw open for a space the gates of our world-sealed imagination, to tenant its vast halls with prophetic echoes of our end? Perhaps it is useless to inquire. The result remains the same; few of us can hear those tones at night without a qualm, and, did we put our thoughts into words, they would run something thus:

"That sound once broke upon the living ears of those who sleep around us. We hear it now. In a little while, hour after hour, it will echo against the tombstones of *our* graves, and new generations, coming out of the silent future, will stand where we stand, and hearken: and muse, as we mused, over the old problems that we have gone to solve; whilst we—shall we not be deaf to hear and dumb to utter?"

Such, at any rate, were the unspoken thoughts that crept into the hearts of Arthur and Angela as the full sound from the belfry thinned itself away into silence. She grew a little pale, and glanced at him, and he gave an involuntary shiver, while even the dog Aleck sniffed and whined uncomfortably.

"It feels cold," he said. "Shall we go?"

They turned and walked towards the gate, and, by the time they reached it, all superstitious thoughts had vanished—at any rate, from Arthur's mind, for he recollected that he had set himself a task to do, and that now would be the time to do it. Absorbed in this reflection, he forgot his politeness, and passed first through the turnstile. On the further side he paused, and looked earnestly into his beloved's face. Their eyes met, and there was that in his that caused her to swiftly drop her own. A silence ensued as they stood by the gate. He broke it.

"It is a lovely night. Let us walk through the ruins."

"I shall wet my feet: the dew must be falling."

"There is no dew falling to-night. Won't you come?"

"Let us go to-morrow. It is later than I generally go in. Pigott will wonder what has become of me."

"Never mind Pigott. The night is too fine to waste asleep; besides, you know, one should always look at ruins by moonlight. Please come."

She looked at him doubtfully, hesitated, and came.

"What do you want to see?" she said, presently, with as near an approach to irritation as he had ever heard her indulge in. "That is the famous window that Mr. Fraser always goes into raptures about."

"It is beautiful. Shall we sit down here and look at it?"

They sat down on a low mass of fallen masonry some fifteen paces from the window. Around them lay a delicate tracery of shadows, whilst they themselves were seated in the eye of the moonlight, and remained for a while as silent and as still as though they had been the shades of the painted figures that had once filled the stony frame above them.

"Angela," he said at length—"Angela, listen, and I will tell you something. My mother, a woman to whom sorrow had become almost an inspiration, when she was dying, spoke to me something thus: 'There is,' she said, 'but one thing that I know of that has the power to make life happy as God meant it to be, and as the folly and weakness of men and women render it nearly impossible for it to be, and that is—love. Love has been the consolation of my own existence in the midst of many troubles; first, the great devotion I bore your father, and then that which I entertain for yourself. Without these two ties, life would indeed have been a desert. And yet, though it is a grief to me to leave you, and though I shrink from the dark passage that lies before me, so far does that first great love outweigh the love I bear you, that in my calmer moments I am glad to go, because I know I am awaited by your father. And from this I wish you to learn a lesson: look for your happiness in life from the love of your life, for there only will you find it. Do not fritter away your heart, but seek out some woman, some one good and pure and true, and in giving her your devotion you will reap a full reward, for her happiness will reflect your own, and, if your choice is right, you will, however stormy your life may be, lay up for yourself, as I feel that I have done, an everlasting joy.'"

She listened to him in silence.

"Angela," he went on, boldly enough, now that the ice was broken, "I have often thought about what my mother said, but until now I have never *quite* understood her meaning. I do understand it now. Angela, do *you* understand me?"

There was no answer; she sat there upon the fallen masonry, gazing at the ruins round her, motionless and white as a marble goddess, forgotten in her desecrated fane.

"Oh, Angela, listen to me—listen to me! I have found the woman of whom my mother spoke, who must be so 'good and pure and true.' You are she. I love you, Angela, I love you with my whole life and soul; I love you for this world and the next. Oh! do not reject me; though I am so little worthy of you, I will try to grow so. Dearest, can you love me?"

Still there was silence, but he thought that he saw her breast heave gently. Then he placed his hand, all trembling with the fierce emotion that throbbed along his veins, upon the palm that hung listless by her side, and gazed into her eyes. Still she neither spoke nor shrank, and, in the imperfect light, her face looked very pale, while her lovely eyes were dark and meaningless as those of one entranced.

Then slowly he gathered up his courage for an effort, and raising his face to the level of her own, he kissed her full upon her lips. She stirred, she sighed. He had broken the spell; the sweet face that had withdrawn itself drew nearer to him; for a second the awakened eyes looked into his own, and filled them with reflected splendor, and then he became aware of a warm arm thrown about his neck, and next—the stars grew dim, and sense and life itself seemed to shake upon their thrones, for a joy almost too great for mortal man to bear took possession of his heart as she laid her willing lips upon his own. And then, before he knew her purpose, she slid down upon her knees beside him, and placed her head upon his breast.

"Dearest," he said, "don't kneel so; look at me."

Slowly she raised her face, wreathed and lovely with many blushes, and looked upon him with tearful eyes. He tried to raise her.

"Let me be," she said, speaking very low. "I am best so; it is the attitude of adoration, and I have found—my divinity."

"But I cannot bear to see you kneel to me."

"Oh! Arthur, you do not understand; a minute since *I* did not understand that a woman is very humble when she really loves."

"Do you—really love me, Angela?"

"I do."

"Have you known that long?"

"I only *knew* it when—when you kissed me. Before then there was something in my heart, but I did not know what it was. Listen, dear," she went on, "for one minute to me first, and I will get up" (for he was again attempting to raise her). "What I have to say is best said upon my knees, for I want to thank God who sent you to me, and to thank you too for your goodness. It is so wonderful that you should love a simple girl like me, and I am so thankful to you. Oh! I have never lived till now, and" (rising to her full stature) "I feel as though I had been crowned a queen of happy things. Dethrone me, desert me, and I will still be grateful to you for this hour of imperial happiness. But if you, after a while, when you know all my faults and imperfections better, can still care for me, I know that there is something in me that will enable me to repay you for what you have given me, by making your whole life happy. Dear, I do not know if I speak as other women do, but, believe me, it is out of the fulness of my heart. Take care, Arthur, oh! take care, lest your fate should be that of the magician you spoke of the other day, who evoked the spirit, and then fell down before it in terror. You have also called up a spirit, and I pray that it was not done in sport, lest it should trouble you hereafter."

"Angela, do not speak so to me; it is I who should have knelt to you. You were right when you called yourself 'a queen of happy things.' You are a queen—"

"Hush! Don't overrate me; your disillusion will be the more painful. Come, Arthur, let us go home."

He arose and went with her, in a dream of joy that for a moment precluded speech. At the door she bade him good-night, and, oh, happiness! gave him her lips to kiss. Then they parted, their hearts too full for words. One thing he asked her, however:

"What was it that took you to your mother's grave to-night?"

She looked at him with a curiously mixed expression of shy love and conviction on her face, and answered:

"Her spirit, who led me to your heart."

CHAPTER XXVII.

GEORGE's recovery, when the doctors had given up all hope, was sufficiently marvellous to suggest the idea that a certain power had determined—on the hangman's principle, perhaps—to give him the longest of ropes; but it could in reality be traced to a more terrestrial influence—namely, Lady Bellamy's nursing. Had it not been for this nursing, it is very certain that her patient would have joined his forefathers in the Bratham churchyard. For whole days and nights she watched and tended him, scarcely closing her own eyes, and quite heedless of the danger of infection; till in the end she conquered the fever, and snatched him from the jaws of the grave. How often has not a woman's devotion been successful in such a struggle!

On the Monday following the events narrated in the last chapter, George, now in advanced stage of convalescence, though forbidden to go abroad for another fortnight, was sitting downstairs enjoying the warm sunshine, and the sensation of returning life and vigor that was creeping into his veins, when Lady Bellamy came into the room, bringing with her some medicine.

"Here is your tonic, George; it is the last dose that I can give you, as I am going back to my disconsolate husband at luncheon-time."

"I can't have you go away yet; I am not well enough."

"I must go, George; people will begin to talk if I stop here any longer."

"Well, if you must, I suppose you must," he answered sulkily. "But I must say I think that you show a great want of consideration for my comfort. Who is to look after me, I should like to know? I am far from well yet—far from well."

"Believe me," she said, softly, "I am very sorry to leave you, and am glad to have been of help to you, though you have never thought much about it."

"Oh, I am sure I am much obliged, but it is not likely that you would leave me to rot of fever without coming to look after me."

She sighed as she answered,

"You would not do as much for me."

"Oh, bother! Anne, don't get sentimental. Before you go, I must speak to you about that girl Angela. Have you taken any steps?"

Lady Bellamy started.

"What, are you still bent upon that project?"

"Of course I am. It seemed to me that all my illness was one long dream of her. I am more bent upon it than ever."

"And do you still insist upon my playing the part you had marked out for me? Do you know, George, that there were times in your illness when, if I had relaxed my care for a single five minutes, it would have turned the scale against you, and that once I did not close my eyes for five nights? Look at me, how thin and worn I am; it is from nursing you. I have saved your life. Surely you will not now force me to do this unnatural thing?"

"If, my dear Anne, you had saved my life fifty times, I would still force you to do it. Ah! it is no use your looking at that safe. I have no doubt that you got my keys and searched it whilst I was ill, but I was too sharp for you. I had the letters moved when I heard that you were coming to nurse me. They are back there now, though. How disappointed you must have been!" And he chuckled.

"I should have done better to let you die, monster of wickedness and ingratitude that you are!" she said, stamping her foot upon the floor, and the tears of vexation standing in her eyes.

"The letters, my dear Anne; remember that you have got to earn your letters. I am very much obliged to you for your nursing, but business is business."

She was silent for a moment, and then spoke in her ordinary tone.

"By the way, talking of letters, there was one came for you this morning in your cousin Philip's handwriting, and with a London postmark. Will you read it?"

"Read it—yes; anything from the father of my inamorata will be welcome."

She fetched the letter and gave it him. He read it aloud. After a page of congratulation on his convalescence, it ended:

"And now I want to make a proposal to you—viz., to buy back the Isleworth lands from you. I know that the place is distasteful to you, and will probably be doubly so after your severe illness; but, if you care to keep the house and grounds, I am not particularly anxious to acquire them. I am prepared to offer a good price," etc., etc.

"I'll see him hanged first," was George's comment. "How did he get the money?"

"Saved it and made it, I suppose."

"Well, at any rate, he shall not buy me out with it. No, no, Master Philip; I am not fond enough of you to do you that turn."

"It does not strike you," she said, coldly, "that you hold in your hands a lever that may roll all your difficulties about this girl out of the way."

"By Jove! you are right, Anne. Trust a woman's brain. But I don't want to sell the estates unless I am forced to."

"Would you rather part with the land, or give up your project of marrying Angela Caresfoot?"

"Why do you ask?"

"Because you will have to choose between the two."

"Then I had rather sell."

"You had better give it up, George. I am not superstitious, but I have knowledge that you do not understand, and I foresee nothing but disaster in this plan."

"Once and for all, Anne, I will not give it up whilst I have any breath left in my body, and I take my oath that unless you help me, and help me honestly, I will expose you."

"Oh, I am your very humble servant; you may count on me. The galley-slave pulls well when the lash hangs over his shoulders," and she laughed coldly.

Just then a servant announced that Mr. Caresfoot was at the door, and anxious to speak to his cousin. He was ordered to show him into the drawing-room. As soon as he had gone on his errand, George said,

"I will not see him; say I am too unwell. But do you go, and see that you make the most of your chance."

Lady Bellamy nodded, and left the room. She found Philip in the drawing-room.

"Ah! how do you do, Mr. Caresfoot? I come from your cousin to say that he cannot see you to-day; he has scarcely recovered sufficiently from the illness through which I have been nursing him; but of course you know all about that."

"Oh, yes, Lady Bellamy, I have heard all about it, including your own brave behavior, to which, the doctor tells me, George owes his life. I am sorry that he cannot see me, though. I have just come down from town, and called in on my way from Roxham. I had some rather important business that I wanted to speak about."

"About your offer to repurchase the Isleworth lands?" she asked.

"Ah! you know of the affair. Yes, that was it."

"Then I am commissioned to give you a reply."

Philip listened anxiously.

"Your cousin absolutely refuses to sell any part of the lands."

"Will nothing change his determination? I am ready to give a good price, and pay a separate valuation for the timber."

"Nothing; he does not intend to sell."

A deep depression spread itself over her hearer's face.

"Then there go the hopes of twenty years," he said. "For twenty long years, ever since my misfortune, I have toiled and schemed to get these lands back, and now it is all for nothing. Well, there is nothing more to be said," and he turned to go.

"Stop a minute, Mr. Caresfoot. Do you know, you interest me very much."

"I am proud to interest so charming a lady," he answered, with a touch of depressed gallantry.

"That is as it should be; but you interest me because you are an instance of the truth of the saying that every man has some ruling passion, if only one could discover it. Why do you want these particular lands? Your money will buy others just as good."

"Why does a Swiss get home-sick? Why does a man defrauded of his own wish to recover it?"

Lady Bellamy mused a little.

"What would you say if I showed you an easy way to get them?"

Philip turned sharply round with a new look of hope upon his face.

"You would earn my eternal gratitude—a gratitude that I should be glad to put into a practical shape."

She laughed.

"Oh! you must speak to Sir John about that. Now listen; I am going to surprise you. Your cousin wants to get married!"

"Get married! George wants to get married!"

"Exactly so; and now I have a further surprise in store for you—he wants to marry your daughter Angela."

This time Philip said nothing, but he started in evident and uncomfortable astonishment. If Lady Bellamy wished to surprise him, she had certainly succeeded.

"Surely you are joking!" he said.

"I never was further from joking in my life; he is desperately in love with her, and wild to marry her."

"Well?"

"Well, don't you now see a way to force your cousin to sell the lands?"

"As the price of Angela's hand?"

"Precisely."

Philip walked up and down the room in thought. Though, as the reader may remember, he had himself, but a month before, been base enough to suggest that his daughter should use her eyes to forward his projects, he had never, in justice to him be it said, dreamt of forcing her into a marriage in every way little less than unnatural. His idea of responsibility towards his daughter was, as regards sins of omission, extremely lax, but there were some of commission that he did not care to face. Certain fears and memories oppressed him too much to allow of it.

"Lady Bellamy," he said, presently, "you have known my cousin George intimately for many years, and are probably sufficiently acquainted with his habits of life to know that such a marriage would be an infamy."

"Many a man who has been wild in his youth makes a good husband," she answered quietly.

"The more I think of it," went on Philip, excitedly, after the fashion of one who would lash himself into a passion, "the more I see the utter impossibility of any such thing, and I must say that I wonder at your having undertaken such an errand. On the one hand, there is a young girl who, though I do not, from force of circumstances, see much of her myself, is, I believe, as good as she is handsome—"

"And on the other," broke in Lady Bellamy, ironically, "are the Isleworth estates."

"And on the other," went on Philip, without paying heed to her remark—"I am going to speak plainly, Lady Bellamy—is a man utterly devoid of the foundations of moral character, whose appearance is certainly against him, who I have good reason to know is not to be trusted, and who is old enough to be her father, and her cousin to boot—and you ask me to forward such a marriage as this! I will have nothing to do with it; my responsibilities as a father forbid it. It would be the wickedest thing I have ever done to put the girl into the power of such a man."

Lady Bellamy burst into a low peal of laughter; she never laughed aloud. She thought that it was now time to throw him a little off his balance.

"Forgive me," she said, with her sweetest smile, "but you must admit that there is something rather ludicrous in hearing the hero of the great Maria Lee scandal talking about moral character, and the father who detests his daughter so much that he fears to look her in the face, and whose sole object is to rid himself of an incumbrance, prating of his paternal responsibilities."

Philip started visibly at her words.

"Ah! Mr. Caresfoot," she went on, "I surprise you by my knowledge, but we women are sad spies, and it is my little amusement to find out other people's secrets, a very useful little amusement. I could tell you many things—"

"I was about to say," broke in Philip, who had naturally no desire to see more of the secrets of his life unveiled by Lady Bellamy, "that, even if I did wish to get rid of Angela, I should have little difficulty in doing so, as young Heigham, who has been stopping at the Abbey House for a fortnight or so, is head over ears in love with her; indeed, I should think it highly probable that they are at this moment engaged."

It was Lady Bellamy's turn to start now.

"Ah!" she said, "I did not know that; that complicates matters." And then, with a sudden change of tone—"Mr. Caresfoot, as a friend, let me beg of you not to throw away such a chance in a hurry for the sake of a few nonsensical ideas about a girl. What is she, after all, that she should stand in the way of such grave interests as you have in hand? I tell you that he is perfectly mad about her. You can make your own terms and fix your own price."

"Price! ay, that is what it would be—a price for her body and soul."

"Well, and what of it? The thing is done every day, only one does not talk of it in that way."

"Who taught you, who were once a young girl yourself, to plead such a cause as this?"

"Nonsense! it is a very good cause—a cause that will benefit everybody, especially your daughter. George will get what he wants; you, with the recovery of the estates, will also recover your lost position and reputation, both to a great extent an affair of landed property. Mr. Heigham will gain a little experience, whilst she will bloom into a great lady, and, like any other girl in the same circumstances, learn to adore her husband in a few months."

"And what will *you* get, Lady Bellamy?"

"I!" she replied, with a gay laugh. "Oh! you know, virtue is its own reward. I shall be quite satisfied in seeing everybody else made happy. Come, I do not want to press you about the matter at present. Think it over at your leisure. I only beg you not to give a decided answer to young Heigham, should he ask you for Angela, till I have seen you again—say in a week's time. Then, if you don't like it, you can leave it alone, and nobody will be a penny the worse."

"As you like; but I tell you that I can never consent;" and Philip took his leave.

"Your cousin entirely refuses his consent, and Angela is by this time probably engaged to your ex-ward, Arthur Heigham," was Lady Bellamy's not very promising report to the interesting invalid in the dining-room.

After relieving his feelings at this intelligence in language more forcible than polite, George remarked that, under these circumstances, matters looked very bad.

"Not at all; they look very well. I shall see your cousin again in a week's time, when I shall have a different tale to tell."

"Why wait a week with that young blackguard making the running on the spot?"

"Because I have put poison into Philip's mind, and the surest poison always works slow. Besides, the mischief has been done. Good-by. I will come and see you in a day or two, when I have made my plans. You see I mean to earn my letters."

CHAPTER XXVIII.

WITH what degree of soundness our pair of lovers slumbered on that memorable Saturday night, let those who have been so fortunate or unfortunate as to have been placed in analogous circumstances form their own opinion.

It is, however, certain that Arthur gazed upon the moon and sundry of the larger planets for some hours, until they unkindly set, and left him, for his candle had burnt out, to find his way to bed in the dark. With his reflections we will not trouble ourselves; or, rather, we will not intrude upon their privacy. But there was another person in the house who also sat at an open window and looked upon the heavens—Angela, to wit. Let us avail ourselves of our rightful privilege, and look into her thoughts.

Arthur's love had come upon her as a surprise, but it had found a perfect home. All the days and hours that she had spent in his company had, unknown to herself, been mysteriously employed in preparing a habitation to receive it. We all know the beautiful Bible story of the Creation, how first there was an empty void, and the Spirit brooding on the waters, then light, and then life, and, last, man coming to turn all things to his uses. Surely that story, which is the type and symbol of many things, is of none more so than of the growth and birth of a perfected love in the human heart.

The soil is made ready in the dead winter, and receives the seed into its bosom. Then comes the spring, and it is clothed with verdure. Space is void till the sun shoots its sudden rays athwart it, and makes it splendid; the heart is cold and unwitting of its ends, till the spirit broods upon it, as upon the waters, and it grows quick with the purposes of life. And then what a change is there! What has the flower in common with the seed from whence it sprang, or the noonday sky with the darkness before the dawn?

Thinking in her chamber, with the night air playing on her hot brow, and her hand pressed upon her heart, as though to still the tumult of its joy, Angela grew vaguely conscious of these things.

"Was she the same in heart and mind that she had been a month ago? No, a thousand times no. Then what was this mysterious change that seemed to shake her inmost life to its foundations? What angel had troubled the waters into which she had so newly plunged? And whence came the healing virtue that she found in them, bringing rest after the vague trouble of the last two weeks, with sight to see the only good—her love, with speed to follow, and strength to hold? O happy, happy world! O merciful Creator, who gave her to drink of such a living spring! O Arthur, beloved Arthur!"

On Sunday mornings it was Pigott's habit to relax the Draconian severity of her laws in the matter of breakfast, which, generally speaking, was not till about half-past eight o'clock. At that hour precisely, on the Sabbath in question, she appeared as usual—no, not as usual, for, it being Sunday, she had on her stiff black gown—and, with all due solemnity, made the tea.

A few minutes elapsed, and Angela entered, dressed in white, and very lovely in her simple, tight-fitting robe, but a trifle pale, and with a shy look upon her face.

She greeted her nurse with a kiss.

"Why, what is the matter with you, dearie?" ejaculated Pigott, whose watchful eye detected a change she could not define; "you look different somehow."

"Hush! I will tell you by and by."

At that moment Arthur's quick step was heard advancing down the passage, together with a pattering noise that announced the presence of Aleck. And, as they came, Angela, poor Angela, grew red and redder, and yet more painfully red, till Pigott, watching her face, was enabled to form a shrewd guess as to what was the cause of her unaccustomed looks.

On came the step and open flew the door, more and more ready to sink into the earth looked Angela, and so interested grew nurse Pigott that she actually poured some hot tea onto her dress, a thing she could never remember having done before.

The first to enter was Aleck, who, following his custom, sprang upon Angela and licked her hand, and behind Aleck, looking somewhat confused, but handsome and happy—for his was one of those faces that become handsome when their owners are happy—came Aleck's master. And then there ensued an infinitesimal but most awkward pause.

On such occasions as the present, namely, the first meeting after an engagement, there is always—especially when it occurs in the presence of a third person—a very considerable difficulty in the minds of the parties to know what demeanor they are to adopt towards one another. Are they to treat the little affair of the previous evening as a kind of confidential communication, not to be alluded to except in private conversation, and to drop into the Mr. and Miss of yesterday ? That would certainly be the easiest, but then it would also be a decided act of mutual retreat. Or are they to rush into each other's arms as becomes betrothed lovers ? This process is so new that they feel that it still requires private rehearsal. And, meanwhile, time presses, and everybody is beginning to stare, and something *must* be done.

These were very much the feelings of Arthur and Angela. He hesitated before her, confused, and she kept her head down over the dog. But presently Aleck, getting bored, moved on, and, as it would have been inane to continue to stare at the floor, she had to raise herself as slowly as she might. Soon their eyes arrived in the same plane, and whether a mutual glance of intelligence was exchanged, or whether their power of attraction overcame his power of resistance, it is not easy to determine, but certain it is that, following a primary natural law, Arthur gravitated towards her, and kissed her on the face.

"My !" exclaimed Pigott, and the milk-jug rolled unheeded on the floor.

"Hum ! I suppose I had better explain—" began he.

"I think you have spilt the milk," added she.

"That we have become engaged and are—"

"All to pieces, I declare," broke in Angela, with her head somewhere near the carpet.

And then they both laughed.

"Well, I never, no, not in all my born days ! Sir and Miss Angela, all I have got to say about this extraordinary proceeding" —they glanced at each other in alarm—"is that I am very glad to hear on it, and I hope and pray how as you may be happy, and, if you treat my Angela right, you'll be just the happiest and luckiest man in the three kingdoms, including Ireland and the Royal Family, and, if you treat her wrong, worse will come to you; and her poor mother's last words, as I heard with my own ears, will come true to you, and serve you right—and there's all the milk upon the floor. And God bless you both, my dears, is the prayer of an old woman."

And here the worthy soul broke down, and began to cry, nor were Angela's eyes free from tears.

After this little episode, breakfast proceeded in something like the usual way. Church was at 10.30, and, a while before the hour, Arthur and Angela strolled down to the spot that had already become as holy ground to them, and looked into each other's eyes, and said again the same sweet words. Then they went on, and mingling with the little congregation—that did not number more than thirty souls—they passed into the cool quiet of the church.

"Lawks!" said a woman, as they went by, "ain't she just a beauty! What a pretty wedding they'd make!"

Arthur overheard it, and noted the woman, and afterwards found a pretext to give her five shillings, because he said it was a lucky omen.

On the communion-table of the pretty little church there was spread the "fair white cloth" of the rubric. It was the day for the monthly celebration of the Sacrament, that met the religious requirements of the village.

"Will you stay to the Sacrament with me?" whispered Angela to her lover, in the interval between their seating themselves and the entry of the clergyman, Mr. Fraser's *locum tenens*.

Arthur nodded assent.

And so, when the time came, those two went up together to the altar-rails, and, kneeling side by side, ate of the bread and drank of the cup, and, rising, departed thence with a new link between them. For, be sure, part of the prayers which they offered up at that high moment were in humble petition to the Almighty to set His solemn seal and blessing on their love. Indeed, so far as Angela was concerned, there were few acts of her simple life that she did not consecrate by prayer; how much more, then, was she bent upon bringing this, the greatest of all her acts, before her Maker's throne!

Strange indeed, and full of a holy promise, is the yearning with which we turn to Heaven to seek sanctification of our deeds, feeling our weakness, and craving strength from the source of strength; a yearning of which the church, with that subtle knowledge of human nature which is one of the mainsprings of its power, has not been slow to avail itself. And this need is more especially felt in matters connected with the noblest of the passions, perhaps because all true love and all true religion come from a common home.

Thus pledged to one another with a new and awful pledge, and knit together in the bonds of an universal love, embracing their poor affection as the wide skies embrace the earth, they rose, and went their ways, purer to worship, and stronger to endure.

That afternoon, Arthur had a conversation with his betrothed, that, partaking of a business nature in the beginning, ended rather oddly.

"I must speak to your father when he comes back to-morrow, dear," he began.

"My father! Oh, yes, I had forgotten about that;" and she looked a little anxious.

"Fortunately, I am fairly well off, so I see no cause why he should object."

"Well, I think that he will be rather glad to get rid of Pigott and myself. You know that he is not very fond of me."

"That is strange want of taste on his part."

"Oh, I don't know. Everybody does not see me with your eyes, Arthur."

"Because they have not the chance. All the world would love you, if it knew you. But, seriously, I think that he can hardly object, or he would not have allowed us to be thrown so much together; for, in nine cases out of ten, that sort of thing has only one result."

"What do you mean?"

"I mean that to import a young fellow into the house, and throw him solely into a daughter's company, is very apt to bring about—well, what has been brought about."

"Then you mean that you think that I should have fallen in love with any gentleman who had come here?"

Arthur, not seeing the slight flash of indignation in her eyes, replied,

"Well, you know there is always a risk, but I should imagine that it would very much depend upon the gentleman."

"Arthur"—with a little stamp—"I am ashamed of you. How can you think such things of me? You must have a very poor opinion of me."

"My dear, why should I suppose myself superior to anybody else, that you should only fall in love with me? You set too high a value on me."

"And you set too low a value upon me; you do not understand me. You are my fate, my other self; how would it have been possible for me to love any one but you? I feel as though I had been travelling to meet you since the beginning of the world, to stand by your side till it crumbles away, yes, for eternity itself. Oh! Arthur, do not laugh at what I say. I am, indeed, only a simple girl, but, as I told you last night, there is something stirring in me now, my real life, my eternal part, something that you have awakened, and with which you have to deal, something apart from the *me* you see before you. As I speak, I feel and know that when we are dead and gone, I shall love you still; when more ages have passed than there are leaves upon that tree, I shall love you still. Arthur, I am yours forever, for the time that is, and is to be."

She spoke with the grand freedom of one inspired, nay, he felt that she was inspired, and the same feeling of awe that had come upon him when first he saw her face again took possession of him. Taking her hand, he kissed it.

"Dearest," he said, "dearest Angela, who am I that you should love me so? What have I done that such a treasure should be given to me? I hope that it may be as you say!"

"It will be as I say," she answered, as she bent to kiss him. And they went on in silence.

CHAPTER XXIX.

PHILIP arrived home about one o'clock on the Monday, and, after their nursery dinner, Arthur made his way to the study, and soon found himself in the dread presence—for what presence is more dread? (most people would rather face a chief-justice with the gout) —of the man whose daughter he was about to ask in marriage.

Philip, whom he found seated by a tray, the contents of which he seemed in no humor to touch, received him with his customary politeness, saying, with a smile, that he hoped he had not come to tell him that he was sick of the place and its inhabitants, and was going away.

"Far from it, Mr. Caresfoot, I come to speak to you on a very different subject."

Philip glanced up with a quick look of expectant curiosity, but said nothing.

"In short," said Arthur, desperately, "I come to ask you to sanction my engagement to Angela."

A pause—a very awkward pause—ensued.

"You are, then, engaged to my daughter?"

"Subject to your consent, I am."

Then came another pause.

"You will understand me, Heigham, when I say that you take me rather by surprise in this business. Your acquaintance with her has been short."

"That is very true, but I have seen a great deal of her."

"Perhaps; but she knows absolutely nothing of the world, and her preference for you—for, as you say you are engaged to her, I presume she has shown a preference—may be a mistake, merely a young girl's romantic idea."

Arthur thought of his conversation of the previous day with Angela, and could not help smiling as he answered,

"I think if you ask her that, she will tell you that is not the case."

"Heigham, I will be frank with you. I like you, and you have, I believe, sufficient means. Of course, you know that my daughter will have nothing—at any rate, till I am dead," he added, quickly.

"I never thought about the matter, but I shall be only too glad to marry her with nothing but herself."

"Very good. I was going to say that, notwithstanding this, marriage is an important matter; and I must have time to think over it before I give you a decided answer, say a week. I shall not, however, expect you to leave here unless you wish to do so, nor shall I seek to place any restrictions on your intercourse with Angela, since it would appear that the mischief is already done. I am flattered by your proposal; but I must have time, and you must understand that in this instance hesitation does not necessarily mean consent."

In affairs of this nature a man is satisfied with small mercies, and willing to put up with inconveniences that appear trifling in comparison with the disasters that might have overtaken him. Arthur was no exception to the general rule. Indeed, he was profuse in his thanks, and, buoyed up with all the confidence of youth, felt sure in his heart that he would soon find a way to extinguish any objections that might still linger in Philip's mind.

His would-be father-in-law contented himself with acknowledging his remarks with courtesy, and the interview came to an end.

Arthur gone, however, his host lost all his calmness of demeanor, and, rising from his untasted meal, paced up and down the room in thought. Everything had, he reflected, fallen out as he wished. Young Heigham wanted to marry his daughter, and he could not wish her a better husband. Save for the fatality which had sent that woman to him on her fiend's errand, he would have given his consent at once, and been glad to give it. Not that he meant to refuse it—he had no such idea. And then he began to think what, supposing that Lady Bellamy's embassy had been of a nature that he could entertain, which it was not, it would mean to him. It would mean the realization of the work and aspirations of twenty years; it would mean his re-entry into the property and position from which he had, according to his own view, been unjustly ousted; it would mean, last but not least, triumph over George. And now chance, mighty chance (as fools call Providence), had at last thrown into his hands a lever with which it would be easy to topple over every stumbling-block that lay in his path to triumph; more, he might even be able to spoil that Egyptian George, giving him less than his due.

Oh! how he hungered for the broad acres of his birthright! longing for them as a lover longs for his lost bride. The opportunity would never come again; why should he throw it away? To do so would be to turn his cousin into an open and implacable foe. Why should he allow this girl, whose birth had bereft him of the only creature he had ever loved, whose sex had alienated the family estates, and for whose company he cared nothing, to come as a destruction on his plans? She would be well-off; the man loved her. As for her being engaged to this young Heigham, women soon got over those things. After all, now that he came to think of the matter calmly, what valid cause was there why the thing should not be?

And as he paced to and fro, and thought thus, an answer came into his mind. For there rose up before him a vision of his dying wife, and there sounded in his ears the murmur of her half-forgotten voice, that, for all its broken softness, had, with its last accents, called down God's winged vengeance and His everlasting doom on him who would harm her unprotected child. And, feeling that if he did this thing, on him would be the vengeance and the doom, he thought of the shadows of the night, and grew afraid.

When Arthur and his host met, according to their custom, that evening, no allusion was made on either side to their conversation of the afternoon, nor did her father even speak a word to Angela on the subject. Life, to all appearance, went on in the old house precisely as though nothing had happened. Philip did not attempt to put the smallest restraint on Arthur and his daughter, and studiously shut his eyes to the pretty obvious signs of their mutual affection. For them, the long June days were golden, but all too short. Every morning found their mutual love more perfect, but when the flakes of crimson light faded from the skies, and night dropped her veil over the tall trees and peaceful lake, by some miracle it had grown deeper and more perfect still. Day by day, Arthur discovered new charms in Angela; here some hidden knowledge, there an unsuspected grace, and everywhere an all-embracing charity and love. Day by day he gazed deeper into the depths of her mind, and still there were more to plumb. For it was a storehouse of noble thoughts and high ambitions—ambitions, many of which could only find fulfilment in another world than this. And the more he saw of her, the prouder he was to think that such a perfect creature should so dearly love himself; and with the greater joy did he look forward to that supreme and happy hour when he should call her his. And so day added itself to day, and found them happy.

Indeed, the aspect of their fortunes seemed as smooth and smiling as the summer surface of the lake. About Philip's final consent to their engagement they did not trouble themselves, judging, not unnaturally, that his conduct was in itself a guarantee of approval. If he meant to raise any serious objections, he would surely have done so before, Arthur would urge, and Angela would quite agree with him, and wonder what parent could find it in his heart to object to her bonnie-eyed lover.

What a merciful provision of Providence it is that throws a veil over the future, only to be pierced by the keenest-eyed of Scotchmen! Where should we find a flavor in those unfrequent cups that the shyest of the gods, Joy, holds to our yearning lips, could we know of the bitter that lurks in the tinselled bowl? Surely we have much to be thankful for, but for nothing should we be so grateful as for this blessed impotence of foresight!

But, as it is often on the bluest days that the mercury begins to sink beneath the breath of far-off hurricane; so there is a warning spirit implanted in sensitive minds that makes them mistrustful of too great happiness. We feel that, for most of us, the wheel of our fortune revolves too quickly to allow of a long continuance of unbroken joy.

"Arthur," said Angela, one morning, when eight days had passed since her father's return from town, "we are too happy. We should throw something into the lake."

"I have not got a ring, except the one you gave me," he answered; for his signet was on her finger. "So unless we sacrifice Aleck or the ravens, I don't know what it is to be."

"Don't joke, Arthur. I tell you we are too happy."

Could Arthur have seen through an ac e or so of undergrowth as Angela uttered these words, he would have perceived a very smart page-boy with the Bellamy crest on his buttons delivering a letter to Philip. It is true that there was nothing particularly alarming about that, but its contents might have given a point to Angela's forebodings. It ran thus:

"Rewtham House, Monday.

"My dear Mr. Caresfoot,

"With reference to our conversation last week about your daughter and G., can you come over and have a quiet chat with me this afternoon?

"Sincerely yours,
"Anne Bellamy."

Philip read this note, and then re-read it, knowing in his heart that now was his opportunity to act up to his convictions, and put an end to the whole transaction in a few decisive words. But a man who has for so many years given place to the devil of avarice, even though it be avarice with a legitimate object, cannot shake himself free from his clutches in a moment; even when, as in Philip's case, honor and right, to say nothing of a still more powerful factor, superstition, speak so loudly in his ears. Surely, he thought, there would be no harm in hearing what she had to say. He could explain his reasons for having nothing to do with the matter so much better in person. Such mental struggles have only one end. Presently the smart page-boy bore back this note:

"Dear Lady Bellamy,

"I will be with you at half-past three. P. C."

It was with very curious sensations that Philip was that afternoon shown into a richly-furnished boudoir in Rewtham House. He had not been in that room since he had talked to Maria Lee, sitting on that very sofa now occupied by Lady Bellamy's still beautiful form, and he could not but feel that it was a place of evil omen for him.

Lady Bellamy rose to greet him with her most fascinating smile.

"This is very kind," she said, as she motioned him to a seat, which Philip afterwards discovered had been carefully arranged so as to put his features in the full light, whilst, sitting on the sofa, her own were concealed. "Well, Mr. Caresfoot," she began, after a little pause, "I suppose I had better come to the point at once. First of all, I presume that, as you anticipated would be the case, there exists some sort of understanding between Mr. Heigham and your daughter."

Philip nodded.

"Well, your cousin is as determined as ever about the matter. Indeed, he is simply infatuated or bewitched, I really don't know which."

"I am sorry for it, Lady Bellamy, as I cannot—"

"One moment, Mr. Caresfoot; first let me tell you his offer then we can talk it over. He offers, conditionally on his marriage with your daughter, to sell you the Isleworth estates at a fair valuation hereafter to be agreed upon, and to make a large settlement."

"And what part does he wish me to play in the matter?"

"This. First, you must get rid of young Heigham, and prevent him from holding *any* communication, either with Angela herself, or with any other person connected with this place, for one year from the date of his departure. Secondly, you must throw no obstacle in George's path. Thirdly, if required, you must dismiss her old nurse Pigott."

"It cannot be, Lady Bellamy. I came here to tell you so. I dare not force my daughter into such a marriage for all the estates in England."

Lady Bellamy laughed.

"It is amusing," she said, "to see a father afraid of his own daughter; but you are over-hasty Mr. Caresfoot. Who asked you to force her? All you are asked to do is not to interfere, and leave the rest to myself and George. You will have nothing to do with it one way or the other, nor will any responsibility rest with you. Besides, it is very probable that your cousin will live down his fancy, or some other obstacle will arise to put an end to the thing, in which case Mr. Heigham will come back at the end of his year's probation, and events will take their natural course. It is only wise and right that you should try the constancy of these young lovers, instead of letting them marry out of hand. If, on the other hand, Angela should in the course of the year declare her preference for her cousin, surely that will be no affair of yours."

"I don't understand what your interest is in this matter, Lady Bellamy."

"My dear Mr. Caresfoot, what does my interest matter to you? Perhaps I have one, perhaps I have not; all women love matchmaking, you know; what really is important is your decision," and she shot a glance at him from the heavy-lidded eyes, only to recognize that he was not convinced by her arguments, or, if convinced, obstinate. "By the way," she went on slowly, "George asked me to make a payment to you on his account, money that has, he says, been long owing, but which it has not hitherto been convenient to repay."

"What is the sum?" asked Philip, abstractedly.

"A large one; a thousand pounds."

It did not require the peculiar intonation she threw into her voice to make the matter clear to him. He was well aware that no such sum was owing.

"Here is the check," she went on; and, taking from her purse a signed and crossed check upon a London banker, she unfolded it and threw it upon the table, watching him the while.

Philip gazed at the money with the eyes of a hungry wolf. A thousand pounds! That might be his for the asking, nay, for the taking. It would bind him to nothing. The miser's greed took possession of him as he looked. Slowly he raised his hand, twitching with excitement, and stretched it out towards the check, but, before his fingers touched it, Lady Bellamy, as though by accident, dropped her white palm upon the precious paper.

"I suppose that Mr. Heigham will leave to-morrow on the understanding we mentioned?" she said, carelessly, but in a significant tone.

Philip nodded.

The hand was withdrawn as carelessly as it had come, leaving the check, blushing in all its naked beauty, upon the table. Philip took it as deliberately as he could, and put it in his pocket. Then, rising, he said good-by, adding, as he passed through the door:

"Remember, I have no responsibility in the matter. I wash my hands of it, and wish to hear nothing about it."

"The thousand pounds has done it," reflected Lady Bellamy. "I told George that he would rise greedily at money. I have not watched him for twenty years for nothing. Fancy selling an only daughter's happiness in life for a thousand pounds, and such a daughter too! I wonder how much he would take to murder her, if he were certain that he would not be found out. Upon my word, my work grows quite interesting. That cur, Philip, is as good as a play," and she laughed her own peculiar laugh.

CHAPTER XXX.

INTO Philip's guilty thoughts, as he wended his homeward way, we will not inquire, and indeed, for all the warm glow that the thousand-pound check in his pocket diffused through his system, they were not to be envied. Perhaps no scoundrel presents at heart such a miserable object to himself and all who know him as the scoundrel who attempts to deceive himself, and, whilst reaping its profits, tries to shoulder the responsibility of his iniquity onto the backs of others!

Unfortunately, in this prosaic world of bargains, one cannot receive checks for one thousand pounds without, in some shape or form, giving a *quid pro quo*. Now, Philip's *quid* was to rid his house and the neighborhood of Arthur Heigham, his guest and his daughter's lover. It was not a task he liked, but the unearned check in his breeches-pocket continually reminded him of the obligation it entailed.

When Arthur came to smoke his pipe with his host that evening, the latter looked so gloomy and depressed, that he wondered to himself if he was going to be treated to a repetition of the shadow-scene, little guessing that there was something much more personally unpleasant before him.

"Heigham," Philip said, suddenly, and looking studiously in the other direction, "I want to speak to you. I have been thinking over our conversation of about a week ago on the subject of your engagement to Angela, and have now come to a final determination. I may say at once that I approve of you in every way" (here his hearer's heart bounded with delight), "but, under all the circumstances, I don't think that I should be right in sanctioning an immediate engagement. You are not sufficiently sure of each other for that. I may seem old fashioned, but I am a great believer in the virtue of constancy, and I'm anxious, in your own interests, to put yours and Angela's to the test. The terms that I can offer you are these: You must leave here to-morrow, and must give me your word of honor as a gentleman—which I know will be the most effectual guarantee that I can take from you—that you will not for the space of a year either attempt to see Angela again, or to hold any written communication with her, or anybody in any way connected with her. The year ended, you can return, and, should you both still be of the same mind, you can then marry her as soon as you like. If you decline to accede to these terms—which I believe to be to your mutual ultimate advantage—I must refuse my consent to the engagement altogether."

A silence followed this speech. The match that Arthur had lit before Philip began burnt itself out between his fingers without his appearing to suffer any particular inconvenience, and now his pipe fell with a crash into the grate, and broke into fragments—a fit symbol of the blow dealt to his hopes. For some moments he was so completely overwhelmed at the idea of losing Angela for a whole long year, losing her as completely as though she were dead, that he could not answer. At length he found his voice, and said, hoarsely:

"Yours are hard terms."

"I cannot argue the point with you, Heigham; such as they are, they are my terms, founded on what I consider I owe to my daughter. Do you accept them?"

"I cannot answer you off-hand. My happiness and Angela's are too vitally concerned to allow me to do so. I must consult her first."

"Very good, I have no objection; but you must let me have your answer by ten to-morrow."

Had Arthur only known his own strength and Philip's weakness—the strength that honesty and honor ever have in the face of dishonor and dishonesty—had he known the hesitating feebleness of Philip's avarice-tossed mind, how easy it would have been for him to tear his bald arguments to shreds, and, by the bare exhibition of unshaken purpose, to confound and disallow his determinations—had he then and there refused to agree to his ultimatum, so divided was Philip in his mind, and so shaken by superstitious fears, that he would have accepted it as an omen, and have yielded to a decision of character that had no real existence in himself. But he did not know; indeed, how could he know? and he was, besides, too thorough a gentleman to allow himself to suspect foul play. And so, too sad for talk, and oppressed by the dread sense of coming separation from her whom he loved more dearly than his life, he sought his room, there to think and pace, to pace and think, until the stars had set.

When, wearied out at length, he threw himself into bed, it was only to exchange bad for worse; for on such occasions sleep is worse than wakefulness, it is so full of dreams, big with coming pain. Shortly after dawn he got up again, and went into the garden and listened to the birds singing their matin hymn. But he was in no mood for the songs of birds, however sweet, and it was a positive relief to him when old Jakes emerged, his cross face set in the gladness of the morning, like a sullen cloud in the blue sky, and began to do something to his favorite bed of cabbages. Not that Arthur was fond of old Jakes; on the contrary, ever since the coffin-stool conversation, which betrayed, he considered, a malevolent mind, he detested him personally; but still he set a fancy value on him because he was connected with the daily life of his betrothed.

And then at last out came Angela, having spied him from behind the curtains of her window, clothed in the same white gown in which he had first beheld her, and which he consequently considered the prettiest of frocks. Never did she look more lovely than when she came walking towards him that morning, with her light, proud step, which was so full of grace and womanly dignity. Never had he thought her more sweet and heart-compelling than when, having first made sure that Jakes had retreated to feed his pigs, she shyly lifted her bright face to be greeted with his kiss. But she was quick of sympathy, and had learned to read him like an open page, and before his lips had fairly fallen on her own she knew that things had gone amiss.

"Oh, what is it, Arthur?" she said, with a little pant of fear.

"Be brave, dear, and I will tell you." And, in somewhat choky tones, he recounted word for word what had passed between her father and himself.

She listened in perfect silence, and bore the blow as a brave woman should. When he had finished, she said, with a little tremor in her voice:

"You will not forget me in a year, will you, Arthur?"

He kissed her by way of answer, and then they agreed to go together to Philip, and try to turn him from his purpose.

Breakfast was not a cheerful meal that day, and Pigott, noticing the prevailing depression, remarked, with sarcasm, that they might, for all appearance to the contrary, have been married for twenty years; but even this spirited sally did not provoke a laugh. Ten o'clock, the hour that was to decide their fate, came all too soon, and it was with very anxious hearts that they took their way to the study. Philip, who was seated in readiness, appeared to view Angela's arrival with some uneasiness.

"Of course, Angela," he said, "I am always glad to see you, but I hardly expected—"

"I beg your pardon for intruding, father," she answered; "but as this is very important to me, I thought that I had better come too, and hear what is settled."

As it was evident that she meant to stay, Philip did not attempt to gainsay her.

"Oh, very well, very well. I suppose you have heard the terms upon which I am prepared to consent to your engagement."

"Yes, Arthur has told me; and it is to implore you to modify them that we have come. Father, they are cruel terms—to be dead to each other for a whole long year."

"I cannot help it, Angela. I am sorry to inflict pain upon either of you; but I have arrived at them entirely in your own interests, and after a great deal of anxious thought. Believe me, a year's probation will be very good for both of you; it is not probable that where my only child is concerned, I should wish to do anything except what is for her happiness!"

Arthur looked rebellion at Angela. Philip saw it, and added:

"Of course you can defy me—it is, I believe, rather the fashion for girls, nowadays, to do so—but, if you do, you must both clearly understand, first, that you cannot marry without my consent till the first of May next, or very nearly a year hence, when Angela comes of age, and that I shall equally forbid all intercourse in the interval; and secondly, that when you do so, it will be against my wish, and that I shall cut her name out of my will, for this property is only entailed in the male line. It now only remains for me to ask you if you agree to my conditions."

Angela answered him, speaking very slowly and clearly:

"I accept them on my own behalf, not because I understand them, or think them right, or because of your threats, but because, though you do not care for me, I am your daughter, and should obey you—and believe that you wish to do what is best for me. That is why I accept, although it will make my life wretched for a year."

"You hear what she says?" said Philip, turning to Arthur. "Do you also agree?"

He answered boldly, and with some temper (how would he have answered could he have seen the thousand-pound check that was reposing upon the table in Philip's rusty pocket-book, and known for what purpose it came there?):

"If it had not been Angela's wish, I would never have agreed. I think your terms preposterous, and I only hope that you have some satisfactory reason for them; for you have not shown us any. But since she takes this view of the matter, and because, so far as I can see, you have completely cornered us, I suppose I must. You are her father, and cannot in nature wish to thwart her happiness; and if you have any plan of causing her to forget me—I don't want to be conceited, but I believe that it will fail." Here Angela smiled somewhat sadly. "So, unless one of us dies before the year is up, I shall come back to be married on the ninth of June next year."

"Really, my dear Heigham, your way of talking is so aggressive, that some fathers might be tempted to ask you not to come back at all; but perhaps it is, under the circumstances, excusable."

"You would probably think so, if you were in my place," blurted out Arthur.

"You give me, then, your word of honor as a gentleman that you will attempt, either in person or by letter, no communication with Angela or with anybody about this place for one year from to-day?"

"On the condition that, at the end of the year, I may return and marry her as soon as I like."

"Certainly; your marriage can take plaçe on the ninth of June next, if you like, and care to bring a license and a proper settlement—say, of half your income—with you," answered Philip, with a half smile.

"I take you at your word," said Arthur, eagerly, "that is, if Angela agrees." Angela made no signs of disagreement. "Then, on those terms, I give you my promise."

"Very good. Then that is settled, and I will send for a dog-cart to take you to the four-o'clock train. I fear you will hardly be ready for the twelve-twenty-five. I shall, however, hope," he added, "to have the pleasure of presenting this young lady to you for good and all on this day next year. Good-by for the present. I shall see you before you go."

It is painful to have to record that when Arthur got outside the door, and out of Angela's hearing, he cursed Philip, in his grief and anger, for the space of some minutes.

To linger over those last hours could only be distressing to the sympathetic reader of this history, more especially if he, or she, has ever had the misfortune to pass through such a time in their own proper persons. The day of any one's departure is always wretched, but much more is it wretched when the person departing is a lover, whose face will not be seen and of whom no postman will bear tidings for a whole long year.

Some comfort, however, these two took in looking forward to that joyous day when the year of probation should have been gathered to its predecessors, and in making the most minute arrangements for their wedding: how Angela was to warn Mr. Fraser that his services would be required; where they should go for their honeymoon, and even of what flowers the wedding bouquet, which Arthur was to bring down from town with him, should be composed.

And thus the hours passed away, all too quickly, and each of them strove to be merry, in order to keep up the spirits of the other. But it is not in human nature to feel cheerful with a lump of ice upon the heart! Dinner was even more dismal than breakfast, and Pigott, who had been informed of the impending misfortune, and who was distrustful of Philip's motives, though she did not like to add to the general gloom by saying so, made, after the manner of half-educated people, a painful and infectious exhibition of her grief.

"Poor Aleck," said Angela, when the time drew near, bending down over the dog to hide a tear, as she had once before bent down to hide a blush; "poor Aleck, I shall miss you almost as much as your master."

"You will not miss him, Angela, because I am going to make you a present of him if you will keep him."

"That is very good of you, dear. I shall be glad to have him for your sake."

"Well, keep him, love, he is a good dog; he will quite have transferred his allegiance by the time I come back. I hope you won't have done the same, Angela."

"Oh, Arthur, why will you so often make me angry by saying such things? The sun will forget to shine before I forget you."

"Hush, love, I did not mean it," and he took her in his arms. And so they sat there together under the oak where first they had met, hand in hand and heart to heart, and it was at this moment that the self-reliant strength and more beautiful serenity of Angela's character as compared with her lover's came into visible play. For whilst, as the moment of separation drew nigh, he could scarcely contain his grief, she on the other hand grew more and more calm, strengthening his weakness with her quiet power; and bidding him seek consolation in his trouble at the hands of Him who for His own purposes decreed it.

"Dearest," she said, in answer to his complainings, "there are so many things in the world that we cannot understand, and yet they must be right and lead to a good end. What may happen to us before this year is out, of course we cannot say, but I feel that all love is immortal, and that there is a perfect life awaiting us, if not in this world, then in the next. Remember, dear, that these few years are, after all, but as a breath to the general air, or as that dew-drop to the waters of the lake, when compared with the future that awaits us there, and that until we attain that future we cannot really know each other, or the true meaning and purpose of our love. So look forward to it without fear, dear heart, and if it should chance that I should pass out of your life, or that other ties should spring up round you that shall forbid the outward expression of our love—" Here Arthur started and was about to interrupt, but she stopped him. "Do not start, Arthur. Who can read the future? Stranger things have happened, and if, I say, such a thing should come about in our case, then remember, I implore you, that in that future lies the answer to the puzzles of the world, and turn your eyes to it, as to the horizon beyond which you will find me waiting for you, and not only me, but all that you have ever loved. Only, dear, try to be a good man and love me always."

He looked at her in wonder.

"Angela," he said, "what has made you so different from other women? With all whom I have known, love is an affair of passion or amusement, of the world and the day, but yours gazes towards heaven, and looks to find its real utterance in the stillness of eternity! To be loved by you, my dear, would be worth a century of sorrows."

At last the moment came, as all moments good and bad must come. To Pigott, who was crying, he gave a hug and a five-pound note, to Aleck a pat on the head, to Philip, who could not look him in the face, a shake of the hand, and to Angela, who bravely smiled into his eyes—a long last kiss.

But when the cruel wheels began to crunch upon the gravel, the great tears welling to her eyes blotted him from sight. Blindly she made her way up to her room, and throwing herself upon the bed let her unrestrained sorrow loose, feeling that she was indeed desolate and alone.

CHAPTER XXXI.

WHEN Angela was still quite a child, the permanent inhabitants of Sherborne Lane, King William Street, in the city of London, used to note a very pretty girl, of small stature and modest ways, passing out—every evening after the city gentlemen had locked up their offices and gone home—from the quiet of the lane into the roar and rush of the city. This young girl was Mildred James, the only daughter of a struggling, a very struggling, city doctor, and her daily mission was to go to the cheap markets, and buy the provisions that were to last the Sherborne Lane household (for her father lived in the same rooms that he practised in) for the ensuing twenty-four hours. The world was a hard place for poor Mildred in those days of provision-hunting, when so little money had to pay for so many necessaries, and to provide also for the luxuries that were necessaries to her invalid mother. Some years later, when she was a sweet maiden of eighteen, her mother died, but medical competition was keen in Sherborne Lane, and her removal did not greatly alleviate the pressure of poverty. At last, one evening, when she was about twenty years of age, a certain Mr. Carr, an old gentleman with whom her father had some acquaintance, sent up a card with a pencilled message on it to the effect that he would be glad to see Dr. James.

"Run, Mildred," said her father, "and tell Mr. Carr that I will be with him in a minute. It will never do to see a new patient in this coat."

Mildred departed, and, gliding into the gloomy consulting-room like a sunbeam, delivered her message to the old gentleman, who appeared to be in some pain, and prepared to return.

"Don't go away," almost shouted the aged patient; "I have crushed my finger in a door, and it hurts most confoundedly. You are something to look at in this hole, and distract my attention."

Mildred thought to herself that this was an odd way of paying a compliment, if it was meant for one; but then old gentlemen with crushed fingers are not given to weighing their words.

"Are you Dr. James's daughter?" he asked, presently.

"Yes, sir."

"Ugh! I have lived most of my life in Sherborne Lane, and never saw anything half so pretty in it before. Confound this finger!"

At this moment the doctor himself arrived, and wanted to dismiss Mildred; but Mr. Carr, who was a headstrong old gentleman, vowed that no one else should hold his injured hand whilst it was dressed, and so she stayed just long enough for him to fall as completely in love with her shell-like face as though he had been twenty instead of nearly seventy.

Now, Mr. Carr was not remarkable for good looks, and, in addition to having seen out so many summers, had also buried two wives. It will, therefore, be clear that he was scarcely the suitor that a lovely girl, conscious of capacities for deep affection, would have selected of her own free will; but, on the other hand, he was honest and kind-hearted, and, what was more to the point, perhaps the wealthiest wine-merchant in the city. Mildred resisted as long as she could, but want is a hard master, and a father's arguments are difficult to answer, and in the end she married him, and, what is more, made him a good and faithful wife.

She never had any cause to regret it, for he was kindness itself towards her, and when he died, some five years afterwards, having no children of his own, he left her sole legatee of all his enormous fortune, bound up by no restrictions as to remarriage. About this time also her father died, and she was left as much alone in the world as it is possible for a young and pretty woman, possessing in her own right between twenty and thirty thousand a year, to be.

Needless to say, Mrs. Carr was thenceforth one of the catches of her generation; but nobody could catch her, though she alone knew how many had tried. Once she made a list of all the people who had proposed to her; it included amongst others a bishop, two peers, three members of parliament, no less than five army officers, an American, and a dissenting clergyman.

"It is perfectly marvellous, my dear," she said to her companion, Agatha Terry, "how fond people are of twenty thousand a year, and yet they all said that they loved me for myself, that is, all except the dissenter, who wanted me to help to 'feed his flock,' and I liked him the best of the lot, because he was the honestest."

Mrs. Carr had a beautiful house in Grosvenor Square, a place in Leicestershire, where she hunted a little, a place in the Isle of Wight that she rarely visited, and, lastly, a place at Madeira where she lived for nearly half the year. There never had been a breath of scandal against her name, nor had she given cause for any. "As for loving," she would say, "the only things she loved were beetles and mummies," for she was a clever naturalist, and a faithful student of the lore of the ancient Egyptians. The beetles, she would explain, had been the connecting link between the two sciences, since beetles had led her to scarabæi, and scarabæi to the human husks with which they are to be found; but this statement, though amusing, was not strictly accurate, as she had in reality contracted the taste from her late husband, who had left her a large collection of Egyptian antiquities.

"I do adore a mummy," she would say; "I am small enough in mind and body already, but it makes me feel inches smaller, and I like to measure my own diminutiveness."

She was not much of a reader; life was, she declared, too short to waste in study; but when she did take up a book, it was generally of a nature that most women of her class would have called stiff, and then she could read it without going to sleep.

In addition to these occupations, Mrs. Carr had had various crazes at different stages in her widowhood, which had now endured for some five years. She had travelled, she had "gone in for art;" once she had speculated a little, but finding that, for a woman, it was a losing game, she was too shrewd to continue this last pastime. But she always came back to her beetles and her mummies.

Still, with all her money, her places, her offers of marriage, and her self-made occupations, Mildred Carr was essentially "a weary woman, sunk deep in ease, and sated with her life." Within that little frame of hers there beat a great active heart, ever urging her onwards towards an unknown end. She would describe herself as an "ill-regulated woman," and the description was not without justice, for she did not possess that placid, even mind which is so necessary to the comfort of English ladies, and which enables many of them to bury a husband or a lover as composedly as they take him. She would have given worlds to be able to fall in love with some one, to fill up the daily emptiness of her existence with another's joys and griefs, but she *could* not. Men passed before her in endless procession, all sorts and conditions of them, and for the most part were anxious to marry her, but they might as well have been a string of wax dolls for aught she could care about them. To her eyes, they were nothing more than a succession of frock-coats and tall hats, full of shine and emptiness, signifying nothing. For their opinion, too, and that of the society which they helped to form, she had a most complete and wrong-headed contempt. She cared nothing for the ordinary laws of social life, and was prepared to break through them on emergency, as a wasp breaks through a spider's web. Perhaps she guessed that a good deal of breaking would be forgiven to the owner of such a lovely face and more than twenty thousand a year. With all this, she was extremely observant, and possessed, unknown to herself, great powers of mind, and great, though dormant, capacities for passion. In short, this little woman, with the baby face, smiling and serene as the blue sky that hides the gathering hurricane, was rather odder than the majority of her sex, which is perhaps saying a great deal.

One day, about a week before Arthur departed from the Abbey House, Agatha Terry was sitting in the blue drawing-room in the house in Grosvenor Square, when Mrs. Carr came in, almost at a run, slammed the door behind her, and plumped herself down in a chair with a sigh of relief.

"Agatha, give orders to pack up. We will go to Madeira by the next boat."

"Goodness gracious, Mildred! across that dreadful bay again; and just think how hot it will be, and the beginning of the season too."

"Now, Agatha, I'm going, and there's an end of it, so it is no use arguing. You can stay here, and give a series of balls and dinners, if you like."

"Nonsense, dear; me give parties indeed, and you at Madeira! Why, it's just as though you asked Ruth to entertain the reapers without Naomi. I'll go and give the orders; but I do hope that it will be calm. Why do you want to go now?"

"I'll tell you. Lord Minster has been proposing to me again, and announces his intention of going on doing so till I accept him. You know, he has just got into the Cabinet, so he has celebrated the event by asking me to marry him, for the third time."

"Poor fellow! Perhaps he is very fond of you."

"Not a bit of it. He is fond of my good looks and my money I will tell you the substance of his speech this morning. He stood like this, with his hands in his pockets, and said, 'I am now a cabinet minister. It is a good thing that a cabinet minister should have somebody presentable to sit at the head of his table. You are presentable. I appreciate beauty, when I have time to think about it. I observe that you are beautiful. I am not very well off for my position. You, on the other hand, are immensely rich. With your money I can, in time, become Prime Minister. It is, consequently, evidently to my advantage that you should marry me, and I have sacrificed a very important appointment in order to come and settle it."

Agatha laughed.

"And how did you answer him?"

"In his own style. 'Lord Minster,' I said, 'I am, for the third time, honored by your flattering proposal, but I have no wish to ornament your table, no desire to expose my beauty to your perpetual admiration, and no ambition to advance your political career. I do not love you, and I had rather become the wife of a crossing-sweeper that I loved than that of a member of the government for whom I have *every* respect but no affection.'

"'As the wife of a crossing-sweeper, it is probable,' he answered, 'that you would be miserable. As my wife, you would certainly be admired and powerful, and consequently happy.'

"'Lord Minster,' I said, 'you have studied human nature but very superficially if you have not learnt that it is better for a woman to be miserable with the man she loves than "admired, powerful, and consequently happy" with one who has no attraction for her.'

"'Your remark is interesting,' he replied; 'but I think that there is something paradoxical about it. I must be going now, as I have only five minutes to get to Westminster; but I will think it over, and answer it when we renew our conversation, which I propose to do very shortly,' and he was gone before I could get in another word "

"But why should that make you go to Madeira?"

"Because, my dear, if I don't, so sure as I am a living woman, that man will tire me out and marry me, and I dislike him, and don't want to marry him. I have a strong will, but his is of iron."

And so it came to pass that the names of Mrs. Carr, Miss Terry, and three servants appeared upon the passenger-list of Messrs. Donald Currie & Co.'s royal mail steamship *Warwick Castle*, due to sail for Madeira and the Cape ports on the 14th of June.

CHAPTER XXXII.

Arthur arrived in town in a melancholy condition. His was a temperament peculiarly liable to suffer from attacks of depression, and he had, with some excuse, a sufficiently severe one on him now. Do what he would, he could not for a single hour free his mind from the sick longing to see or hear from Angela, that, in addition to the mental distress it occasioned him, amounted almost to a physical pain. After two or three days of lounging about his club—for he was in no mood for going out—he began to feel that this sort of thing was intolerable, and that it was absolutely necessary for him to go somewhere or do something.

It so happened that, just after he had come to this decision, he overheard two men, who were sitting at the next table to him in the club dining-room, talking of the island of Madeira, and speaking of it as a charming place. He accepted this as an omen, and determined that to Madeira he would go. And, indeed, the place would suit him as well as any other to get through a portion of his year of probation in, and, whilst affording a complete change of scene, would not be too far from England.

And so it came to pass that on the morrow Arthur found himself in the office of Messrs. Donald Currie for the purpose of booking his berth in the vessel that was due to sail on the 14th. There he was informed by the very affable clerk who assisted him to choose his cabin that the vessel was unusually empty, and that up to the present time berths had been taken only for five ladies, and two of them Jewesses.

"However," the clerk added, by way of consolation, "this one," pointing to Mrs. Carr's name on the list, "is as good as a cargo," and he whistled expressively.

"What do you mean?" asked Arthur, his curiosity slightly excited.

"I mean—my word! here she comes."

At that moment the swing-doors of the office were pushed open, and there came through them one of the sweetest, daintiest little women Arthur had ever seen. She was no longer quite young; she might be eight-and-twenty or thirty; but, on the other hand, maturity had but added to the charms of youth. She had big brown eyes that Arthur thought could probably look languishing, if they chose, and that even in repose were full of expression; a face soft and blooming as a peach and round as a baby's, surmounted by a quantity of nut-brown hair; the very sweetest mouth, the lips rather full and just showing a line of pearl; and lastly, what looked rather odd on such an infantile countenance, a firm, square, and very determined, if very diminutive, chin. For the rest, it was difficult to say which was the most perfect, her figure or her dress.

All of which, of course, had little interest for Arthur; but what did rather startle him was her voice, when she spoke. From such a woman one would naturally have expected a voice of a corresponding nature, namely, one of the soft and murmuring order. But hers, on the contrary, though sweet, was decided, and clear as a bell, and with a peculiar ring in it that he would have recognized amongst a thousand others.

On her entrance, Arthur stepped on one side.

"I have come to say," she said, with a slight bow of recognition to the clerk, "that I have changed my mind about my berth; instead of the starboard deck cabin I should like to have the port, I think that it will be cooler at this time of the year; and also will you please make arrangements for three horses?"

"I am excessively sorry, Mrs. Carr," the clerk answered; "but the port cabin is engaged—in fact, this gentleman has just taken it."

"Oh, in that case"—with a little blush—"there is an end of the question."

"By no means," interrupted Arthur. "It is a matter of perfect indifference to me where I go. I beg that you will take it."

"Oh, thank you. You are very good, but I could not think of robbing you of your cabin."

"I must implore you to do so. Rather than there should be any difficulty, I will go below." And then, addressing the clerk, "Be so kind as to change the cabins."

"I owe you many thanks for your courtesy," said Mrs. Carr, with a little courtesy.

Arthur took off his hat.

"Then we will considered that settled. Good-morning, or perhaps I should say *Au revoir;*" and, bowing again, he left the office.

"What is that gentleman's name?" Mrs. Carr asked, when he was gone.

"Here it is, madam, on the list. 'Arthur Preston Heigham, passenger for Madeira.'"

"Arthur Preston Heigham!" Mrs. Carr said to herself, as she made her way down to her carriage in Fenchurch Street. "Arthur is pretty, and Preston is pretty, but I don't much like Heigham. At any rate, there is no doubt about his bieng a gentleman. I wonder what he is going to Madeira for? He has an interesting face. I think I am glad we are going to be fellow-passengers."

The two days that remained to him in town Arthur spent in making his preparations for departure; getting money, buying, after the manner of young Englishmen starting on a voyage to foreign parts, a large and fearfully sharp hunting-knife, as though Madeira were the home of wild beasts, and laying in a stock of various other articles of a useless description, such as impenetrable sun-helmets and leather coats.

The boat was to sail at noon on Friday, and on Thursday evening he left Paddington by the mail that reaches Dartmouth about midnight. On the pier he and one or two other fellow-passengers found a boat waiting to take them to the great vessel, that, painted a dull gray, lay still and solemn in the harbor as they were rowed up to her, very different from the active, living thing that she was destined to become within the next twenty-four hours. The tide ebbing past her sides, the fresh, strong smell of the sea, the tall masts pointing skywards like gigantic fingers, the chime of the bell upon the bridge, the sleepy steward, and the stuffy cabin, were all a pleasant variation from the every-day monotony of existence, and contributed towards the conclusion that life was still partially worth living, even when it could not be lived with Angela. Indeed, so much are we the creatures of circumstance, and so liable to be influenced by surroundings, that Arthur, who, a few hours before, had been plunged into the depths of depression, turned into his narrow berth, after a tremendous struggle with the sheets—which stewards arrange on a principle incomprehensible to landlubbers, and probably only partially understood by themselves—with considerable satisfaction and a pleasurable sense of excitement.

The next morning, or rather the earlier part of it, he devoted, when he was not thinking about Angela, to arranging his goods and chattels in his small domain, to examining the lovely scenery of Dartmouth harbor—the sight of which is enough to make any outward-bound individual bitterly regret his determination to quit his native land—and to inspecting the outward man of his fellow-passengers with that icy stolidity which characterizes the true-born Briton. But the great event of the morning was the arrival of the mail train, bringing the bags destined for various African ports, loose letters for the passengers, and a motley contingent of the passengers themselves. Amongst these latter, he had no difficulty in recognizing the two Jewesses of whom the clerk in the office had spoken, who were accompanied by individuals presumably their husbands, and very remarkable for the splendor of their diamond studs and the dirtiness of their nails. The only other specimen of saloon-passenger womankind that he could see was a pretty, black-eyed girl of about eighteen, who was, as he afterwards discovered, going out under the captain's care to be a governess at the Cape, and who, to judge from the intense melancholy of her countenance, did not particularly enjoy the prospect. But, with the exception of some heavy baggage that was being worked up from a cargo-boat by the donkey-engine, and a luxurious cane-chair on the deck that bore her name, no signs were there of Mrs. Carr.

Presently the purser sent round the head steward, a gentleman whom Arthur mistook for the first mate, so smart was his uniform, to collect the letters, and it wrung him not a little to think that he alone could send none. The bell sounded to warn all not sailing to hurry to their boats, but still there was nothing to be seen of his acquaintance of the office; and, to speak the truth, he was just a little disappointed, for what he had seen of her had piqued his curiosity and made him anxious to see more.

"I can't wait any longer," he heard the captain say; "she must come on by the *Kinfauns.*"

It was full twelve o'clock, and the last rope was being loosed from the moorings. "Ting-ting," went the engine-room bell. "Thud-thud," started the great screw that would not stop again for so many restless hours. The huge vessel shuddered throughout her frame like an awakening sleeper, and, growing quick with life, forged an inch or two ahead. Next a quartermaster came with two men to hoist up the gangway, when suddenly a boat shot alongside and hooked on, amongst the occupants of which Arthur had no difficulty in recognizing Mrs. Carr, who sat laughing, like Pleasure, at the helm. The other occupants of the boat, who were not laughing, he guessed to be her servants and the lady who figured on the passenger-list as Miss Terry, a stout, solemn-looking person in spectacles.

"Now, then, Agatha," called out Mrs. Carr from the stern-sheets, "be quick and jump up."

"My dear Mildred, I can't go up there; I can't, indeed. Why, the thing's moving."

"But you must go up, or else be pulled with a rope. Here, I will show the way," and, moving down the boat, she sprang boldly, as it rose with the swell, into the stalwart arms of the sailor who was waiting on the gangway landing-stage, and thence ran up the steps to the deck.

"Very well, I am going to Madeira. I don't know what you are going to do; but you must make up your mind quick."

"Can't hold on much longer, mum," said the boatman; "she's getting way on now."

"Come on, mum; I won't let you in," said the man of the ladder, seductively.

"Oh dear, oh dear! what shall I do?" groaned Miss Terry, wringing the hand that was not employed in holding on.

"John," called Mrs. Carr to a servant who was behind Miss Terry, and looking considerably alarmed, "don't stand there like a fool; put Miss Terry onto that ladder."

Mrs. Carr was evidently accustomed to be obeyed, for, thus admonished, John seized the struggling and shrieking Miss Terry and bore her to the edge of the boat, where she was caught by two sailors and, amidst the cheers of excited passengers, fairly dragged onto the deck.

"Oh, Mrs. Carr," said the chief officer, reproachfully, when Miss Terry had been satisfactorily deposited on a bench, "you are late again; you were late last voyage."

"Not at all, Mr. Thompson. I hate spending longer than is necessary aboard ship, so, when the train got in, I took a boat and went for a row in the harbor. I knew that you would not go without me."

"Oh, yes, we should have, Mrs. Carr; the skipper heard about it because he waited for you before."

"Well, here I am, and I promise that I won't do it again."

Mr. Thompson laughed, and passed on. At this moment Mrs. Carr perceived Arthur, and, bowing to him, they fell into conversation about the scenery through which the boat was passing on her way to the open sea. Before very long, indeed, as soon as the vessel began to rise and fall upon the swell, this talk was interrupted by a voice from the seat where Miss Terry had been placed.

"Mildred," it said, "I do wish you would not come to sea; I am beginning to feel ill."

"And no wonder, if you will insist upon coming up ladders head downwards. Where's John? He will help you to your cabin; the deck one, next to mine."

But John had vanished with a parcel.

"Mildred, send some one quick, I beg of you," remarked Miss Terry, in the solemn tones of one who feels that a crisis is approaching.

"I can't see anybody except a very dirty sailor."

"Permit me," said Arthur, stepping to the rescue.

"You are very kind; but she can't walk. I know her ways; she has got to the stage when she must be carried. Can you manage her?"

"I think so," replied Arthur, "if you don't mind holding her legs, and provided that the vessel does not roll," and, with an effort, he hoisted Miss Terry baby-fashion into his arms, and staggered off with her towards the indicated cabin, Mrs. Carr, as suggested, holding the lower limbs of the prostrate lady. Presently she began to laugh.

"If you only knew how absurd we look," she said.

"Don't make me laugh," answered Arthur, puffing; for Miss Terry was by no means light, "or I shall drop her."

"If you do, young man," ejaculated his apparently unconscious burden with wonderful energy, "I will never forgive you."

A remark the suddenness of which so startled him, that he very nearly did.

"Thank you. Now lay her quite flat, please. She won't get up again till we drop anchor at Madeira."

"If I live so long," murmured the invalid.

Arthur now made his bow and departed, wondering how two women so dissimilar as Mrs. Carr and Miss Terry came to be living together. As it is a piece of curiosity that the reader may share, perhaps it had better be explained.

Miss Terry was a middle-aged relative of Mrs. Carr's late husband, who had by a series of misfortunes been left quite destitute. Her distress having come to the knowledge of Mildred Carr, she, with the kind-hearted promptitude that distinguished her, at once came to her aid, paid her debts, and brought her to her own house to stay, where she had remained ever since under the title of companion. These two women, living thus together, had nothing whatsoever in common, save that Miss Terry took some reflected interest in beetles. As for travelling, having been brought up and lived in the same house of the same county town until she reached the age of forty-five, it was, as may be imagined, altogether obnoxious to her. Indeed, it is more than doubtful if she retained any clear impression whatsoever of the places she visited. "A set of foreign holes!" as she would call them, contemptuously. Miss Terry was, in short, neither clever nor strong-minded, but so long as she could be in the company of her beloved Mildred, whom she regarded with mingled reverence and affection, she was perfectly happy. Oddly enough, this affection was reciprocated, and there probably was nobody in the world for whom Mrs. Carr cared so much as her cousin by marriage, Agatha Terry. And yet it would be impossible to imagine two women more dissimilar.

Not long after they had left Dartmouth, the afternoon set in dull, and towards evening the sea freshened sufficiently to send most of the passengers below, leaving those who remained to be finally dispersed by the penetrating drizzle that is generally to be met with off the English coast. Arthur, left alone on the heaving deck, surveyed the scene, and thought it very desolate. Around was a gray waste of tossing waters, illumined here and there by the setting rays of an angry sun, above a wild and windy sky, with not even a sea-gull in all its space, and in the far distance a white and fading line, which was the shore of England.

Faint it grew, and fainter yet, and, as it disappeared, he thought of Angela, and a yearning sorrow fell upon him. When, he wondered sadly, should he again look into her eyes, and hold that proud beauty in his arms; what fate awaited them in the future that stretched before them, dim as the darkening ocean, and more uncertain? Alas! he could not tell; he only felt that it was very bitter to be parted thus from her to whom had been given his whole heart's love, to know that every fleeting moment widened a breach already far too wide, and not to know if it would again be narrowed, or if this farewell would be the last. Then he thought, if it should be the last, if she should die or desert him, what would his life be worth to him? A consciousness within him answered, "Nothing." And, in a degree, his conclusion was right; for, although it is, fortunately, not often in the power of any single passion to render life altogether worthless; it is certain that, when it strikes in youth, there is no sickness so sore as that of the heart; no sorrow more keen, and no evil more lasting, than those connected with its disappointments and its griefs. For other sorrows, life has salves and consolations, but a noble and enduring passion is not all of this world, and to cure its sting we must look to something beyond this world's quackeries. Other griefs can find sympathy and expression, and become absorbed little by little in the variety of life's issues. But love, as it is and should be understood—not the faint ghost that arrays itself in stolen robes, and says, "I am love," but love the strong and the immortal, the pass-key to the happy skies, the angel cipher we read but cannot understand—such love as this, and there is none other true, can find no full solace here, not even in its earthly satisfaction.

For still it beats against its mortal bars and rends the heart that holds it; still strives like a meteor flaming to its central star, or a new-loosed spirit seeking the presence of its God, to pass hence with that kindred soul to the inner heaven whence it came, there to be wholly mingled with its other life and clothed with a divine identity—there to satisfy the aspirations that now vaguely throb within their fleshly walls, with the splendor and the peace and the full measure of the eternal joys it knows await its coming.

And is it not a first-fruit of this knowledge that the thoughts of those who are plunged into the fires of a pure devotion fly upwards as surely as the sparks? Nothing but the dross, the grosser earthly part is purged away by their ever-chastening sorrow, which is, in truth, a discipline for finer souls. For did there ever yet live the man or woman who, loving truly, has suffered and, the fires burnt out, has not risen Phœnix-like from the ashes, purer and better, and holding in the heart a bright, undying hope? Never; for these have walked barefooted upon the holy ground: it is the flames from the Altar that have purged them and left their own light within! And surely this holds also good of those who have loved and lost, of those who have been scorned or betrayed; of the suffering army that cry aloud of the empty bitterness of life and dare not hope beyond. They do not understand that having once loved truly it is not possible that they should altogether lose: that there is to their pain and the dry-rot of their hopes, as to everything else in Nature, an end and object. Shall the soul be immortal, and its best essence but a thing of air? Shall the one thought by day and the one dream by night, the ethereal star which guides us across life's mirage, and which will still shine serene at the moment of our fall from the precipice of Time—shall this alone, amidst all that makes us what we are, be chosen out to see corruption, to be cast off and forgotten in the grave? Never! There, by the workings of a Providence we cannot understand, that mighty germ awaits fruition. There, too, shall we know the wherefore of our sorrow at which, sad-eyed, we now so often wonder; there shall we kiss the rod that smote us, and learn the glorious uses and pluck the glowing fruits of an affliction, that on earth filled us with such sick longing; and such an aching pain.

Let the long-suffering reader forgive these pages of speculative writing, for the subject is a tempting one, and full of interest fot us mortals. Indeed, it may chance that, if he or she is more than five-and-twenty, these lines may even have been read without impatience, for there are many who have the memory of a lost Angela hidden away somewhere in the records of their past, and who are fain, in the breathing-spaces of their lives, to dream that they will find her wandering in that wide Eternity where "all human barriers fall, all human relations end, and love ceases to be a crime."

CHAPTER XXXIII.

THE morning after the vessel left Dartmouth brought with it lovely weather, brisk and clear, with a fresh breeze that just topped the glittering swell with white. There was, however, a considerable roll on the ship, and those poor wretches who for their sins are given to sea-sickness were not yet happy. Presently Arthur observed the pretty black-eyed girl—poor thing, she did not look very pretty now—creep on to the deck and attempt to walk about, an effort which promptly resulted in a fall into the scuppers. He picked her up, and asked if she would not like to sit down, but she faintly declined, saying that she did not mind falling so long as she could walk a little—she did not feel so sick when she walked. Under these circumstances he could hardly do less than help her, which he did in the only way at all practicable with one so weak namely, by walking her about on his arm.

In the midst of his interesting peregrinations he observed Mrs. Carr gazing out of her deck-cabin window, looking, he thought, pale, but sweetly pretty, and rather cross. When that lady saw that she was observed, she pulled the curtain with a jerk and vanished. Shortly after this Arthur's companion vanished too, circumstances over which she had no control compelling her, and Arthur himself sat down rather relieved.

But he was destined that day to play knight-errant to ladies in distress. Presently Mrs. Carr's cabin-door opened, and that lady herself emerged therefrom, holding on to the side-rail. He had just begun to observe how charmingly she was dressed, when some qualm seized her, and she turned to re-enter the cabin. But the door had swung-to with the roll of the vessel, and she could not open it. Impelled by an agony of doubt, she flew to the side, and, to his horror, sprang with a single bound on to the broad rail that surmounted the bulwark netting, and remained seated there, holding only to a little rope that hung down from the awning-chain. The ship, which was at the moment rolling pretty heavily, had just reached the full angle of her windward roll, and was preparing for a heavy swing to leeward. Arthur, seeing that Mrs. Carr would in a few seconds certainly be flung out to sea, rushed promptly forward and lifted her from the rail. It was none too soon, for next moment down the great ship went with a lurch into a trough of the sea, hurling him, with her in his arms, up against the bulwarks, and, to say truth, hurting him considerably. But, if he expected any thanks for this exploit, he was destined to be disappointed, for no sooner had he set his lovely burden down than she made use of her freedom to stamp upon the deck.

"How could you be so foolish?" said he. "In another moment you would have been flung out to sea!"

"And pray, Mr. Heigham," she answered, in a cutting and sarcastic voice, "is that my business or your own? Surely it would have been time enough for you to take a liberty when I asked you to jump over after me."

Arthur drew himself up to his full height and looked dignified—he could look dignified when he liked.

"I do not quite understand you, Mrs. Carr," he said, with a little bow. "What I did, I did to save you from going overboard. Next time that such a little adventure comes in my way, I hope, for my own sake, that it may concern a lady possessed of less rudeness and more gratitude."

And then, glaring defiance at each other, they separated; she marching off with all the dignity of an offended queen to the "sweet seclusion that a cabin grants," whilst he withdrew moodily to a bench, comforted, however, not a little by the thought that he had given Mrs. Carr a Roland for her Oliver.

Mrs. Carr's bound onto the bulwarks had been the last effort of that prince of demons, Sea-sickness, rending her ere he left. When the occasion for remaining there had thus passed away, she soon tired of her cabin and of listening to the inarticulate moans of her beloved Agatha, who was a most faithful subject of the fiend, one who would never desert his banner so long as he could roll the tiniest wave, and, sallying forth, took up her position in the little society of the ship.

But between Arthur and herself there was no attempt at reconciliation. Each felt their wrongs to be eternal as the rocks. At luncheon they looked unutterable things from different sides of the table; going into dinner, she cut him with the sweetest grace, and on the following morning they naturally removed to situations as remote from each other as the cubic area of a mail-steamer would allow.

"Pretty, very much so, but ill-mannered; not quite a lady, I should say," reflected Arthur to himself, with a superior smile.

"I detest him," said Mrs. Carr to herself; "at least, I think I do; but how neatly he put me down! There is no doubt about his being a gentleman, though insufferably conceited."

These uncharitable thoughts rankled in their respective minds about 12 A.M. What, then, was Arthur's disgust, on descending a little late to luncheon that day, to be informed by the resplendent chief-steward—who, for some undiscovered reason, always reminded him of Pharaoh's butler—that the captain had altered the places at table, and that this alteration involved his being placed next to none other than Mrs. Carr. Everybody was already seated, and it was too late to protest, at any rate for that meal; so he had to choose between submission and going without his luncheon.

Being extremely hungry, he decided for the first alternative, and reluctantly brought himself to a halt next his avowed enemy.

But surprises, like sorrows, come in battalions—a fact that he very distinctly realized when, having helped himself to some chicken, he heard a clear voice at his side address him by name.

"Mr. Heigham," said the voice, "I have not yet thanked you for your kindness to Miss Terry. I am commissioned to assure you that she is very grateful, since she is prevented by circumstances from doing so herself."

"I am much gratified," he replied, stiffly; "but really I did nothing to deserve thanks; and if I had," he added, with a touch of sarcasm, "I should not have expected any."

"Oh, what a cynic you must be!" she answered with a rippling laugh, "as though women, helpless as they are, were not always thankful for the tiniest attention. Did not the pretty girl with the black eyes thank you for your attentions yesterday, for instance?"

"Did the lady with the brown eyes thank me for my attentions —my very necessary attentions—yesterday, for instance?" he answered somewhat mollified, for the laugh and the voice would have thawed a human icicle, and, with all his faults, Arthur was not an icicle.

"No, she did not; she deferred doing so in order that she might do it better. It was very kind of you to help me, and I dare say that you saved my life, and I—I beg your pardon for being so cross, but being sea-sick always makes me cross, even to those who are kindest to me. Do you forgive me? Please forgive me; I really am quite unhappy when I think of my behavior." And Mrs. Carr shot a glance at him that would have cleared the North-West Passage for a man-of-war.

"Please don't apologize," he said, humbly. "I really have nothing to forgive. I am aware that I took a liberty, as you put it, but I thought that I was justified by the circumstances."

"It is not generous of you, Mr. Heigham, to throw my words into my teeth. I had forgotten all about them. But I will set your want of feeling against my want of gratitude, and we kiss and be friends."

"I can assure you, Mrs. Carr, that there is nothing in the world I should like better. When shall the ceremony come off?"

"Now you are laughing at me, and actually interpreting what I say literally, as though the English language were not full of figures of speech. By that phrase," and she blushed a little—that is, her cheek took a deeper shade of coral—"I meant that we would not cut each other after lunch."

"You bring me from the seventh heaven of expectation into a very prosaic world; but I accept your terms, whatever they are. I am conquered."

"For exactly half an hour. But let us talk sense. Are you going to stop at Madeira?"

"Yes."

"For how long?"

"I don't know; till I get tired of it, I suppose. Is it nice, Madeira?"

"Charming. I live there half the year."

"Ah! then I can well believe that it is charming."

"Mr. Heigham, you are paying compliments. I thought that you looked above that sort of thing."

"In the presence of misfortune and of beauty"—here he bowed—"all men are reduced to the same level. Talk to me from behind a curtain, or let me turn my back upon you, and you may expect to hear work-a-day prose; but face to face, I fear that you must put up with compliment."

"A neat way of saying that you have had enough of me. Your compliments are two-edged. Good-by for the present." And she rose, leaving Arthur—well, rather amused.

After this they saw a good deal of each other—that is to say, they conversed together for at least thirty minutes out of every sixty during an average day of fourteen hours, and in the course of these conversations she learned nearly everything about him, except his engagement to Angela, and she shrewdly guessed at that, or, rather, at some kindred circumstance in his career. Arthur, on the other hand, learned quite everything about her, for her life was open as the day, and would have borne reporting in the *Times* newspaper. But nevertheless he found it extremely interesting.

"You must be a busy woman," he said one morning, when he had been listening to one of her rattling accounts of her travels and gayeties, sprinkled over as it was with the shrewd remarks, and illumined by the keen insight into character, that made her talk so charming.

"Busy, no; one of the idlest in the world, and a very worthless one to boot," she answered, with a little sigh.

"Then why don't you change your life? it is in your own hands, if ever anybody's was."

"Do you think so? I doubt if anybody's life is in their own hands. We follow an appointed course; if we did not, it would be impossible to understand why so many sensible, clever people make such a complete mess of their existence. They can't do it from choice."

"At any rate, you have not made a mess of yours, and your appointed course seems a very pleasant one."

"Yes; and the sea beneath us is very smooth, but it has been rough before, and will be rough again—there is no stability in the sea. As to making a mess of my life, who knows what I may not accomplish in that way? Prosperity cannot shine down fear of the future, it only throws it into darker relief. Myself I am afraid of the future—it is unknown, and to me what is unknown is not magnificent, but terrible. The present is enough for me. I do not like speculation, and I never loved the dark."

And, as they talked, Madeira, in all its summer glory, loomed up out of the ocean, for they had passed the "Desertas" and "Porto Santo" by night, and for a while they were lost in the contemplation of one of the most lovely and verdant scenes that the world can show. Before they had well examined it, however, the vessel had dropped her anchor, and was surrounded by boats full of custom-house officials, boats full of diving boys, of vegetables, of wicker chairs and tables, of parrots, fruit, and "other articles too numerous to mention," as they say in the auctioneers' catalogues, and they knew that it was time to go ashore.

"Well, it has been a pleasant voyage," said Mrs. Carr. "I am glad you are not going on."

"So am I."

"You will come and see me to-morrow, will you not? Look, there is my house," and she pointed to a large white house opposite Leuw Rock, that had a background of glossy foliage, and commanded a view of the sea. "If you come, I will show you my beetles. And if you care to come next day, I will show you my mummies."

"And if I come the next, what will you show me?"

"So often as you may come," she said, with a little tremor in her voice, "I shall find something to show you."

Then they shook hands and took their respective ways, she—together with the unfortunate Miss Terry, who looked like a resuscitated corpse—in the steam-launch that was waiting for her, and he in the boat belonging to Miles's Hotel.

CHAPTER XXXIV.

A MINUTE or two after the boat in which Arthur was being piloted to the shore, under the guidance of the manager of Miles's Hotel, had left the side of the vessel, Mrs. Carr's steam-launch shot up alongside of them, its brass-work gleaming in the sunlight like polished gold. On the deck, near the little wheel, stood Mrs. Carr herself, and by her side, her martial cloak around her, lay Miss Terry, still as any log.

"Mr. Heigham," said Mrs. Carr, in a voice that sounded across the water like a silver bell, "I forgot that you will not be able to find your way to my place by yourself to-morrow, so I will send down a bullock-cart to fetch you; you have to travel about with bullocks here, you know. Good-by," and, before he could answer, the launch's head was round, and she was tearing through the swell at the rate of fourteen knots.

"That's her private launch," said the manager of the hotel to Arthur; "it is the quickest in the island, and she always goes at full steam. She must have come some way round to tell you that, too. There's her place, over there."

"Mrs. Carr comes here every year, does she not?"

"Oh, yes, every year; but she is very early this year; our season does not begin yet, you know. She is a great blessing to the place, she gives so much away to the poor peasants. At first she used to come with old Mr. Carr, and a wonderful nurse they say she made the old gentleman till he died."

"Does she entertain much?"

"Not as a rule, but sometimes she gives great balls, splendid affairs, and a series of dinner-parties that are the talk of the island. She hardly ever goes out anywhere, which makes the ladies in the place angry, but I believe that they all go to her balls and dinners. Mostly, she spends her time up in the hills, collecting butterflies and beetles. She has got the most wonderful collection of Egyptian curiosities up at the house there, too, though why she keeps them here instead of in England I am sure I don't know. Her husband began the collection when he was a young man, and collected all his life, and she has gone on with it since."

"I wonder that she has not married again."

"Well, it can't be for want of asking, if half of what they say is true; for, according to that, every single gentleman under fifty who has been at Madeira during the last five years has had a try at her, but she wouldn't look at one of them. But of course that is gossip—and here we are at the landing-place. Sit steady, sir; those fellows will pull the boat up."

Had it not been for the preoccupied and uncomfortable state of his mind, that took the flavor out of all that he did, and persistently thrust a skeleton amidst the flowers of every landscape, Arthur should by rights have enjoyed himself very much at Madeira.

To live in one of the lofty rooms of "Miles's Hotel," protected by thick walls and cool, green shutters, to feel that you are enjoying all the advantages of a warm climate without its drawbacks, and that, too, however much people in England may be shivering—which they mostly do all the year round—is in itself a luxury. And so it is, if the day is hot, to dine chiefly off fish and fruit, and such fruit! and then to exchange the dining-room for the cool portico, with the sea-breeze sweeping through it, and, pipe in hand, to sink into a slumber that even the diabolical shrieks of the parrots, tied by the leg in a line below, are powerless to disturb. Or if you be energetic—I speak of Madeira energy—you may stroll down the little terraced walk, under the shade of your landlord's vines, and contemplate the glowing mass of greenery that in this heavenly island makes a garden. You can do more than this, even; for, having penetrated through the brilliant flower-beds, and recruited exhausted nature under a fig-tree, you can engage, in true English fashion, in a game of lawn-tennis, which done you will again seek the shade of the creeping vines or spreading bananas, and in a springy hammock take your well-earned repose.

All these things are the quintessence of luxury, so much so that he who has once enjoyed them will long to turn lotus-eater, forget the painful and laborious past, and live and die at "Miles's Hotel." O Madeira! gem of the ocean, land of pine-clad mountains that foolish men love to climb, valleys where wise ones much prefer to to rest, and of smells that both alike abhor; Madeira of the sunny sky and azure sea, land flowing with milk and honey, and overflowing with population, if only you belonged to the country on which you depend for a livelihood, what a perfect place you would be, and how poetical one could grow about you!—a consummation which, fortunately for my readers, the recollection of the open drains, the ill-favored priests and Pòrtuguese officials effectually prevents.

On the following morning, at twelve punctually, Arthur was informed that the conveyance had arrived to fetch him. He went down, and was quite appalled at its magnificence. It was sledge-like in form, built to hold four, and mounted on wooden runners that glided over the round pebbles with which the Madeira streets are paved, with scarcely a sound, and as smoothly as though they ran on ice. The chariot, as Arthur always called it afterwards, was built of beautiful woods, and lined and curtained throughout with satin, whilst the motive power was supplied by two splendidly-harnessed white oxen. Two native servants, handsome young fellows, dressed in a kind of white uniform, accompanied the sledge, and saluted Arthur on his appearance with much reverence.

It took him, however, some time before he could make up his mind to embark in a conveyance that reminded him of the description of Cleopatra's galley, and smelt more sweet; but finally he got in, and off he started, feeling that he was the observed of all observers, and followed by at least a score of beggars, each afflicted with some peculiar and dreadful deformity or disease. And thus, in triumphal guise, they slid down the quaint and narrow streets, squeezed in for the sake of shade between a double line of tall, green-shuttered houses; over the bridges that span the vast open drains; past the ochre-colored cathedral; down the promenade, edged with great magnolia-trees, that made the air heavy with their perfume, and where twice a week the band plays, and the Portuguese officials march up and down in all the pomp and panoply of office; onward through the dip, where the town slopes downwards to the sea; then up again through more streets, and past a stretch of dead wall, after which the chariot wheels through some iron gates, and he is in fairyland. On each side of the carriage-way there spreads a garden calculated to make English horticulturists gnash their teeth with envy, through the bowers of which he could catch peeps of green turf and of the blue sea beyond.

Here the cabbage-palm shot its smooth and lofty trunk high into the air, there the bamboo waved its leafy ostrich-plumes, and all about and around the soil was spread like an Indian shawl, with many a gorgeous flower and many a splendid fruit. Arthur thought of the Garden of Eden and the Isles of the Blest, and whilst his eyes, accustomed to nothing better than our poor English roses, were still fixed upon the blazing masses of pomegranate-flower, and his senses were filled with the sweet scent of orange and magnolia blooms, the oxen halted before the portico of a stately building, white-walled and green-shuttered like all Madeira houses.

Then the slaves of the chariot assisted him to descend, whilst other slaves of the door bowed him up the steps, and he stood in a great cool hall, dazzling dark after the brilliancy of the sunlight. And here no slave awaited him, but the princess of this fair domain—none other than Mildred Carr herself, clad all in summer white, and with a smile of welcome in her eyes.

"I am so glad that you have come. How do you like Madeira? Do you find it very hot?"

"I have not seen much of it yet; but this place is lovely; it is like fairyland, and I believe that you," he added, with a bow, "are the fairy queen."

"Compliments again, Mr. Heigham. Well, I was the sleeping beauty last time, so one may as well be a queen for a change. I wonder what you will call me next?"

"Let me see: shall we say—an angel?"

"Mr. Heigham, stop talking nonsense, and come into the drawing-room."

He followed her, laughing, into an apartment that, from its noble proportions and beauty, might fairly be called magnificent. Its ceiling was panelled with worked timber, and its floor beautifully inlaid with woods of various hue, whilst the walls were thickly covered with pictures, chiefly sea-pieces, and all by good masters. He had, however, but little time to look about him, for a door opened at the further end of the room and admitted the portly person of Miss Terry, arrayed in a gigantic sun-hat and a pair of green spectacles. She seemed very hot, and held in her hand a piece of brown paper, inside of which something was violently scratching.

"I've caught him at last," she said, "though he did avoid me all last year. I've caught him."

"Good gracious! caught what?" asked Arthur, with great interest.

"What! why him that Mildred wanted," she replied, regardless of grammar in her excitement. "Just look at him, he's beautiful."

Thus admonished, Arthur carefully undid the brown paper, and next moment started back with an exclamation, and began to dance about with an enormous red beetle grinding its jaws into his finger.

"Oh, keep still, do, pray!" called Miss Terry, in alarm, "don't shake him off on any account, or we shall lose him for the want of a little patience, as I did when he bit my finger last year. If you'll keep him quite still, he won't leave go, and I'll ring for John to bring the chloroform-bottle."

Arthur, feeling that the interests of science were matters of a higher importance than the well-being of his finger, obeyed her injunction to the letter, hanging his arm (and the beetle) over the back of a chair, and looking the picture of silent misery.

"Quite still, if you please, Mr. Heigham, quite still; is not the animal's tenacity interesting?"

"No doubt to you, but I hope your pet beetle is not poisonous, for he is gnashing his pincers together inside my finger."

"Never mind, we will treat you with caustic presently. Mildred, don't laugh so much, but come and look at him; he's lovely. John, please be quick with that chloroform-bottle."

"If this sort of thing happens often, I don't think that I should collect beetles from choice, at least not large ones," groaned Arthur.

"Oh, dear!" laughed Mrs. Carr, "I never saw anything so absurd. I don't know which looks most savage, you or the beetle."

"Don't make all that noise, Mildred, you will frighten him; and if once he flies, we shall never catch him in this big room."

Here, fortunately for Arthur, the servant arrived with the required bottle, into which the ferocious insect was triumphantly stoppered by Miss Terry.

"I am so much obliged to you, Mr. Heigham, you are a true collector."

"For the first and last time," mumbled Arthur, who was sucking his finger.

"I am infinitely obliged to you, too, Mr. Heigham," said Mrs. Carr, as soon as she had recovered from her fit of laughing; "the beetle is really very rare; it is not even in the British Museum. But come, let us go in to luncheon."

After that meal was over, Mrs. Carr asked her guest which he would like to see, her collection of beetles or of mummies.

"Thank you, Mrs. Carr, I have had enough of beetles for one day, so I vote for the mummies."

"Very well. Will you come, Agatha?"

"Now, Mildred, you know very well that I won't come. Just think, Mr. Heigham: I only saw the nasty things once, and then they gave me the creeps every night for a fortnight. As though those horrid Egyptian 'fellahs' weren't ugly enough when they are alive, without going and making great skin-and-bone dolls of them —pah!"

"Agatha persists in believing that my mummies are the bodies of people like she saw in Egypt last year."

"And so they are, Mildred. That last one you got is just like the boy who used to drive my donkey at Cairo—the one that died, you know—I believe they just stuffed him, and said that he was an ancient king. Ancient king, indeed!" And Miss Terry departed in search for more beetles.

"Now, Mr. Heigham, you must follow me. The museum is not in the house. Wait, I will get a hat."

In a minute she returned, and led the way across a strip of garden to a detached building, with a broad veranda, facing the sea. Scarcely ten feet from this veranda, and on the edge of the sheer precipice, was built a low wall, leaning over which Arthur could hear the wavelets lapping against the hollow rock two hundred feet beneath him. Here they stopped for a moment to look at the vast expanse of ocean, glittering in the sunlight like a sea of molten sapphires and heaving as gently as an infant's bosom.

"It is very lovely; the sea moves just enough to show that it is only asleep."

"Yes; but I like it best when it is awake, when it blows a hurricane—it is magnificent. The whole cliff shakes with the shock of the waves, and sometimes the spray drives over in sheets. That is when I like to sit here; it exhilarates me, and makes me feel as though I belonged to the storm, and was strong with its strength. Come, let us go in."

The entrance to the veranda was from the end that faced the house, and to gain it they passed under the boughs of a large magnolia-tree. Going through glass doors that opened outwards into the veranda, Mrs. Carr entered a room luxuriously furnished as a boudoir. This had apparently no other exit, and Arthur was beginning to wonder where the museum could be, when she took a tiny bramah key from her watch-chain, and with it opened a door that was papered and painted to match the wall exactly. He followed her, and found himself in a stone passage, dimly lighted from above, and sloping downwards, that led to a doorway graven in the rock, on the model of those to be seen at the entrance of Egyptian temples.

"Now, Mr. Heigham," she said, flinging open another door, and stepping forward, "you are about to enter 'The Hall of the Dead.'"

He went in, and a strange sight met his gaze. They were standing in the centre of one side of a vast cave, that ran right and left at right angles to the passage. The light poured into it in great rays from skylights in the roof, and by it he could see that it was hollowed out of the virgin rock, and measured some sixty feet or more in length, by about forty wide, and thirty high. Down the length of each side of the great chamber ran a line of six polished sphinxes, which had been hewn out of the surrounding granite, on the model of those at Carnac, whilst the walls were elaborately painted after the fashion of an Egyptian sepulchre. Here Osiris held his dread tribunal on the spirit of the departed; here the warrior sped onward in his charging chariot; here the harper swept his sounding chords; and here, again, crowned with lotus-flowers, those whose corpses lay around held their joyous festivals.

In the respective centres of each end of the stone chamber a colossus towered in its silent and unearthly grandeur. That to the right was a statue of Osiris, judge of the souls of the dead, seated on his judgment-seat, and holding in his hand the scourge and the bent-headed sceptre. Facing him at the other end of the hall was the effigy of the mighty Ramses, his broad brow encircled by that kingly symbol which few in the world's history have worn so proudly, and his noble features impressing those who gaze upon them from age to age with a sense of scornful power and melancholy calm, such as does not belong to the countenances of the men of their own time. And all around, under this solemn guardianship, each upon a polished slab of marble, and inclosed in a case of thick glass, lay the corpses of the Egyptian dead, swathed in numberless wrappings, as in their day the true religion that they held was swathed in symbols and in mummeries.

Here were to be found the high-priest of the mysteries of Isis the astronomer whose lore could read the prophecies that are written in the stars, the dark magician, the renowned warrior, the noble, the musician with his cymbals by his side, the fair maiden who had—so said her cedar coffin-boards—died of love and sorrow, and the royal babe, all sleeping the same sleep, and waiting the same awakening. This princess must have been well known to Joseph; that may have been her who rescued Moses from the waters, whilst the babe belongs to a dynasty of which the history was already merging into tradition when the great pyramid reared its head on Egypt's fertile plains.

Arthur stood, awed at the wonderful sight.

"Never before," said he, in that whisper which we involuntarily use in the presence of the dead, "did I realize my own insignificance."

The thought was abruptly put, but the words represented well what was passing in his mind, what must pass in the mind of any man of culture and sensibility when he gazes on such a sight. For in such presences the human mite of to-day, fluttering in the sun and walking on the earth that these have known and walked four thousand years ago, must indeed learn how infinitely small is the place that he occupies in the tale of things created; and yet, if to his culture and sensibility he adds religion, a word of living hope hovers on those dumb lips. For where are the spirits of those that lie before him in their eternal silence? Answer, withered lips, and tell us what judgment has Osiris given, and what has Thoth written in his awful book? Four thousand years! Old human husk, if thy dead carcass can last so long, what limit is there to the life of the soul it held?

"Did you collect all these?" asked Arthur, when he had made a superficial examination of the almost countless treasures of the museum.

"Oh, no; Mr. Carr spent half of his long life, and more money than I can tell you, in getting this collection together. It was the passion of his life, and he had this cave hollowed at enormous cost, because he thought that the air here would be less likely to injure them than the English fogs. I have added to it, however. I got those papyri and that beautiful bust of Berenice, the one in black marble. Did you ever see such hair?"

Arthur thought to himself that he had at that moment some not far from his heart that must be quite as beautiful, but he did not say so.

"Look, here are some curious things;" and she opened an air-tight case that contained some discolored grains and a few lumps of shrivelled substance.

"What are they?"

"This is wheat taken from the inside of a mummy, and those are supposed to be hyacinth-bulbs. They came from the mummy-case of that baby prince, and I have been told that they would still grow if planted."

"I can scarcely believe that: the principle of life must be extinct."

"Wise people say, you know, that the principle of life can never become extinct in anything that has once lived, though it may change its form; but I do not pretend to understand these things. However, we will settle the question, for we will plant one, and, if it grows, I will give the flower to you. Choose one."

Arthur took the biggest lump from the case, and examined it curiously.

"I have not much faith in your hyacinth; I am sure that it is dead."

"Ah! but many things that seem more dead than that have the strangest way of suddenly breaking into life," she said, with a little sigh. "Give it to me; I will have it planted;" and then, with a quick glance upwards, "I wonder if you will be here to see it bloom."

"I don't think that either of us will see it bloom in this world," he answered, laughing, and took his leave.

CHAPTER XXXV.

HAD Arthur been a little less wrapped up in thoughts of Angela, and a little more alive to the fact that being engaged or even married to one woman does not necessarily prevent complications arising with another, it might have occurred to him to doubt the prudence of the course of life that he was pursuing at Madeira. And, as it is, it is impossible to acquit him of showing a want of knowledge of the world amounting almost to folly, for he should have known upon general principles that, for a man in his position, a grizzly bear would have been a safer daily companion than a young and lovely widow, and the North Pole a more suitable place of residence than Madeira. But he simply did not think about the matter, and, as thin ice has a treacherous way of not cracking till it suddenly breaks, so outward appearances gave him no indication of his danger.

And yet the facts were full of evil promise, for, as time went on, Mildred Carr fell headlong in love with him. There was no particular reason why she should have done so. She might have had scores of men, handsomer, cleverer, more distinguished, for the asking, or, rather, for the waiting to be asked. Beyond a certain ability of mind, a taking manner, and a sympathetic, thoughtful face, with that tinge of melancholy upon it which women sometimes find dangerously interesting, there was nothing so remarkable about Arthur that a woman possessing her manifold attractions and opportunities, should, unsought and without inquiry, lavish her affection upon him. There is only one satisfactory explanation of the phenomenon, which, indeed, is a very common one, and that is, that he was her fate, the one man whom she was to love in the world, for no woman worth the name ever *loves* two, however many she may happen to marry. For this curious difference would appear to exist between the sexes. The man can attach himself, though in a varying degree, to several women in the course of a lifetime, whilst the woman, the true, pure-hearted woman, cannot so adapt her best affection. Once given, like the law of the Medes and Persians it altereth not.

Mildred felt, when her eyes first met Arthur's in Donald Currie's office, that this man was for her different from all other men, though she did not put the thought in words even to herself. And from that hour till she embarked on board the boat he was continually in her mind, a fact which so irritated her that she nearly missed the steamer on purpose, only changing her mind at the last moment. And then, when she had helped him to carry Miss Terry to her cabin, their hands had accidentally met, and the contact had sent a thrill through her frame such as she had never felt before. The next development that she could trace was her jealousy of the black-eyed girl whom she saw him helping about the deck, and her consequent rudeness.

Up to her present age Mildred Carr had never known a single touch of love; she had not even felt particularly interested in her numerous admirers; but now this marble Galatea had by some freak of fate found a woman's heart, awkwardly enough, without the semblance of a supplication on the part of him whom she destined to play Pygmalion. And when she examined herself by the light of the flame thus newly kindled, she shrank back dismayed, like one who peeps over the crater of a volcano commencing its fiery work. She had believed her heart to be callous to all affection of this nature; it had seemed as dead as the mummied hyacinth: and now it was a living, suffering thing, and all alight with love. She had tasted of a new wine, and it burnt her, and was bitter-sweet, and yet she longed for more. And thus, by slow and sad degrees, she learned that her life, which had for thirty years flowed on its quiet way unshadowed by Love's wing, must henceforth own his dominion, and be a slave to his sorrows and caprices. No wonder that she grew afraid!

But Mildred was a woman of keen insight into character, and it did not require that her powers of observation should be sharpened by the condition of her affections to show her that, however deeply she might be in love with Arthur Heigham, he was not one little bit in love with her. Knowing the almost irresistible strength of her own beauty and attractions, she quickly came to the conclusion —and it was one that sent a cold chill through her—that there must be some other woman blocking the path to his heart. For some reason or other, Arthur had never spoken to her of Angela, either because a man very rarely volunteers information to a woman concerning his existing relationship with another of her sex, knowing that to do so would be to depreciate his value in her eyes, or from an instinctive knowledge that the subject would not be an agreeable one, or perhaps because the whole matter was too sacred to him. But she, on her part, was determined to probe his secret to the bottom. So one sleepy afternoon, when they were sitting on the museum veranda, about six weeks after the date of their arrival in the island, she took her opportunity.

Mildred was sitting, or rather half lying, in a cane-work chair, gazing out over the peaceful sea, and Arthur, looking at her, thought what a lovely little woman she was, and wondered what it was that had made her face and eyes so much softer and more attractive of late. Miss Terry was also there, complaining of the heat, but presently she moved off after an imaginary beetle, and they were alone.

"Oh, by-the-bye, Mr. Heigham," Mildred said presently, "I was going to ask you a question, if only I can remember what it is."

"Try to remember what it is about. 'Shoes, sealing-wax, cabbages, or kings.' Does it come under any of those heads?"

"Ah, I remember now. If you had added 'queens,' you would not have been far out. What I wanted to ask you—" and she turned her large brown eyes full upon him, and yawned slightly. "Dear me, Agatha is right; it *is* hot!"

"Well, I am waiting to give you any information in my power."

"Oh! to be sure, the question. Well, it is a very simple one. Who are you engaged to?"

Arthur nearly sprang off his chair with astonishment.

"What makes you think that I am engaged?" he asked.

She broke into a merry peal of laughter. Ah! if he could have known what that laugh cost her.

"What makes me think that you are engaged!" she answered, in a tone of raillery. "Why, of course you would have been at my feet long ago if it had not been so. Come, don't be reticent. I shall not laugh at you. What is she like?" (Generally a woman's first question about a rival.) "Is she as good-looking—well, as I am, say—for, though you may not think it, I have been thought good-looking."

"She is quite different from you; she is very tall and fair, like an angel in a picture, you know."

"Oh! then there is a 'she,' and a 'she like an angel.' Very different *indeed* from me, I should think. How nicely I caught you out;" and she laughed again.

"Why did you want to catch me out?" said Arthur, on whose ear Mrs. Carr's tone jarred; he could not tell why.

"Feminine curiosity, and a natural anxiety to fathom the reasons of your sighs, that is all. But never mind, Mr. Heigham, you and I shall not quarrel because you are engaged to be married. You shall tell me the story when you like, for I am sure there is a story—no, not this afternoon; the sun has given me a headache, and I am going to sleep it off. Other people's love-stories are very interesting to me, the more so because I have reached the respectable age of thirty without being the subject of one myself;" and again she laughed, this time at her own falsehood. But when he had gone there was no laughter in her eyes, nothing but tears, bitter, burning tears.

"Agatha," said Mildred that evening, "I am sick of this place. I want to go to the Isle of Wight. It must be quite nice there now. We will go by the next Currie boat."

"My dear Mildred," replied Miss Terry, aghast, "if you were going back so soon, why did you not leave me behind you? And just as we were getting so nicely settled here too, and I shall be so sorry to say good-by to that young Heigham, he is such a nice young man! Why don't you marry him? I really thought you liked him. But perhaps he is coming to the Isle of Wight too. Oh, that dreadful bay!"

Mildred winced at Miss Terry's allusions to Arthur, of whom that lady had grown extremely fond.

"I am very sorry, dear," she said, hastily; "but I am bored to death, and it is such a bad insect year: so really you must begin to pack up."

Miss Terry began to pack up accordingly, but when next she alluded to the subject of their departure Mildred affected surprise, and asked her what she meant. The astonished Agatha referred her to her own words, and was met by a laughing disclaimer.

"Why, you surely did not think that I was in earnest, did you? I was only a little cross."

"Well, really, Mildred, you've got so strange lately, that I never know when you are in earnest and when you are not, though, for my part, I am very glad to stay in peace and quiet."

"Strange, grown strange, have I!" said Mrs. Carr, looking dreamily out of a window that commanded the carriage-drive, with her hands crossed behind her. "Yes, I think that you are right. I think that I have lost the old Mildred somewhere or other, and picked up a new one whom I don't understand."

"Ah, indeed," remarked Miss Terry, in the most matter-of-fact way, without having the faintest idea of what her friend was driving at.

"How it rains! I suppose that he won't come to-day."

"He! Who's he?"

"Why, how stupid you are! Mr. Heigham, of course!"

"So you always mean him when you say 'he!'"

"Yes, of course I do, if it isn't ungrammatical. It is miserable this afternoon. I feel wretched. Why, actually, here he comes!" and she tore off like a school-girl into the hall, to meet him.

"Ah, indeed!" again remarked Miss Terry, solemnly, to the empty walls. "I am not such a fool as I look. I suppose that Mr. Heigham wouldn't come to the Isle of Wight."

It is perhaps needless to say that Mrs. Carr had never been more in earnest in her life than when she announced her intention of departing to the Isle of Wight. The discovery that her suspicions about Arthur had but too sure a foundation had been a crushing blow to her hopes, and she had formed a wise resolution to see no more of him. Happy would it have been for her if she could have found the moral courage to act up to it, and go away, a wiser, if a sadder, woman. But this was not to be. The more she contemplated it, the more did her passion—which was now both wild and deep—take hold upon her heart, eating into it like acid into steel, and graving one name there in ineffacable letters. She could not bear the thought of parting from him, and felt, or thought she felt, that her happiness was already too deeply pledged to allow her to throw up the cards without an effort.

Fortune favors the brave. Perhaps, after all, it would declare itself for her. She was modest in her aspirations. She did not expect that he would ever give her the love he bore this other woman; she only asked to live in the sunlight of his presence, and would be glad to take him at his own price, or indeed at any price. Man, she knew, is by nature as unstable as water, and will mostly melt beneath the eyes of more women than one, as readily as ice before a fire when the sun has hid his face. Yes, she would play the game out: she would not throw away her life's happiness without an effort. After all, matters might have been worse: he might have been actually married.

But she knew that her hand was a difficult one to lead from, though she also knew that she held the great trumps—unusual beauty, practically unlimited wealth, and considerable fascination of manner. Her part must be to attract without repelling, charm without alarming, fascinate by slow degrees, till at length he was involved in a net from which there was no escape, and, above all, never to allow him to suspect her motives till the ripe moment came. It was a hard task for a proud woman to set herself, and in a manner, she was proud; but, alas! with the best of us, when love comes in at the door, pride, reason, and sometimes honor, fly out of the window.

And so Miss Terry heard no more talk of the Isle of Wight.

Thenceforward, under the frank and open guise of friendship, Mildred contrived to keep Arthur continually at her side. She did more. She drew from him all the history of his engagement to Angela, and listened, with words of sympathy on her lips, and wrath and bitter jealousy in her heart, to his enraptured descriptions of her rival's beauty and perfections. So benighted was he, indeed, that once he went so far as to suggest that he should, when he and Angela were married, come to Madeira to spend their honeymoon, and dilated on the pleasant trips which they three might take together.

"Truly," thought Mildred to herself, "that would be delightful."

Once, too, he even showed her a tress of Angela's hair, and, strange to say, she found that there still lingered in her bosom a sufficient measure of vulgar first principles to cause her to long to snatch it from him and throw it into the sea. But, as it was, she smiled faintly, and admired openly, and then went to the glass to look at her own nut-brown tresses. Never had she been so dissatisfied with them, and yet her hair was considered lovely, and an æsthetic hair-dresser had once called it a "poem."

"Blind fool!" she muttered, stamping her little foot upon the floor, "why does he torture me so?"

Mildred forgot that all love is blind, and that none was ever blinder or more headstrong than her own.

And so this second Calypso of a lovely isle set herself almost as unblushingly as her prototype to get our very unheroic Ulysses into her toils. And Penelope, poor Penelope, she sat at home and span, and defied her would-be lovers.

But as yet Ulysses—I mean Arthur—was conscious of none of these things. He was by nature an easy-going young gentleman, who took matters as he found them, and asked no questions. And he found them very pleasant at Madeira, or rather at the Quinta Carr, for he did everything except sleep there. Within its precincts he was everywhere surrounded with that atmosphere of subtle and refined flattery, flattery addressed chiefly to the intellect, that is one of the most effective weapons of a clever woman. Soon the drawing-room tables were loaded with his favorite books, and no songs but such as he approved were ordered from London.

He discovered one evening, for instance, that Mildred looked best at night in black and silver, and next morning Mr. Worth received a telegram requesting him to forward without delay a large consignment of dresses in which those colors predominated. On another occasion he casually threw out a suggestion about the erection of a terrace in the garden, and shortly afterwards was surprised to find a small army of Portuguese laborers engaged upon the work. He had made this suggestion in total ignorance of the science of garden-engineering, and its execution necessitated the removal of vast quantities of soil and the blasting of many tons of rock. The contractor employed by Mrs. Carr pointed out how the terrace could be made equally well at a fifth of the expense, but it did not happen to take exactly the direction that Arthur had indicated, so she would have none of it. His word was law, and, because he had spoken, the whole place was for a month overrun with dirty laborers, whilst, to the great detriment of Miss Terry's remaining nerves, and even to the slight discomfort of His Royal Highness himself, the air resounded all day long with the terrific bangs of the blasting-powder.

But, so long as he was pleased with the progress of the improvement, Mildred felt no discomfort, nor would she allow any one else to express any. It even aggravated her to see Miss Terry put her hands to her head and jump whenever a particularly large piece of ordnance was discharged, and she would vow that it must be affectation because she never even noticed it.

In short, Mildred Carr possessed to an extraordinary degree

that faculty for blind, unreasoning adoration which is so characteristic of the sex, an adoration that is at once magnificent in the entirety of its own self-sacrifice and extremely selfish. When she thought that she could please Arthur, the state of Agatha's nerves became a matter of supreme indifference to her, and in the same way, had she been an absolute monarch, she would have spent the lives of thousands, and shaken empires till thrones came tumbling down like apples in a wind, if she had believed that she could thereby advance herself in his affections.

But, as it never occurred to Arthur that Mrs. Carr might be in love with him, he saw nothing abnormal about all this. Not that he was conceited, for nobody was ever less so, but it is wonderful what an amount of flattery and attention men will accept from women as their simple right. If the other sex possesses the faculty of admiration, we in compensation are perfectly endowed with that of receiving it with careless ease, and when we fall in with some goddess who is foolish enough to worship *us*, and to whom *we* should be on our knees, we merely label her "sympathetic," and say that she "understands us."

From all of which wise reflections the reader will gather that our friend Arthur was not a hundred miles from an awkward situation.

CHAPTER XXXVI.

One day, some three weeks after Arthur had gone, Angela strolled down the tunnel-walk, now, in the height of summer, almost dark with the shade of the lime-trees, and settled herself on one of the stone seats under Caresfoot's Staff.

She had a book in hand, but it soon became clear that she had come to this secluded spot to think rather than read, for it fell unopened from her hand, and her gray eyes were full of a far-off look as they gazed across the lake glittering in the sunlight, away towards the hazy purple outline of the distant hills. Her face was quite calm, but it was not that of a happy person; indeed, it gave a distinct idea of mental suffering. All grief, however acute, is subject to fixed gradations, and Angela was as yet in the second stage. First there is the acute stage, when the heart aches with a physical pain, and the mind, filled with a wild yearning or tortured by an unceasing anxiety, well-nigh gives beneath the abnormal strain. This does not last long, or it would kill or drive us to the mad-house. Then comes that long epoch of dull misery, enduring till at last kindly nature in pity rubs off the rough extremes of our calamity, and by slow but sure degrees softens agony into sorrow.

This was what she was now passing through, and—as all highly-organized natures like her own are, especially in youth, very sensitive to those more exquisite vibrations of pain and happiness that leave minds of a coarser fibre comparatively unmoved—it may be taken for granted that she was suffering sufficiently acutely.

Perhaps she had never quite realized how necessary Arthur had become to her, how deep his love had sent its fibres into her heart and inner self until he was violently wrenched away from her and she lost all sight and knowledge of him in the darkness of the outside world. Still she had made no show of her sorrow; but once, when Pigott told her some pathetic story of the death of a little child in the village, she burst into a paroxysm of weeping. The pity for another's pain had loosed the floodgates of her own, but it was a performance that she did not repeat.

But Angela had her anxieties as well as her griefs, and it was over these former that she was thinking as she sat on the great stone under the oak. Love is a wonderful quickener of the perceptions, and, ignorant as she was of all the world's ways, the more she thought over the terms imposed by her father upon her engagement, the more distrustful did she grow. Lady Bellamy, too, had been to see her twice, and on each occasion had inspired her with a lively sense of fear and repugnance. During the first of these visits she had shown a perfect acquaintance with the circumstances of her engagement, her "flirtation with Mr. Heigham," as she was pleased to call it. During the second call, too, she had been full of strange remarks about her cousin George, talking mysteriously of a "change" that had come over him since his illness, and of his being under a "new influence." Nor was this all; for, on the very next day when she was out walking with Pigott in the village, she had met George himself, and he had insisted upon entering into a long rambling conversation with her, and on looking at her in a way that made her feel perfectly sick.

"Oh, Aleck," she said, aloud, to the dog that was sitting by her side with his head upon her knee, for he was now her constant companion, "I wonder where your master is, your master and mine, Aleck. Would to God that he were back here to protect me, for I am growing afraid, I don't know of what, Aleck, and there are eleven long silent months to wait." At this moment the dog raised his head, listened, and sprang round with an angry "woof." Angela rose up with a flash of hope in her eyes, turned, and faced George Caresfoot.

He was still pale and shrivelled from the effects of his illness, but otherwise little changed, except that the light-blue eyes glittered with a fierce determination, and that the features had attained that fixity and strength which sometimes come to those who are bent heart and soul upon an enterprise, be it good or evil.

"So I have found you out at last, Cousin Angela. What, are you not going to shake hands with me?"

Angela touched his fingers with her own.

"My father is not here," she said.

"Thank you, my dear cousin, but I did not come to see your father, of whom I have seen plenty in the course of my life, and shall doubtless see more; I came to see you, of whom I can never see enough."

"I don't understand you," said Angela, defiantly, folding her arms across her bosom and looking him full in the face with fearless eyes, for her instinct warned her that she was in danger, and also that, whatever she might feel, she must not show that she was afraid.

"I shall hope to make you do so before long," he replied, with a meaning glance; "but you are not very polite; you do not offer me a seat."

"I beg your pardon, I did not know that you wanted to sit down. I can only offer you a choice of those stones."

"Then call that brute away, and I will sit down."

"The dog is not a brute, as you mean it. But I should not speak of him like that, if I were you. He is sensible as a human being, and might resent it."

Angela knew that George was a coward about dogs; and at that moment, as though to confirm her words, Aleck growled slightly.

"Ah, indeed; well, he is certainly a handsome dog;" and he sat down suspiciously. "Won't you come and sit down?"

"Thank you. I prefer to stand."

"Do you know what you look like, standing there with your arms crossed? You look like an angry goddess."

"If you mean that seriously, I don't understand you. If it is a compliment, I don't like compliments."

"You are not very friendly," said George, whose temper was fast getting the better of him.

"I am sorry. I do not wish to be unfriendly."

"So I hear that my ward has been staying here whilst I was ill."

"Yes, he was staying here."

"And I am also told that there was some boy-and-girl love affair between you. I suppose that he indulged in a flirtation to while away the time."

Angela turned upon him, too angry to speak.

"Well, you need not look at me like that. You surely never expect to see him again, do you?"

"If we both live, I shall certainly see him again; indeed, I shall in any case."

"You will never see him again."

"Why not?"

"Because he was only flirting and playing the fool with you. He is a notorious flirt, and, to my certain knowledge, has been engaged to two women before."

"I do not believe that that is true, or, if it is true, it is not all the truth; but, true or untrue, I am not going to discuss Mr. Heigham with you, or allow myself to be influenced by stories told behind his back."

"Angela," said George, rising, and seizing her hand.

She turned quite pale, and a shudder passed over her frame.

"Leave my hand alone, and never dare to touch me again. This is the second time that you have tried to insult me."

"So!" answered George, furious with outraged pride and baffled passion, "you set up your will against mine, do you? Very well, you shall see. I will crush you to powder. Insult you, indeed! How often did that young blackguard insult you? I warrant he did more than take your hand."

"If," answered Angela, "you mean Mr. Heigham, I shall leave you to consider whether that term is not more applicable to the person who does his best to outrage an unprotected woman, and take advantage of the absent, than to the gentleman against whom you have used it;" and, darting on him one glance of supreme contempt, she swept away like an angry queen.

Left to his meditations, George shook his fist towards where she had vanished.

"Very well, my fine lady, very well," he said, aloud. "You treat me as so much dirt, do you? You shall smart for this, so sure as my name is George Caresfoot. Only wait till you are in my power, and you shall learn that I was never yet defied with impunity. Oh, and you shall learn many other things also."

From that time forward, Angela was, for a period of two months or more, subjected to an organized persecution as harassing as it was cruel. George waylaid her everywhere, and twice actually succeeded in entering into conversation with her, but on both occasions she managed to escape from him before he could proceed any further. So persistently did he hunt her, that at last the wretched girl was driven to hide herself away in odd corners of the house and woods, in order to keep out of his way. Then he took to writing her letters and sending handsome presents, all of which she returned.

Poor Angela! It was hard both to lose her lover and to suffer daily from the persecutions of her hateful cousin, which were now pushed forward so openly and with such pertinacity as to fill her with vague alarm. What made her position worse was that she had no one in whom to confide, for Mr. Fraser had not yet returned. Pigott indeed knew more or less what was going on, but she could do nothing, except bewail Arthur's absence, and tell her "not to mind." There remained her father, but with him she had never been on sufficiently intimate terms for confidences. Indeed, as time went on, the suspicion gathered strength in her mind that he was privy to George's advances, and that those advances had something to do with the harsh terms imposed upon Arthur and herself. But at last matters grew so bad that, having no other refuge, she determined to appeal to him for protection.

"Father," she said, boldly, one day to Philip, as he was sitting writing in his study, "my cousin George is persecuting me every day. I have borne it as long as I can, but I can bear it no longer. I have come to ask you to protect me from him."

"Why, Angela, I should have thought that you were perfectly capable of protecting yourself. What is he persecuting you about? What does he want?"

"To marry me, I suppose," answered Angela, blushing to her eyes.

"Well, that is a very complimentary wish on his part, and I can tell you what it is, Angela, if only you could get that young Heigham out of your head, you might do a deal worse."

"It is quite useless to talk to me like that," she answered, coldly.

"Well, that is your affair; but it is very ridiculous of you to come and ask me to protect you. The woman must, indeed, be a fool who cannot protect herself."

And so the interview ended.

Next day Lady Bellamy called again.

"My dear child," she said to Angela, "you are not looking well; this business worries you, no doubt; it is the old struggle between duty and inclination that we have most of us gone through. Well, there is one consolation, nobody who ever did his or her duty, regardless of inclination, ever regretted it in the end."

"What do you mean, Lady Bellamy, when you talk about my duty?"

"I mean the plain duty that lies before you of marrying your cousin George, and of throwing up this young Heigham."

"I recognize no such duty."

"My dear Angela, do look at the matter from a sensible point of view; think what a good thing it would be for your father, and remember, too, that it would reunite all the property. If ever a girl had a clear duty to perform, you have."

"Since you insist so much upon my 'duty,' I must say that it seems to me that an honest girl in my position has three duties to consider, and not one, as you say, Lady Bellamy. First, there is her duty to the man she loves, for her the greatest duty of any in the world; next, her duty to herself, for her happiness and self-respect are involved in her decision; and, lastly, her duty to her family. I put the family last, because, after all, it is she who gets married, not her family."

Lady Bellamy smiled a little.

"You argue well; but there is one thing that you overlook, though I am sorry to have to pain you by saying it; young Mr. Heigham is no better than he should be. I have made inquiries about him, and think that I ought to tell you that."

"What do you mean?"

"I mean that his life, young as he is, has not been so creditable as it might have been. He has been the hero of one or two little affairs. I can tell you about them if you like."

"Lady Bellamy, your stories are either true or untrue. If true, I should take no notice of them, because they must have happened before he loved me; if untrue, they would be a mere waste of breath, so I think that we may dispense with the stories—they would influence me no more than the hum of next summer's gnats."

Lady Bellamy smiled again.

"You are a curious woman," she said; "but, supposing that there were to be a repetition of these little stories *after* he loved you, what would you say then?"

Angela looked troubled, and thought awhile.

"He could never go far from me," she answered.

"What do you mean?"

"I mean that I hold the strings of his heart in my hands, and I have only to lift them to draw him back to me—so. No other woman, no living force, can keep him from me, if I choose to bid him come."

"Supposing that to be so, how about the self-respect you spoke of just now? Could you bear to take your lover back from the hands of another woman?"

"That would entirely depend upon the circumstances, and upon what was just to the other woman."

"You would not then throw him up without question?"

"Lady Bellamy, I may be very ignorant and simple, but I am neither mad nor a fool. What do you suppose that my life would be worth to me if I threw Arthur up? If I remained single, it would be an aching void, as it is now; and if I married any other man whilst he still lived, it would become a daily and shameful humiliation such as I had rather die than endure."

Lady Bellamy glanced up from under her heavy-lidded eyes; a thought had evidently struck her, but she did not express it.

"Then I am to tell your cousin George that you will have absolutely nothing to do with him?"

"Yes, and beg him to cease persecuting me; it is quite useless; if there were no Arthur and no other man in the world, I would not marry him. I detest him—I cannot tell you how I detest him."

"It is amusing to hear you talk so, and to think that you will certainly be Mrs. George Caresfoot within nine months."

"Never!" answered Angela, passionately stamping her foot upon the floor. "What makes you say such horrible things?"

"I reflect,' answered Lady Bellamy, with an ominous smile, "that George Caresfoot has made up his mind to marry you, and that I have made up mine to help him to do so, and that your will, strong as it certainly is, is, as compared with our united wills, what a straw is to a gale. The straw cannot travel against the wind, it *must* go with it, and you *must* marry George Caresfoot. You will as certainly come to the altar-rails with him as you will to your death-bed. It is written in your face. Good-by."

For the first time Angela's courage really gave way as she heard these dreadful words. She remembered how she herself had called Lady Bellamy an embodiment of the "Spirit of Power," and now she felt that the comparison was just. The woman was power incarnate, and her words, which from anybody else she would have laughed at, sent a cold chill through her.

"She is a fine creature both in mind and body," reflected Lady Bellamy, as she stepped into her carriage. "Really, though I try to hate her, I can find it in my heart to be sorry for her. Indeed, I am not sure that I do not like her; certainly I respect her. But she has come in my path and must be crushed—my own safety demands it. At least, she is worth crushing, and the game is fair, for perhaps she will crush me. I should not be surprised; there is a judgment in those gray eyes of hers—Qui vivra verra. Home, William."

CHAPTER XXXVII.

ANGELA'S appeal for protection set Philip thinking.

As the reader is aware, his sole motive in consenting to become, as it were, a sleeping partner in the shameful plot, of which his innocent daughter was the object, was to obtain possession of his lost inheritance, and it now occurred to him that even should that plot succeed, which he very greatly doubted, nothing had as yet been settled as to the terms upon which it was to be reconveyed to him. The whole affair was excessively repugnant to him; indeed, he regarded the prospect of its success with little less than terror, only his greed overmastered his fear.

But on one point he was very clear: it should not succeed except upon the very best of terms for himself; his daughter should not be sacrificed unless the price paid for the victim was positively princely: such guilt was not to be incurred for a bagatelle. If George married Angela, the Isleworth estates must pass back into his hands for a very low sum indeed. But would his cousin be willing to accept such a sum? That was the rub, and that, too, was what must be made clear without any further delay. He had no wish to see Angela put to needless suffering—suffering which would not bring an equivalent with it, and which might, on the contrary, entail consequences upon himself that he shuddered to think of.

Curiously enough, however, he had of late been signally free from his superstitious fears; indeed, since the night when he had so astonished Arthur by his outbreak about the shadows on the wall, no fit had come to trouble him, and he was beginning to look upon the whole thing as an evil dream, a nightmare that he had at last lived down. But still the nightmare might return, and he was not going to run the risk unless he was very well paid for it. And so he determined to offer a price so low for the property that no man in his senses would accept it, and then wrote a note to George asking him to come over on the following evening after dinner, as he wished to speak to him on a matter of business.

"There," he said to himself, "that will make an end of the affair, and I will get young Heigham back and they can be married. George can never take what I mean to offer; if he should, the Egyptian will be spoiled indeed, and the game will be worth the candle. Not that I have any responsibility about it, however; I shall put no pressure on Angela; she must choose for herself." And Philip went to bed, quite feeling as though he had done a virtuous action.

George came punctually enough on the following evening, which was that of the day of Lady Bellamy's conversation with Angela, a conversation which had so upset the latter that she had already gone to her room, not knowing anything of her cousin's proposed visit.

The night was one of those dreadfully oppressive ones that sometimes visit us in the course of an English summer. The day had been hot and sultry, and with the fall of the evening the little breeze that stirred in the thunder-laden air had died away, leaving the temperature at much the same point that is to be expected in a tropical valley, and rendering the heat of the house almost unbearable.

"How do you do, George?" said Philip. "Hot, isn't it?"

"Yes, there will be a tempest soon."

"Not before midnight, I think. Shall we go and walk down by the lake? it will be cooler there, and we shall be quite undisturbed. Walls have ears sometimes, you know."

"Very well; but where is Angela?"

"I met her on the stairs just now, and she said that she was going to bed—got a headache, I believe. Shall we start?"

So soon as they were well away from the house, Philip broke the ice.

"Some months back, I had a conversation with Lady Bellamy on the subject of a proposal that you made to me through her for Angela's hand. It is about that I wish to speak to you now. First, I must ask you if you still wish to go on with the business?"

"Certainly; I wish it more than ever."

"Well, as I intimated to Lady Bellamy, I do not at all approve of your suit. Angela is already, subject to my consent, very suitably engaged to your late ward, a young fellow whom, whatever you may think about him, I like very much; and I can assure you that it will require the very strongest inducements to make me even allow such a thing. In any case, I will have nothing to do with influencing Angela; she is a perfectly free agent."

"Which means, I suppose, that you intend to screw down the price?"

"In wanting to marry Angela," went on Philip, "you must remember that you fly high. She is a very lovely woman, and, what is more, will some day or other be exceedingly well off, whilst you—you must excuse my being candid, but this is a mere matter of business, and I am only talking of you in the light of a possible son-in-law—you are a middle-aged man, not prepossessing in appearance, broken in health, and, however well you may have kept up your reputation in these parts, as you and I well know, without a single shred of character left; altogether not a man to whom a father would marry his daughter of his own free will, or one with whom a young girl is likely to find happiness."

"You draw a flattering picture of me, I must say."

"Not at all, only a true one."

"Well, if I am all you say, how is it that you are prepared to allow your daughter to marry me at all?"

"I will tell you: because the rights of property should take precedence of the interests of a single individual. Because my father and you between you cozened me out of my lawful own, and this is the only way that I see of coming by it again."

"What does it matter? in any case, after your death the land will come back to Angela and her children."

"No, George, it will not; if ever the Isleworth estates come into my hands, they shall not pass again to any child of yours."

"What would you do with them, then?"

"Marry, and get children of my own."

George whistled.

"Well, I must say that your intentions are amiable; but you have not got the estates yet, my dear cousin."

"No, and never shall have, most likely; but let us come to the point. Although I do not approve of your advances, I am willing to waive my objections and accept you as a son-in-law, if you can win Angela's consent, provided that before the marriage you consent to give me clear transfer, at a price, of all the Isleworth estates, with the exception of the mansion and the pleasure-grounds."

"Very good; but now about the price. That is the real point."

They had taken a path that ran down through the shrubberies to the side of the lake, and then turned up towards Caresfoot's Staff. Before answering George's remark, Philip proposed that they should sit down, and, suiting the action to the word, placed himself upon the trunk of a fallen tree that lay by the water's edge, just outside the spread of the branches of the great oak, and commanding a view of the area beneath them.

"The moon will come out again presently," he said, when George had followed his example. "She has got behind that thunder-cloud. Ah!" as a bright flash of lightning passed from heaven to earth, "I thought that we should get a storm; it will be here in half an hour."

All this Philip said to gain time; he had not quite made up his mind what price to offer.

"Never mind the lightning. What do you offer for the property, inclusive of timber, and with all improvements—just as it stands, in short?"

"One hundred thousand pounds cash," said Philip, deliberately.

George sprang from his seat and sat down again before he answered:

"Do you think that I am drunk, or a fool, that you come to me with such a ridiculous offer? Why, the probate valuation was two hundred thousand, and that was very low."

"I offer one hundred thousand, and am willing to settle thirty thousand absolutely on the girl should she marry you, and twenty thousand more on my death. That is my offer—take it, or leave it."

"Talk sense, man; your terms are preposterous."

"I tell you that, preposterous or not, I will not go beyond them. If you don't like them, well and good, leave them alone, and I'll put myself in communication with young Heigham to-morrow, and tell him that he can come and marry the girl as soon as he likes. For my part, I am very glad to have the business settled."

"You ask me to sacrifice half my property," groaned George.

"My property, you mean, that you stole. But I don't ask you to do anything one way or the other. Am I to understand that you refuse my offer?"

"Give me a minute to think," and George hid his face in his hand, and Philip, looking at him with hatred gleaming in his dark eyes, muttered between his teeth:

"I believe that my turn has come at last."

When some thirty seconds had passed in silence, the attention of the pair was attracted by the cracking of dead leaves that sounded quite startling in the intense stillness of the night, and next second a tall figure in white glided up to the water's edge, and stood still within half a dozen paces of them.

Involuntarily Philip gripped his cousin's arm, but neither of them moved. The sky had rapidly clouded up, and the faint light that struggled from the moon only served to show that the figure appeared to be lifting its arms. In another second that was gone too, and the place was totally dark.

"Wait till the moon comes out, and we shall see what it is," whispered George, and, as he spoke, there came from the direction of the figure a rustling sound as of falling garments.

"What can it be?" whispered Philip.

They were not left long in doubt, for at that instant a vivid flash from the thunder-cloud turned the darkness into the most brilliant day, and revealed a woman standing up to her knees in the water, with her arms lifted, knotting her long hair. It was Angela. For one moment the fierce light shone upon the stately form that gleamed whiter than ivory—white as snow against the dense background of the brushwood, and, as it passed, they heard her sink into the water softly as a swan, and strike out with steady strokes towards the centre of the lake.

"It is only Angela," said Philip, when the sound of the strokes grew faint. "Phew! what a start she gave me."

"Is she safe?" asked George, in a husky voice. "Hadn't I better get a boat?"

"She needs no help from you; she is quite capable of looking after herself, especially in the water, I can tell you," Philip answered, sharply.

Nothing more was said till they reached the house, when, on entering the lighted study, Philip noticed that his cousin's face was flushed, and his hands shaking like aspen leaves.

"Why, what is the matter with you, man?" he asked.

"Nothing—nothing. I am only rather cold. Give me some brandy."

"Cold on such a night as this? That's curious," said Philip, as he got the spirit from a cupboard.

George drank about a wine-glassful neat, and seemed to recover himself.

"I accept your offer for the land, Philip," he said, presently.

His cousin looked at him curiously, and a brilliant idea struck him.

"You agree, then, to take *fifty* thousand pounds for the Isleworth estates in the event of your marrying my daughter, the sale to be completed before the marriage takes place?"

"Fifty thousand! No, a hundred thousand—you said a hundred thousand just now."

"You must have misunderstood me, or I must have made a mistake; what I meant and mean is *fifty thousand*, and you to put a thousand down as earnest-money—to be forfeited whether the affair comes off or not."

George ground his teeth and clutched at his red hair, proceedings that his cousin watched with a great deal of quiet enjoyment. When at length he spoke, it was in a low, hoarse voice; quite unlike his usual hard tones:

"Damn you!" he said, "you have me at your mercy. Take the land for the money, if you like, though it will nearly ruin me. That woman has turned my head; I *must* marry her or I shall go mad."

"Very good; that is your affair. Remember that I have no responsibility in the matter, and that I am not going to put any pressure on Angela. If you want to marry her, you must win her within the next eight months. Then that is settled. I suppose that you will pay in the thousand to-morrow. The storm is coming up fast, so I won't keep you. Good night," and they separated, George to drive home—with fever in his heart, and the thunderstorm, of which he heard nothing, rattling round him—and Philip to make his way to bed, with the dream of his life advanced a step nearer realization.

"That was a lucky swim of Angela's to-night," he thought. "Fifty thousand pounds for the estate. He is right; he must be going mad. But will he get her to marry him, I wonder. If he does, I shall cry quits with him, indeed."

CHAPTER XXXVIII.

George had spoken no falsehood when he said that he felt as though he must marry Angela or go mad. Indeed, it is a striking proof of how necessary he thought that step to be to his happiness, that he had been willing to consent to his cousin's Shylock-like terms about the sale of the property, although they would in their result degrade him from his position as a large landed proprietor, and make a comparatively poor man of him. The danger or suffering that could induce a Caresfoot to half ruin himself with his eyes open had need to be of an extraordinarily pressing nature.

Love's empire is this globe and all mankind; the most refined and the most degraded, the cleverest and the most stupid, are all liable to become his faithful subjects. He can alike command the devotion of an archbishop and a South-Sea Islander, of the most immaculate maiden lady (whatever her age) and of the savage Zulu girl. From the pole to the equator, and from the equator to the further pole, there is no monarch like Love. Where he sets his foot, the rocks bloom with flowers, or the garden becomes a wilderness according to his good will and pleasure, and at his whisper all other allegiances melt away like ropes of sand. He is the real arbiter of the destinies of the world.

But to each nature of all the millions beneath his sway, Love comes in a fitting guise, to some as an angel messenger, telling of sympathy and peace, and a strange new hope; to others draped in sad robes indeed, but still divine. Thus when he visits such a one as George Caresfoot, it is as a potent fiend, whose mission is to enter through man's lower nature, to torture and destroy; to scorch the heart with fearful heats, and then to crush it, and leave its owner's bosom choked with bitter dust.

And, so far as George is concerned, there is no doubt but what the work was done right well, for under the influence of what is, with doubtful propriety, known as the "tender passion," that estimable character was rapidly drifting within a measurable distance of a lunatic asylum. The checks and repulses that he had met with, instead of cooling his ardor, had only the effect of inflaming it to an extraordinary degree. Angela's scornful dislike, as water thrown upon burning oil, did but diffuse the flames of his passion throughout the whole system of his mind, till he grew wild with its heat and violence. Her glorious beauty daily took a still stronger hold upon his imagination, till it scorched into his very soul. For whole nights he could not sleep, for whole days he would scarcely eat or do anything but walk, walk, walk, and try to devise means to win her to his side. The irritation of his mind produced its natural effects upon his conduct, and he would burst into fits of the most causeless fury. In one of these he dismissed every servant in the house, and so evil was his reputation among that class, that he had great difficulty in obtaining others to take their places. In another he hurled a heavy pot containing an azalea-bush at the head of one of the gardeners, and had to compromise an action for assault. In short, the lunatic asylum loomed very near indeed.

For a week or so after the memorable night of his interview with Philip, an interview that he, at least, would never forget, George was quite unable, try as he would, to get a single word with Angela.

At last, one day, when he was driving, by a seldom-used road, past the fields near the Abbey House on his way from Roxham, chance gave him the opportunity that he had for so long sought without success. For, far up a by-lane that led to a turnip-field, his eye caught sight of the flutter of a gray dress vanishing round a corner, something in the make of which suggested to him that Angela was its wearer. Giving the reins to the servant, and bidding him drive on home, he got out of the dog-cart and hurried up the grassy track, and on turning the corner came suddenly upon the object of his search. She was standing on the bank of the hedge-row, and struggling with a bough of honeysuckle from which she wished to pluck its last remaining autumn bloom. So engaged was she that she did not hear his step, and it was not until his hard voice grated on her ear that she knew that she was trapped.

"Caught at last. You have given me a pretty hunt, Angela."

The violent start she gave effectually carried out her purpose as regards the honeysuckle, which snapped in two under the strain of her backward jerk, and she turned round upon him panting with fear and exertion, the flowery bough grasped within her hand.

"Am I, then, a wild creature, that you should hunt me so?"

"Yes, you are the loveliest and the wildest of creatures, and, now I have caught you, you must listen to me."

"I will not listen to you; you have nothing to say to me that can interest me. I will not listen to you."

George laughed a little—a threatening, nervous laugh.

"I am accustomed to have my own way, Angela, and I am not going to give it up now. You must and you shall listen. I have got my opportunity at last, and I mean to use it. I am sorry to have to speak so roughly, but you have only yourself to thank; you have driven me to it."

His determination frightened her, and she took refuge in an armor of calm and freezing contempt.

"I don't understand you," she said.

"On the contrary, you understand me very well. You always avoid me; I can never see you, try how I will. Perhaps," he went on, still talking quite quietly, "if you knew what a hell there is in my heart and brain you would not treat me so. I tell you that I am in torture," and the muscles of the pallid face twitched in a way that went far to confirm his words.

"I do not understand your meaning, unless, indeed, you are trying to frighten and insult me, as you have done before," answered Angela.

Poor girl, she did not know what else to say; she was not of a nervous disposition, but there was something about George's manner that alarmed her very much, and she glanced anxiously around to see if any one was within call, but the place was lonely as the grave.

"There is no need for you to look for help, I wish neither to frighten nor insult you; my suit is an honorable one enough. I wish you to promise to marry me, that is all; you must and shall promise it, I will take no refusal. You were made for me and I for you; it is quite useless for you to resist me, for you must marry me at last. I love you, and by that right you belong to me. I love you—I love you."

"You—love—me—you—"

"Yes, I do, and why should you look at me like that? I cannot help it, you are so beautiful; if you knew your own loveliness, you would understand me. I love those gray eyes of yours, even when they flash and burn as they do now. Ah! they shall look softly at me yet, and those sweet lips that curl so scornfully shall shape themselves to kiss me. Listen, I loved you when I first saw you there in the drawing-room at Isleworth, I loved you more and more all the time that I was ill, and now I love you to madness. So you see, Angela, you *must* marry me soon."

"*I* marry you!"

"Oh! don't say you won't, for God's sake, don't say you won't," said George, with a sudden change of manner from the confident to the supplicatory. "Look, I beg you not to, on my knees," and he actually flung himself down on the grass roadway and grovelled before her in an abandonment of passion hideous to behold.

She turned very pale, and answered him in a cold, quiet voice, every syllable of which fell upon him like the stroke of a knife.

"Such a thing would be quite impossible for many reasons, but I need only repeat you one that you are already aware of. I am engaged to Mr. Heigham."

"Bah, that is nothing. I know that; but you will not throw away such a love as I have to offer for the wavering affection of a boy. We can soon get rid of him. Write and tell him that you have changed your mind. Listen, Angela," he went on, catching her by the skirt of her dress; "he is not rich, he has only got enough for a bare living. I have five times the money, and you shall help to spend it. Don't marry a young beggar like that; you won't get value for yourself. It will pay you ever so much better to marry me."

George was convinced from his experience of the sex that every woman could be bought if only you bid high enough; but, as the sequel showed, he could not well have used a worse argument to a person like Angela, or one more likely to excite the indignation that fear of him, together with a certain respect for the evident genuineness of his suffering, had hitherto kept in suppression. She wrenched her dress free from him, leaving a portion of its fabric in his hand.

"Are you not ashamed?" she said, her voice trembling with indignation and her eyes filled with angry tears; "are you not ashamed to talk to me like this, *you*, my own father's cousin, and yourself old enough to be my father? I tell you that my love is already given, which would have been a sufficient answer to any *gentleman*, and you reply by saying that you are richer than the man I love. Do you believe that a woman thinks of nothing but money? or do you suppose that I am to be bought like a beast at the market? Get up from the ground, for, since your brutality forces me to speak so plainly in my own defence, I must tell you once and for all that you will get nothing by kneeling to me. Listen: I would die rather than be your wife; rather than always see your face about me, I would pass my life in prison; I had sooner be touched by a snake than by you. You are quite hateful to me.

Now you have your answer, and I beg that you will get up and let me pass!"

Drawn up to the full height of her majestic stature, her face flushed with emotion, and her clear eyes flashing scornful fire, whilst in her hand she still held the bough of sweet honeysuckle, Angela formed a strange contrast to the miserable man crouched at her feet, swaying himself to and fro and moaning, his hat off and his face hidden in his trembling hands.

As he would not, or could not move, she left him there, and slipping through a neighboring gap vanished from sight. When she was fairly gone, he stirred, and having risen and recovered his hat, which had fallen off in his excitement, his first action was to shake his fist in the direction in which she had vanished, his next to frantically kiss the fragment of her dress that he still held in his hand.

"You *shall* marry me yet, my fine lady," he hissed between his teeth; "and, if I do not repay your gentle words with interest, my name is not George Caresfoot;" and then, staggering like a drunken man, he made his way home.

"Oh, Arthur," thought Angela, as she crept quite broken in spirit to the solitude of her room, "if I only knew where you were, I think that I would follow you, promise or no promise. There is no one to help me, no one; they are all in league against me—even my own father."

CHAPTER XXXIX.

NOTWITHSTANDING his brave threats made behind Angela's back, about forcing her to marry him in the teeth of any opposition that she could offer, George reached home that night very much disheartened about the whole business. How was he to bow the neck of this proud woman to his yoke, and break the strong cord of her allegiance to her absent lover. With many girls it might have been possible to find a way, but Angela was not an ordinary girl. He had tried, and Lady Bellamy had tried, and they had both failed, and as for Philip, he would take no active part in the matter. What more could be done? Only one thing that he could think of: he could force Lady Bellamy to search her finer brains for a fresh expedient. Acting upon this idea, he at once despatched a note to her, requesting her to come and see him at Isleworth on the following morning.

That night passed very ill for the love-lorn George. Angela's vigorous and imaginative expression of her entire loathing of him had pierced even the thick hide of his self-conceit, and left him sore as a whipped hound—altogether too sore to sleep. When Lady Bellamy arrived on the following morning, she found him marching up and down the dining-room, in the worst of his bad tempers, and that was a very shocking temper indeed. His light-blue eyes were angry and bloodshot, his general appearance slovenly to the last degree, and a red spot burned upon each sallow cheek.

"Well, George, what is the matter? You don't look quite so happy as a lover should."

He grunted by way of answer.

"Has the lady been unkind, failed to appreciate your advances, eh?"

"Now look here, Anne," he answered. savagely, "if I have to put up with things from that confounded girl, I am not going to stand your jeers, so stop them once and for all."

"It is very evident that she has been unkind. Supposing that instead of abusing me you tell me the details. No doubt they are interesting," and she settled herself in a low chair, and glanced at him keenly from under her heavy eyelids.

Thus admonished, George proceeded to give her such a version of his melancholy tale as best suited him, needless to say not a full one, but his hearer's imagination easily supplied the gaps, and, as he proceeded, a slow smile crept over her face as she conjured up the suppressed details of the scene in the lane.

"Curse you! what are you laughing at? You came here to listen, not laugh," broke out George furiously, when he saw it.

She made no answer, and he continued his thrilling tale without comment on her part.

"Now," he said, when it was finished, "what is to be done?"

"There is nothing to be done; you have failed to win her affections, and there is an end of the matter."

"Then you mean I must give it up?"

"Yes, and a very good thing too, for the ridiculous arrangement that you have entered into with Philip would have half-ruined you, and you would be tired of the girl in a month."

"Now, look you here, Anne," said George, in a sort of hiss, and standing over her in a threatening attitude, "I have suspected for some time that you were playing me false in this business, and now I am sure of it. You have put the girl up to treating me like this, you treacherous snake; you have struck me from behind, you Red Indian in petticoats. But, look here, I will be square with you; you shall not have all the laugh on your side."

"George, you must be mad."

"You shall see whether I am mad or not. Did you see what the brigands did to a fellow they caught in Greece the other day for whom they wanted ransom? First, they sent his ear to his friends, then his nose, then his foot, and last of all, his head—all by post, mark you. Well, dear Anne, that is just how I am going to pay you out. You shall have a week to find a fresh plan to trap the bird you have frighted, and, if you find none, first, I shall post one of those interesting letters that I have yonder to your husband—anonymously, you know—not a very compromising one, but one that will pique his curiosity and set him making inquiries; then I shall wait another week."

Lady Bellamy could bear it no longer. She sprang up from her chair, pale with anger.

"You fiend in human form, what is it, I wonder, that has kept me so long from destroying you and myself too? Oh! you need not laugh; I have the means to do it, if I choose: I have had them for twenty years."

George laughed again hoarsely.

"Quite penny-dreadful, I declare. But I don't think you will come to that; you would be afraid, and, if you do, I don't much care—I am pretty reckless, I can tell you."

"For your threats," she went on, without heeding him, "I care nothing, for, as I tell you, I have their antidote at hand. You have known me for many years, tell me, did you ever see my nerve desert me? Do you suppose that I am a woman who would bear failure when I could choose death? No, George, I had rather pass into eternity on the crest of the wave of my success, such as it has been, and let it break and grind me to powder there, or else bear me to greater heights. All that should have been a woman's better part in the world you have destroyed in me. I do not say that it was altogether your fault, for an evil destiny bound me to you, and it must seem odd to you when I say that, knowing you for what you are, I still love you. And to fill up this void, to trample down those surging memories, I have made myself a slave to my ambition, and the acquisition of another power that you cannot understand. The man you married me to is rich and a knight to-day. I made him so. If I live another twenty years, his wealth shall be colossal and his influence unbounded, and I will be one of the most powerful women in the kingdom. Why do you suppose that I so fear your treachery? Do you think that I should mind its being known that I had thrown aside that poor fig-leaf, virtue—the green garment that marks a coward or a fool; for, mark you, all women, or nearly all, would be vicious if they dared. Fear and poverty of spirit restrain them, not virtue. Why, it is by their vices, properly managed, that women always have risen, and always will rise. To be really great, I think that a woman must be vicious with discrimination, and I respect vice accordingly. No, it is not that I fear. I am afraid because I have a husband whose bitter resentment is justly piling up against me from year to year, who only lies in wait for an opportunity to destroy me. Nor is he my only enemy. In his skilful hands, the letters you possess can, as society is in this country, be used so as to make me powerless. Yes, George, all the good in me is dead; the mad love I have given you is hourly outraged, and yet I cannot shake it off. *There* alone my strength fails me, and I am weak as a child. Only the power to exercise my will, my sense of command over the dullards round me, and a yet keener pleasure you do not know of, are left to me. If these are taken away, what will my life be? A void, a waste, a howling wilderness, a place where I will not stay! I had rather tempt the unknown. Even in Hell there must be scope for abilities such as mine!"

She paused awhile, as if for an answer, and then went on—

"And as for you, poor creature that you are, words cannot tell how I despise you. You discard me and my devotion, to follow a nature, in its way, it is true, greater even than my own, representing the principle of good, as I represent the principle of evil, but one to which yours is utterly abhorrent. Can you mix light with darkness, or filthy oil with water? As well hope to merge your life, black as it is with every wickedness, with that of the splendid creature you would defile. Do you suppose that a woman such as she is will ever be really faithless to her love, even though you trap her into marriage? Fool, her heart is as far above you as the stars; and without a heart a woman is a husk that none but such miserables as yourself would own. But go on—dash yourself against a white purity that will, in the end, blind and destroy you. Dree your own doom! I will find you expedients; it is my business to obey you. You shall marry her, if you will, and taste of the judgment that will follow. Be still, I will bear no more of your insolence to-day." And she swept out of the room, leaving George looking somewhat scared.

When Lady Bellamy reached Rewtham House, she went straight to her husband's study. He received her with much politeness, and asked her to sit down.

"I have come to consult you on a matter of some importance," she said.

"That is, indeed, an unusual occurrence," answered Sir John, rubbing his dry hands and smiling.

"It is not my own affair: listen," and she gave him a full, accurate, and clear account of all that had taken place with reference to George's determination to marry Angela, not omitting the most trivial detail. Sir John expressed no surprise; he was a very old bird was Sir John, one for whom every net was spread in vain, whether in or out of his sight. Nothing in this world, provided that it did not affect his own comfort or safety, could affect his bland and appreciative smile. He was never surprised. Once or twice he put a shrewd question to elucidate some point in the narrative, and that was all. When his wife had finished, he said,

"Well, Anne, you have told a very interesting and amusing little history, doubly so, if you will permit me to say it, seeing that it is told of George Caresfoot by Lady Bellamy; but it seems that your joint efforts have failed. What is it that you wish me to do?"

"I wish to ask you if you can suggest any plan that will not fail. You are very cunning in your way, and your advice may be good."

"Let me see, young Heigham is in Madeira, is he not?"

"I am sure I do not know."

"But I do," and he extracted a note-book from a drawer. "Let me see, I think I have an entry somewhere here. Ah! here we are. 'Arthur P. Heigham, Esq., passenger, per *Warwick Castle*, to Madeira, June 16.' (Copied from passenger-list, *Western Daily News*.) His second name is Preston, is it not? Lucky I kept that.

Now, the thing will be to communicate with Madeira, and see if he is still there. I can easily do that; I know a man there."

"Have you formed any plan, then?"

"Yes," answered Sir John, with great deliberation, "I think I see my way; but I must have time to think of it. I will speak to you about it to-morrow."

When Lady Bellamy had gone, the little man rose, peeped round to see that nobody was within hearing, and then, rubbing his dry hands with infinite zest, said aloud, in a voice that was quite solemn in the intensity of its satisfaction:

"The Lord hath delivered mine enemies into mine hand."

CHAPTER XL.

Two days after Sir John had been taken into confidence, Philip received a visit from Lady Bellamy that caused him a good deal of discomfort. After talking to him on general subjects for awhile, she rose to go.

"By the way, Mr. Caresfoot," she said, "I really had almost forgotten the object of my visit. You may remember a conversation we had together some time ago, when I was the means of paying a debt owing to you?"

Philip nodded.

"Then you will not have forgotten that one of the articles of our little verbal convention was, that if it should be considered to the interest of all the parties concerned, your daughter's old nurse was not to remain in your house?"

"I remember."

"Well, do you know, I cannot help thinking that it must be a bad thing for Angela to have so much of the society of an ill-educated and not very refined person like Pigott. I really advise you to get rid of her."

"She has been with me for twenty years, and my daughter is devoted to her. I can't turn her off."

"It is always painful to dismiss an old servant—almost as bad as discarding an old dress; but when a dress is worn out it must be thrown away. Surely the same applies to servants."

"I don't see how I am to send her away."

"I can quite understand your feelings; but then, you see, an agreement implies obligations on both sides, doesn't it? especially an agreement 'for value received,' as the lawyers say."

Philip winced perceptibly.

"I wish I had never had anything to do with your agreements."

"Oh! if you think it over, I don't think that you will say so. Well, that is settled. I suppose she will go pretty soon. I am glad to see you looking so well—very different from your cousin, I assure you. I don't think much of his state of health.

Good-by; remember me to Angela. By the way, I don't know if you have heard that George has met with a repulse in that direction; he does not intend to press matters anymore at present; but, of course, the agreement holds all the same. Nobody knows what the morrow may bring forth."

"Where you and my amiable cousin are concerned, I shall be much surprised if it does not bring forth villany," thought Philip, as soon as he heard the front door close. "I suppose that it must be done about Pigott. Curse that woman, with her sorceress face. I wish I had never put myself into her power; the iron hand can be felt pretty plainly through her velvet glove."

Life is never altogether clouded over, and that morning Angela's horizon had been brightened by two big rays of sunshine that came to shed their cheering light on the gray monotony of her surroundings. For of late, notwithstanding its occasional spasms of fierce excitement, her life had been as monotonous as it was miserable. Always the same anxious grief, the same fears, the same longing pressing hourly round her like phantoms in the mist—no, not like phantoms, like real living things peeping at her from the dark. Sometimes, indeed, the presentiments and intangible terrors that were gradually strengthening their hold upon her would get beyond her control, and arouse in her a restless desire for action—any action, it did not matter what—that would take her away out of these dull hours of unwholesome mental growth. It was this longing to be doing something that drove her, fevered physically with the stifling air of the summer night, and mentally by thoughts of her absent lover and recollections of Lady Bellamy's ominous words, down to the borders of the lake on the evening of George's visit to her father, and once there, prompted her to try to forget her troubles for awhile in the exercise of an art of which she had from childhood been a mistress.

The same feeling it was, too, that led her to spend long hours of the day and even of the night, when by rights she should have been asleep, immersed in endless mathematical studies, and in solving, or attempting to solve, almost impossible problems. She found that the strenuous effort of the brain acted as a counter-irritant to the fretting of her troubles, and, though it may seem an odd thing to say, mathematics alone, owing to the intense application they required, exercised a soothing effect upon her. But, as one cannot constantly enjoy sleep induced by chloral without paying for it in some shape or form, Angela's relief from her cares was obtained at no small cost to her health. When the same brain, however well developed it may be, has both to study hard and suffer much, there must be a waste of tissue somewhere. In Angela's case the outward and visible result of this state of things was to make her grow thinner, and the alternate mental effect to increasingly rarefy an intellect already too ethereal for this work-a-day world, and to plunge its owner into fits of depression which were rendered dreadful by sudden forebodings of evil that would leap to life in the recesses of her mind, and for a moment cast a lurid glare upon its gloom, such as at night the lightning gives to the blackness which surrounds it.

It was in one of the worst of these fits, her "cloudy days" as she would call them to Pigott, that good news found her. As she was dressing, Pigott brought her a letter, which, recognizing Lady Bellamy's bold handwriting, she opened in fear and trembling. It contained a short note and another letter. The note ran as follows:

"Dear Angela,

"I inclose you a letter from your cousin George, which contains what I suppose you will consider good news. *For your own sake* I beg you not to send it back unopened as you did the last.

"A. B."

For a moment Angela was tempted to mistrust this inclosure, and almost come to the determination to throw it into the fire, feeling sure that a serpent lurked in the grass and that it was a cunningly disguised love-letter. But curiosity overcame her, and she opened it as gingerly as though it were infected, unfolding the sheet with the handle of her hair-brush. Its contents were destined to give her a surprise. They ran thus:

"Isleworth Hall, September 20.

"My dear Cousin.

"After what passed between us a few days ago, you will perhaps be surprised at hearing from me, but, if you have the patience to read this short letter, its contents will not, I fear, be altogether displeasing to you. They are very simple. I write to say that I accept your verdict, and that you need fear no further advances from me. Whether I quite deserved all the bitter words you poured out upon me I leave you to judge at leisure, seeing that my only crime was that I loved you. To most women the offence would not have seemed so unpardonable. But that is as it may be. After what you said there is only one course left for a man who has any pride—and that is to withdraw. So let the past be dead between us. I shall never allude to it again. Wishing you happiness in the path of life which you have chosen,

"I remain,

"Your affectionate cousin,

"George Caresfoot."

It would have been difficult for any one to have received a more perfectly satisfactory letter than this was to Angela.

"Pigott," she called out, feeling the absolute necessity of a confidant in her joy, and forgetting that that worthy soul had nothing but the most general knowledge of George's advances, "he has given me up; just think, he is going to let me alone. I declare I feel quite fond of him."

"And who might you be talking of, miss?"

"Why, my cousin George, of course; he is going to let me alone, I tell you."

"Which, seeing how as he isn't fit to touch you with a pair of tongs, is about the least as he can do, miss, and, as for letting you alone, I didn't know as he ever proposed doing anything else. But that reminds me, miss, though I am sure I don't know why it should, how as Mrs. Hawkins, as was put in to look after the vicarage while the Reverend Fraser was away, told me last night how as she had got a telegraft the sight of which, she said, knocked her all faint-like, till she turned just as yellow as the cover, to say nothing of four-and-six porterage, the which, however, she intends to recover from the Reverend—Lord, where was I?"

"I am sure I don't know, Pigott, but I suppose you were going to tell me what was in the telegram."

"Yes, miss, that's right; but my head does seem to wool up somehow so at times that I fare to lose my way."

"Well, Pigott, what was in the telegram?"

"Lord, miss, how you do hurry one, begging your pardon; only that the Reverend Fraser—not but what Mrs. Hawkins do say that it can't be true, because the words warn't in his writing nor nothing like, as she has good reason to know, seeing that—"

"Yes, but what about Mr. Fraser, Pigott? Isn't he well?"

"The telegraft didn't say, as I remembers, miss; bless me, I forget if it was to-day or to-morrow."

"Oh, Pigott," groaned Angela, "do tell me what was in the telegram."

"Why, miss, surely I told you that the thing said, though I fancy likely to be in error—"

"What?" almost shouted Angela.

"Why, that the Reverend Fraser would be home by the midday train, and would like a beefsteak for lunch, not mentioning, however, anything about the onions, which is very puzzling to Mrs.—"

"Oh, I am glad; why could you not tell me before? Cousin George disposed of and Mr. Fraser coming back. Why, things are looking quite bright again; at least they would be if only Arthur were here," and her rejoicing ended in a sigh.

As soon as she thought that he would have finished his beefsteak, with or without the onions, Angela walked down to the vicarage and broke in upon Mr. Fraser with something of her old gladsome warmth. Running up to him without waiting to be announced, she seized him by both hands.

"And so you are back at last! What a long time you have been away! Oh, I am so glad to see you!"

Mr. Fraser, who, it struck her, looked older since his absence, turned first a little red and then a little pale, and said:

"Yes, Angela, here I am back again in the old shop; it is very good of you to come so soon to see me. Now, sit down and tell me all about yourself whilst I go on with my unpacking. But, bless me, my dear, what is the matter with you? You look thin, and as though you were not happy, and—where has your smile gone to, Angela?"

"Never mind me, you must tell me all about yourself first.

Where have you been; and what have you been doing, all these long months?"

"Oh, I have been enjoying myself over half the civilized globe," he answered, with a somewhat forced laugh. "Switzerland, Italy, and Spain have all been benefited by my presence, but I got tired of it, so here I am back in my proper sphere, and delighted to again behold these dear familiar faces," and he pointed to his ample collection of classics. "But let me hear about yourself, Angela. I am tired of Number One, I can assure you."

"Oh, mine is a long story; you will scarcely find patience to listen to it."

"Ah, I thought that there was a story, from your face; then I think that I can guess what it is about. Young ladies' stories generally turn upon the same pivot," and he laughed a little softly, and sat down in a corner well out of the light. "Now, my dear, I am ready to give you my best attention."

Angela blushed very deeply and, looking studiously out of the window, began, with many hesitations, to tell her story.

"Well, Mr. Fraser, you must understand first of all—I mean, you know, that I must tell you that—" desperately, "that I am engaged."

"Ah!"

There was something so sharp and sudden about this exclamation that Angela turned round quickly.

"What's the matter—have you hurt yourself?"

"Yes; but go on, Angela."

It was an awkward story to tell, especially the George complication part of it, and to any one else she felt that she would have found it almost impossible to tell it; but in Mr. Fraser she was, she knew, sure of a sympathetic listener. Had she known, too, that the mere mention of her lover's name was a stab to her listener's heart, and that every expression of her own deep and enduring love and each tone of endearment were new and ingenious tortures, she might well have been confused.

For so it was. Although he was fifty years of age, Mr. Fraser had not educated Angela with impunity. He had paid the penalty that must have resulted to any heart-whole man not absolutely a fossil who had been brought into close contact with such a woman as Angela. Her loveliness appealed to his sense of beauty, her goodness to his heart, and her learning to his intellectual sympaties. What wonder that he learnt by imperceptible degrees to love her! The wonder would have been if he had not.

The reader need not fear, however; he shall not be troubled with any long account of Mr. Fraser's misfortune, for it never came to light or obtruded itself upon the world, or even upon its object. His was one of those earnest, secret, and self-sacrificing passions of which, if we only knew it, there exist a good many round about us, passions which to all appearance tend to nothing and are entirely without object, unless it be to make the individuals on whom they are inflicted a little less happy, or a little more miserable, as the case may be, than he or she would otherwise have been. It was to strive to conquer this passion, which in his heart he called dishonorable, that Mr. Fraser had gone abroad, right away from Angela, where he had wrestled with it, and prayed against it, and at last, as he thought, subdued it. But now, on his first sight of her, it rose again in all its former strength, and rushed through his being like a storm, and he realized that such love is of those things that cannot die. And perhaps it is a question if he really wished to lose it. It was a poor thing indeed, a very poor thing, but his own. There is something so divine about all true love that there lurks a conviction at the bottom of the hearts of most of us that it is better to love, however much we suffer, than not to love at all. Perhaps, after all, those really to be pitied are the people who are not capable of any such sensation.

But what Mr. Fraser suffered listening that autumn afternoon to Angela's tale of another's love and of her own deep return of that love, no man but himself ever knew. Yet still he heard and was not shaken in his loyal-heartedness, and comforted and consoled her, giving her the best advice in his power, like the noble Christian gentleman that he was; showing her, too, that there was little need of anxiety and every ground for hope that things would come to a happy and successful issue. The martyr's abnegation of self is not yet dead in the world.

At last Angela came to the letter that she had that very morning received from George. Mr. Fraser read it carefully.

"At any rate," he said, "he is behaving like a gentleman now. On the whole, that is a nice letter. You will be troubled with him no more."

"Yes," answered Angela, and then flushing up at the memory of George's arguments in the lane, "but it is certainly time that he did, for he had no business, oh, he had no business to speak to me as he spoke, and he a man old enough to be my father."

Mr. Fraser's pale cheeks colored a little.

"Don't be hard upon him because he is old, Angela—which, by the way, he is not; he is nearly ten years my junior—for I fear that old men are just as liable to be made fools of by a pretty face as young ones."

From that moment, not knowing the man's real character, Mr. Fraser secretly entertained a certain sympathy for George's sufferings, arising no doubt from a fellow-feeling. It seemed to him that he could understand a man going very far indeed when his object was to win Angela: not that he would have done it himself, but he knew the temptation and what it cost to struggle against it.

It was nearly dark when at length Angela, rising to go, warmly pressed his hand, and thanked him in her own sweet way for his goodness and kind counsel. And then, declining his offer of escort, and saying that she would come and see him again on the morrow, she departed on her homeward path.

The first thing that met her gaze on the hall-table at the Abbey

House was a note addressed to herself in a handwriting that she had seen in many washing bills, but never before on an envelope. She opened it in vague alarm. It ran as follows:

"Miss,—Yore father has just dismissed me, saying that he is too pore to keep me any longer, which is a matter as I holds my own opinion on, and that I am too uneddicated to be in yore company, which is a perfect truth. But, miss, not feeling any how ekal to bid you good-by in person after bringing you up by hand and doing for you these many years, I takes the liberty to write you, miss, to say good-by and God bless you, my beautiful angel, and I shall be to be found down at the old housen at the end of the drift as my pore husband left me, which is fortinately just empty, and p'raps you will come and see me at times, miss.

"Yore obedient servant,

"PIGOTT.

"I opens this again to say how as I have tidied up your things a bit afore I left leaving mine till to-morrow, when, if living, I shall send for them. If you please, miss, you will find yore clean night-shift in the left-hand drawyer, and sorry am I that I can't be there to lay it out for you. I shall take the liberty to send up for your washing, as it can't be trusted to any one."

Angela read the letter through, and then sank back upon a chair and burst into a storm of tears. Partially recovering herself, however, she rose and entered her father's study.

"Is this true?" she asked, still sobbing.

"Is what true?" asked Philip, indifferently, and affecting not to see her distress.

"That you have sent Pigott away?"

"Yes, yes; you see, Angela—"

"Do you mean that she is really to stop away?"

"Of course I do. I really must be allowed, Angela—"

"Forgive me, father, but I do not want to listen to your reasons and excuses." Her eyes were quite dry now. "That woman nursed my dying mother, and played a mother's part to me. She is, as you know, my only woman friend, and yet you throw her away like a worn-out shoe. No doubt you have your reasons, and I hope that they are satisfactory to you, but I tell you, reasons or no reasons, you have acted in a way that is cowardly and cruel;" and casting one indignant glance at him, she left the room.

Philip quailed before his daughter's anger.

"Thank goodness she's gone, and that job is done with. I am downright afraid of her, and the worst of it is she speaks the truth," said Philip to himself, as the door closed.

Ten days after this incident, Angela heard casually from Mr. Fraser that Sir John and Lady Bellamy were going on a short trip abroad for the benefit of the former's health. If she thought about the matter at all, it was to feel rather glad. Angela did not like Lady Bellamy, indeed she feared her. Of George she neither heard nor saw anything. He had also gone away.

CHAPTER XLI.

Meanwhile at Madeira matters were going on much as we left them; there had indeed been little appreciable change in the situation.

For his part, our friend Arthur continued to dance or rather stroll along the edge of his flowery precipice, and found the view pleasant and the air bracing.

And no doubt things were very nicely arranged for his satisfaction, and had it not been for the ever-present thought of Angela—for he did think of her a great deal and with deep longing—he should have enjoyed himself thoroughly, for every day was beautiful, and every day brought its amusements with it. Perhaps on arriving at the Quinta Carr about eleven o'clock, he would find that the steam-launch was waiting for them in a little bay where the cliff on which the house stood curved inwards. Then, a merry party of young English folks all collected together by Mrs. Carr that morning by the dint of superhuman efforts, they would scramble down the steps cut in the rock and steam off to some neighboring islet to eat luncheon and wander about collecting shells and flowers and beetles till sunset, and then steam back again through the spicy evening air, laughing and flirting and making the night melodious with their songs. Or else the horses would be ordered out and they would wander over the lonely mountains in the interior of the island, talking of mummies and all things human, of Angela and all things divine. And sometimes, in the course of these conversations, Arthur would in a brotherly way call Mrs. Carr "Mildred," while occasionally, in the tone of a spinster aunt, she would address him as "Arthur," a practice that, once acquired, she soon found was, like all other bad habits, not easy to get rid of. For somehow in all these expeditions she was continually at his side, striving, and not without success, to weave herself into the substance of his life, and to make herself indispensable to him, till at last he grew to look upon her almost as a sister.

But beyond this he never went, and to her advances he was as cold as ice, simply because he never noticed them, and she was afraid of making them more obvious for fear that she would frighten him away. He thought it the most natural thing in the world that he and Mildred should live together like brother and sister, and be very fond of each other as "sich," whilst she thought him—just what he was—the blindest of fools, and then loved him the more for his folly. The sisterly relationship did not possess the same charms for Mildred that it did for Arthur; they looked at matters from different points of view.

One morning, peeping through a big telescope that was fixed in the window of the little boudoir which formed an entrance-lobby to the museum, Mrs. Carr saw a cloud of smoke upon the horizon. Presently the point of a mast poked up through the vapor as though the vessel were rising out of the ocean, then two more mastheads and a red and black funnel, and last of all a great gray hull.

"Hurrah!" called out Mrs. Carr, with one eye still fixed to the telescope and the remainder of her little face all screwed up in her efforts to keep the other closed, "it's the mail; I can see the Donald Currie flag, a white C on a blue ground."

"Well, I am sure, Mildred, there's no need for you to make your face look like a monkey, if it is; you look just as though the corner of your mouth were changing places with your eyebrow."

"Agatha, you are dreadfully rude; when the fairies took your endowment in hand, they certainly did not forget the gift of plain speech. I shall appeal to Mr. Heigham; do I look like a monkey, Mr. Heigham? No, on second thoughts, I won't wait for the inevitable compliment. Arthur, hold your tongue and I will tell you something. That must be the new boat, the *Garth Castle*, and I want to see over her. Captain Smithson, who is bringing her out, has got a box of things for me. What do you say if we kill two birds with one stone—go and see the vessel and get our luncheon on board?"

"I am at your ladyship's service," answered Arthur, lazily; "but would you like to have the compliment apropos of the monkey? I have thought of something extremely neat now."

"Not on any account; I hate compliments that are not meant," and her eyes gave a little flash which put a point to her words. "Agatha, I suppose that you will come?"

"Well, yes, dear; the bay looks pretty smooth."

"Smooth; yes, you might sail across it in a paper ship," yawned Arthur.

"For goodness' sake don't look so lazy, Mr. Heigham, but ring the bell—not that one, the electric one—and let us order the launch at once. The mail will be at anchor in about an hour."

Arthur did as he was bid, and within that time they were steaming through the throng of boats already surrounding the steamer.

"My gracious, Mildred!" suddenly exclaimed Agatha, "do you see who that is there, leaning over the bulwarks? Oh, he's gone; but so sure as I am a living woman, it was Lord Minster and Lady Florence Thingumebob, his sister—you know, the pretty one."

Mildred looked vexed, and glanced involuntarily at Arthur, who was steering the launch. For a moment she hesitated about going on, and glanced again at Arthur. The look seemed to inspire her, for she said nothing, and presently he brought the boat deftly alongside the gangway ladder.

The captain of the ship had already come to the side to meet her, having recognized her from the bridge; indeed there was scarcely a man in Donald Currie's service who did not know Mrs. Carr, at any rate, by sight.

"How do you do, Mrs. Carr? Are you coming on to South Africa with us?"

"No, Captain Smithson; I, or rather we, are coming to lunch, and to see your new boat, and last, but not least, to claim my box."

"Mrs. Carr, will you ever forgive me? I have lost it!"

"Produce my box, Captain Smithson, or I will never speak to you again. I'll do more. I'll go over to the Union line."

"In which case, I am afraid Donald Currie would never speak to me again. I must certainly try to find that box," and he whispered an order to a quartermaster. "Well, it is very kind of you to come and lunch, and I hope that you and your friends will do so with me. Till then, good-by, I must be off."

As soon as they got on the quarter-deck, Arthur perceived a tall, well-preserved man with an eye-glass, whom he seemed to know, bearing down upon them, followed by a charming-looking girl, about three-and-twenty years of age, remarkable for her pleasant eyes and the humorous expression of her mouth.

"How do you do, Mrs. Carr?" said the tall man. "I suppose that you heard that we were coming; it is very good of you to come and meet us."

"I had not the slightest idea that you were coming, and I did not come to meet you, Lord Minster; I came to lunch," answered Mrs. Carr, rather coldly.

"Nasty one for James that, very," murmured Lady Florence; "hope it will do him good."

"I was determined to come and look you up as soon as I got time, but the House sat very late. However, I have got a fortnight here now, and shall see plenty of you."

"A good deal too much I dare say, Lord Minster; but let me introduce you to Mr. Heigham."

Lord Minster glanced casually at Arthur, and, lifting his hat about an eighth of an inch, was about to resume his conversation, when Arthur, who was rather nettled by this treatment, said,

"I think I have had the pleasure of meeting you before, Lord Minster; we were stopping together at the Stanley Foxes last autumn."

"Stanley Foxes, ah, quite so, forgive my forgetfulness, but one meets so many people, you see," and he turned round to where Mrs. Carr had been, but that lady had taken the opportunity to retreat. Lord Minster at once followed her.

"Well, if my brother has forgotten you, Mr. Heigham, I have not," said Lady Florence, now coming forward for the first time. "Don't you remember when we went nutting together, and I tumbled into the pond?"

"Indeed I do, Lady Florence, and I can't tell you how pleased I am to see you again. Are you here for long?"

"An indefinite time: an old aunt of mine, Mrs. Velley, is coming out by next mail, and I am going to stop with her when my brother goes back. Are you staying with Mrs. Carr?"

"Oh no, only I know her very well."

"Do you admire her?"

"Immensely."

"Then you won't like James—I mean my brother."

"Why not?"

"Because he also admires her immensely."

"We both admire the view from here very much indeed, but that is no reason why you and I should not like each other."

"No, but then you see there is a difference between lovely scenery and lovely widows."

"Perhaps there is," said Arthur.

At this moment Lord Minster returned with Mrs. Carr.

"How do you do, Lady Florence?" said the latter; "let me introduce you to Mr. Heigham. What, do you already know each other?"

"Oh, yes, Mrs. Carr, we are old friends."

"Oh, indeed, that is very charming for you."

"Yes, it is," said Lady Florence, frankly.

"Well, we must be off now, Florence."

"All right, James, I'm ready."

"Will you both come and dine with me to-night sans façon, there will be nobody else except Agatha and Mr. Heigham?" asked Mrs. Carr.

'We shall be delighted," said Lord Minster.

"Au revoir, then," nodded Lady Florence to Arthur, and they separated.

When, after lunching and seeing round the ship, Miss Terry and Arthur found themselves in the steam launch waiting for Mrs. Carr, who was saying good-by to the captain and looking after her precious box, Arthur took the opportunity to ask his companion what she knew of Lord Minster.

"Oh, not much, that is, nothing in particular, except that he is the son of a sugar-broker or something, who was made a peer for some reason or other, and I suppose that is why he is so stuck up, because all the other peers I ever met are just like other people. He is very clever, too, is in the government now, and always hanging about after Mildred. He wants to marry her, you know, and I expect that he will at last, but I hope he won't. I don't like him; he always looks at one as though one were dirt."

"The deuce he does!" ejaculated Arthur, his heart filling on the instant with envy, hatred, malice, and all uncharitableness towards Lord Minster. He had not the slightest wish to marry Mildred himself, but he boiled at the mere thought of anybody else doing so. Lady Florence was right, there is a difference between ladies and landscapes.

At that moment Mildred herself arrived, but so disgusted was he that he would scarcely speak to her, and on arriving at the landing-stage he at once departed to the hotel, and even tried to get out of coming to dinner that night, but this was overruled.

"Good," said Mildred to herself, with a smile; "I have found out how to vex him."

At dinner that evening Lord Minster, who had of course taken his hostess in, opened the conversation by asking her how she had been employing herself at Madeira.

"Better than you have at St. Stephen's, Lord Minster; at any rate, I have not been forwarding schemes for highway robbery and the national disgrace," she answered, laughing.

"I suppose that you mean the Irish Land Act and the Transvaal Convention. I have heard several ladies speak of them like that, and I am really coming to the conclusion that your sex is entirely devoid of political instinct."

"What do you mean by political instinct, Lord Minster?" asked Arthur.

"By political instinct," he replied, "I understand a proper appreciation of the science and objects of government."

"Goodness me, what are they?" asked Mrs. Carr.

"Well, the science of government consists, roughly speaking, in knowing how to get into office, and remain there when once in; its objects are to guess and give expression to the prevailing popular feeling or whim with the loss of as few votes as possible."

"According to that definition," said Arthur, "all national questions are, or should be, treated by those who understand the 'science and objects of government' on a semi-financial basis. I mean, they should be dealt with as an investor deals with his funds, in order to make as much out of them as possible, not to bring real benefit to the country."

"You put the matter rather awkwardly, but I think I follow you. I will try to explain. In the first place, all the old-fashioned Jingo nonsense about patriotism and the 'honor of the country' has, if people only knew it, quite exploded; it only lingers in a certain section of the landed gentry and a proportion of the upper middle class, and has no serious weight with leading politicians."

"How about Lord Beaconsfield?"

"Well, he was perhaps an exception; but then he was a man with so large a mind—I say it, though I detested him—that he could actually, by a sort of political prescience, see into the far future, and shape his course accordingly. But even in his case I do not believe that he was actuated by patriotism, but rather by a keener insight into human affairs than most men possess."

"And yet he came terribly to grief."

"Because he outflew his age. The will of the country—which means the will of between five hundred thousand and a million hungry fluctuating electors—could not wait for the development of his imperial schemes. They wanted plunder in the present, not honor and prosperity for the Empire in the future. The instinct of robbery is perhaps the strongest in human nature, and those who would rule humanity on its present basis must pander to it or fail. The party of progress means the party that can give most spoil, taken from those that have, to those who have not. That is why Mr. Gladstone is such a truly great man; he understands better than any one of his age how to excite the greed of hungry voters and to guide it for his own ends. What was the Midlothian campaign but a crusade of plunder? First he excited the desire, then he promised to satisfy it. Of course that is impossible, but at the time he was believed, and his promises floated us triumphantly into power. The same arguments apply to that body of electors whose motive power is sentiment—their folly must be pandered to. For instance, the Transvaal Convention that Mrs. Carr mentioned is an admirable example of how such pandering is done. No man of experience can have believed that such an agreement could be wise, or that it can result in anything but trouble and humiliation; but the trouble and humiliation will not come just yet, and in the meanwhile a sop is thrown to Cerberus. Political memories are short, and when exposure comes it will be easy to fix the blame upon the other side. It is because we appreciate these facts that in the end we must prevail. The Liberal party, or rather the Radical section, which is to the great Liberal party what the helm is to the ship, appeals to the baser instincts and more pressing appetites of the people; the Conservative only to their traditions and higher aspirations, in the same way that religion appeals to the spirit, and the worship of Mammon to the senses. The shibboleth of the one is 'self-interest;' of the other, 'national honor.' The first appeals to the many, the second to the finer few, and I must leave you to judge which will carry the day."

"And if ever you become Prime Minister, shall you rule England upon these principles?" asked Mrs. Carr.

"Certainly; it is because I have mastered them that I am what I am. I owe everything to them, consequently in my view they are the finest of all principles."

"Then Heaven help England!" soliloquized Arthur, rudely.

"And so say we all," added Lady Florence, who was a strong Conservative.

"My dear young people," answered Lord Minster, with a superior smile, "England is quite capable of looking after herself. I have to look after myself. She will, at any rate, last my time, and my motto is that one should get something out of one's country, not attempt to do her services that would in all probability never be recognized, or, if recognized, left unrewarded."

Arthur was about to answer, with more sharpness than discretion, but Mrs. Carr interposed.

"Well, Lord Minster, we have to thank you for a very cynical and lucid explanation of the objects of your party, if they really are its objects. Will you give me some wine?"

After dinner Mrs. Carr devoted herself almost exclusively to Lord Minster, leaving Arthur to talk to Lady Florence. Lord Minster was not slow to avail himself of the opportunity.

"I have been thinking of your remark to me in London about the crossing-sweeper," he began.

"Oh, for Heaven's sake don't drag that wretched man out of his grave, Lord Minster. I really have forgotten what I said about him."

"I hope, Mrs. Carr, that you have forgotten a good deal you said that day. I may as well take this opportunity—"

"No, please don't, Lord Minster," she answered, knowing very well what was coming; "I am so tired to-night."

"Oh, in that case I can easily postpone my statement. I have a whole fortnight before me."

Mrs. Carr secretly determined that it should remain as much as possible at his own exclusive disposal, but she did not say so.

Shortly after this, Arthur took his leave, after shaking hands very coldly with her. Nor did he come to the Quinta next day, as he had conceived too great a detestation of Lord Minster to risk meeting him, a detestation which he attributed solely to that rising member of the Government's political principles, which jarred very much with his own.

"Better and better," said Mrs. Carr to herself, as she took off her dress, "but Lord Minster is really odious; I cannot stand him for long."

CHAPTER XLII.

"Why, Arthur, I had almost forgotten what you are like," said Mildred, when that young gentleman at last put in an appearance at the Quinta. "Where have you been to all this time?"

"I—oh, I have been writing letters," said Arthur.

"Then they must have been very long ones. Don't tell fibs, Arthur; you have not stopped away from here a day and a half in order to write letters. What is the matter with you?"

"Well, if you must know, Mildred, I detest your friend Lord Minster; the mere sight of him sets my teeth on edge, and I did not want to meet him. I only came here to day because Lady Florence told me that they were going up to the Convent this afternoon."

"So you have been to see Lady Florence?"

"No, I met her buying fruit yesterday, and went for a walk with her."

"In the intervals of the letter-writing?"

"Yes."

"Well, do you know I detest Lady Florence?"

"That is very unkind of you. She is charming."

"From your point of view, perhaps, as her brother is from mine."

"Do you mean to tell me that you think that horrid fellow charming?" asked Arthur in disgust.

"Why should I not?"

"Oh, for the matter of that there is no reason why you should not, but I can't congratulate you either on your friend or your taste."

"Leaving my taste out of the question, why do you call Lord Minster my friend?"

"Because Miss Terry told me that he was; she said that he was always proposing to you, and that you would probably marry him in the end."

Mildred blushed faintly.

"She has no business to tell you; but, for the matter of that, so have many other men. It does not follow that, because they choose to propose to me, they are my friends."

"No, but then they have not married you."

"No more has he; but, while we are talking of it, why should I not marry Lord Minster? He can give me position, influence, everything that is dear to a woman, except the rarest of all gifts—love."

"But is love so rare, Mildred?"

"Yes, the love that it can satisfy a woman either to receive or to give, especially the latter, for in this we are more blessed in giving than in receiving. It is but very rarely that the most fortunate of us get a chance of accepting such love as I mean, and we can only give it once in our lives. But you have not told me your reasons against my marrying Lord Minster."

"Because he is a mean-spirited, selfish man. If he were not, he could not have talked as he did last night. Because you do not love him, Mildred, you cannot love such a man as that, if he were fifty times a member of the Government."

"What does it matter to you, Arthur," she said, in a voice of indescribable softness, bending her sunny head low over her work, "whether I love him or not; my doing so would not make your heart beat the faster."

"I don't wish you to marry him," he said, confusedly.

She raised her head and looked full at him with eyes which shone like stars through a summer mist.

"That is enough, Arthur," she answered, in a tone of gentle submission, "if you do not wish it, I will not," and, rising, she left the room.

Arthur blushed furiously at her words, and a new sensation crept over him.

"Surely," he said to himself, "she cannot— No, of course, she only means that she will take my advice."

But, though he dismissed the suspicion thus readily, it left something that he could not quite define behind it. He had, after the manner of young men where women are concerned, thought that he understood Mildred thoroughly; now he came to the modest conclusion that he knew very little about her.

On the following afternoon, when he was at the Quinta talking as usual to Mrs. Carr, he saw Lord Minster coming up the steps of the portico, dressed in much the same way and with exactly the same air as he was accustomed to assume when he mounted those of the "Reform," or, occasionally, if he thought that the "hungry electors" wanted "pandering" to, those of the new "National Club."

"Hullo," said Arthur, "here comes Lord Minster in his war-paint, frock coat, tall hat, eye-glass and all. Good-by."

"Why do you go away, Arthur? Stop and protect me," said Mildred, laughing.

"Oh, no, indeed, I don't want to spoil sport. I would not interfere with your amusement on any account."

Mildred looked a little vexed.

"Well, you will come back to dinner?"

"That depends upon what happens."

"I told you what would happen, Arthur. Good-by."

"Perhaps it is as well to get it over at once," thought Mildred.

In the hall Arthur met Lord Minster, and they passed with a gesture of recognition so infinitesimally small that it almost faded into the nothingness of a "cut." So far as he could condescend to notice so low a thing at all, his lordship had conceived a great dislike for Arthur.

"How do you do, Lord Minster?" said Mildred cordially. "I hear that you went to the Convent yesterday; what did you think of the view?"

"The view, Mrs. Carr—was there a view? I did not notice it; indeed, I only went up there at all to please Florence. I don't like that sort of thing."

"If you don't like roughing it, I am afraid that you did not enjoy your voyage out."

"Well, no, I don't think I did, and there was a low fellow on board who had been ruined by the retrocession of the Transvaal, and who, hearing that I was in the Government, took every possible opportunity to tell me publicly that his wife and children were almost in a state of starvation, as though I cared about his confounded wife and children. He was positively brutal. No, certainly I did not enjoy it. However, I am rewarded by finding you here."

"I am very much flattered."

Lord Minster fixed his eye-glass firmly in his eye, planted his hands at the bottom of his trousers pockets, and, clearing his throat, placed himself in the attitude that was so familiar to the House, and began.

"Mrs. Carr, I told you, when last I had the pleasure of seeing you, that I should take the first opportunity of renewing a conversation which I was forced to suspend in order to attend, if my memory serves me, a very important committee meeting. I was therefore surprised, indeed I may almost say hurt, when I found that you had suddenly flitted from London."

"Indeed, Lord Minster?"

"I will not, however, take up the time of this—I mean your time by recapitulating all that I told you on that occasion; the facts are, so to speak, all upon the table, and I will merely touch upon the main heads of my case. My prospects are these: I am now a member of the Cabinet, and enjoy, owing to the unusual but calculated recklessness of my non-official public utterances, an extraordinary popularity with a large section of the country, the hungry section to which I alluded last night. It is probable that the course of the present Government is pretty nearly run; the country is sick of it, and those who put it into power have not got enough out of it. A dissolution is therefore an event of the near future; the Conservatives will come in, but they have no power of organization, and very little political talent at their backs; above all, they are deficient in energy, probably because there is nothing that they can destroy and therefore no pickings to struggle for. In short, they are not 'capaces imperii.' The want of these qualities and of leaders will very soon undermine their hold upon the country, always a slight one, and, assisted by a few other pushing men, I anticipate, by carefully playing into the hands of the Irish party, which will really rule England in the future, being able, as one of the leaders of the Opposition, to consummate their downfall. Then will come my opportunity, and, if luck goes with me, I shall be first Lord of the Treasury within half a dozen years. But now comes the difficulty. Though I am so popular with the country, I am, for some reason quite inexplicable to myself, rather at a—hum—a discount amongst my colleagues and that influential section of society to which they belong. Now, in order to succeed to the full extent that I have planned, it is absolutely essential that I should win the countenance of this class, and the only way that I can see of doing it is by marrying some woman charming enough to disarm dislike, beautiful enough to command admiration, rich enough to entertain profusely, and clever enough to rule England. Those desiderata are all to a striking degree united in your person, Mrs. Carr, and I have therefore much pleasure in asking you to become my wife."

"You have, as I understand you, Lord Minster, made a very admirable statement of how desirable it is for yourself that you should marry me, but it is not so clear what advantage I should reap by marrying you."

"Why, the advantages are obvious: if by your help I can become Prime Minister, you would become the wife of the Prime Minister."

"The prospect fails to dazzle me. I have everything that I want; why should I strive to reach a grandeur to which I was not born, and which, to speak the truth, I regard with a very complete indifference? But there is another point. In all your speech you have said nothing of any affection that you have to offer, not a single word of love—you have been content to expatiate on the profits that a matrimonial investment would bring to yourself and, by reflection, to the other contracting party."

"Love?" asked Lord Minster, with an expression of genuine surprise; "why, you talk like a character in a novel; now tell me, Mrs. Carr, *what* is love?"

"It is difficult to define, Lord Minster; but as you ask me to do so, I will try. Love to a woman is what the sun is to the world; it is her life, her animating principle, without which she must droop, and, if the plant be very tender, die. Except under its influence, a woman can never attain her full growth, never touch the height of her possibilities, or bloom into the plenitude of her moral beauty.

A loveless marriage dwarfs our natures; a marriage where love is develops them to their utmost."

"And what is love to a man?"

"Well, I should say that nine of a man's passions are merely episodes in his career, the mile-stones that mark his path; the tenth, or the first, is his philosopher's stone that turns all things to gold, or, if the charm does not work, leaves his heart, broken and bankrupt, a cold monument of failure."

"I don't quite follow you, and I must say that, speaking for myself, I never felt anything of all this," said Lord Minster, blankly.

"I know that you do not, Lord Minster; your only passions tend towards political triumphs and personal aggrandisement; we are at the two poles, you see, and I fear that we can never, never meet upon a common matrimonial line. But don't be down-hearted about it; you will find plenty more women who fulfil all your requirements and will be very happy to take you at your own valuation. If only a woman is necessary to success, you need not look far, and forgive me if I say that I believe it will not make much difference to you who she is. But all the same, Lord Minster, I will venture to give you a piece of advice: next time you propose, address yourself a little more to the lady's affections and a little less to her interests," and Mrs. Carr rose as though to show that the interview was at an end.

"Am I then to understand that my offer is definitely refused?" asked Lord Minster, stiffly.

"I am afraid so; and I am sure that you will, on reflection, see how utterly unsuited we are to each other."

"Possibly, Mrs. Carr, possibly; at present all that I see is that you have had a great opportunity, and have failed to avail yourself of it. My only consolation is that the loss will be yours, and my only regret that I have had the trouble of coming to this place for nothing. However, there is a ship due to-morrow, and I shall sail in her."

"I am sorry to have been the cause of bringing you here, Lord Minster, and still more sorry that you should feel obliged to cut short your stay. Good by, Lord Minster; we part friends, I hope?"

"Oh, certainly, Mrs. Carr. I wish you a very good morning, Mrs. Carr," and his lordship marched out of Mildred's life.

"There goes my chance of becoming the wife of a Prime Minister, and making a figure in history," said that lady, as she watched his tall figure stalking stiffly down the avenue. "Well, I am glad of it. I would just as soon have married a speech-making figurehead stuffed full of the purest Radical principles."

On the following day Arthur met Lady Florence again in the town.

"Where have you been to, Lady Florence?" he said.

"To see my brother off," she answered, without any signs of deep grief.

"What, has he gone already?"

"Yes; your friend Mrs. Carr has been too many for poor James."

"What! do you mean that he has been proposing?"

"Yes, and got more than he bargained for."

"Is he cut up?"

"He? no, but his vanity is. You see, Mr. Heigham, it is this way. My brother may be a very great man and a pillar of the State, and all that sort of thing. I don't say he isn't; but from personal experience I *know* that he is an awful prig, and thinks that all women are machines constructed to advance the comfort of your noble sex. Well, he has come down a peg or two, that's all, and he don't like it. Good-by; I'm in a hurry."

Lady Florence was nothing if not outspoken.

CHAPTER XLIII.

A WEEK or so after the departure of Lord Minster, Mildred suggested that they should, on the following day, vary their amusements by going up to the Convent, a building perched on the hills some thousand feet above the town of Funchal, in palanquins, or rather hammocks swung upon long poles. Arthur, who had never yet travelled in these luxurious conveyances, jumped at the idea; and even Miss Terry, when she discovered that she was to be carried, made no objection. The party was completed by the addition of a newly-married couple of whom Mrs. Carr had known something at home, and who had come to Madeira to spend the honeymoon. Lady Florence also had been asked, but, rather to Arthur's disappointment, she could not come.

When the long line of swinging hammocks, each with its two sturdy bearers, were marshalled, and the adventurous voyagers had settled themselves in them, they really formed quite an imposing procession, headed as it was by the extra-sized one that carried Miss Terry, who complained bitterly that "the thing wobbled and made her feel sick."

But to Arthur's mind there was something effeminate in allowing himself, a strong, active man, to be carted up hills as steep as the side of a house by two perspiring wretches; so, hot as it was, he, to the intense amusement of his bearers, elected to get out and walk. The newly-married man followed his example, and for a while they went on together, till presently the latter gravitated towards his wife's palanquin, and, overcome at so long a separation, squeezed her hand between the curtains. Not wishing to intrude himself on their conjugal felicity, Arthur in his turn gravitated to the side of Mrs. Carr, who was being lightly swung along in the second palanquin some twenty yards behind Miss Terry's. Shortly afterwards they observed a signal of distress being flown by that lady, whose arm was to be seen violently agitating her green veil from between the curtains of her hammock, which immediately came to a dead stop.

"What is it?" cried Arthur and Mildred, in a breath, as they arrived on the scene of supposed disaster.

"My dear Mildred, will you be so kind as to tell that man" (pointing to her front bearer, a stout, flabby individual) "that he must not go on carrying me. I must have a cooler man. It makes me positively ill to see him puffing and blowing and dripping under my nose like a fresh-basted joint."

Miss Terry's realistic description of her bearer's appearance, which was, to say the least of it, limp and moist, was no exaggeration. But then she herself, as Arthur well remembered, was no featherweight, especially when, as in the present case, she had to be carted up the side of a nearly perpendicular hill some miles long, a fact very well exemplified by the condition of the bearer.

"My dear Agatha," replied Mildred, laughing, "what is to be done? Of course the man is hot, you are not a feather-weight; but what is to be done?"

"I don't know, but I won't go on with him, it's simply disgusting; he might let himself out as a watering-cart."

"But we can't get another here."

"Then he must cool himself; the others might come and fan him. I won't go on till he is cool, and that's flat."

"He will take hours to cool, and meanwhile we are boiling on this hot road. You really must come on, Agatha."

"I have it," said Arthur. "Miss Terry must turn herself round with her head towards the back of the hammock, and then she won't see him."

To this arrangement the aggrieved lady was after some difficulty persuaded to accede, and the procession started again.

Their destination reached, they picknicked as they had arranged, and then separated, the bride and bridegroom strolling off in one direction, and Mildred and Arthur in another, whilst Miss Terry mounted guard over the plates and dishes.

Presently Arthur and Mildred came to a little English-looking grove of pine and oak, that extended down a gentle slope and was bordered by a steep bank, at the foot of which great ferns and beautiful Madeira flowers twined themselves into a shelter from the heat. Here they sat down and gazed at the splendid and many-tinted view set in its background of emerald ocean.

"What a view it is!" said Arthur. "Look, Mildred, how dark the clumps of sugar-cane look against the green of the vines, and how pretty the red roofs of the town are peeping out of the groves of fruit-trees. Do you see the great shadow thrown upon the sea by that cliff? How deep and cool the water looks within it, and how it sparkles where the sun strikes!"

"Yes, it is beautiful, and the pines smell sweet."

"I wish Angela could see it," he said, half to himself. Mildred, who was lying back lazily among the ferns, her hat off, her eyes closed, so that the long dark lashes lay upon her cheek, and her head resting on her arm, suddenly started up.

"What is the matter?"

"Nothing; you woke me from a sort of dream, that's all."

"This spring I remember going with her to look at a view near the Abbey House, and saying—what I often think when I look at anything beautiful and full of life—that it depressed one to know that all this was so much food for death, and its beauty a thing that to-day is and to-morrow is not."

"And what did she say?"

"She said that to her it spoke of immortality, and that in everything around her she saw evidences of eternal life."

"She must be very fortunate. Shall I tell you of what it reminds me?"

"What?"

"Of neither death nor immortality, but of the full, happy, pulsing existence of the hour, and of the beautiful world that pessimists like yourself and mystics like your Angela think so poorly of, but which is really so glorious and so rich in joy. Why, this sunlight and those flowers, and the wide sparkle of that sea, are each and all a happiness, and the health in our veins and the beauty in our eyes, deep pleasures that we never realize till we lose them. Death, indeed, comes to us all, but why add to its terrors by thinking of them whilst it is far off? And, as for life after death, it is a faint, vague thing, more likely to be horrible than happy. This world is our only reality, the only thing that we can grasp; here alone we *know* that we can enjoy, and yet how we waste our short opportunities for enjoyment! Soon youth will have slipped away, and we shall be too old for love. Roses fade fastest, Arthur, when the sun is bright; in the evening when they have fallen, and the ground is red with withering petals, do you not think we shall wish that we had gathered more?"

"Yours is a pleasant philosophy, Mildred," he said, struggling faintly in his own mind against her conclusions.

But at that moment, somehow, his fingers touched her own and were presently locked fast within her little palm, and for the first time in his life they sat hand in hand. But, happily for him, he did not venture to look into her eyes, and, before many minutes had passed, Miss Terry's voice was heard calling him loudly.

"I suppose that you must go," said Mildred, with a shade of vexation in her voice and a good many shades upon her face, "or she will be blundering down here. I will come, too; it is time for tea."

On arriving at the spot whence the sounds proceeded, they found Miss Terry surrounded by a crowd of laughing and excited bearers, and pouring out a flood of the most vigorous English upon an unfortunate islander, who stood, a silver mug in each hand, bowing and shrugging his shoulders, and enunciating with every variety of movement indicative of humiliation, these mystic words:

"Mee washeeuppee, signora, washeeuppee—e."

"What *is* the matter now, Agatha?"

"Matter, why I woke up and found this man stealing the cups; I charged him at once with my umbrella, but he dodged and I fell down, and the umbrella has gone over the rock there. Take him up at once, Arthur—there's the stolen property on his person. Hand him over to justice."

"Good gracious, Agatha, what are you thinking about? The poor man only wants to wash the things out."

"Then I should like to know why he could not tell me so in plain English," said Miss Terry, retiring discomfited amidst shouts of laughter from the whole party, including the supposed thief.

After tea they all set out on a grand beetle-hunting expedition, and so intent were they upon this fascinating pursuit that they did not note the flight of time, till suddenly Mildred, pulling out her watch, gave a pretty cry of alarm.

"Do you know what time it is, good people? Half-past six, and the Custances are to dine with us at a quarter-past seven. It will take us a good hour to get down; what *shall* we do?"

"I know," said Arthur, "there are two sledges just below; I saw them as we came up. They will take us down to Funchal in a quarter of an hour, and we can get to the Quinta by about seven."

"Arthur, you are invaluable; the very thing. Come on, all of you, quick."

Now these sledges are peculiar to Madeira, being made on the principle of the bullock car, with the difference that they travel down the smooth, stoned paved roadways by their own momentum, guided by two skilled conductors, each with one foot naked to prevent his slipping, who hold the ropes, and when the sledge begins to travel more swiftly than they can follow, mount upon the projecting ends of the runners and are carried with it. By means of the swift and exhilarating rush of these sledges, the traveller traverses the distance, that it takes some hours to climb, in a very few minutes. Indeed, his journey up and down may be very well compared with that of the well-known British sailor who took five hours to get up Majuba mountain, but according to his own forcibly told story, came down again with an almost incredible rapidity. It may therefore be imagined that sledge-travelling in Madeira is not very well suited to nervous voyagers.

Miss Terry had at times seen these wheelless vehicles shoot from the top of a mountain to the bottom like a balloon with the gas out, and had also heard of occasional accidents in connection with them. Stoutly she vowed that nothing should induce her to trust her neck to one of them.

"But you must, Agatha, or else be left behind. They are as safe as a church, and I can't leave the Custances to wait till half-past eight for dinner. Come, get in. Arthur can go in front and hold you; I will sit behind."

Thus admonished—Miss Terry entered groaning, Arthur taking his seat beside her, and Mrs. Carr hers in a sort of dickey behind. The newly-married pair, who did not half like it, possessed themselves of the smaller sledge, determined to brave extinction in each other's arms. Then the conductors seized the ropes, and, planting their one naked foot firmly before them, awaited the signal to depart.

"Stop," said Miss Terry, lifting the recovered umbrella, "that man has forgotten to put on his shoe and stocking on his right leg. He will cut his foot, and, besides, it doesn't look respectable to be seen flying through a place with a one-legged ragamuffin—"

"Let her go," shouted Arthur, and they did, to some purpose, for in a minute they were passing down that hill like a flash of light. Woods and houses appeared and vanished like the visions of a dream, and the soft air went singing away on either side of them as they clove it, flying downwards at an angle of thirty degrees, and leaving nothing behind them but the sound of Miss Terry's lamentations. Soon they neared the bottom, but there was yet a dip—the deepest of them all, with a sharp turn at the end of it—to be traversed.

Away went the little connubial sledge in front like a pigeon down the wind; away they sped after it like an eagle in pursuit; *crack* went the little sledge into the corner, and out shot the happy pair; *crash* went the big sledge into it, and Arthur became conscious of a wild yell, of a green veil fluttering through the air, and of a fall as on to a feather-bed. Miss Terry's superior weight had brought her to her mother earth the first, and he, after a higher heavenward flight, had lit upon the top of her. He picked her up and sat her down against a wall to recover her breath, and then fished Mildred, dirty and bruised, but as usual laughing, out of a gutter; the loving pair had already risen and in an agony of mutual anxiety were rubbing each other's shins. And then he started back with a cry, for there before him, surveying the disaster with an air of mingled amusement and benevolence, stood—Sir John and Lady Bellamy.

Had it been the Prince and Princess of Evil—if, as is probable, there is a Princess—Arthur could scarcely have been more astounded. Somehow he had always in his thoughts regarded Sir John and Lady Bellamy, when he thought about them at all, as possessing indeed individual characters and tendencies, but as completely "adscripti glebæ" of the neighborhood of the Abbey House as that house itself. He would as soon have expected to see Caresfoot's Staff re-rooted in the soil of Madeira, as to find them strolling about Funchal. He rubbed his eyes; perhaps, he thought, he had been knocked silly and was laboring under a hallucination. No, there was no doubt about it; there they were, just the same as he had seen them at Isleworth, except that if possible Sir John looked even more like a ripe apple than usual, while the sun had browned his wife's Egyptian face and given her a last finish as a perfect type of Cleopatra. Nor was the recognition on his side only, for next second his hand was grasped first by Sir John and then by Lady Bellamy.

"When we last met, Mr. Heigham," said the gentleman, with a benevolent beam, "I think I expressed a wish that we might soon renew our acquaintance, but I little thought under what circumstances our next meeting would take place, and he pointed to the overturned sledges and the prostrate sledgers.

"You have had a very merciful escape," chimed in Lady Bellamy, cordially; "with so many hard stones about, affairs might have ended differently."

"Now then, Mr. Heigham, we had better set to and run, that is, if Agatha has got a run left in her, or we shall be late after all. Thank goodness nobody is hurt; but we must find a hammock for Agatha, for to judge from her groans she thinks she is. Is my nose— Oh, I beg your pardon," and Mrs. Carr stopped short, observing for the first time that he was talking to strangers.

"Do not let me detain you, if you are in a hurry. I am so thankful that nobody is hurt," said Lady Bellamy. "I believe that we are stopping at the same hotel, Mr. Heigham, I saw your name in the book, so we shall have plenty of opportunities of meeting."

But Arthur felt that there was one question which he must ask before he went on, whether or no it exceeded the strict letter of his agreement with Philip; so, calling to Mrs. Carr that he was coming, he said, with a blush.

"How was Miss Caresfoot when—when last you saw her, Lady Bellamy?"

"Perfectly well," she answered, smiling.

"And more lovely than ever," added her husband.

"Thank you for that news; it is the best I have heard for some time. Good-by for the present, we shall meet to-morrow at breakfast," and he ran on after the others, happier than he had been for months, feeling that he had come again within call of Angela, and as though he had never sat hand in hand with Mildred Carr.

CHAPTER XLIV.

At breakfast on the following morning Arthur, as he had anticipated, met the Bellamys. Sir John came down first, arrayed in true English fashion, in a tourist suit of gray, and presently Lady Bellamy followed. As she entered, dressed in trailing white, and walked slowly up the long table, every eye was turned upon her, for she was one of those women who attract attention as surely and unconsciously as a magnet attracts iron. Arthur, looking with the rest, thought that he had never seen a stranger, or at the same time a more imposing-looking, woman. Time had not yet touched her beauty or impaired her vigorous constitution, and at forty she was still at the zenith of her charms. The dark hair, that threw out glinting lights of copper when the sun struck it, still curled in its clustering ringlets and showed no line of gray, while the mysterious heavy-lidded eyes and the coral lips were as full of rich life and beauty as they had been when she and Hilda von Holtzhausen first met at Rewtham House.

On her face, too, was the same expression of quiet power, of conscious superiority and calm command, that had always distinguished it. Arthur tried to think what it reminded him of, and remembered that the same look was to be seen upon the stone features of some of the Egyptian statues in Mildred's museum.

"How splendid Lady Bellamy looks!" he said, almost unconsciously, to his neighbor.

Sir John did not answer; and Arthur, glancing up to learn the reason, saw that he also was watching the approach of his wife, and that his face was contorted with a sudden spasm of intense malice and hatred, whilst his little pig-like eyes glittered threateningly. He had not even heard the remark. Arthur would have liked to whistle; he had surprised a secret.

"How do you do, Mr. Heigham? I hope that you are not bruised after your tumble yesterday. Good-morning, John."

Arthur rose and shook hands.

"I never was more surprised in my life," he said, "than when I saw you and Sir John at the top of the street there. May I ask what brought you to Madeira?"

"Health, sir, health," answered the little man. "Cough, catarrh, influenza, and all that's damn—ah! infernal!"

"My husband, Mr. Heigham," struck in Lady Bellamy, in her full, rich tones, "had a severe threatening of chest-disease, and the doctor recommended a trip to some warmer climate. Unfortunately, however, his business arrangements will not permit of a long stay. We only stop here three weeks at most."

"I am sorry to hear that you are not well, Sir John."

"Oh! it is nothing very much," answered Lady Bellamy for him; "only he requires care. What a lovely garden this is—is it not? By the way, I forgot to inquire after the ladies who shared your tumble. I hope that they were none the worse. I was much struck with one of them, the very pretty person with the brown hair whom you pulled out of the gutter."

"Oh, Mrs. Carr. Yes, she is pretty."

After breakfast, Arthur volunteered to take Lady Bellamy round the garden, with the ulterior object of extracting some more information about Angela. It must be remembered that he had no cause to mistrust that lady, nor had he any knowledge of the events which had recently happened in the neighborhood of the Abbey House. He was therefore perfectly frank with her.

"I suppose that you have heard of my engagement, Lady Bellamy?"

"Oh, yes, Mr. Heigham; it is quite a subject of conversation in the Roxham neighborhood. Angela Caresfoot is a sweet and very beautiful girl, and I congratulate you much."

"You know, then, of its conditions?"

"Yes, I heard of them, and thought them ridiculous. Indeed I tried, at Angela's suggestion, to do you a good turn with Philip Caresfoot, and get him to modify them; but he would not. He is a curious man, Philip, and when he once gets a thing into his head, it is beyond the power of most people to drive it out again. I suppose that you are spending your year of probation here?"

"Well, yes—I am trying to get through the time in that way; but it is slow work."

"I thought you seemed pretty happy yesterday," she answered, smiling.

Arthur blushed.

"Oh, yes, I may appear to be. But tell me all about Angela."

"I have really very little to tell. She seems to be living as usual, and looks well. Her friend Mr. Fraser has come back. But I must be going in; I have promised to go out walking with Sir John. Au revoir, Mr. Heigham."

Left to himself, Arthur remembered that he also had an appointment to keep—namely, to meet Mildred by the Cathedral steps, and go with her to choose some Madeira jewelry, an undertaking which she did not feel competent to carry out without his assistance.

When he reached the Cathedral, he found her rather cross at having been kept waiting for ten minutes.

"It is very rude of you," she said; "but I suppose that you were so taken up with the conversation of your friends that you forgot the time. By the way, who are they? anybody you have told me about?"

In the pauses of selecting the jewelry, Arthur told her all he knew about the Bellamys, and of their connection with the neighborhood of the Abbey House. The story caused Mildred to open her brown eyes and look thoughtful. Just as they came out of the shop, who should they run into but the Bellamys themselves, chaffering for Madeira work with a woman in the street! Arthur stopped and spoke to them, and then introduced Mrs. Carr, who, after a little conversation, asked them up to lunch.

After this Mildred and Lady Bellamy met a good deal. The two women interested each other.

One night, when the Bellamys had been about ten days in Madeira, the conversation took a personal turn. Sir John and Arthur were sitting over their wine (they were dining with Mrs. Carr), Agatha Terry was fast asleep on a sofa, so that Lady Bellamy and Mildred, seated upon lounging-chairs, by a table with a light on it, placed by an open window, were practically alone.

"Oh, by the way, Lady Bellamy," said Mildred, after a pause, "I believe that you are acquainted with the young lady to whom Mr. Heigham is engaged?" She had meant to say, "to be married," but the words stuck in her throat.

"Oh, yes, I know her well."

"I am so glad. I am quite curious to hear what she is like; one can never put much faith in lovers' raptures, you know."

"Do you mean in person or in character?"

"Both."

"Well, Angela Caresfoot is as lovely a woman as ever I saw, with a noble figure, well-set head, and magnificent eyes and hair."

Mildred turned a little pale and bit her lips.

"As to her character, I can hardly describe it. She lives in an atmosphere of her own, an atmosphere that I cannot reach, or, at any rate, cannot breathe. But if you can imagine a woman whose mind is enriched with learning as profound as that of the first classical scholars of the day, and tinged with an originality all her own; a woman whose faith is as steady as that star, and whose love is as deep as the sea and as definite as its tides; who lives to higher ends than those we strive for; whose whole life, indeed, gives one the idea that it is the shadow—imperfect, perhaps, but still the shadow—of an immortal light,—then you will get some idea of Angela Caresfoot. She is a woman intellectually, physically, and spiritually immeasurably above the man on whom she has set her affections."

"That cannot be," said Mildred, softly; "like draws to like: she must have found something in him, some better part, some affinity of which you know nothing."

After this she fell into silence. Presently Lady Bellamy raised her eyes, just now filled up with the great pupils, and fixed them on Mildred.

"You are thinking," she said, slowly, "that Angela Caresfoot is a formidable rival."

Mildred started.

"How can you pretend to read my thoughts?"

She laughed a little.

"I am an adept at the art. Don't be down-hearted. I should not be surprised if, after all, the engagement between Mr. Heigham and Angela Caresfoot should come to nothing. Of course, I speak in perfect confidence."

"Of course."

"Well, the marriage is not altogether agreeable to the father, who would prefer another and more suitable match. But, unfortunately, there is no way of shaking the young lady's determination."

"Indeed!"

"But I think that, with assistance, a way might be found."

Their eyes met, and this time Mildred took up the parable.

"Should I be wrong, Lady Bellamy, if I supposed that you have not come to Madeira solely for pleasure?"

"A wise person always tries to combine business and pleasure."

"And in this case the business combined is in connection with Mr. Heigham's engagement?"

"Exactly."

"And supposing that I were to tell him this?"

"Had I not known that you would on no account tell Mr. Heigham, I should not have told you."

"And how do you know that?"

"I will answer your question by another. Did you ever yet know a woman who loved a man willingly help him to the arms of a rival,—unless indeed she was forced to it?" she added, with something like a sigh.

Mildred Carr's snowy bosom heaved tumultuously, and the rose-leaf hue faded from her cheeks.

"You mean that I am in love with Arthur Heigham. On what do you base that belief ?"

"On a base as broad as the pyramids of which you were talking at dinner. Public report, not nearly so misleading a guide as people think, your face, your voice, your eyes, all betray you. Why do you always try to get near him to touch him?—answer me that. I have seen you do it three times this evening. Once you handed him a book in order to touch his hand beneath it; but there is no need to enumerate what you doubtless very well remember. No nice woman, Mrs. Carr, ever likes to continually touch a man unless she loves him. You are always listening for his voice and step, you are listening for them now. Your eyes follow his face as a dog does his master's; when you speak to him, your voice is a caress in itself. Shall I go on?"

"I think that it is unnecessary. Whether you be right or not, I will give you the credit of being a close observer."

"To observe with me is at once a task and an amusement, and the habit is one that leads me to accurate conclusions, as I think you will admit. The conclusion I have come to in your case is that you do not wish to see Arthur Heigham married to another woman. I spoke just now of assistance—"

"I have none to give; I will give none. How could I look him in the face?"

"You are strangely scrupulous for a woman in your position."

"I have always tried to behave like an honorable woman, Lady Bellamy, and I do not feel inclined to do otherwise now."

"Perhaps you will think differently when it comes to the point. But in the mean while remember that people who will not help themselves cannot expect to be helped."

"Once and for all, Lady Bellamy, understand me. I fight for my own hand with the weapons which Nature and fortune have given me, and by myself I will stand or fall. I will join in no schemes to separate Arthur from this woman. If I cannot win him for myself by myself, I will at any rate lose him fairly. I will respect what you have told me, but I will do no more."

Lady Bellamy smiled as she answered—

"I really admire your courage. It is quite quixotic. Hush, here come the gentlemen."

CHAPTER XLV.

A FEW days after the dinner at the Quinta Carr, the Bellamys' visit to Madeira drew to a close. On the evening before their departure, Arthur volunteered to take Lady Bellamy down to the parade to hear the band play. After they had walked about a while under the shade of the magnolia-trees, which were starred all over with creamy cups of bloom, and sufficiently inspected the gay throng of Portuguese inhabitants and English visitors, made gayer still by the amazingly gorgeous uniforms of the officials, Arthur spied two chairs in a comparatively quiet corner, and suggested that they should sit down.

"Lady Bellamy," he said, after hesitating awhile, "you are a woman of the world, and I believe a friend of my own. I want to ask your advice about something."

"It is entirely at your service, Mr. Heigham."

"Well, really it is very awkward—"

"Shall I turn my head so as not to see your blushes?"

"Don't laugh at me, Lady Bellamy. Of course you will say nothing of this."

"If you doubt my discretion, Mr. Heigham, do not choose me as a confidante. You are going, unless I am mistaken, to speak to me about Mrs. Carr."

"Yes, it is about her. But how did you know that? You always seem to be able to read one's thoughts before one speaks. Do you know, sometimes I think that she has taken a fancy to me, do you see, and I wanted to ask what you thought about it."

"Well, supposing that she had, most young men, Mr. Heigham, would not talk of such a thing in a tone befitting a great catastrophe. But, if I am not entering too deeply into particulars, what makes you think you so?"

"Well, really, I don't exactly know. She sometimes gives me a general idea."

"Oh, then, there has been nothing tangible."

"Well, yes, once she took my hand, or I took hers, I don't know which; but I don't think much of that, because it's the sort of thing that's always happening, don't you know, and nine times out of ten means nothing at all. But why I ask you about it is that, if there is anything of the sort, I had better cut and run out of this, because it would not be fair to stop, either to her, or to Angela, or myself. It would be dangerous, you see, playing with such a woman as Mildred."

"So you would go away if you thought that she took any warmer interest in you than ladies generally do in men engaged to be married."

"Certainly I should."

"Well, then, I think that I can set your mind at ease. I have observed Mrs. Carr pretty closely, and in the way you suppose she cares for you no more than she does for your coat. She is, no doubt, a bit of a flirt, and very likely wishes to get you to fall in love with her—a natural ambition on the part of a woman; but, as for being in love with you herself, the idea is absurd. Women of the world do not fall in love so readily; they are too much taken up with thinking about themselves to have time to think about anybody else. With them it is all self, self, self, from morning till night. Besides, look at the common-sense side of the thing. Do you suppose it likely that a person of Mrs. Carr's wealth and beauty, who has only to lift her hand to have all London at her feet, is likely to fix her affections upon a young man whom she knows is already engaged to be married, and who—forgive me if I say so—has not got the same recommendations to her favor that many of her suitors have? It is, of course, quite possible that Mrs. Carr's society may be dangerous for you, in which case it might be wise for you to go; but I really do not think that you need feel any anxiety on her account. She finds you a charming companion, and in some ways a useful one, and that is all. When you go, somebody else will soon fill the vacant space."

"Then that's all right," said Arthur, though somehow he did not feel as wildly delighted as he should have done at hearing it so clearly demonstrated that Mildred did not care a brass button about him; but then that is human nature. Between eighteen and thirty-five, ninety per cent of the men in the world would like to centre in themselves the affections of every young and pretty woman they know, even if there was not the ghost of a chance of their marrying one of them. The same tendency is to be observed conversely in the other sex, only in their case with a still smaller proportion of exceptions.

"By the way," asked Arthur, presently, "how is my late guardian, Mr. George Caresfoot?"

"Not at all well, I am sorry to say. I am very anxious about his health. He is in the south of England now for a change."

"I am sorry he is ill. Do you know, I dare say you will think me absurd; but you have taken a weight off my mind. I always had an idea that he wanted to marry Angela, and sometimes I am afraid that I have suspected that Philip Caresfoot carted me off in order to give him a chance. You see, Philip is uncommonly fond of money, and George is rich."

"What an absurd idea, Mr. Heigham! Why, George looks upon matrimony as an institution of the evil one. He admires Angela, I know—he always does admire a pretty face; but as for dreaming of marrying a girl half his age, and his own cousin into the bargain, it is about the last thing that he would do."

"I am glad to hear it. I am sure I have been uncomfortable enough thinking about him sometimes. Lady Bellamy, will you do something for me?"

"What is that, Mr. Heigham?"

"Tell Angela all about me."

"But would that be quite honorable, Mr. Heigham—under the conditions of your engagement, I mean?"

"You never promised not to talk about me; I only promised not to attempt verbal or written communication with Angela."

"Well, I will tell her that I met you, and that you are well, and, if Philip will allow me, I will tell her more; but of course I don't know if he will or not. What ring is that you wear?"

"It is one that Angela gave me when we became engaged. It was her mother's."

"Will you let me look at it?"

Arthur held out his hand. The ring was an antique, a large emerald, cut like a seal and heavily set in a band of dull gold. On the face of the stone were engraved some mysterious characters.

"What is that engraved on the stone?"

"I am not sure; but Angela told me that Mr. Fraser had taken an impression of it, and forwarded it to a great Oriental scholar. His friend said that the stone must be extremely ancient, as the character is a form of Sanscrit, and that he believed the word to mean 'Forever' or 'Eternity.' Angela said that it had been in her mother's family for generations, and was supposed to have been brought from the East about the year 1700. That is all I know about it."

"The motto is better suited to a wedding-ring than to an engagement stone," said Lady Bellamy, with one of her dark smiles.

"Why?"

"Because engagements are like promises and pie-crust, made to be broken."

"I hope that will not be the case with ours, however," said Arthur, attempting a laugh.

"I hope not, I am sure; but never pin your faith absolutely to any woman, or you will regret it. Always accept her oaths and protestations as you would a political statement, politely, and with an appearance of perfect faith, but with a certain grain of mistrust. Woman's fidelity is in the main a fiction. We are faithful just as men are, so long as it suits us to be so; with this difference however, men play false from passion or impulse, women from calculation."

"You do not draw a pleasing picture of your own sex."

"When is the truth pleasing? It is only when we clothe its nakedness with the rags of imagination, or sweeten it with fiction, that it can please. Of itself, it is so ugly a thing that society in its refinement will not even hear it, but prefers to employ a corresponding formula. Thus all passion, however vile, is called by the name of 'love,' all superstitious terror and grovelling attempts to conciliate the unseen are known as 'religion,' while selfish greed and the hungry lust for power masquerade as laudable 'ambition.' Men and women, especially women, hate the truth, because, like the electric light, it shows them as they are, and that is vile. It has grown so strange to them from disuse that, like Pilate, they do not even know what it is! I was going to say, however, that if you care to trust me with it, I think I see how I can take a message to Angela for you—without either causing you to break your promise or doing anything dishonorable myself."

"How?"

"Well, if you like, I will take her that ring. I think that is a very generous offer on my part, for I do not like the responsibility."

"But what is the use of taking her the ring?"

"It is something that there can be no mistake about, that is all, a speaking message from yourself. But don't give it me if you do not like; perhaps you had rather not!"

"I don't like parting with it at all, I confess, but I should dearly like to send her something. I suppose that you would not take a letter?"

"You would not write one, Mr. Heigham!"

"No, of course, I forgot that accursed promise. Here, take the ring, and say all you can to Angela with it. You promise that you will?"

"Certainly, I promise that I will say all I can."

"You are very good and kind. I wish to Heaven that I were going to Marlshire with you. If you only knew how I long to see her again. I think that it would break my heart if anything happened to separate us," and his lips quivered at the thought.

Lady Bellamy turned her sombre face upon him—there was compassion in her eyes.

"If you bear Angela Caresfoot so great a love, be guided by me and shake it off, strangle it—be rid of it anyhow; for fulfilled affection of that nature would carry a larger happiness with it than is allowed in a world planned expressly to secure the greatest misery of the greatest number. There is a fate which fights against it; its ministers are human folly and passion. You have seen many marriages: tell me, how many have you known, out of a novel, where the people married their true loves? In novels they always do, it is another of society's pleasant fictions, but real life is like a novel without the third volume. I do not want to alarm you, Mr. Heigham; but, because I like you, I ask you to steel your mind to disappointments, so that, if a blow comes, it may not crush you."

"What do you mean, Lady Bellamy? do you know of any impending trouble?"

"I? Certainly not. I only talk on general principles. Do not be over-confident, and *never* trust a woman. Come let us get home."

Next morning, when Arthur came down to breakfast, the Bellamys had sailed. The mail had come in from the Cape at midnight, and left again at dawn, taking them with it.

CHAPTER XLVI.

THE departure of the Bellamys left Arthur in very low spirits. His sensations were similar to those which one can well imagine an ancient Greek might have experienced who, having sent to consult the Delphic oracle, had got for his pains a very unsatisfactory reply, foreshadowing evils but not actually defining them. Lady Bellamy was in some way connected with the idea of an oracle in his mind. She looked, oracular. Her dark face and inscrutable eyes, the stamp of power upon her brow, all suggested that she was a mistress of the black arts. Her words, too, were mysterious, and fraught with bitter wisdom and a deep knowledge distilled from the poisonous weeds of life.

Arthur felt with something like a shudder that if Lady Bellamy prophesied evil, evil was following hard upon her words. And in warning him not to place his whole heart's happiness upon one venture, lest it should meet with shipwreck, he was sure that she was prophesying with a knowledge of the future denied to ordinary mortals. How earnestly, too, she had cautioned him against putting absolute faith in Angela—so earnestly, indeed, that her talk had left a flavor of distrust in his mind! Yet how could he mistrust Angela?

Nor was he comforted by a remark that fell from Mildred Carr the afternoon following the departure of the mail. Raising her eyes, she glanced at his hand.

"What are you looking at?" he said.

"Was not that queer emerald you wore your engagement-ring?"

"Yes."

"What have you done with it?"

"I gave it to Lady Bellamy to give to Angela."

"What for?"

"To show her that I am alive and well! I may not write, you know."

"You are very confiding."

"What do you mean?"

"Nothing. At least, I mean that I don't think that I should care to hand over my engagement-ring so easily. It might be misapplied, you know."

This view of the matter helped to fill up the cup of Arthur's nervous anxiety, and he vainly plied Mildred with questions to get her to elucidate her meaning, and state her causes of suspicion, if she had any; but she would say nothing more on the subject, which then dropped, and was not alluded to again between them.

After the Bellamys' departure, the time wore on at Madeira without bringing about any appreciable change in the situation. But Mildred saw that their visit had robbed her of any advantages she had gained over Arthur, for they had, as it were, brought Angela's atmosphere with them, and, faint though it was, it sufficed to overpower her influence. He made no move forward, and seemed to have entirely forgotten the episode on the hills when he had gone so very near disaster. On the contrary, he appeared to her to grow increasingly preoccupied as time went on, and to look upon her more and more in the light of a sister, till at length her patience wore thin.

As for her passion, it grew almost unrestrainable in its confinement. Now she drifted like a rudderless vessel on a sea which raged continuously and knew no space of calm. And so little oil was poured upon the troubled waters, there were so few breaks in the storm-walls that rose black between her and the desired haven of her rest. Indeed, she began to doubt if even her poor power of charming him, as at first she had been able to do, with the sparkle of her wit and the half-unconscious display of her natural grace, was not on the wane, and if she was not near to losing her precarious foothold in his esteem and affection. The thought that he might be tiring of her struck her like freezing wind, and for a moment turned her heart to ice.

Poor Mildred! higher than ever above her head bloomed that "blue rose" she longed to pluck. Would she ever reach it after all her striving, even to gather one poor leaf, one withered petal? The path which led to it was very hard to climb, and below the breakers boiled. Would it, after all, be her fate to fall, down into that gulf of which the sorrowful waters could bring neither death nor forgetfulness?

And so Christmas came and went.

One day, when they were all sitting in the drawing-room, some eight weeks after the Bellamys had left, and Mildred was letting her mind run on such thoughts as these, Arthur, who had been reading a novel, got up and opened the folding-doors at the end of the room which separated it from the second drawing-room, and also the further doors between that room and the dining-room. Then he returned, and, standing at the top of the big drawing-room, took a bird's-eye view of the whole suite.

"What *are* you doing, Arthur?"

"I am reflecting, Mildred, that, with such a suite of apartments at your command, it is a sin and a shame not to give a ball."

"I will give a ball, if you like, Arthur. Will you dance with me if I do?"

"How many times?" he said, laughing.

"Well, I will be moderate—three times. Let me see—the first waltz, the waltz before supper, and the last galop."

"You will dance me off my head. It is dangerous to waltz with any one so pretty," he said, in that bantering tone he often took with her, and which aggravated her intensely.

"It is more likely that my own head will suffer, as I dance so rarely. Then, that is a bargain?"

"Certainly."

"Dear me, Mildred, how silly you are; you are like a school-girl!" said Miss Terry.

"Agatha is put out because you do not offer to dance three times with her."

"Oh! but I will, though, if she likes; three quadrilles."

And so the matter passed off in mutual badinage; but Mildred did not forget her intention. On the contrary, "society" at Madeira was soon profoundly agitated by the intelligence that the lady Crœsus, Mrs. Carr, was about to give a magnificent ball, and so ill-natured—or, rather, so given to jumping to conclusions—is society, that it was freely said it was in order to celebrate her engagement to Arthur Heigham. Arthur heard nothing of this; one is always the last to hear things about one's self. Mildred knew of it, however; but, whether from indifference or from some hidden motive, she neither took any steps to contradict it herself, nor would she allow Miss Terry to do so.

"Nonsense," she said; "let them talk. To contradict such things only makes people believe them the more. Mind now, Agatha, not a word of this to Mr. Heigham; it would put him out."

"Well, Mildred, I should have thought that you would be put out too."

"I!—oh, no! Worse things might happen;" and she shrugged her shoulders.

At length the much-expected evening came, and the arriving guests found that the ball had been planned on a scale such as Madeira had never before beheld. The night was lovely and sufficiently still to admit of the illumination of the gardens by means of Chinese lanterns that glowed all around in hundreds, and were even hung like golden fruit amongst the topmost leaves of the lofty cabbage palms, and from the tallest sprays of the bamboos. Within, the scene was equally beautiful. The suite of three reception-rooms had been thrown into one, two for dancing, and one for use as a sitting-room. They were quite full, for the Madeira season was at its height, and all the English visitors who were "anybody" were there. There happened, too, to be a man-of-war in the harbor, every man-jack, or, rather, every officer-jack of which, with the exception of those on watch—and they were to be relieved later on—was there, and prepared to enjoy himself with a gusto characteristic of the British sailor-man.

The rooms, too, were by no means devoid of beauty, but by far the loveliest woman in them was Mrs. Carr herself. She was simply dressed in a perfectly-fitting black satin gown, looped up with diamond stars that showed off the exquisite fairness of her skin to great perfection. Her ornaments were also diamonds, but such diamonds—not little flowers and birds constructed of tiny stones, but large single gems, each the size of a hazel-nut. On her head she wore a tiara of these, eleven stones in all, five on each side, and surmounted over the centre of the forehead by an enormous gem as large as a small walnut, which, standing by itself above the level of the others, flashed and blazed like a fairy star. Around her neck, wrists, and waist were similar points of concentrated light, that, shining against the black satin as she moved, gave her a truly magnificent appearance. Never before had Mildred Carr looked so perfectly lovely, for her face and form were well worthy of the gems and dress; indeed, most of the men there that night thought her eyes as beautiful as her diamonds.

The ball opened with a quadrille, but in this Mrs. Carr did not dance, being employed in the reception of her guests. Then followed a waltz, and, as its first strains struck up, several applicants came to compete for the honor of her hand; but she declined them all, saying that she was already engaged; and presently Arthur, looking very tall and quite the typical young Englishman in his dress-clothes, came hurrying up.

"You are late, Mr. Heigham," she said; "the music has begun."

"Yes; I am awfully sorry. I was dancing with Lady Florence, and could not find her old aunt."

"Indeed, to me Mrs. Velley is pretty conspicuous, with that green thing on her head; but come along, we are wasting time."

Putting his arm round her waist, they sailed away together amidst the murmurs of the disappointed applicants.

"Lucky dog," said one.

"Infernal puppy," muttered another.

Arthur enjoyed his waltz very much, for the rooms, though full, were not crowded, and Mildred waltzed well. Still he was a little uneasy, for he felt that, in being chosen to dance the first waltz with the giver of this splendid entertainment over the heads of so many of his superiors in rank and position, he was being put rather out of his place. He did not as a rule take any great degree of notice of Mildred's appearance, but to-night it struck him as unusually charming.

"You look very beautiful to-night, Mildred," he said, when they halted for breath; "and what splendid diamonds you have on!"

She flushed with pleasure at his compliment.

"You must not laugh at my diamonds. I know that I am too insignificant to wear such jewels. I had two minds about putting them on."

"Laugh at them, indeed. I should as soon think of laughing at the Bank of England. They are splendid."

"Yes," she said, bitterly; "they would be splendid on your Angela. They want a splendid woman to carry them off."

Oddly enough, he was thinking the same thing: so, having nothing to say, he went on dancing. Presently the waltz came to an end, and Mildred was obliged to hurry off to receive the Portuguese Governor, who had just put in an appearance. Arthur looked at his card, and found that he was down for the next galop with Lady Florence Claverley.

"Our dance again, Lady Florence."

"Really, Mr. Heigham, this is quite shocking. If everybody did not know that you belonged body and soul to the lovely widow, I should be accused of flirting with you."

"Who was it made me promise to dance five dances?"

"I did. I want to make Mrs. Carr angry."

"Why should my dancing five or fifty dances with you make Mrs. Carr angry?"

Lady Florence shrugged her pretty shoulders.

"Are you blind?" she said.

Arthur felt uncomfortable.

In due course, however, the last waltz before supper came round, and he, as agreed upon, danced it with his hostess. As the strains of the music died away, the doors of the supper-room and tent were thrown open.

"Now, Arthur," said Mildred, "take me in to supper."

He hesitated.

"The Portuguese Governor—" he began.

She stamped her little foot, and her eyes gave an ominous flash.

"Must I ask you twice?" she said.

Then he yielded, though the fact of being for the second time that night placed in an unnecessarily prominent position made him feel more uncomfortable than ever, for they were seated at the head of the top table. Mildred Carr was in the exact centre, with himself on her right and the Portuguese Governor on the left. To Arthur's left was Lady Florence, who took an opportunity to assure him solemnly that he really "bore his blushing honors very nicely," and to ask him "how he liked the high places at feasts?"

The supper passed off as brilliantly as most successful suppers do. Mrs. Carr looked charming, and her conversation sparkled like her own champagne; but it seemed to him that, as in the case of the wine, there was too much sting in it. The wine was a little too dry, and her talk a little too full of suppressed sarcasm, though he could not quite tell what it was aimed at, any more than he could trace the source of the champagne bubbles.

Supper done, he led her back to the ball-room. The second extra was just beginning, and she stood as though she were expecting him to ask her to dance it.

"I am sorry, Mildred, but I must go now. I am engaged this dance."

"Indeed—who to?" This was very coolly said.

"Lady Florence," he answered, confusedly, though there really was no reason why he should be confused.

She looked at him steadily.

"Oh! I forgot, for to-night you are her monopoly. Good-by."

A little while after this, Arthur thought that he had had about enough dancing for awhile, and went and sat by himself in a secluded spot under the shadow of a tree-fern in a temporary conservatory put up outside a bow-window. The Chinese lantern that hung upon the fern had gone out, leaving his chair in total darkness. Presently a couple, whom he did not recognize for he only saw their backs, strayed in, and placed themselves on a bench before him in such a way as to entirely cut off his retreat. He was making up his mind to disturb them, when they began a conversation, in which the squeezing of hands and mild terms of endearment played a part. Fearing to interrupt, lest he should disturb their equanimity, he judged it best to stop where he was. Presently, however, their talk took a turn that proved intensely interesting to him. It was something as follows:

She. "Have you seen the hero of the evening?"

He. "Who? Do you mean the Portuguese Governor in his war-paint?"

She. "No, of course not. You don't call him a hero, do you? I mean our hostess's *fiancé*, the nice-looking young fellow who took her in to supper."

He. "Oh, yes. I did not think much of him. Lucky dog! but he must be rather mean. They say that he is engaged to a girl in England, and has thrown her over for the widow."

She. "Ah, you're jealous! I know that you would like to be in his shoes. Come, confess."

He. "You are very unkind. Why should I be jealous when—"

She. "Well, you need not hurt my hand, and will you *never* remember that black shows against white!"

He. "It's awfully hot here; let's go into the garden." [*Exeunt.*]

CHAPTER XLVII.

ARTHUR emerged from his hiding-place, horror-struck at learning what was being said about him, and wondering, so far as he was at the moment capable of accurate thought, how long this report had been going about, and whether by any chance it had reached the ears of the Bellamys. If it had, the mischief might be very serious. In the confusion of his mind, only two things were clear to him—one was, that both for Mildred's and his own sake, he must leave Madeira at once; and, secondly, that he would dance no more with her that night.

Meanwhile the ball was drawing to a close, and presently he heard the strains of the last galop strike up. After the band had been playing for a minute or so, a natural curiosity drew him to the door of the ball-room, to see if Mildred was dancing with anybody else. Here he found Lady Florence, looking rather disconsolate.

"How is it that you are not dancing?" she asked.

He murmured something inaudible about "partner."

"Well, we are in the same box. What do you think? I promised this galop to Captain Clemence, and now there he is, vainly trying to persuade Mrs. Carr, who won't look at him, and appears to be waiting for somebody else—you, I should think—to give him the dance. I will be even with him, though."

Just then the music reached a peculiarly seductive passage.

"Oh, come along!" said Lady Florence, quite regardless of the proprieties; and, before Arthur well knew where he was, he was whirling round the room.

Mrs. Carr was standing at the top corner, where the crush obliged him to slacken his pace, and, as he did so, he caught her eye. She was talking to Lady Florence's faithless partner, with a smile upon her lips; but one glance at her face sufficed to tell him that she was in a royal rage, and, what was more, with himself. His partner noticed it, too, and was amused.

"Unless I am mistaken, Mr. Heigham, you have come into trouble. Look at Mrs. Carr." And she laughed.

But that was not all. Either from sheer mischief, or from curiosity to see what would happen, she insisted upon stopping, as the dance drew to a close, by Mildred's corner. That lady, however, proved herself equal to the occasion.

"Mr. Heigham," she said sweetly, "do you know that that was our dance?"

"Oh, was it?" he replied, feeling very much a fool.

"Yes, certainly it was; but with such a temptation to error"—and she smiled towards Lady Florence—"it is not wonderful that you made a mistake, and, as you look so contrite, you shall be forgiven. Agatha, there's a dear, just ask that man to go up to the band, and tell them to play another waltz, 'La Berceuse,' before 'God save the Queen.'"

Arthur felt all the while, though she was talking so suavely, that she was in a state of suppressed rage; once he glanced at her, and saw that her eyes seemed to flash. But her anger only made her look more lovely, supplying as it did an added dignity and charm to her sweet features. Nor did she allow it to have full play.

Mildred felt that the crisis in her fortunes was far too serious to admit of being trifled with. She knew how unlikely it was that she would ever have a better chance with Arthur than she had now, for the mirrors told her that she was looking her loveliest, which was very lovely indeed. In addition, she was surrounded by every seductive circumstance that could assist to compel a young man, however much engaged, to commit himself by some act or words of folly. The sound and sights of beauty, the rich odor of flowers, the music's voluptuous swell, and last, but not least, the pressure of her gracious form and the glances from her eyes, which alone were enough to make fools of ninety-nine out of every hundred young men in Europe—all these things combined to help her. And to them must be added her determination, that concentrated strength of will employed to a single end, which, if there be any truth in the theories of the action of mind on mind, cannot fail to influence the individual on whom it is directed.

"Now, Arthur."

The room was very nearly clear, for it was drawing towards daylight when they floated away together. Oh! what a waltz that was! The incarnate spirit of the dance took possession of them. She waltzed divinely, and there was scarcely anything to check their progress. On, on they sped with flying feet as the music rose and fell above them. And soon things began to change for Arthur. All sense of embarrassment and regret vanished from his mind, which now appeared to be capable of holding but one idea of the simplest and yet the most soaring nature. He thought that he was in heaven with Mildred Carr. On, still on; now he saw nothing but her shell-like face and the large flash of the circling diamonds, felt nothing but the pressure of her form and her odorous breath upon his cheek, heard nothing but the soft sound of her breathing. Closer he clasped her; there was no sense of weariness in his feet or oppression in his lungs; he could have danced forever. But all too soon the music ceased with a crash, and they were standing with quick breath and sparkling eyes by the spot that they had started from. Close by Miss Terry was sitting yawning.

"Agatha, say good-by to those people for me. I must get a breath of fresh air. Give me a glass of water, please, Arthur."

He did so, and, by way of composing his own nerves, took a tumbler of champagne. He had no longer any thought of anxiety or danger, and he, too, longed for air. They passed out into the garden, and, by a common consent, made their way to the museum veranda, which was, as it proved, quite deserted.

The night, which was drawing to its close, was perfect. Far over the west the setting moon was sinking into the silver ocean, whilst the first primrose hue of dawn was creeping up the eastern sky. It was essentially a dangerous night, especially after dancing and champagne—a night to make people do and say regrettable things; for, as one of the poets—is it not Byron?—has profoundly remarked, there is the very devil in the moon at times.

They stood and gazed a while at the softness of its setting splendors, and listened to the sounds of the last departing guests fading into silence, and to the murmurs of the quiet sea. At last she spoke, very low and musically.

"I was angry with you. I brought you here to scold you; but on such a night I cannot find the heart."

"What did you want to scold me about?"

"Never mind; it is all forgotten. Look at that setting moon and the silver clouds above her," and she dropped her hand, from which she had slipped the glove, upon his own.

"And now look at me and tell me how I look, and how you liked the ball. I gave it to please you."

"You look very lovely, dangerously lovely, and the ball was splendid. Let us go."

"Do you think me lovely, Arthur?"

"Yes; who could help it? But let us go in."

"Stay a while, Arthur; do not leave me yet. Tell me, is not this necklace undone? Fasten it for me, Arthur."

He turned to obey, but his hand shook too much to allow him to do so. Her eyes shone into his own, her fragrant breath played upon his brow, and her bosom heaved beneath his shaking hand. She too was moved; light tremors ran along her limbs, the color came and went upon her neck and brow, and a dreamy look had gathered in her tender eyes. Beneath them the sea made its gentle music, and above the wind was whispering to the trees. Presently his hand dropped, and he stood fascinated.

"I cannot. What makes you look like that? You are bewitching me."

Next moment he heard a sigh, the next Mildred's sweet lips were upon his own, and she was in his arms. She lay there still, quite still, but even as she lay there rose, as it were, in the midst of the glamour and confusion of his mind, that made him see all things distraught, and seemed to blot out every principle of right and honor, another and far different scene. For, as in a vision, he saw a dim English landscape and a gray ruin, and himself within its shadows with a nobler woman in his arms. "Dethrone me," said a remembered voice, "desert me, and I will still thank you for this hour of imperial happiness." The glamour was gone, the confusion made straight, and clear above him shone the light of duty.

"Mildred, dear Mildred, this cannot be. Sit down. I want to speak to you."

She turned quite white, and sank from his arms without a word.

"Mildred, you know that I am engaged."

The lips moved, but no sound issued from them. Again she tried.

"I know."

"Then why do you tempt me? I am only a man, and weak as water in your presence. Do not make me dishonorable to myself and her.'

"I love you as well as she. There—take the shameful truth."

"Yes, but—forgive me if I pain you, for I must, I must. I love *her*."

The beautiful face hid itself in the ungloved hands. No answer came, only the great diamond sparkled and blazed in the soft light like a hard and cruel eye.

'Do not, Mildred, for pity's sake, involve us all in shame and ruin, but let us part now. If I could have foreseen how this would end! But I have been a blind and selfish fool. I have been to blame."

She was quite calm now, and spoke in her usual singularly clear voice.

"Arthur dear, I do not blame you. Loving *her*, how was it likely that you should think of love from *me?* I only blame myself. I have loved you, God help me, ever since we met—loved you with a despairing, desperate love such as I hope that you may never know. Was I to allow your phantom Angela to snatch the cup from my lips without a struggle, the only happy cup I ever knew? For, Arthur, at the best of times, I have not been a happy woman; I have always wanted love, and it has not come to me.

Perhaps I should be, but I am not—a high ideal being. I am as Nature made me, Arthur, a poor creature, unable to stand alone against such a current as has lately swept me with it. But you are quite right, you must leave me, we *must* separate, you *must* go; but oh God! when I think of the future, the hard, loveless future—"

She paused a while, and then went on—

"I did not think to harm you or involve you in trouble, though I hoped to win some small portion of your love, and I had something to give you in exchange, if beauty and great wealth are really worth anything. But you must go, dear, now, whilst I am brave. I hope that you will be happy with your Angela. When I see your marriage in the paper, I shall send her this tiara as a wedding present. I shall never wear it again. Go, dear; go quick."

He turned to leave, not trusting himself to speak, for the big tears stood in his eyes, and his throat was choked. When he had reached the steps, she called him back.

"Kiss me once before you go, and I see your dear face no more. I used to be a proud woman, and to think that I can stoop to rob a kiss from Angela. Thank you; you are very kind. And now one word; you know a woman always loves a last word. Sometimes it happens that we put up idols, and a stronger hand than ours shatters them to dust before our eyes. I trust this may not be your lot. I love you so well that I can say that honestly; but, Arthur, if it should be, remember that in all the changes of this cold world there is one heart which will never forget you, and never set up a rival to your memory, one place where you will always find a home. If anything should ever happen to break your life, come back to me for comfort, Arthur. I can talk no more; I have played for high stakes—and lost. Good-by."

He went without a word.

CHAPTER XLVIII.

READER, have you ever, in the winter or early spring, come from a hot-house where you have admired some rich tropical bloom, and then, in walking by the hedgerows, suddenly seen a pure primrose opening its sweet eye, and looking bravely into bitter weather's face? If so, you will, if it is your habit to notice flowers, have experienced some such sensation as takes possession of my mind when I pass from the story of Mildred as she was then, storm-tossed and loving, to Angela, as loving indeed, and yet more anxious, but simple-minded as a child, and not doubtful for the end. They were both flowers indeed, and both beautiful, but between them there was a wide difference. The one, in the richness of her splendor, gazed upon the close place where she queened it, and was satisfied with the beauty round her, or, if not satisfied, she could imagine none different. The limits of that little spot formed the horizon of her mind—she knew no world beyond. The other, full of possibilities, shed sweetness even on the blast which cut her, and looked up for shelter towards the blue sky she knew endured eternally above the driving clouds.

Whilst Sir John Bellamy's health was being recruited at Madeira, Angela's daily life pursued an even and, comparatively speaking, a happy course. She missed Pigott much, but then she often went to see her, and by way of compensation, if she had gone, so had George Caresfoot and Lady Bellamy. Mr. Fraser, too, had come back to fill a space in the void of her loneliness, and for his presence she was very grateful. Indeed none but herself could know the comfort and strength she gathered from his friendship, none but himself could know what it cost him to comfort her. But he did not shrink from the duty; indeed, it gave him a melancholy satisfaction. He loved her quite as dearly, and with as deep a longing, as Mildred Carr did Arthur; but how different were his ends! Of ultimately supplanting his rival he never dreamt; his aim was to assist him, to help to bring the full cup of joy, untainted, to his lips. And so he read with her and talked with her, and was sick at heart; and she thanked him, and consecrating all her most sacred thoughts to the memory of her absent lover, and all her quick energies to self-preparation for his coming, possessed her soul in patience.

And thus her young life began to bloom again with a fresh promise. The close of each departing day was the signal for the lifting of a portion of her load, for it brought her a day nearer to her lover's arms, subtracting something from the long tale of barren hours; since to her all hours seemed most barren that were not quickened by his presence. Indeed, no Arctic winter could be colder and more devoid of light and life than this time of absence was to her, and, had it not been for the warm splendor of her hopes, shooting its beautiful promise in unreal gleams across the blackness of her horizon, she felt as though she must have frozen and died. For Hope, elusive as she is, often bears a fairer outward mien than the realization to which she points, and, like a fond deceiver, serves to keep the heart alive till the first bitterness is overpast, and, schooled in trouble, it can know her false, and yet remain unbroken.

But sometimes Angela's mood would change, and then, to her strained and sensitive mind, this dead calm and cessation of events would seem to resemble that ominous moment when, in tropic seas, the fierce outrider of the tempest has passed howling away clothed in flying foam. Then comes a calm, and for a space there is blue sky, and the sails flap drearily against the mast, and the vessel only rocks from the violence of her past plunging, while the scream of the sea-bird is heard with unnatural clearness, for there is no sound nor motion in the air. Intenser still grows the silence, and the waters almost cease from tossing; but the seaman knows that presently, with a sudden roar, the armies of the winds and waves will leap upon him, and that a struggle for life is at hand.

Such fears, however, did not often take her, for, unlike Arthur, she was naturally of a hopeful mind, and, when they did, Mr. Fraser would find means to comfort her. But this was soon to change.

One afternoon—it was Christmas Eve—Angela went down the village to see Pigott, now comfortably established in the house her long departed husband had left her. It was a miserable December day, a damp, unpleasant ghost of a day, and all the sky was packed with clouds, while the surface of the earth was wrapped in mist. Rain and snow fell noiselessly by turns; indeed, the only sound in the air was the loud dripping of water from the trees on the dead leaves beneath. The whole outlook was melancholy in the extreme. While Angela was in her old nurse's cottage, the snow fell in earnest for an hour or so, and then held up again, and when she came out the mist had recovered its supremacy, and the snow was melting.

"Come, miss, you must be getting home, or it will be dark. Shall I come with you a bit?"

"No, thank you, Pigott. I am not afraid of the dark, and I ought to know my way about these parts. Good-night, dear."

The prevailing dismalness of the scene depressed her, and she made up her mind to go and see Mr. Fraser, instead of returning at present to her lonely home. With this view, leaving the main road that ran through Rewtham, Bratham, and Isleworth to Roxham, she turned up a little by-lane which led to the foot of the lake. Just as she did so, she heard the deadened footfall of a fast-trotting horse, accompanied by the faint roll of carriage-wheels over the snow. As she turned half involuntarily to see who it was that travelled so fast, the creeping mist was driven aside by a puff of wind, and she saw a splendid blood-horse drawing an open victoria trotting past her at, at least, twelve miles an hour. But, quickly as it passed, it was not too quick for her to recognize Lady Bellamy wrapped up in furs, her dark, stern face looking on straight before her, as though the mist had no power to dim *her* sight. Next second the dark closed in, and the carriage had vanished like a dream in the direction of Isleworth.

Angela shivered; the dark afternoon seemed to have grown darker to her.

"So she *is* back," she said to herself. "I felt that she was back. She makes me feel afraid."

Going on her way, she came to a spot where the path forked, one track leading to a plank with a hand-rail spanning the stream that fed the lake, and the other to some stepping-stones, by crossing which and following the path on the other side a short cut could be made to the rectory. The bridge and the stepping-stones were not more than twenty yards apart, but so intent was Angela upon her own thoughts and upon placing her feet accurately on the stones that she did not notice a little man with a red comforter, who was leaning on the hand-rail, engaged apparently in meditation. The little man, however, noticed her, for he gave a violent start, and apparently was about to call out to her, when he changed his mind. He was Sir John Bellamy.

"Better let her go perhaps, John," he said, addressing his own effigy in the water. "After all, it will be best for you to let things take their course, and not to burn your own fingers or commit yourself in any way, John. You will trap them more securely so. If you were to warn the girl now, you would only expose them; if you wait till he has married her, you will altogether destroy them with the help of that young Heigham. And perhaps by that time you will have touched those compromising letters, John, and made a few other little arrangements, and then you will be able to enjoy the sweets of revenge meted out with a quart measure, not in beggarly ones or twos. But you are thinking of the girl—eh, John? Ah! you always were a pitiful beggar; but tread down the inclination, decline to gratify it. If you do, you will spoil your own hand. The girl must take her chance—oh! clearly the girl must take her chance. But all the same, John, you are very sorry for her—very. Come, come, you must be off, or her ladyship and the gentle George will be kept waiting," and away he went at a brisk pace, cheerfully singing a verse of a comic song. Sir John was a merry little man.

In due course Angela reached the rectory, and found Mr. Fraser seated in his study reading.

"Well, my dear, what brings you here? What a dreary night!"

"Yes, it is dreadfully damp and lonesome; the people look like ghosts in the mist, and their voices sound hollow. A proper day for evil things to creep home," and she laughed drearily.

"What do you mean?" he answered, with a quick glance at her face, which wore an expression of nervous anxiety.

"I mean that Lady Bellamy has come home. Is she not an evil thing?"

"Hush, Angela; you should not talk so. You are excited, dear. Why should you call her evil?"

"I don't know; but have you never noticed her? Have you never seen her creep, creep, like a tiger on its prey? Watch her dark face, and see the bad thoughts come and peep out of her eyes as the great black pupils swell and then shrivel, till they are no larger than the head of this black pin, and you will know that she is evil, and does evil work."

"My dear, my dear, you are upset to talk so."

"Oh, no! I am not upset; but did you ever have a presentiment?"

"Plenty; but never one that came true."

"Well, I have a presentiment now—yes, a presentiment—it caught me in the mist."

"What is it? I am anxious to hear."

"I don't know—I cannot say; it is not clear in my mind. I cannot see it, but it is evil, and it has to do with that evil woman."

"Come, Angela, you must not give way to this sort of thing;

you will make yourself ill. Sit down, there is a good girl, and have some tea."

She was standing by the window staring out into the mist, her fingers alternately intertwining and unlacing themselves, whilst an unusual—almost an unearthly—expression played upon her face. Turning, she obeyed him.

"You need not fear for me. I am tough, and growing used to troubles. What was it you said? Oh! tea. Thank you; that reminds me. Will you come and have dinner with me to-morrow after church? It is Christmas Day, you know. Pigott has given me a turkey she has been fatting, and I made the mincemeat myself, so there will be plenty to eat if we can find the heart to eat it."

"But your father, my dear?"

"Oh! you need not be afraid. I have got permission to ask you. What do you think? I actually talked to my father for ten whole minutes yesterday; he wanted to avoid me when he saw me, but I caught him in a corner. He took advantage of the opportunity to try to prevent me from going to see Pigott, but I would not listen to him, so he gave it up. What did he mean by that? Why did he send her away? What does it all mean? Oh! Arthur, when will you come back, Arthur?" and, to Mr. Fraser's infinite distress, she burst into tears.

CHAPTER XLIX.

PRESENTIMENTS are no doubt foolish things, and yet, at the time that Angela was speaking of hers to Mr. Fraser, a consultation was going on in a back study at Isleworth that might almost have justified it. The fire was the only light in the room; and gathered round it, talking very low, their features thrown alternately into strong light and dark shadow, were George Caresfoot and Sir John and Lady Bellamy. It was evident from the strong expression of interest, almost of excitement, on their faces that they were talking of some matter of great importance.

Sir John was, as usual, perched on the edge of his chair, rubbing his dry hands and eliciting occasional sparks in the shape of remarks, but he was no longer merry; indeed, he looked ill at ease. George, his red hair all rumpled up, and his long limbs thrust out towards the fire, spoke scarcely at all, but glued his little bloodshot eyes alternately on the faces of his companions, and only contributed an occasional chuckle. But the soul of this witches' gathering was evidently Lady Bellamy. She was standing up and energetically detailing some scheme, the great pupils of her eyes expanding and contracting as the unholy flame within them rose and fell.

"Then that is settled," she said at last.

George nodded. Bellamy said nothing.

"I suppose that silence gives consent. Very well, I will take the first step to-morrow. I do not like Angela Caresfoot, but, upon my word, I shall be sorry for her before she is twenty-four hours older. She is made of too fine a material to be sold into such hands as yours, George Caresfoot."

George looked up menacingly, but said nothing.

"I have often urged you to give this up; now I urge no more—the thing is done in spirit, it may as well be done in reality. I told you long ago that it was a most dreadfully wicked thing, and that nothing but evil can come of it. Do not say that I have not warned you."

"Come, stop that devil's talk," growled George.

"Devil's talk!—that is a good word, George, for it is of the devil's wages that I am telling you. Now listen, I am going to prophesy. A curse will fall upon this house and all within it. Would you like to have a sign that I speak the truth? Then wait." She was standing up, her hand stretched out, and in the dim light she looked like some heathen priestess urging a bloody sacrifice to her gods. Her forebodings terrified her hearers, and, by a common impulse, they rose and moved away from her.

At that moment a strange thing happened. A gust of wind, making its way from some entrance in the back of the house, burst open the door of the room in which they were, and entered with a cold flap as of wings. Next second a terrible crash resounded from the other end of the room. George turned white as a sheet, and sank into a chair, cursing feebly. Bellamy gave a sort of howl of terror, and shrank up to his wife, almost falling into the fire in his efforts to get behind her. Lady Bellamy alone, remaining erect and undaunted, laughed aloud.

"Come, one of you brave conspirators against a defenceless girl, strike a light, for the place is as dark as a vault, and let us see what has happened. I told you that you should have a sign."

After several efforts, George succeeded in doing as she bade him, and held a candle forward in his trembling hand.

"Come, don't be foolish," she said; "a picture has fallen, that is all."

He advanced to look at it, and then benefited his companions with a further assortment of curses. The picture, on examination, proved to be a large one that he had, some years previously, had painted of Isleworth, with the Bellamys and himself in the foreground. The frame was shattered, and all the centre of the canvas torn out by the weight of its fall onto a life-sized and beautiful statue of Andromeda chained to a rock, awaiting her fate with a staring look of agonized terror in her eyes.

"An omen, a very palpable omen," said Lady Bellamy, with one of her dark smiles. "Isleworth and ourselves destroyed by being dashed agrinst a marble girl, who rises uninjured from the wreck. Eh, John?"

"Don't touch me, you sorceress!" replied Sir John, who was shaking with fear. "I believe that you are Satan in person."

"You are strangely complimentary, even for a husband."

"Perhaps I am; but I know your dark ways, and your dealings with your master, and I tell you both what it is; I have done with the job. I will have nothing more to do with it. I will know nothing more about it."

"You hear what he says," said Lady Bellamy to George. "John does not like omens. For the last time, will you give it up, or will you go on?"

"I can't give her up—I can't indeed; it would kill me," answered George, wringing his hands. "There is a fiend driving me along this path."

"Not a doubt of it," said Sir John, who was staring at the broken picture with chattering teeth, and his eyes almost starting out of his head; "but if I were you, I should get him to drive me a little straighter, that's all."

"You are poor creatures, both of you," said Lady Bellamy; "but we will, then, decide to go on."

"Fiat 'injuria' ruat cœlum," said Sir John, who knew a little Latin; and, frightened as he was, could not resist the temptation to air it.

And then they went and left George still contemplating the horror-stricken face of the nude marble virgin whose eyes appeared to gaze upon the ruins of his picture.

Next morning being Christmas Day, Lady Bellamy went to church, as behooves a good Christian, and listened to the divine message of peace on earth and good-will towards men. So, for the matter of that, did George, and so did Angela. After church, Lady Bellamy went home to lunch, but she was in no mood for eating, so she left the table, and ordered the victoria to be round in half an hour.

After church, too, Angela and Mr. Fraser ate their Christmas dinner. Angela's melancholy had to some extent melted beneath the genial influence of the Christmas-tide, and her mind had taken comfort from the words of peace and everlasting love that she had heard that morning, and for a while, at any rate, she had forgotten her forebodings. The unaccustomed splendor of the dinner, too, had diverted her attention, for she was easily pleased with such things, and altogether she was in a more comfortable frame of mind than she had been on the previous evening, and was inclined to indulge in a pleasant talk with Mr. Fraser upon various subjects, mostly classical and Arthurian. She had already cracked some filberts for him, plucked by herself in the autumn, and specially saved in a damp jar, and was about to settle herself in a chair by the fire, when suddenly she turned white and stood quite still.

"Hark!" she said, "do you hear it?"

"Hear what?"

"Lady Bellamy's horse—the big black horse that trots so fast."

"I can hear nothing, Angela."

"But I can. She is on the high-road yet; she will be here very soon; that horse trots fast."

"Nonsense, Angela; it is some other horse."

But, as he spoke, the sound of a powerful animal trotting very rapidly became distinctly audible.

"It has come—the evil news—and she has brought it."

"Rubbish, dear; somebody to see your father, no doubt."

A minute elapsed, and then Mrs. Jakes, now the only servant in the house, was heard shuffling along the passage, followed by a firm, light step.

"Don't leave me," said Angela to Mr. Fraser. "God give me strength to bear it," she went on, beneath her breath. She was still standing staring vacantly towards the door, pale, and her bosom heaving. The intensity of her anxiety had to some extent communicated itself to Mr. Fraser, for there are few things so catching as anxiety, except enthusiasm; he, too, had risen, and was standing in an attitude of expectancy.

"Lady Bellamy to see yer," said Mrs. Jakes, pushing her head through the half-opened door.

Next second she had entered.

"I must apologize for disturbing you at dinner, Angela," she began hurriedly, and then stopped and also stood still. There was something very curious about her reception, she thought; both Mr. Fraser and Angela might have been cut out of stone, for neither moved.

Standing thus in the silence of expectancy, the three made a strange picture. On Lady Bellamy's face there was a look of stern determination and suppressed excitement such as became one about to commit a crime.

At last she broke the silence.

"I come to bring you bad news, Angela," she said.

"What have you to say? tell me, quick! No, stop; hear me before you speak. If you have come here with any evil in your heart, or with the intention to deceive or betray, pause before you answer. I am a lonely and almost friendless woman, and have no claim except upon your compassion; but it is not always well to deal ill with such as I, since we have at the last a friend whose vengeance you too must fear. So, by the love of Christ and by the presence of the God who made you, speak to me only such truth as you will utter at His judgment. Now answer; I am ready."

At her words, spoken with an earnestness and in a voice which made them almost awful, a momentary expression of fear swept across Lady Bellamy's face, but it went as quickly as it came, and the hard, determined look returned. The mysterious eyes grew cold and glittered, the head erected itself. At that moment Lady Bellamy distinctly reminded Mr. Fraser of a hooded cobra about to strike.

"Am I to speak before Mr. Fraser?"

"Speak!"

"What is the good of this high-flown talk, Angela? You seem to know my news before I give it, and believe me it pains me very much to have to give it. *He is dead, Angela.*"

The cobra had struck, but as yet the poison had scarcely begun to work. There was only numbness. Mr. Fraser gave a gasp and half dropped, half fell, into his chair. The noise attracted Angela's attention, and pressing her hand to her forehead she turned towards him with a ghost of a laugh.

"Did I not tell you that this evil woman would bring evil news." Then addressing Lady Bellamy, "But stop, you forget what I said to you, you do not speak the truth. Arthur dead! How can Arthur be dead and I alive? How is it that I do not know he is dead? Oh, for shame, it is not true, he is not dead."

"This seems to me to be a thankless as well as a painful task," said Lady Bellamy, hoarsely, "but, if you will not believe me, look here: you know this, I suppose? I took it, as he asked me to do, from his dead hand that it might be given back to you."

"If Mr. Heigham is dead," said Mr. Fraser, "how do you know it? where did he die, and what of?"

"I know it, Mr. Fraser, because it was my sad duty to nurse him through his last illness at Madeira. He died of enteric fever. I have got a copy of his burial certificate here which I had taken from the Portuguese books. He seems to have had no relations living, poor young man, but Sir John communicated with the family lawyer. Here is the certificate," and she handed Mr. Fraser a paper written in Portuguese and officially stamped.

"You sáy," broke in Angela, "that you took this ring from his dead hand—the hand on which I placed it. I do not believe you. You beguiled it from his living hand. It cannot be that he is dead; for, if he were, I should have felt it. Oh, Arthur!" and in her misery she stretched out her arms and turned her agonized eyes upwards, "if you are dead, come to me, let me see your spirit face, and hear the whisper of your wings. Have you no voice in the silence? You see he does not come, he is not dead; if he were dead, Heaven could not hold him from my side, or, if it could, it would have drawn me up to his."

"My love, my love," said Mr. Fraser, in a scared voice, "it is not God's will that the dead should come back to us thus—"

"My poor Angela, why will you not believe me? This is so very painful, do you suppose that I want to torture you by saying what is not true about your lover? The idea is absurd. I had meant to keep it till you were calmer; but I have a letter for you. Read it and convince yourself."

Angela almost snatched the paper from her outstretched hand. It ran thus, in characters almost illegible from weakness:

"DEAREST—Good-by. I am dying of fever. Lady Bellamy will take back your ring when it is over. Try to forget me, and be happy. Too weak to write more. Good-by. God —"

At the foot of this broken and almost illegible letter was scrawled the word, "ARTHUR."

Angela read it slowly, and then at length the poison did its work. She did not speak wildly any more, or call upon Arthur; she was stung back to sense, but all the light went out of her eyes."

"It is his writing," she said, slowly. "I beg your pardon. It was good of you to nurse him."

Then, pressing the paper to her bosom with one hand, with the other she groped her way towards the door.

"It is very dark," she said.

Lady Bellamy's eyes gave a flash of triumph, and then she stood watching the pitiable exhibition of human misery as curiously as ever a Roman matron did an expiring gladiator. When Angela was near the door, the letter still pressed against her heart, she spoke again.

"The blow comes from God, Angela, and the religion and spiritual theories which you believe in will bring you consolation. Most likely it is a blessing in disguise—a thing that you will in time even learn to be thankful for."

Lady Bellamy had overacted her part. The words did not ring true, they jarred upon Mr. Fraser; much more did they jar upon Angela's torn nerves. Her pale cheek flushed, and she turned and spoke, but there was no anger in her face, nothing but sorrow that dignified, and unfathomable love lost in its own depths. Only the eyes seemed as sightless as those of one walking in her sleep.

"When your hour of dreadful trouble comes, as it will come, pray God that there may be none to mock you as you mock me." And she turned like a stricken thing, and went slowly out, blindly groping her way along.

Her last words had hit the victor hard. Who can say what hidden string they touched, or what prescience of evil they awakened? But they went nigh to felling her. Clutching the mantelpiece, Lady Bellamy gasped for air; then, recovering a little, she said:

"Thank God, that is over."

Mr. Fraser scarcely saw this last incident. So overwhelmed was he at the sight of Angela's agony that he had covered his face with his hand. When he lifted it again, Lady Bellamy was gone and he was alone.

CHAPTER L.

THREE months had passed since that awful Christmas Day. Angela was heart-broken, and, after the first burst of her despair, turned herself to the only consolation which was left her. It was not of this world.

She did not question the truth of the dreadful news that Lady Bellamy had brought her, and, if ever a doubt did arise in her breast, a glance at the ring and the letter effectually quelled it. Nor did she get brain-fever or any other illness; her young and healthy frame was too strong a citadel to be taken out of hand by sorrow. And this to her was one of the most wonderful things in her affliction. It had come and crushed her, and life still went on much as before. The sun of her system had fallen, and yet the system was not appreciably deranged. It was dreadful to her to think that Arthur was dead, but an added sting lay in the fact that she was not dead too. Oh! how glad she would have been to die, since death had become the gate through which she needs must pass to reach her lover's side.

For it had been given to Angela, living so much alone and thinking so long and deeply upon these great mysteries of our being, to soar to the heights of a noble faith. To the intense purity of her mind, a living heaven presented itself, a comfortable place, very different from the vague and formularized abstractions with which we are for the most part satisfied; where Arthur and her mother were waiting to greet her, and where the great light of the Godhead would shine around them all. She grew to hate her life, the dull barrier of the flesh that stood between her and her ends. Still she ate and drank enough to support it, still dressed with the same perfect neatness as before, still lived, in short, as though Arthur had not died, and the light and color had not gone out of her world.

One day—it was in March—she was sitting in Mr. Fraser's study reading the "Shakespeare" which Arthur had given her, and in the woes of others striving to forget her own. But the attempt proved a failure; she could not concentrate her thoughts, they would continually wander away into space in search of Arthur.

She was dressed in black; from the day that she heard her lover was dead, she would wear no other color, and as she gazed, with her hands idly clasped before her, out at the driving sleet and snow, Mr. Fraser thought that he had never seen statue, picture, or woman of such sweet, yet majestic beauty. But it had been filched from the features of an immortal. The spirit-look which at times had visited her from a child now continually shone upon her face, and to the sight of sinful men her eyes seemed almost awful in their solemn calm and purity. She smiled but seldom now, and, when she did, it was in those gray eyes that the radiance began: her features scarcely seemed to move.

"What are you thinking of, Angela?"

"I am thinking, Mr. Fraser, that it is only fourteen weeks to-day since Arthur died, and that it is very likely that I shall live another forty or fifty years before I see him. I am only twenty-one, and I am so strong. Even this shock has not hurt me."

"Why should you want to die?"

"Because all the beauty and light has gone out of my life; because I prefer to trust myself into the hands of God rather than to the tender mercies of the world; because he is there, and I am here, and I am tired of waiting."

"Have you no fear of death?"

"I have never feared death, and least of all do I fear it now. Why, the veriest coward would not shrink back when the man she loved was waiting for her. And I am not a coward, and if I were told that I must die within an hour, I could say: 'How beautiful upon the mountains are the feet of Him that bringeth good tidings, that publisheth peace!' Cannot you understand me? If all your life and soul were wrapped up in one person, and she died, would you not long to go to her."

Mr. Fraser made no reply for awhile, but in his turn gazed out at the drifting snow, surely not more immaculately pure than this woman who could love with so divine a love. At length he spoke.

"Angela, do you know that it is wrong to talk so? You have no right to set yourself up against the decrees of the Almighty. In His wisdom He is working out ends of which you are one of the instruments. Who are you that you should rebel?"

"No one—a grain, an atom, a wind-tossed feather; but what am I to do with my life, how am I to occupy all the coming years?"

"With your abilities, that is a question easy to answer. Work, write, take the place in scholastic or social literature which I have trained you to fill. For you, fame and fortune lie in an inkstand; your mind is a golden key that will open to your sight all that is worth seeing in the world, and pass you into its most pleasant places. You can become a famous woman, Angela."

She turned upon him sadly.

"I had such ideas; for Arthur's sake I wished to do something great; indeed I had already formed a plan. But, Mr. Fraser, like many another, when I lost my love I lost my ambition too; both lie buried in his grave. I have nothing left to work for; I do not care for fame or money for myself, they would only have been valuable to give to him. At twenty-one I seem to have done with the world's rewards and punishments, its blanks and prizes, its satisfactions and desires, even before I have learnt what they are.

My hopes are as dull and leaden as that sky, and yet the sun is behind it. Yes, that is my only hope, the sun is behind it though we cannot see it. Do not talk to me of ambition, Mr. Fraser. I am broken-spirited, and my only ambition is for rest, the rest He gives to His beloved—"

"Rest, Angela! that is the cry of us all; we strive for rest, and here we never find it. You suffer, but do not think that you are alone; everybody suffers in their degree, though perhaps such as you, with the nerves of your mind bared to the roughness of the world's weather, feel mental pain the more acutely. But, my dear, there are few really refined men and women of sensitive organization who have not at times sent up that prayer for rest, any rest, even eternal sleep. It is the price they pay for their refinement. But they are not alone. If the heart's cry of every being who endures in this great universe could be collected into a single prayer, that prayer would be, 'Thou who made us, in pity give us rest.'"

"Yes, we suffer, no doubt, all of us, and implore a peace that does not come. We must learn

'How black is night when golden day is done,
How drear the blindness that hath seen the sun!'

You can tell me that; but tell me, you who are a clergyman, and stronger to stand against sorrow than I, how can we win even a partial peace, and draw the sting from suffering? If you know a way, however hard, tell it me, for do you know," and she put her hand to her head and a vacant look came into her eyes, "I think that if I have to endure much more of the anguish which I sometimes suffer, or get any more shocks, I shall go mad? I try to look to the future only and to rise superior to my sorrows, and to a certain extent I succeed, but my mind will not always carry the strain put upon it, but falls heavily to earth like a winged bird. Then it is that, deprived of its higher food, and left to feed upon its own sadness and to brood upon the bare fact of the death of the man I loved—I sometimes think, as men are not often loved—that my spirit almost breaks down. If you can tell me any cure, anything which will bring me comfort, I shall indeed be grateful to you."

"I think I can, Angela. If you will no longer devote yourself to study, you have only to look round to find another answer to your question as to what you are to do. Are there no poor in these parts for you to visit? Cannot your hands make clothes to cover those who have none? Is there no sickness that you can nurse, no sorrow that you can comfort? I know that even in this parish there are many homes where your presence would be as welcome as a sunbeam in winter. Remember, Angela, that grief can be selfish as well as pleasure."

"You are right, Mr. Fraser, you always are right, I think I am selfish in my trouble, but it is a fault that I will try to mend.

Indeed, to look at it in that light only, my time is of no benefit to myself, I may as well devote it to others."

"If you do, your labor will bring its own reward, for in helping others to bear their load you will wonderfully lighten your own. Nor need you go far to begin. Why do you not see more of your own father? You are naturally bound to love him. Yet it is but rarely that you speak to him."

"My father! you know he does not like me, my presence is always a source of irritation to him, he cannot even bear me to look at him."

"Oh, surely that must be your fancy; probably he thinks you do not care about him. He has always been a strange and wayward man, I know; but you should remember that he has had bitter disappointments in life, and try to soften him and win him to other thoughts. Do this, and you will soon find that he will be glad enough of your company."

"I will try to do as you say, Mr. Fraser, but I confess I have only small hopes of any success in that direction. Have you any parish work I can do?"

Nor did the matter end there, as is so often the case where parish work and young ladies are concerned. Angela set to her charitable duties with a steady determination that made her services very valuable. She undertook the sole management of a clothing club, in itself a maddening thing to ordinary mortals, and had an eye to the distribution of the parish coals. Of mothers' meetings and other cheerful parochial entertainments she became the life and soul. Giving up her mathematics and classical reading, she took to knitting babies' vests and socks instead; indeed, the number of articles which her nimble fingers turned out in a fortnight was a pleasant surprise for the cold toes of the babies. And, as Mr. Fraser had prophesied, she found that her labor was of a sort which brought a certain reward.

CHAPTER LI.

On one point, however, Angela's efforts failed completely: she could make no headway with her father. He shrank more than ever from her society, and at last asked her to oblige him by allowing him to follow his own path in peace. Of Arthur's death he had never spoken to her, or she to him, but she knew that he had heard of it.

Philip had heard of it thus. On that Christmas afternoon he had been taking his daily exercise when he met Lady Bellamy returning from the Abbey House. The carriage stopped, and she got out to speak to him.

"Have you been to the Abbey House to pay a Christmas visit?"

he asked. "It is very kind of you to come and see us so soon after your return."

"I am the bearer of bad news, so I did not loiter."

"Bad news! what was it?"

"Mr. Heigham is dead," she answered, watching his face narrowly.

"Dead—impossible!"

"He died of enteric fever at Madeira. I have just been to break the news to Angela."

"Oh, indeed, she will be pained; she was very fond of him, you know."

Lady Bellamy smiled contemptuously.

"Did you ever see any one put to the extremest torture? If you have, you can guess how your daughter was 'pained.'"

Philip winced.

"Well, I can't help it; it is no affair of mine. Good-by;" and then, as soon as she was out of hearing; "I wonder if she lies, or if she has murdered him. George must have been putting on the screw."

Into the particulars of Arthur Heigham's death, or supposed death, he never inquired. Why should he? It was no affair of his; he had long ago washed his hands of the whole matter, and left things to take their chance. If he was dead, well and good; he was very sorry for him; if he was alive, well and good also. In that case, he would no doubt arrive on the appointed date to marry Angela.

But, notwithstanding all this unanswerable reasoning, he still found it quite impossible to look his daughter in the face. Her eyes still burnt him, ay, more than ever did they burn, for her widowed dress and brow were agony to him, and rent his heart, not with remorse but fear. But still his greed kept the upper hand, though death by mental torture must result, yet he would glut himself with his desire. More than ever he hungered for those wide lands which, if only things fell out right, would become his at so ridiculous a price. Decidedly Arthur Heigham's death was "no affair of his."

About six weeks before Angela's conversation with Mr. Fraser which ended in her undertaking parish work, a rumor had got about that George Caresfoot had been taken ill, very seriously ill. It was said that a chill had settled on his lungs, which had never been very strong since his fever, and that he had, in short, gone into a consumption.

Of George, Angela had neither seen nor heard anything for some time—not since she received the welcome letter in which he relinquished his suit. She had, indeed, with that natural readiness of the human mind to forget unpleasant occurrences, thought but little about him of late, since her mind had been more fully occupied with other and more pressing things. Still she vaguely wondered at times if he was really so ill as her father thought.

One day she was walking home by the path round the lake, after paying a visit to a sick child in the village, when she suddenly came face to face with her father. She expected that he would as usual pass on without addressing her, and drew to one side of the path to allow him to do so, but to her surprise he stopped.

"Where have you been, Angela?"

"To see Ellen Mim; she is very ill, poor child."

"You had better be careful; you will be catching scarlet fever or something—there is a great deal about."

"I am not at all afraid."

"Yes; but you never think that you may bring it home to me."

"I never thought that there was any likelihood of my bringing anything to you. We see so little of each other."

"Well, well, I have been to Isleworth to see your cousin George; he is very ill."

"You told me that he was ill some time back. What is it that is really the matter with him?"

"Galloping consumption. He cannot last long."

"Poor man, why does he not go to a warmer climate?"

"I don't know—that is his affair. But it is a serious matter for me. If he dies under present circumstances, all the Isleworth estates, which are mine by right, must pass away from the family forever."

"Why must they pass away?"

"Because your grandfather, with a refined ingenuity, made a provision in his will that George was not to leave them back to me, as he was telling me this afternoon he is anxious to do. If he were to die now with a will in my favor, or without any will at all, they would all go to some far-away cousins in Scotland."

"He died of heart-disease, did he not?—my grandfather I mean?"

"Philip's face grew black as night, and he shot a quick glance of suspicion at his daughter.

"I was saying," he went on, without answering her question, "that George may sell the land or settle it, but must not leave it to me or you, nor can I take under an intestacy."

Angela did not understand these legal intricacies, and knew about as much about the law of intestacy as she did of Egyptian inscriptions.

"Well," she said, consolingly, "I am very sorry, but it can't be helped, can it?"

"The girl is a born fool," muttered Philip beneath his breath, and passed on.

A week or so afterwards, just when the primroses and Lent-lilies were at the meridian of their beauty and all the air was full of song, Angela heard more about her cousin George. Mr. Fraser was one day sent for to Isleworth; Lady Bellamy brought him the message, saying that George was in such a state of health that he wished to see a clergyman.

"I never saw a worse case," he said to Angela on his return. "He does not leave the house, but lies in a darkened room coughing and spitting blood. He is, I should say, going off fast; but he refuses to see a doctor. His frame of mind, however, is most Christian, and he seems to have reconciled himself to the prospect of a speedy release."

"Poor man!" said Angela, sympathetically; "he sent and asked to see you, did he not?"

"Well—yes; but when I got there he talked more about the things of this world than of the next. He is greatly distressed about your father. I dare say you have heard how your cousin George supplanted your father in the succession to the Isleworth estates. Your grandfather disinherited him, you know, because of his marriage with your mother. Now that he is dying he sees the injustice of this, but is prevented by the terms of your grandfather's will from restoring the land to your branch of the family, so it must pass to some distant cousins—at least, so I understand the matter."

"You always told me that it is easy to drive a coach and four through wills and settlements and legal things. If he is so anxious to do so, can he not find a way out of the difficulty—I mean, some honorable way?"

"No, I believe not, except an impossible one," and Mr. Fraser smiled a rather forced smile.

"What is that?" asked Angela carelessly.

"Well, that he should—should marry *you* before he dies. At least, you know, he says that that is the only way in which he could legally transfer the estates."

Angela started and turned pale.

"Then I am afraid the estates will never be transferred. How would that help him?"

"Well, he says he could then enter into a nominal sale of the estates to your father and settle the money on you."

"And why could he not do this without marrying me?"

"I don't know, I don't understand much about these things, I am not a business man; but it is impossible for some reason or another. But of course it is absurd. Good-night, my dear. Don't overdo it in the parish."

Another week passed without any particular news of George's illness, except that he was getting weaker, when one day Lady Bellamy appeared at the Abbey House, where she had not been since that dreadful Christmas Day. Angela felt quite cold when she saw her enter, and her greeting was as cold as herself.

"I hope that you bring me no more bad news," she said.

"No, Angela, except that your cousin George is dying, but that is scarcely likely to distress you."

"I am sorry."

"Are you? There is no particular reason why you should be. You do not like him."

"No, I do not like him."

"It is a pity though, because I have come to ask you to marry him."

"Upon my word, Lady Bellamy, you seem to be the chosen messenger of everything that is wretched. Last time you came to this house it was to tell me of dear Arthur's death, and now it is to ask me to marry a man whom I detest. I thought that I had told both you and him that I will not marry him. I have gone as near marrying as I ever mean to in this world."

"Really, Angela, you are most unjust to me. Do you suppose that it was any pleasure to me to have such a sad duty to perform? However, it is refreshing to hear you talk so vigorously. Clearly the loss of your lover has not affected your spirits."

Angela winced beneath the taunt, but made no reply.

"But, if you will condescend to look at the matter with a single grain of common-sense, you will see that circumstances have utterly changed since you refused to marry George. Then Mr. Heigham was alive, poor fellow, and then, too, George wanted to marry you as a wife; now he is merely anxious to marry you that he may be enabled to make reparation to your father. He is a fast-dying man. You would never be his wife except in name. The grave would be his only marriage-bed. Do you not understand the difference?"

"Perfectly, but do *you* not understand that whether in deed or in name I cannot outrage my dead Arthur's memory by being for an hour the wife of that man? Do *you* not know that the marriage service requires a woman to swear to 'Love, honor, and obey,' till death parts, whether it be a day or a lifetime away? Can I, even as a mere form, swear to love when I loathe, honor when I despise, obey when my whole life would rise in rebellion against obedience! What are these estates to me that I should do such violence to my conscience and my memories? Estates—of what use are they to one whose future lies in the wards of a hospital or a sisterhood? I will have nothing to do with this marriage, Lady Bellamy."

"Well, I must say, Angela, you do not make much ado about ruining your father to gratify your own sentimental whims. It must be a comfortable thing to have children to help one in one's old age."

Angela reflected on Mr. Fraser's words about her duty to her father, and for the second time that day she winced beneath Lady Bellamy's taunt; but, as she returned no answer, her visitor had no alternative but to drop the subject and depart.

Before she went, however, she had a few words with Philip, urging the serious state of George's health and the terms of his grandfather's will, which prevented him from leaving the estates to himself, as a reason why he should put pressure on Angela. Somewhat, but not altogether to her surprise, he refused in these terms:

"I don't know to what depths you have gone in this business, and it is no affair of mine to inquire, but I have kept to my share of the bargain and I expect you to keep to yours. If you can bring about the marriage with George, well or ill, on the terms I have agreed upon with him, I shall throw no obstacle in the way; but as for my trying to force Angela into it, I should never take the responsibility of doing so, nor would she listen to me. If she speaks to me on the subject I shall point out how the family will be advantaged, and leave the matter to her. Further I will not go."

CHAPTER LII.

THREE days after her conversation with Lady Bellamy, Angela received the following letter:

"Isleworth Hall, Roxham, May 2.

"DEAR COUSIN ANGELA,

"My kind and devoted friend, Lady Bellamy, has told me that she has spoken to you on a subject which is very near to my heart, and that you have distinctly declined to have anything to do with it. Of course I know that the matter lies entirely within your own discretion, but I still venture to lay the following points before you. There have, I am aware, been some painful passages between us—passages which, under present circumstances, had much better be forgotten. So, first, I ask you to put them quite out of your mind, and to judge of what I have to propose from a different point of view.

"I write, Angela, to ask you to marry me it is true (since, unfortunately, my health will not allow me to ask you in person), but it is a very different offer from that which I made you in the lane when you so bitterly refused me. Now I am solely anxious that the marriage should take place in order that I may be enabled to avoid the stringent provisions of your grandfather's will, which, whilst forbidding me to leave these estates back to your father or his issue, fortunately does not forbid a fictitious sale and the settlement of the sum, or otherwise. But I will not trouble you with these legal details.

"In short, I supplanted your father in youth, and I am now anxious to make every reparation in my power, and at present I am quite unable to make any. Independently of this, it pains me to think of the estate passing away from the old stock, and I should like to know that you, who have been the only woman whom I have felt true affection for, will one day come into possession of it. Of course, as you understand, the marriage would be *nothing but a form*, and if, as I am told, you object to its being gone through with the ceremonies of the Church, it could be made equally legal at a registry office.

"But please understand, Angela, that I do not wish to press you: it is for you to judge. Only you must judge quickly, for I am a fast-dying man, and am anxious to get this matter off my mind one way or other, in order that I may be able to give it fully to the consideration of subjects of more vital importance to one in my condition, than marrying and giving in marriage.

"Ever, dear cousin Angela,
"Affectionately yours,
GEORGE CARESFOOT.

"P.S.—Remember you have your father to consider in this matter as well as yourself."

The receipt of this letter plunged Angela into the greatest distress of mind. It was couched in a tone so courteous and so moderate that it carried with it conviction of its sincerity and truth. If she only had been concerned, she would not long have hesitated, but the idea of her duty to her father rose up before her like a cloud. What was her true duty under the circumstances? There was the rub!

She took the letter to Mr. Fraser and asked his advice. He read it carefully, and thought a long while before he answered. The idea of Angela being united to anybody in marriage, even as a matter of form, was naturally abominable to him, but he was far too honorable and conscientious a man to allow his personal likes or dislikes to interfere with whatever he considered to be his duty. But in the end he found it impossible to give any fixed opinion.

"My dear," he said, "all that I can suggest is that you should take it to your father and hear what he has got to say. After all, it is he who must have your true welfare most at heart. It was into his hands that I heard your mother, in peculiarly solemn words, consign you and your interests. Take it to your father, dear; there is no counsel like that of a father."

Had Mr. Fraser been the father, this would, doubtless, have been true enough. But though he had known him for so many years, and was privy to so much of his history, he did not yet understand Philip Caresfoot. His own open and guileless nature did not easily suspect evil in another, more especially when that other was the father of her whom he looked upon as the earthly incarnation of all that was holy and pure.

Angela sighed and obeyed—sighed from doubt, obeyed from duty. She handed the letter to Philip without a word—without a word he read it.

"I want your opinion, father," she said. "I wish to do what is right. You know how painful what has happened has been for me. You know—or, if you do not know, you must have guessed—how completely shattered my life is. As for this marriage, the whole thing is repugnant to me; personally, I had rather sacrifice fifty properties than go through it, but I know that I ought to think of others. Mr. Fraser tells me that it is my duty to consult you, that you will naturally have my interest most at heart, that it was into your hands and to your care that my mother consigned me on her deathbed. Father"—and she clasped her hands and looked him full in the face with her earnest eyes—"Mr. Fraser is right, it must be for you to decide. I will trust you entirely, and leave the burden of decision to your honor and generosity; only I say, spare me if you can."

Philip rose and went to look out of the window, that he might hide the evident agitation of his face and the tremor of his limbs. He felt that the crucial moment had come. All his poor sophistry, all his miserable shuffling and attempts to fix the responsibility of his acts on others, had recoiled upon his own head. She had come to him and laid the burden on his heart. What should he answer? For a moment the shades—for with him they were only shades—of good angels gained the upper hand, and he was about to turn and look her in the face—for then he felt he could have looked her in the face—and bid her have nothing to do with George and his proposals. But, even in the act of turning to obey the impulse, his eye fell upon the roof of Isleworth Hall, which, standing on an eminence, could easily be seen from the Abbey House, and his mind, quicker than the eye, flew to the outlook place upon that roof where he had so often climbed as a boy, and surveyed the fair champaign country beyond it: meadow and wood, fallow and corn-land, all of which were for him involved in that answer. He did not stop turning, but—so quick is the working of the mind—he changed the nature of his answer. The real presence of the demon of greed chased away the poor angelic shades.

"It would not be much of a sacrifice for you, Angela, to go through this form; he is a dying man, and you need not even change your name. The lands are mine by right, and will be yours. It will break my heart to lose them, after all these years of toiling to save enough to buy them. But I do not wish to force you. In short, I leave the matter to your generosity, as you would have left it to mine."

"And supposing that I were to marry my cousin George, and he were not to die after all, what would be my position then? You must clearly understand that, to save us all from starvation, I would never be his wife."

"You need not trouble yourself with the question. He is a dead man; in two months' time he will be in the family vault."

She bowed her head and left him—left him with his hot and glowing greed, behind which crept a terror.

Next morning George Caresfoot received the following letter:

"Bratham Abbey, May 5.

"DEAR COUSIN GEORGE,

"In reply to your letter, I must tell you that I am willing to go through the form of marriage with you—at a registry-office, not in church—in order to enable you to carry out the property arrangements you wish to make. You must, however, clearly understand that I do not do this on my own account, but simply and solely to benefit my father, who has left the matter to my 'generosity.' I must ask you as a preliminary step to make a copy of and sign the enclosed letter addressed to me. Our lives are in the hand of God, and it is possible that you might be restored to health. In such an event, however improbable it may seem, it cannot be made too plain that I am not, and have never in any sense undertaken to be, your wife.

"Truly yours,

"Angela Caresfoot.

The enclosure ran as follows:

"I, George Caresfoot, hereby solemnly promise before God that under no possible circumstance will I attempt to avail myself of any rights over my cousin, Angela Caresfoot, and that I will leave her as soon as the formal ceremony is concluded, and never again attempt to see her except by her own wish; the so-called marriage being only contemplated in order to enable me to carry out certain business arrangements which, in view of the failing state of my health, I am anxious to enter into."

This letter and its curious enclosure, surely the oddest marriage contract which was ever penned, George, trembling with excitement, thrust into the hands of Lady Bellamy. She read them with a dark smile.

"The bird is springed," she said, quietly. "It has been a close thing, but I told you that I should not fail, as I have warned you of what will follow your success. Sign this paper—this waste-paper—and return it."

CHAPTER LIII.

By return of post Angela received her strange agreement, duly copied and signed, and after this the preparations for the marriage went on rapidly. But where such a large transaction is concerned as the sale of between three and four thousand acres of land, copyhold and freehold, together with sundry rent-charges and the lordship of six manors, things cannot be done in a minute.

Both George and Philip and their respective lawyers—Sir John would have nothing to do with the matter—did their best to expedite matters, but unfortunately some legal difficulty arose in connection with the transfer, and who can hurry the ponderous and capricious machinery of the law?

At length it became clear to all concerned, except Angela, that it would be impossible for the marriage to take place before the eighth of June, and it also became clear that that was the last possible day on which it could take place. George begged Philip (by letter, being too ill to come and see him) to allow the marriage to be gone through with at once, and have the business transactions finished afterwards. But to this Philip would not consent; the title-deeds, he said, must be in his possession before it took place, otherwise he would have no marriage. George had therefore no option but to accept his terms.

When Angela was told of the date fixed for the ceremony—she would not allow the word marriage to be mentioned in connection with it—she at first created considerable consternation by quietly announcing that she would not have it performed until the tenth of June. At last, however, when matters were growing serious, and when she had treated all the pressure that it was possible to put upon her with quiet indifference—for, as usual, her father declined to interfere, but contented himself with playing a strictly passive part—she suddenly, of her own mere motion, abolished the difficulty by consenting to appear before the registrar on the eighth of June, as George wished.

Her reasons for having objected to this date in the first instance will be easily guessed. It was the day before the anniversary of Arthur's departure, an anniversary which it was her fancy to dedicate solely to his memory. But as the delay appeared—though she could not altogether understand why—to put others to great inconvenience, and as George's state of health had become such as to render postponement even for a couple of days of doubtful expediency, and as, moreover, she decided on reflection that she could better give her thoughts to her dead lover when she had gone through with the grim farce that hung over her, she suddenly changed her mind.

Occasionally they brought her documents to sign, and she signed them without a question, but on the whole she treated the affair with considerable apathy, the truth being that it was repugnant to her mind, which she preferred to occupy with other and very different thoughts. So she let it go. She knew that she was going to do a thing which was dreadful to her, because she believed it to be her duty, but she comforted herself with the reflection that she was amply secured against all possible contingencies by her previous agreement with George. Angela's knowledge of the marriage-law of her country and of what constituted a legal document was not extensive.

For this same reason, because it was distasteful, she had never said anything of her contemplated marriage to Pigott, and it was quite unknown in the neighborhood. Since the Miss Lee scandal and his consequent disinheritance, nobody had visited Philip Caresfoot, and those who took interest in him or his affairs were few. Indeed the matter had been kept a dead secret. But on the seventh of June, being the day previous to the ceremony, Angela went down to her nurse's cottage and told her what was about to be done, suppressing, however, from various motives, all mention of her agreement with George. It added to her depression to find that Pigott was unaccountably disturbed at the news.

"Well, miss," she said,—"Lord, to think that I sha'n't be able to call you that no longer—I haven't got nothing in particular to say agin it, seeing that sure enough the man's a-dying, as I has on good authority from my own aunt's cousin, her that does the servants' washing up at the Hall, and mighty bad she does it, begging of her pardon for the disparagement, and so he won't trouble you for long, and somehow it do seem as though you hadn't no choice left in the matter, just as though everybody and everything was a-quietly pushing you into it. But, miss, somehow I don't like it, to be plain; a marriage as ain't no marriage ain't altogether natural like, and in an office, too, along with a man as you would not touch with a pair of tongs; and that man on his last leg. I'm right down sorry if I makes you feel uncomfortable, dearie; but, bless me, I don't know how it is, but, when a thing sticks in my mind, I'm as bound to hawk it up as though it were a bone in my throat."

"I don't like it any more than you do, nurse, but perhaps you don't understand all about the property being concerned, and about its having to pass away from my father, if I don't do this. I care nothing about the property, but he left it to 'my generosity!' Arthur is dead; and he left it to 'my generosity,' nurse. What could I do?"

"Well, miss, you're acting according to what you thinks right and due to your father, which is more nor I does; and poor, dead Mr. Arthur up in Heaven there will make a note of that, there ain't no manner of doubt. And somehow it do seem that things can't be allowed to go wrong with you, my dear, seeing how you're a-sacrificing of yourself and of your wishes to benefit others."

This conversation did not tend to put Angela into better spirits, but she felt that it was now too late to recede.

Whilst Angela was talking to Pigott, Sir John and Lady Bellamy were paying a call at Isleworth. They found George lying on the sofa in the dining-room, in which, though it was the first week in June, a fire was burning on the hearth. He bore all the signs of a man in the last stage of consumption. The hollow cough, the emaciation, and the hectic hue upon his face, all spoke with no uncertain voice.

"Well, Caresfoot, you scarcely look like a bridegroom, I must say," said little Sir John, looking as pleased as though he had made an eminently cheerful remark.

"No, but I am stronger than I look; marriage will cure me."

"Humph! will it? Then you will be signally fortunate."

"Don't croak, Bellamy. I am happy to-day—there is fire dancing along my veins. Just think, this time to-morrow Angela will be my legal wife!"

"Well, you appear to have given a good price for the privilege, if what Anne tells me is correct. To sell the Isleworth estates for fifty thousand, is to sell them for a hundred and fifty thousand less than they are worth. Consequently, the girl costs you a hundred and fifty thousand pounds—a long figure that for one girl."

"Bah! you are a cold-blooded fellow, Bellamy. Can't you understand that there is a positive delight in ruining one's self for the woman one loves? And then, think how she will love me, when she comes to understand what she has cost me. I can see her now. She will come and kiss me—mind you, kiss me of her own free will—and say, 'George, you are a noble fellow; George, you are a lover that any woman may be proud of; no price was too heavy for you.' Yes, that is what she will say, that sort of thing, you know."

Sir John's merry little eye twinkled with inexpressible amusement, and his wife's full lip curled with unutterable contempt.

"You are counting your kisses before they are paid for, she said. "Does Philip come here this afternoon to sign the deeds."

"Yes; they are in the next room. Will you come and see them?"

"Yes, I will. Will you come, John?"

"No, thank you. I don't wish to be treated to any more of your ladyship's omens. I have long ago washed my hands of the whole business. I will stop here and read the *Times*."

They went out, George leaning on Lady Bellamy's arm.

No sooner had they gone than Sir John put down the *Times*, and listened intently. Then he rose, and slipped the bolt of that door which opened into the hall, thereby halving his chances of interruption. Next, listening at every step, his round face, which was solemn enough now, stretched forward, and looking for all the world like that of some whiskered puss advancing on a cream-jug, he crept on tiptoe to the iron safe in the corner of the room. Arrived there, he listened again, and then drew a little key from his pocket, and inserted it in the lock; it turned without difficulty.

"Beau-ti-ful," murmured Sir John; "but now comes the rub." Taking another key, he inserted it in the lock of the subdivision. It would not turn. "One more chance," he said, as he tried a second. "Ah!" and open came the lid. Rapidly he extracted two thick bundles of letters. They were in Lady Bellamy's handwriting. Then he relocked the subdivision, and the safe itself, and put the keys away in his trousers and the packets in his coat-tail pockets, one in each, that they might not bulge suspiciously. Next he unbolted the door, and returning, gave way to paroxysms of exultation too deep for words.

"At last," he said, stretching out his fat little fist towards the room where George was with Lady Bellamy, "at last, after twenty years of waiting, you are in my power, my lady. Time *has* brought its revenge, and if before you are forty-eight hours older you do not make acquaintance with a bitterness worse than death, then my name is not John Bellamy. I will repay you every jot, and with interest, too, my lady!"

Then he calmed himself, and ringing a bell, told the servant to tell Lady Bellamy that he had walked on home. When, an hour and a half later, she reached Rewtham House, she found that her husband had been suddenly summoned to London on a matter of business.

That night in her desolation Angela cast herself upon the floor with outstretched arms and wept for her dead lover, and for the shame which overshadowed her. And the moon travelling up the sky, struck her, shining coldly on her snowy robe and rounded form—glinting on the stormy gold of her loosed hair—flooding all the room with light; till the white floor gleamed like a silver shrine, and she lay there a weeping saint. Then she rose and crept to such rest as utter weariness of body and mind can give.

All that night, too, George Caresfoot paced, hungry-eyed, up and down, up and down the length of his great room, his gaze fixed on the windows which commanded Bratham, like that of some caged tiger on a desired prey.

"To-morrow," he kept muttering; till the first ray of the rising sun fell blood-red upon his wasted form, and then, bathing his thin hands in its beams, he sank down exhausted, crying exultingly, "not to-morrow, but *to-day*."

That night Lady Bellamy sat at an open window, rising continually to turn her dark eyes upon the starry heavens above her.

"It is of no use," she said at last, "my knowledge fails me, my calculations are baffled by a quantity I cannot trace. I am face to face with a combination that I cannot solve. Let me try once more! Ah, supposing that the unknown quantity is a directing will which at the crisis shatters laws, and overrides even the immutability of the unchanging stars! I have heard of such a thing. Let me change the positions of our opposing planets and then, see, it would all be as clear as day. George vanishes; that I knew before. She sails triumphant through overshadowing influences towards a silver sky. And I—is it death that awaits me? No, but some great change; there the pale light of my fading star would fall into her bright track. Bah! my science fails me; I can no longer prophesy. My knowledge only tells me of great events; of what use is such knowledge as that? Well, come what may, Fate will find one spirit that does not fear him. As for this," and she pointed towards the symbols and calculations, "I have done with it. Henceforth I will devote myself to the only real powers which can enlighten us. Yet there is humiliation in failure after so many years of study. It is folly to follow a partial truth of which we miss the keynote, though we sometimes blunder on its harmonies."

CHAPTER LIV.

THE arrangement for the morrow was that Angela and her father were to take a fly to Roxham, where the registry office was, and whither George was also to be conveyed in a close carriage; that the ceremony was then to be gone through, after which the parties were to separate and return to their respective homes. Mr. Fraser had been asked to attend, but had excused himself from doing so.

In pursuance of this programme, Angela and her father left the Abbey House about ten o'clock, and drove in silence to the town. Strange as it may seem, Angela had never been in a town before, and, in the curious condition of her mind, the new sight of busy streets interested her greatly, and served to divert her attention till they reached the door of the office. She alighted and was shown with Philip into a waiting-room. And here, for some unexplained reason, a great fear took hold of her, a terror of this ceremony which now loomed large and life-like before her.

"Father," she said, suddenly, after a moment of irresolution, "I am going home. I will not go on with this business."

"What can you mean, Angela?"

"I mean what I say. I never realized how dreadful it all was till now; it has come upon me like a revelation. Come, I am going."

"Angela, don't be a fool. You forget that George will be here in a minute, and that the settlements are all signed."

"Then he can go back again and the settlements can be torn up. I will not go on with it."

Philip was by this time almost beside himself with anxiety. After having thus with thought and toil, and by the aid of a blessed chance, lifted this delicious cup to his lips, was it to be dashed from him? Were the sweet dreams so near approaching to realization, in which he had been wrapped for so many days, all to be dissipated into thin air? Was he to lose the land after all, after he had fingered—oh, how lovingly!—the yellow title-deeds? For, alas! the sale depended on the marriage. It could not be; neither fate nor Angela could be so cruel. He turned upon her with the boldness of despair.

"Angela, you must not go on like this, after having agreed to the thing of your own free will. Think of what it involves for me. If you refuse to marry him now at the last moment, I shall lose the Isleworth estates. Heavens! to think that so much property should be dependent upon the mere whim of a girl! Cannot you have a little consideration for others beside yourself? Do you really mean to sacrifice the hopes of my whole life, to throw away the only opportunity I can ever have of righting my wrongs, in order to gratify a sentimental whim? For God's sake, think a little first before you sacrifice me. You promised to do it."

Never before had Angela seen her father so strongly excited; he was positively shaking with agitation. She looked at him steadily, and with such contempt that, even in his excitement, he quailed before her.

"Very well, then, I will carry out my promise, dreadful as it is to me; but remember that it is only because you beg it, and that the responsibility of its consequences must always remain with you. Now, are you satisfied?—you will get your land."

Philip's dark face assumed a look of fervent gratitude, but before he had time to reply, a messenger came to say that "the gentleman" was waiting.

Her resolve once taken, Angela followed him with an untroubled face into the room where the registrar, a gentleman neatly dressed in black, was sitting at a sort of desk. Here the first thing her glance fell upon was the person of George Caresfoot. Although it was now the second week in June, he wore a respirator over his mouth and a scarf round his neck, and coughed very much. These were the first things she noticed. The next was that he was much thinner, so thin that the cheek-bones stood quite out from the level of his face, whilst the little bloodshot eyes seemed to protrude, giving to his general appearance, even with the mouth (his worst feature) hidden by the respirator, an unusually repulsive look. He was leaning on the arm of Lady Bellamy, who greeted Angela with a smile which the latter fancied had something of triumph in it.

With the exception of the messenger, who played the part of clerk in this civil ceremony, there was nobody else in the room. No greetings were interchanged, and in another moment Angela was standing, dressed in her funereal black, by George's side before the registrar, and the ceremony had begun.

But from that moment, although her beautiful face preserved its composure, she scarcely saw or heard anything of what was going on. It was as though all the streams of thought in her brain had burst their banks and mingled in a great and turbulent current. She was filled with thought, but could seize upon no one idea, whilst within her mind she heard a sound as of the continuous whirring of broken machinery.

Objects and individuals, real and imagined, presented themselves before her mental vision, expanded till they filled the heavens with their bulk, and then shrank and shrank, and vanished into nothing. The word "wife" struck upon her ears, and seemed to go wailing away, "wife, wife, wife," through all the illimitable halls of sound, till they were filled with echoes, and sound itself fell dead against the silence of the stars.

It was done. She awoke to find herself a married woman. Lady Bellamy stepped forward with the same half-triumphant smile with which she had greeted Angela hovering about her lips.

"Let me congratulate you, *Mrs.* Caresfoot," she said; "indeed, I think I am privileged to do so, for, if I remember right, I was the first to prophesy this happy event;" and then, dropping her voice so that Angela alone could hear her, "Do you not remember that I told you that you would as certainly come to the altar-rails within nine months with George Caresfoot as you would to your death-bed? I said that nine months ago to-day."

Angela started as though she had been stung.

"Events have been too strong for me," she murmured; "but all this is nothing but a form, a form that can now be forgotten."

Again Lady Bellamy smiled as she answered,

"Oh, of course, Mrs. Caresfoot, nothing but a form."

Angela's eye fell upon the ring on her finger. She tore it off.

"Take this back," she said; "I have done with it."

"A married woman must wear a ring, Mrs. Caresfoot."

She hurled it upon the floor.

Just then George and Philip returned from a little back room, where they had been with the registrar, who still remained behind, to sign the certificates. George advanced upon his wife with a dreadful smile on his features, removing the respirator as he came. His object was to kiss her, but she divined it and caught her father by the arm.

"Father," she said, "protect me from this man."

"Protect you, Angela! Why, he is your husband!"

"My husband! Have you all agreed to drive me mad?"

Lady Bellamy saw that if something were not done quickly there would be a shocking scene, which was the last thing she wanted, so she seized George and whispered in his ear, after which he followed her sulkily, turning round from time to time to look at Angela.

On her way from Roxham, Lady Bellamy stopped her carriage at the telegraph-office and went in and wrote a telegram.

"I respect that woman, and she shall have her chance," she said, as she re-read it previous to handing it to the clerk.

Three hours later Mildred Carr received the following message at Madeira:

"From A. B. to Mrs. Carr, Quinta Carr, Madeira:
"Angela C. married her cousin G. C. this morning."

That night Lady Bellamy dined at Isleworth with George Caresfoot. The dinner passed over in almost complete silence; George was evidently plunged in thought, and could not eat, though he drank a good deal. Lady Bellamy ate and thought too. After the servants had gone, she began to speak.

"I want my price, George," she said.

"What do you mean?"

"I mean what I say. You are now Angela Caresfoot's husband; give me back those letters as you promised; I am impatient to break my chains." He hesitated. "George," she said, in a warning voice, "do not dare to play with me; I warn you that your power over me is not what it used to be. Give me back those letters. I have done your wicked work for you and will have my pay."

"All right, Anne, and so you shall; when will you have them?"

"Now, this instant."

"But I have not got my keys."

"You forget your keys are on your watch-chain."

"Ah! to be sure; so they are. You won't turn round on me when you get them, will you, Anne?"

"Why should I turn on you? I wish to get the letters, and, if I can, to have done with you."

He went with a somewhat hesitating step to the iron safe in the corner of the room and opened it. Then he opened the subdivision and rummaged about there for a while. At last he looked up.

"It is very curious, Anne," he said, in a half-frightened voice, "but I can't find them."

"George, give me those letters."

"I can't find them, Anne, I can't find them. If you don't believe me, come and look for yourself. Somebody must have taken them."

She advanced and did as he said. It was evident that the letters were not there.

"Once before when you were ill you hid them. Where have you hidden them now?"

"I haven't hidden them, Anne; I haven't, indeed."

She turned slowly and looked him full in the eyes. Her own face was ashy pale with fury, but she said never a word. Her silence was more terrible than words. Then she raised her hands and covered her eyes for a while. Presently she dropped them, and said, in a singularly soft voice:

"It is over now."

"What do you mean?" he asked, fearfully, for she terrified him.

"I mean a great deal, George Caresfoot. I mean that something has snapped the bond which bound me to you. I mean that I no longer fear you, that I have done with you. Use your letters, if you will; you can harm me no more· I have passed out of the region of your influence, out of the reach of your revenge. I look on you now and wonder what the link was between us, for there was a mysterious link. That I cannot tell. But this I can tell you. I have let go your hand, and you are going to fall down a great precipice, George, a precipice of which I cannot see the foot. Yes, it is right that you should cower before me now; I have cowered before you for more than twenty years. You made me what I am. I am going into the next room now till my carriage comes, I did not order it till half-past ten. Do not follow me. But before I go I will tell you something, and you know I do not make mistakes. You will never sleep under this roof again, George Caresfoot, and we shall not meet again alive. You have had a long day, but your hour has struck."

"Who told you that, woman?" he asked, furiously.

"Last night I read it in the stars; to-night I read it in your face."

And again she looked at him, long and steadily, as he crouched in the chair before her, and then slowly left the room.

After a while he roused himself, and began to drink wine furiously.

"Curse her," he said, as the fumes mounted into his brain, "curse her. She is trying to frighten me with her infernal magic, but she sha'n't. I know what she is at; but I will be beforehand with her." And, staggering under the mingled influence of drink and excitement, he rose and left the house.

Lady Bellamy sat in the drawing-room and waited for her carriage; at last she heard the wheels upon the gravel. Then she rose, and rapidly did something to the great lamp upon the paper-strewn table. As she shut the door she turned.

"That will do," she said.

In the hall she met the servant coming to announce the carriage.

"Is your master still in the dining-room ?" she asked.

"No, my lady."

She laughed a little, and civilly bade the man good-night.

CHAPTER LV.

OUTSIDE the door of the registry-office, Angela and her father had to make their way through a crowd of small boys, who had by some means or other found out that a wedding was going on inside, and stood waiting there, animated by the intention of cheering the bride and the certain hope of sixpences. But when they saw Angela, her stately form robed in black, and her sweet face betraying the anguish of her mind, the sight shocked their sense of the fitness of things, and they slipped off without a word. Indeed, a butcher's boy, with a turn for expressive language, remarked in indignation to another of his craft, so soon as they had recovered their spirits,

"Call that a weddin', Bill? why, it's more like a—funeral with the plumes off; and as for the gal, though she's a 'clipper,' her face was as pale as a 'long un's.'"

Angela never quite knew how she got back to the Abbey House. She only remembered that she was by herself in the fly, her father preferring to travel on the box along with the coachman. Nor could she ever quite remember how she got through the remainder of that day. She was quite mazed. But at length it passed, and the night came, and she was thankful for the night.

About nine o'clock she went up to her bedroom at the top of the house. It had served as a nursery for many generations of Caresfoots; indeed, during the last three centuries hundreds of little feet had pattered over the old worm-eaten boards. But the little feet had long since gone to dust, and the only signs of children's play and merriment left about the place were the numberless scratches, nicks, and letters cut in the old panelling, and even on the beams which supported the low ceiling.

It was a lonesome room for a young girl, or, indeed, for anybody whose nerves were not of the strongest. Nobody slept upon that floor or in the rooms beneath it, Philip occupying a little closet which joined his study on the ground-floor. All the other rooms were closed, and tenanted only by rats that made unearthly noises in their emptiness. As for Jakes and his wife, the only servants on the place, they occupied a room over the washhouse, which was separate from the main building. Angela was therefore practically alone in a great house, and might have been murdered a dozen times over without the fact being discovered for hours. This did not, however, trouble her much, simply because she paid no heed to the noises in the house, and was singularly free from fear of any kind.

On reaching her room, she sat down and began to think of Arthur, and, as she thought, her mind grew clearer, and more at peace. Indeed, it seemed to her that her dead lover was near, and as though she could distinguish distinct pulsations of thought which came from him, impinging on her system, and bringing his presence with them. It is a common sensation, and occurs to many people of sensitive organization when asleep or thinking on some one with whom they are in a high state of sympathy, and doubtless indicates some occult communication. But, as it chanced, it had never before visited Angela in this form, and she abandoned herself to its influence with delight. It thrilled her through and through.

How long she sat thus she could not tell, but presently the communication, whatever it was, stopped as suddenly as though the connecting link had been severed. The currents directed by her will would no longer do her bidding; they could not find their object, or, frighted by some adverse influence, recoiled in confusion on her brain. Several times she tried to renew this subtle intercourse that was so palpable and real, and yet so different from anything else in the world, but failed. Then she rose, feeling very tired, for those who thus draw upon the vital energies must pay the penalty of exhaustion. She took her Bible and read her nightly chapter, and then undressed and said her prayers, praying with unusual earnestness that it might please the Almighty in His wisdom to take her to where her lover was. Her prayers done, she rose, put on a white dressing wrapper, and, seating herself before the glass, unloosed her hair. Then she began to brush it, pausing presently to think how Arthur had admired its color and the ripples on it. She had been much more careful of her hair since then, and smiled sadly to herself at her folly for being so.

Thinking thus, she fell into a reverie, and sat so still that a great gray rat came noiselessly out of his hole in a corner of the room, and, advancing into the circle of light round the dressing-table, sat up on his hind legs to see if he was alone. Suddenly he turned and scuttled back to his hole in evident alarm, and at the same second Angela thought that she heard a sound of a different character from those she was accustomed to in the old house—a sound like the creaking of a boot. It passed, however, but left an indefinable dread creeping over her, and chilling the blood in her veins. She began to expect something, she knew not what, and was fascinated by the expectation. She would have risen to lock the door, but all strength seemed to have left her; she was paralyzed by the near sense of evil. Then came a silence as intense as it was lonely.

It was a ghastly moment.

Her back was towards the doorway, for her dressing-table was immediately opposite the door, which was raised some four feet above the level of the landing, and approached by as many steps.

Gradually her eyes became riveted on the glass before her, for in it she thought that she saw the door move. Next second she was sure that it *was* moving, very slowly; the hinges took an age to turn. What could be behind it? At last it was open, and in the glass Angela saw framed in darkness *the head and shoulders of George Caresfoot.* At first she believed that her mind deceived her. that it was an apparition. No, there was no mistake. But the respirator, the hollow cough and decrepitude of the morning—where were they?

With horror in her heart, she turned and faced him. Seeing that he was observed, he staggered into the room with a step which was half drunken and half jaunty, but which belied the conflict of passions written on his brow. He spoke—his voice sounded hoarse and hollow, and was ill-tuned to his words.

"You did not expect me, perhaps—wonder how I got here! Jakes let me in; he has got a proper respect for marital rights, has Jakes. You looked so pretty, I could not make up my mind to disturb you. Quite a romantic meeting, is it not?"

"You are a dying man. How did you come here?"

"Dying! my dear wife; not a bit of it. I am no more dying than you are. I have been ill, it is true, but that is only because you have fretted me so. The dying was only a little ruse to get your consent. All is fair in love and war, you know; and of course you never really believed in that precious agreement. That was nothing but a bit of maidenly shyness, eh?"

Angela stood still as stone, a look of horror on her face.

"Then you don't know what you have cost me. Your father's price was a hundred and fifty thousand, at least that is what it came to, the old shark! It isn't every man who would come down like that for a girl, now is it? It shows a generous mind, doesn't it?"

Still she uttered not a syllable.

"Angela," he said, changing his tone to one of hoarse earnestness, "don't look at me like that, because, even if you are a bit put out at the trick I have played you, just think it was because I loved you so, Angela. I couldn't help it, I couldn't really. It is not every man who would go through all that I have gone through for you; it is no joke to sham consumption for three months, I can tell you; but we will have many a laugh over that. Why don't you answer me, instead of standing there just like the Andromeda in my study?"

The simile was an apt one; the statue of the girl awaiting her awful fate wore the same hopeless, helpless look of vacant terror which was upon Angela's face now. But its mention recalled Lady Bellamy and the ominous incident in which that statue had figured, and he hastened to drown recollection in action.

"Come," he said, "you will forgive me, won't you? It was all done for love of you." And he moved towards her.

As he came she seemed to collect her energies; the fear left her face, and in its stead there shone a great and awful blaze of indignation.

Her brush was still in her hand, and as he drew near she dashed it full into his face. It was but a light thing, and only staggered him, but it gave her time to pass him, and reach the still open door. Barefooted, she fled like the wind down the passages, and down the stairs. Uttering an oath, he followed her. But, as she went, she remembered that she could not run upon the gravel with her naked feet, and, with this in her mind, she turned to bay by a large window that gave light to the first-floor landing, immediately opposite which was the portrait of "Devil" Caresfoot. It was unbolted, and with a single movement of the hand she flung it open, and stood panting by it in the full light of the moon. In another moment he was upon her, furious at the blow, and his face contorted with passion.

."Stop," she cried, "and listen to me. Before I will allow you to touch me with a single finger, I will spring from here. I would rather thrust myself into the hands of Providence than into yours, monster and perjured liar that you are!"

He stopped as she bade him, and commenced to pace round and round her in a semicircle, glaring at her with wild eyes.

"If you jump from there," he said, "you will only break your limbs; it is not high enough to kill you. You are my wife, don't you understand? You are my legal wife; the law is on my side. No one can help you, no one; you are mine in the sight of the whole world."

"But not yours in the sight of God. It is to Him that I now appeal. Get back!"

She stretched out her arm, and with her golden hair glimmering in the moonlight, her white robes, and the anger on her face, looked like some avenging angel driving a fiend to hell. He shrank away before her, and there came a pause, and, save for their heavy breathing, stillness again fell upon the house, whilst the picture that hung above them seemed, in the half-light, to follow them with its fierce eyes as though it were a living thing.

The landing where they stood looked upon the hall below, at the end of which was Philip's study. Suddenly its door burst open, and Philip himself passed through it, grasping a candlestick in one hand and some parchments in the other. His features were dreadful to see, resembling those of a dumb thing in torture; his eyes protruded, his livid lips moved, but no sound came from them. He staggered across the hall with terror staring from his face.

"Father, father," called Angela; but he took no notice—he did not even seem to hear.

Presently they heard the candlestick thrown with a clash upon the hall pavement, then the front door slammed, and he was gone, and at that moment a great ruddy glow shot up the western sky, then a tongue of flame, then another and another.

"See," said Angela, with a solemn laugh, "I did not appeal for help in vain."

Isleworth Hall was in flames.

CHAPTER LVI.

ARTHUR did not delay his departure from Madeira. The morning following Mildred's ball he embarked on board a Portuguese boat, a very dirty craft which smelt of garlic and rancid oil, and sailed for Lisbon. He arrived there safely, and mooned about that city for a while, himself a monument of serious reflections, and then struck across into Spain, where he spent a month or so inspecting the historical beauties of that fallen country. Thence he penetrated across the Pyrenees into Southern France, which was pleasant in the spring months. Here he remained another month, meeting with no adventures worthy of any note, and improving his knowledge of the French language. Tiring at last of this, he travelled to Paris, and went to the theatres, but found his own thoughts too absorbing to allow of his taking any keen interest in their sensationalisms; so, after a brief stay, he made his way up to Brittany and Normandy, and went in for inspecting old castles and cathedrals, and finally ended up his continental travels by spending a week on the island-rock of Saint Michel.

This place pleased him more than any he had visited. He liked to wander about among the massive granite pillars of that noble ecclesiastical fortress, and at night to watch the phosphoric tide come rushing in with all the speed of a race-horse over the wide sands which separate it from the mainland. There the thirty-first day of May found him, and he bethought him that it was time to return to London and see about getting the settlements drawn and ordering the wedding bouquet. To speak the truth, he thought more about the bouquet than the settlements.

He arrived in London on the first of June, and went to see his family lawyer, a certain Mr. Borley, who had been solicitor to the trust during his minority.

"Bless me, Heigham, how like your father you have grown!" said that legal gentleman, as soon as Arthur was ensconced in the client's chair—a chair that, had it been endowed with the gift of speech, could have told some surprising stories. "It seems only the other day that he was sitting there dictating the terms of his will, and yet that was before the Crimean war, more than twenty years ago. Well, my boy, what is it?"

Arthur, thus encouraged, entered into a rather blundering recital of the circumstances of his engagement.

Mr. Borley did not say much, but, from his manner and occasional comments, it was evident that he considered the whole story very odd—regarding it, indeed, with some suspicion.

"I must tell you frankly, Heigham," he said at last, "I don't quite understand this business. The young lady, no doubt, is charming—young ladies, looking at them from my clients' point of view, always are—but I can't say I like your story about her father. Why did you not tell me all this before? I might then have been able to give you some advice worth having, or, at any rate, to make a few confidential"—he laid great emphasis on the word "confidential"—"inquiries."

Arthur replied that it had not occurred to him to do so.

"Umph! pity—great pity; but there is no time for that sort of thing now, if you think you are going to get married on the tenth; so I suppose the only thing to do is to go through with it and await the upshot. What do you wish done?"

Arthur explained his views, which apparently included settling all his property on his bride in the most absolute fashion possible. To this Mr. Borley forcibly objected, and in the end Arthur had to give way and make such arrangements as the old gentleman thought proper—arrangements differing considerably from those proposed by himself.

This interview over, he had other and pleasanter duties to perform, such as ordering his wedding clothes, making arrangements with a florist for the bridal bouquet, and, last but not least, having his mother's diamonds reset as a present for his bride.

But still the days went very slowly; there seemed to be no end to them. He had no relations to go and see, and in his present anxious, excited state he preferred to avoid his friends and club acquaintances. Fifth, sixth, seventh; never did a schoolboy await the coming of the day that marked the advent of his holidays with such intense anxiety.

At length the eighth of June arrived. Months before, he had settled what his programme should be on that day. His promise, as the reader may remember, forbade him to see Angela till the ninth, that is, any hour after twelve on the night of the eighth, or, practically, as early as possible on the following morning. Now the earliest train would not get him down to Roxham till eleven o'clock, which would involve a wicked waste of four or five hours of daylight that might be spent with Angela; so he wisely resolved to start on the evening of the eighth, by a train leaving Paddington at six o'clock, and reaching Roxham at nine.

The day he spent in signing the settlements, finally interviewing the florist, and giving him directions as to forwarding the wedding bouquet, which was to be composed of orange-blossoms, lilies of the valley, and stephanotis, and in getting the marriage-license. But, notwithstanding these manifold employments, he managed to be three quarters of an hour before his train, the longest forty-five minutes he ever spent.

He had written to the proprietor of the inn at Rewtham, where he had slept a year ago the night after he had left Isleworth, to send a gig to meet him at the station; and on arriving at Roxham, a porter told him that a trap was waiting for him. On emerging from the station, even in the darkness, he was able to recognize the outlines of the identical vehicle which had conveyed him to the Abbey House some thirteen months ago, whilst the sound of an ancient, quavering voice informed him that the John was likewise the same. His luggage was soon bundled up behind, and the steady-going old nag departed into the darkness.

"Well, Sam, do you remember me?"

"Well, no, sir, I can't rightly say how as I do: wait a bit; bean't you the gemmen as travels in the dry line, and as I seed a-kissing the chambermaid?"

"No, I don't travel at present, and I have not kissed a chambermaid for some time. Do you remember driving a gentleman over to the Abbey House a year or so ago?"

"Why, yes, in course I does. Lor', now, and be you he? and we seed old Devil Caresfoot's granddaughter. Ah! many's the time that he has damned me, and all so soft and pleasant like; but it was his eyes that did the trick. They was awful, just awful. And you gave me half-a-crown, you did. But somehow I thought I heard summat about you, sir, but I can't rightly remember what it be, my head not being so good as it used to."

"Perhaps you heard that I was going to be married?"

"No, I don't think how as it was that neither."

"Well, never mind me; have you seen Miss Caresfoot—the young lady you saw the day you drove me to the Abbey House—anywhere about lately?"

Arthur waited for the old man's lingering answer with all his heart upon his lips.

"Lor', yes, sir, that I have; I saw her this morning driving through the Roxham market-place."

"And how did she look?"

"A bit pale, I thought, sir; but well enough, and wonnerful handsome."

Arthur gave a sigh of relief. He felt like a man who has just come scathless through some horrible crisis and once more knows the sweet sensation of safety. What a load the old man's words had lifted from his mind! In his active imagination he had pictured all sorts of evils which might have happened to Angela during his year of absence. Lovers are always prone to such imaginings, and not altogether without reason, for there would seem to be a special power of evil that devotes itself to the derangement of their affairs and the ingenious disappointment of their hopes. But now the vague dread was gone; Angela was not spirited away or dead, and to know her alive was to know her faithful.

As they drove along, the old ostler continued to volunteer various scraps of information which fell upon his ears unheeded, till presently his attention was caught by the name Caresfoot.

"What about him?" he asked, quickly.

"He be a-dying, they do say."

"Which of them?"

"Why, the red-haired one—him as lives up at the Hall yonder."

"Poor fellow!" said Arthur, feeling quite fond of George in his happiness.

They had by this time reached the inn, where he had some supper, for old Sam's good news had brought back his appetite, which of late had not been quite up to par, and then went straight to his room that faced towards the Abbey House. It was, he noticed, the same in which he had slept the year before, and, looking at the bed, he remembered his dream, and smiled as he thought that the wood was passed, and before him lay nothing but the flowery meadows. Mildred Carr, too, crossed his mind, but of her he did not think much; not that he was by any means heartless—indeed, what had happened had pained him acutely, the more so because his own conscience told him he had been a fool. He was very sorry, but, love being here below one of the most selfish of the passions, he had not time to be sorry just then.

For just on the horizon he could distinguish a dense mass which was the trees surrounding the Abbey House, and between the trees there glimmered a faint light which might proceed from some rising star, or from Angela's window. He preferred to believe it was the latter. The propinquity made him very happy. What was she doing? he wondered—sitting by her window and thinking of him! He would ask her on the morrow. It was worth while going through that year of separation in order to taste the joy of meeting. It seemed like a dream to think that within six-and-thirty hours he would probably be Angela's husband, and how nobody in the world would be able to take her away from him. He stretched out his arms towards her.

"My darling, my darling!" he cried aloud into the still night.

"My darling, my darling!" the echo answered sadly.

CHAPTER LVII.

THAT night Arthur dreamed no evil dreams, but he thought he heard a sound outside his door, and some one speak of fire. Hearing nothing more, he turned and went to sleep again. Waking in the early dawn, he felt, ere yet his senses fully came, a happy sense of something, he knew not what—a rosy shadow of coming joy, such as will, only with more intensity, fall upon our quickened faculties when, death ended, our souls begin to stir as we awaken to Eternity.

He sprang from his bed, and his eye fell on a morocco case upon the dressing-table. It contained the diamonds which he had had reset as a wedding present to Angela. They were nothing compared with Mildred Carr's, but still extremely handsome, their beauty being enhanced by the elegance of the setting, which was in the shape of a snake with emerald head and ruby eyes, so constructed as to clasp tightly round Angela's shapely throat.

The sight of the jewelry at once recalled his present circumstances, and he knew that the long hour of trial was passed—he was about to meet Angela. Having dressed himself as quickly as he could, he took up the jewel-case, but, finding it too large to stow away, he opened it, and, taking out the necklace, crammed it into his pocket. Thus armed he slipped down the stairs, past the open common room where the light shone through the cracks in the shutters on a dismal array of sticky beer-mugs and spirit-glasses, down the sanded passage into the village street.

It was full daylight now, and the sun never looked upon a lovelier morning. The air was warm, but there was that sharp freshness in it which is needful to make summer weather perfect, and which we always miss by breakfasting at nine o'clock. The sky was blue, just flecked with little clouds; the dewdrops sparkled upon every leaf and blade of grass; touches of mist clung about the hollows. and the sweet breath of the awakened earth was full of the perfect scent of an English June, which is in its way even more delicious than the spicy odors of the tropics. It was a morning to make sick men well, sad men happy, and atheists believers in a creative hand. How much more, then, did it fire Arthur's pulses, already bounding with youth and health, with an untold joy!

He felt like a child again, so free from care, so happy, except that his heart swelled with a love beyond the knowledge of children. His quick temperament had rebounded from the depths of unequal depression, into which it so often fell, to the heights of a happy assurance. The Tantalus cup was at his lips at last, and he would drink his full, be sure! His eyes flashed and sparkled, his foot fell light and quick as an antelope's, his brown cheek glowed—never had he looked so handsome. Angela would not forget her promise; she would be waiting for him by the lake, he was sure of that: and thither he made his way through the morning sunshine. They were happy moments.

Presently he passed into the parish at Bratham, and his eye fell upon a neat red-brick cottage, a garden planted with sunflowers, hollyhocks, and sweet annunciation lilies, now breaking into bloom, and a bright gravel-path running to the rustic gate. He thought the garden charmingly old-fashioned, and had just entered a mental note to ask Angela who lived there, when the door opened, and a figure he knew emerged, bearing a mat in one hand and a mopstick in the other. He was some way off, and at first could not quite distinguish who it was; but before she had come to the gate he recognized Pigott. By this time she had stepped into the road, and was making elaborate preparations to dust her mat, so that she did not see him till he spoke to her.

"How are you, Pigott? What may you be doing down here? Why are you not up at the Abbey?"

She gave a cry, and the mat and mopstick fell from her hands.

"Mr. Heigham!" she said, in an awed voice that chilled his blood, "what has brought you back, and why do you come to me? I never wronged you."

"What are you talking about? I have come to marry Angela, of course. We are going to be married to-morrow."

"Oh, then it's really *you*, sir! *And she married yesterday—oh, good God!*"

"Don't laugh at me, nurse—please don't laugh. It—it upsets me. Why do you shake so? What do you mean?"

"Mean! I mean that my Angela *married her cousin, George Caresfoot, at Roxham, yesterday.* Heaven forgive me for having to tell it you!"

Reader, have you ever mortally wounded a head of large game? You hear your bullet thud upon the living flesh, and see the creature throw up its head and stagger for a moment, and then plunge forward with desperate speed, crashing through bush and reeds as though they were meadow-grass. Follow him awhile, and you will find him standing quite still, breathing in great sighs, his back humped and his eye dim, the gore trickling from his nostrils. He is dying—but be careful: he means mischief before he dies.

Any great shock, mental or physical, is apt to reduce man to the level of his brother-beasts. Arthur, for instance, behaved very much like a wounded buffalo as soon as the stun of the blow passed away and the rending pain began to make itself felt. For a few seconds he gazed before him stupid and helpless, then his face turned quite gray, the eyes and nostrils gaped wide, and a curious rigidity took possession of his muscles.

The road he was following led to a branching lane, the same that Angela was turning up that misty Christmas Eve when she saw Lady Bellamy glide past in her carriage. This lane had in former ages, no doubt, to judge from its numerous curves, been an ancient forest-path, and it ran to the little bridge over the stream that fed the lake—a point that, by travelling as the crow flies from Pigott's cottage, might be reached in half the time. This fact Arthur seemed at that dreadful moment to suddenly realize, more probably from natural instinct than from any particular knowledge of the lay of the land. He did not again speak to Pigott, and she was too frightened at his face to speak to him. He only looked at her, but she never forgot that look so long as she lived. Then he turned like a mad thing, and went *crash* through the thick fence that hedged the road, and ran at full speed towards the lake, diverging neither to the right nor to the left, but breaking his way without the slightest apparent difficulty through everything that opposed him.

Very soon he came to the little bridge, and here, struck by some new instinct, he halted. He did not appear to be out of breath, but he leaned on the rail of the bridge and groaned like a dying man. His ghastly face made a blot in the mimic scenery of the place, which was really very pretty. The bridge commanded no view, for the little creek it spanned, and into which the stream ran, gave a turn before it grew into the neck of the lake; but it was hedged in by greenery, and the still pool beneath it was starred with water-lilies, turning their innocent eyes up to the blue sky, and looking as peaceful as though there were no stormy winds or waters in the world to toss them. Amongst these water-lilies a moorhen had built her nest, and presently she came clucking out right under Arthur's feet, followed by ten or a dozen little hurrying black balls, each tipped with sealing-wax red. She looked very happy with her brood—as happy as the lilies and the blue sky—and the sight made him savage. He took up a large stone that lay by him and threw it at her. It hit her on the back and killed her, and Arthur laughed loud as he watched her struggle and then lie still, while the motherless chicks hurried, frightened, away. And yet since he was a boy he had never till now wantonly injured any living creature.

Presently the dead water-hen floated out of sight, and he roused himself, straightened his clothes, which had been somewhat torn and deranged, and, with a steady step and a fixed smile upon his lips, went forward, no longer at a run, but walking quietly up the path that led to the big oak and shaded glen. In five minutes he was there.

Again he paused and looked. There was something to see. On one of the stone seats, dressed in black, her face deathly pale, her head resting on her hand, and trouble in her eyes, sat Angela. On the other was her constant companion, the dog which he had given her. He remembered how, a little more than a year before, she had surprised him in the same way, and he had looked upon her and loved her. He could even smile at the strange irony of fate that had, under such curiously reversed circumstances, brought him back to surprise her, to look upon her, and hate her.

She moved uneasily, and glanced round, but he was hidden by a bush. Then she half rose, paused irresolutely, and, as though struggling against something foolish, sat determinedly down again. When Arthur had done smiling, he came forward a few steps into the open, feeling that his face was all drawn and changed, as indeed it was. It was the face of a man of fifty. His eyes were fire, and his heart was ice.

She turned her head, and looked up with a shrinking in her eyes, as though she feared to see something hateful—a shrinking which turned first to wonder, then to dread, then to a lively joy, and then again to awe. She rose mechanically, with a great gasp; her lips parted, as though to speak, but no words came. The dog, too, saw him, and growled, then ran up and sniffed, and leaped upon him with a yelp of joy. He waved it down, and there was something in the gesture that frightened the beast. It shrank behind him. Then he spoke in a clear, hard tone—not his own voice, she thought.

"Angela, is this true? Are you *married?*"

"Oh, no;" and her voice came stealing to his senses like half-forgotten music; "that is, yes, alas! But is it really you? Oh, Arthur, my darling, have you come back to me?" and she moved towards him with outstretched arms.

Already they were closing round him, and he could feel her

breath upon his cheek, when the charm broke, and he wrenched himself free.

"Get back; do not dare to touch me. Do you know what you are? The poor lost girl is not fallen so low as you. She must get her bread; but, at any rate, I could have given you bread. What! fresh from your husband's arms, and ready to throw yourself into mine! Shame upon you! Were you not married yesterday?"

"Oh, Arthur, have pity! You do not understand. Oh, merciful God—"

"Have pity! What need for pity? Were you not married yesterday?" and he laughed bitterly. "I come—I come from far to congratulate the new-made wife. It is a little odd, though; I thought to marry you myself. See, here was my wedding present;" and he tore the diamond necklace from his pocket. "A snake, you see; a good emblem! Away with it, its use is gone!"

The diamonds went flashing through the sunlight, and fell with a little splash into the lake.

"What! are you not sorry to see so much valuable property wasted? You have a keen appreciation of property!"

Angela sank down on her knees before him, like a broken lily. Her looks grew faint and despairing. The stately head bowed itself to his feet, and all the golden weight of hair broke loose. But he did not pause or spare her. He ground his teeth. No one could have recognized in this maddened, passion-inspired man the pleasant, easy-tempered Arthur of an hour before. His nature was stirred to its depths, and they were deep.

"You miserable woman! do not kneel to me. If it were not unmanly, I could spurn you with my foot. Do you know, girl, you who swore to love me till time had passed—yes, and for all eternity, you who do love me at this moment—and therein lies your shame—that you have killed me? You have murdered my heart. I trusted you, Angela, I trusted you; I gave you all my life, all that was best in me; and now in reward—degraded as you are—I must always love you as much as I despise you. Even now I feel that I *cannot* hate you and forget you. I *must* love you, and I *must* despise you."

She gazed up at him like a dumb beast at its butcher; she could not speak, her voice had gone.

"And yet, when I think of it, I have something to thank you for. You have cleared my mind of illusions. You have taught me what a woman's purity is worth. You did the thing well, too! You did not crush me by inches with platitudes, bidding me forget you and not think of you any more, as though forgetfulness were possible, and thought a tangible thing that one could kill. You struck home in silence, once and for all. Thank you for *that*, Angela. What, are you crying? Go back to the brute whom you have chosen, the brute whose passion or whose money you could prefer to me; tell him that they are tears of happiness, and let him kiss them quite away."

"Oh, Arthur—cruel—Arthur!" and nature gave way. She fell fainting on the grass.

Then, when he saw that she could not understand or feel any more, his rage died, and he too broke down and sobbed—great, gasping sobs. And the frightened dog crept up and licked first her face and then his hand.

Kneeling down, Arthur raised her in his arms and strained her to his heart, kissing her thrice upon the forehead—the lips he could not touch. Then he placed her on the seat, leaning her weight against the tree, and, motioning back the dog, he went his way.

CHAPTER LVIII.

Arthur took the same path by which he had come—all paths were alike to him now—but before he had gone ten yards he saw the figure of George Caresfoot, who appeared to have been watching him. In George's hand was a riding-whip, for he had ridden from the scene of the fire, and was all begrimed with smoke and dirt. But this Arthur did not notice.

"Hullo!" he began; "what—" and then he hesitated; there was a look in Arthur's eyes which he did not like.

But, if George hesitated, Arthur did not. He sprang at him like a wild cat, and in a second had him by the throat and shoulder. For a moment he held him there, for in his state of compressed fury George was like a child in his hands. And as he held him, a fierce and almost uncontrollable desire took possession of him to kill this man, to throw him down and stamp the life out of him. He conquered it, however, and loosed the grip on his throat.

"Let me go!" shrieked George, as soon as he could get breath.

Arthur cut short his clamors by again compressing his windpipe.

"Listen," he said; "a second ago I was very near killing you, but I remember now that, after all, it is she, not you, who are chiefly to blame. You only followed your brutal nature, and nothing else can be expected of a brute. Very likely you put pressure on her, like the cad that you are, but that does not excuse her, for, if she could not resist pressure, she is a fool in addition to being what she is. I look at you and think that soon *she* will come down to *your* level, the level of my successful rival. To be mated to a man like you would drag an angel down. That will be punishment enough. Now go, you cur!"

He swung him violently from him. His fall was broken by a bramble-bush. It was not exactly a bed of roses, but George thought it safer to lie there till his assailant's footsteps had grown faint—he did not wish to bring him back again. Then he crept out of the bush smarting all over. Indeed, his frame of mind was altogether not of the most amiable. To begin with, he had just seen his house—which, as luck would have it, was the only thing he had not sold to Philip, and which was also at the moment uninsured, owing to the confusion arising from the transfer of the property—entirely burnt down. All its valuable contents, too, including a fine collection of pictures and private papers he by no means wished to lose, were irretrievably destroyed.

Nor was his mood improved by the recollection of the events of the previous night, or by the episode of the bramble-bush, illuminated as it was by Arthur's vigorous language; or by what he had just witnessed, for he had arrived in time to see, though from a distance, the last act of the interview between Arthur and Angela.

He had seen him lift her in his arms, kiss her, and place her on the stone seat, but he did not know that she had fainted. The sight had roused his evil passions until they raged like the fire he had left. Then Arthur came out upon him and he made acquaintance with the bramble-bush as already described. But he was not going to be cheated out of his revenge; the woman was still left for him to wreak it on.

By the time he reached Angela, her faculties were reawakening; but, though insensibility had yielded, sense had not returned. She sat upon the stone seat, upright indeed, but rigid and grasping its angles with her hands. The dog had gone. In the undecided way common to dogs, when two people to whom they are equally attached separate, it had at that moment taken it into its head to run a little way after Arthur.

George marched straight up to her, livid with fury.

"So this is how you go on when your husband is away, is it? I saw you kissing that young blackguard, though I am not good enough for you. What, won't you answer? Then it is time that I taught you obedience."

Swish! went the heavy whip through the air, and fell across her fair cheek.

"Will that wake you up, eh, or must I repeat the dose?"

The pain of the blow seemed to rouse her. She rose, her loosed hair falling round her like a golden fleece, and a broad blue stripe across her ghastly face. She stretched out her hands; she opened her great eyes, and in them blazed the awful light of madness.

He was standing, whip in hand, with his back to the lake; she faced him, a breathing, beautiful vengeance, and, in a whisper so intense that the air was full of it, commenced a rambling prayer.

"O God," she said, "bless my dear Arthur! O Almighty Father, avenge our wrongs!"

She paused and fixed her eyes upon him, and they held him so that he could not stir. Then, in strange contrast to the hissing whisper, there broke from her lips a ringing and unearthly laugh that chilled him to the marrow. So they stood for some seconds.

The sound of angry voices had brought the bull-dog back at full speed, and, at the sight of George's threatening attitude, it halted.

It had always hated him, and now it straightway grew more like a devil than a dog. The innate fierceness of the great brute awoke; it bristled with fury till each separate hair stood on end, the eyes grew inflamed and rolled, the muscles stood out in knots against the skin, and saliva ran from its twitching jaws.

George did not know that it was near him, but Angela's wild eye fell upon it. Slowly raising her hand, she pointed at it.

"Look behind you," she cried.

The sound of her voice broke the spell that was upon him.

"Come, give me no more of your nonsense," he said, and then, as much from vague fear and rampant brutality as from any other reason, again struck her with the whip.

Next second he was aware of a tremendous shock. The dog had seen the blow, and had instantly launched itself, with all the blind courage of its race, straight at the striker's throat. It missed its aim, however, only carrying away a portion of George's under-lip. He yelled with pain, and struck at it with the whip, and then began a scene which, in its grotesque horror, beggars all description. Again and again the dog flew at him, its perfect silence contrasting strangely with George's shrieks of terror, and the shrill peals of horrible laughter that came hurrying from Angela's lips as she watched the struggle.

At last the dog gripped the man by the forearm, and, sinking its great teeth into the flesh, hung its weight upon it. In vain did George, maddened by the exquisite pain, dash himself and the dog against the ground: in vain did he stagger round and round the glen, tearing at its throat with his uninjured hand. The brute hung grimly on. Presently there came an end. As he reeled along, howling for help and dragging his fierce burden with him, George stumbled over a dead bough which lay upon the bank of the lake, and fell backwards into the water, exactly at the spot where the foundations of the old boat-house wall rose to within a few inches of the surface. His head struck heavily against the stonework, and he and the dog, who would not lose his grip, lay on it for a moment, then they rolled off together into the deep pool, the man dragging the dog with him. There were a few ripples, stained with little red filaments, a few air-bubbles that marked the exhalation of his last breath, and George's spirit had left its inclosing body, and gone—whither? Ay, reader, whither had it gone?

The outcry brought Philip and old Jakes running down to the lake. They found Angela standing alone on the brink and laughing her wildest.

"See," she cried, as they came panting up, "the bridegroom cometh from his chamber," and at that moment some unreleased air within the body brought it up for an instant to the surface, so that the torn and ghastly face and head emerged for a second as though to look at them. Then it sank again.

"The brave dog holds him well—ha, ha, ha! He cannot catch

me now—ha, ha, ha! Nor you, Judas, who sold me. Judas! Judas! Judas!" and, turning, she fled with the speed of the wind.

Mr. Fraser had but just come down, and was walking in his garden, when he saw this dreadful figure come flying towards him with streaming hair.

"*Betrayed!*" she cried, in a voice which rang like the wail of a lost soul, and fell on her face at his feet.

When she came back to life they found that she was mad.

CHAPTER LIX.

The news of George Caresfoot's tragic death was soon common property, and following as it did so hard upon his marriage, which now was becoming known, and within a few hours of the destruction of his house by fire, it caused no little excitement. It cannot be said that the general feeling was one of very great regret; it was not. George Caresfoot had commanded deference as a rich man, but he certainly had not won affection. Still, his fate excited general interest and sympathy, though some people were louder in their regrets over the death of such a plucky dog as Aleck than over that of the man he killed; but then these had a personal dislike to George. When, however, it came to be rumored that the dog had attacked George because George had struck the dog's mistress, general sympathy veered decidedly towards the dog. By and by, as some of the true facts of the case came out, namely, that Angela Caresfoot had gone mad, that her lover, who was supposed to be dead, had been seen in Rewtham on the evening of the wedding, that the news of Mr. Heigham's death had been concocted to bring about the marriage, and, last but not least, that the Isleworth estates had passed into the possession of Philip Caresfoot, public opinion grew very excited, and the dog Aleck was well spoken of.

When Sir John Bellamy stepped out on the platform at Roxham on his return from London that day, his practised eye saw at once that something unusual had occurred. A group of county magistrates returning from quarter sessions were talking excitedly together whilst waiting for their train. He knew them all well, but at first they seemed inclined to let him pass without speaking to him. Presently, however, one of them turned, and spoke to him.

"Have you heard about this, Bellamy?"

"No; what?"

"George Caresfoot is dead; killed by a bull-dog, or something. They say he was thrashing the girl he married yesterday, his cousin's daughter, with a whip, and the dog made for him, and they both fell into the water together and were drowned. The girl has gone mad."

"Good heavens! you don't say so!"

"Yes, I do, though; and I'll tell you what it is, Bellamy, they say that you and your wife went to Madeira and trumped up a story about her lover's death in order to take the girl in. I tell you this as an old friend."

"What? I certainly went to Madeira, and I saw young Heigham there, but I never trumped up any story about his death. I never mentioned him to Angela Caresfoot, for two reasons: first, because I have not come across her; and secondly, because I understood that Philip Caresfoot did not wish it."

"Well, I'm glad to hear it, for your sake; but I have just seen Fraser, and he tells me that Lady Bellamy told the girl of this young Heigham's death in his own presence, and, what is more, he showed me a letter they found in her dress purporting to have been written by him on his death-bed which your wife gave her."

"Of what Lady Bellamy has or has not said or done, I know nothing. I have no control over her actions."

"Well, I should advise you to look into the business, because it will all come out at the inquest," and they separated.

Sir John drove homewards, thoughtful, but by no means unhappy. The news of George's agonizing death was balm to him; he only regretted that he had not been there, somewhere well out of the way of the dog,—up a tree, for instance—to see it.

As soon as he got home, he sent a message to Lady Bellamy to say he wished to speak to her. Then he seated himself at his writing-desk, and waited. Presently he heard his wife's firm step upon the stairs. He rubbed his dry hands, and smiled a half-frightened, wicked little smile.

"At last," he said. "And now for revenge."

She entered the room, looking rather pale, but calm and commanding as ever.

"So you have come back," she said.

"Yes. Have you heard the news? *Your flame*, George Caresfoot, is dead."

"I knew that he was dead. How did he die?"

"Who told you he was dead?"

"No one; I knew it. I told him he would die last night, and I felt him die this morning. Did she kill him or did Arthur Heigham?"

"Neither; that bull-dog flew at him and he fell into the lake."

"Oh! I suppose Angela set it on. I told him that she would win. You remember the picture falling in the study at Isleworth. It has been a true omen, you see."

"Angela is mad. The story is all over the country and travelling like wild-fire. The letter you forged has been found. Heigham was down here this morning and has gone again, and you, Lady Bellamy, are a disgraced and ruined woman."

She did not flinch a muscle.

"I know it; it is the result of pitting myself against that girl. But pray, Sir John, what are you? Was it not you who devised the scheme?"

"You are right: I did—to trap two fools. Anne, I have waited twenty years, but you have met your master at last."

Lady Bellamy made a slight exclamation and relapsed into silence.

"My plot has worked well. Already one of you is dead, and for you a fate is reserved that is worse than death. You are henceforth a penniless outcast, left at forty-two to the tender mercies of the wide world."

"Explain yourself a little."

"With pleasure. For years I have submitted to your contumely, longing to be revenged, waiting to be revenged. You thought me a fool, I know, and compared with you I am; but you do not understand what an amount of hatred even a fool is capable of. For twenty years, Lady Bellamy, I have hated you, you will never know how much, though perhaps what I am going to say may give you some idea. I very well know what terms you were on with George Caresfoot; you never took any pains to hide them from me, you only hid the proofs. I soon discovered, indeed, that your marriage to me was nothing but a blind; that I was being used as a screen, forsooth. But your past I could never fathom. I don't look like a revengeful man, do I? but for all that I have for years sought many ways to ruin you both. Yet from one thing and another they all failed, till a blessed chance made that brute's blind passion the instrument of his own destruction, and put you into my hands. You little thought when you told me all that story, and begged my advice, how I was revelling in the sense that, proud woman as you are, it must have been an agony of humiliation to you to have to tell it. It was an instructive scene, that; it assured me of what I suspected before, that George Caresfoot must have you bound to him by some stronger ties than those of affection; that he must hold you in a grip of iron. It made me think, too, that if by any means I could acquire the same power, I too should be able to torture you."

For the first time Lady Bellamy looked up.

"Am I tiring you," he said, politely, "or shall I go on?"

"Go on."

"With your permission, I will ring for a glass of sherry—no, claret; the day is too hot for sherry," and he rang.

The claret was brought and he drank a glass, remarking with an affectation of coolness that it was a sound wine for a pound a dozen; then he proceeded.

"The first thing I have to call your attention to is this Arthur Heigham plot. At first it may appear that I am involved with you; I am not. There is not, now that George Caresfoot is dead, one tittle of evidence against me except your own, and who will believe *you?* You are inculpated up to the eyes; you delivered the forged letter; I can prove that you cozened the ring out of Heigham, and you told Philip. There is no escape for you, and I have already taken an opportunity to renounce any responsibility for your acts At the inquest I shall appear to give evidence against you, and then I shall abandon you to your fate."

"Is that all?"

"No, woman. *I have your letters!*"

She sprang up with a little scream and stood over him with dilated eyes. Sir John leaned back in his chair, rubbed his hands, and watched her tortured face with evident satisfaction.

"Yes, you may well scream," he said, "for I not only possess them, but I have read and re-read them. I know all your story, the name of the husband you deserted and of the child who died of your neglect. I have even sent an agent to identify the localities. Yes, you may well scream, for I have read them all, and really they are most instructive documents, and romantic enough for a novel; such fire, such passionate invective, such wild despair. But since I learnt how and why you married me, I will tell you what I have made up my mind to do. I am going after the inquest to turn you out of this house, and give you a pittance to live on so long as you remain here. I wish you to become a visible moral, a walking monument of disgrace in the neighborhood you ruled. Should you attempt to escape me, the payment will be stopped; should you obtain employment, your character shall be exposed. At every turn you shall be struck down till you learn to kiss the hand that strikes you and beg for pity on your knees. My revenge, Anne, shall be to break your spirit."

"And are you not perhaps afraid that I may turn upon you? You know me to be a woman of strong will and many resources, some of which you do not even understand."

"No, I am not afraid, because I still have a reserve force; I still hold the letters that I stole two days ago; and, even should you murder me, I have left directions that will insure your exposure."

A pause ensued.

"Have you nothing more to say?" he said, at last.

"Nothing."

"Supposing, Anne, that I were to tell you that I have been trying to frighten you, and that if you were to go down on your knees before me now, and beg my forgiveness, I would forgive you —no, not forgive you, but let you off with easier terms—would you do it?"

"No, John, I would not. Once I went on my knees to a man, and I have not forgotten the lesson he taught me. Do your worst."

"Then you understand my terms, and accept them?"

"Understand them? yes. I understand that you are a little-minded man, and, like all little-minded men, cruel, and desirous of exacting the uttermost farthing in the way of revenge, forgetting that you owe everything to me. I do not wish to exculpate myself, mind you. Looking at the case from your point of view, and in your own petty way, I can almost sympathize with you. But as for accepting your terms—do you know me so little as to think that I could do so? Have you not learnt that I may break, but shall never bend? And, if I choose now to face the matter out, I should beat you, even now when you hold all the cards in your hand; but I am weary of it all, especially weary of you and your little ways, and I do not choose. You will injure me enough to make the great success I planned for us both impossible, and I am tired of everything except the success which crowns a struggle. Well, I have ways of escape you know nothing of. Do your worst; I am not afraid of you;" and she leaned back easily in her chair, and looked at him with wearied and indifferent eyes.

Little Sir John ground his teeth, and twisted his pippin-like face into a scowl that looked absurdly out of place on anything so jovial.

"Curse you!" he said, "even now you dare to defy me. Do you know, you woman-fiend, that at this moment I almost think I love you?"

"Of course I know it. If you did not love me, you would not take all this trouble to try to crush me. But this conversation is very long; shall we put an end to it?"

Sir John sat still a moment thinking, and gazing at the splendid Sphinx-browed creature before him with a mixture of hatred and respect. Then he rose, and spoke.

"Anne, you are a wonderful woman! I cannot do it; I cannot utterly ruin you. You must be exposed—I could not help that, if I would—and we must separate; but I will be generous to you: I will allow you five hundred a year, and you shall live where you like. You shall not starve."

She laughed a little as she answered:

"I am starving now; it is long past luncheon-time. As for your five hundred a year that you will give me out of the three or four thousand I have given you, I care nothing for it. I tell you I am tired of it all, and I never felt more superior to you than I do now in the moment of your triumph. It wants a stronger hand than yours to humble me. I may be a bad woman, I dare say I am; but you will find, too late, that there are few in the world like me. For years you have shone with a reflected light; when the light goes out, you will go out too. Get back into your native mud, the mental slime out of which I picked you, contemptible creature that you are! and when you have lost me, learn to measure the loss by the depths to which you will sink. I reject your offers. I mock at your threats, for they will recoil on your own head. I despise you, and I have done with you. John Bellamy, good-by;" and, with a proud courtesy, she swept from the room.

That evening it was rumored that Sir John Bellamy had separated from his wife, owing to circumstances which had come to his knowledge in connection with George Caresfoot's death.

CHAPTER LX.

THAT same afternoon, Lady Bellamy ordered out the victoria with the fast-trotting horse, and drove to the Abbey House. She found Philip pacing up and down the gravel in front of the gray old place, which had that morning added one more to the long list of human tragedies its walls had witnessed. His face was pale and contorted by mental suffering, and, as soon as he recognized Lady Bellamy, he made an effort to escape. She stopped him.

"I suppose it is here, Mr. Caresfoot?"

"It! What?"

"The body."

"Yes."

"I wish to see it."

Philip hesitated a minute, and then led the way to his study. The corpse had been laid upon the table just as it had been taken from the water; indeed, the wet still fell in heavy drops from the clothes onto the ground. It was to be removed to Roxham that evening, to await the inquest on the morrow. The shutters of the room had been closed, lest the light should strike too fiercely on the ghastly sight; but even in the twilight Lady Bellamy could discern every detail of its outline clearly marked by the wet patches on the sheet which was thrown loosely over it. On a chair by the side of the table, above the level of which its head rose, giving it the appearance of being in the act of climbing onto it, lay the carcass of the dog, its teeth still firmly set in the dead man's arm. They had been unable to unlock the savage grip without hacking its jaws asunder, and this it was not thought advisable to do till after the inquest.

At the door Philip paused, as though he did not mean to enter.

"Come in," said Lady Bellamy; "surely you are not afraid of a dead man."

"I fear the dead a great deal more than I do the living," he muttered, but came in and shut the door.

As soon as her eyes had grown accustomed to the light, Lady Bellamy went up to the body, and, drawing off the sheet, gazed long and steadily at the mutilated face, on the lips of which the bloody froth still stood.

"I told him last night," she said presently to Philip, "that we should never meet again alive, but I did not think to see him so soon like this. Do you know that I once loved that thing? That shattered brain directed the only will to which I ever bowed. But the love went out for ever last night, the chain snapped; and now I can look upon this sight without a single sigh or a regret, with nothing but loathing and disgust. There lies the man who ruined me—did you know it? I do not care who knows it now—ruined me with his eyes open, not caring anything about me; there lies the hard taskmaster whom I served through so many years, the villain who drove me against my will into this last crime which has thus brought its reward. The dog gave him his just due; look, its teeth still hold him, as fast, perhaps, as the memories of his crimes will hold him where he has gone. Regret him! sorrow for him! no, oh no! I can curse him as he lies, villain, monster, devil that he was!"

She paused, and even in the dim light Philip could see her bosom heave and her great eyes flash with the fierceness of her excitement.

"You should not talk so of the dead," he said.

"You are right," she answered; "he has gone beyond the reach of my words; but the thought of all the misery I have suffered at his hands made me for a moment mad. Cover it up again, the vile frame which held a viler soul: to the earth with the one, to undreamed-of sorrow with the other, each to its appointed place. How does it run?—'The wages of sin is death.' Yes, that is right. He is dead; the blow fell first on him, that was right, and I am about to die; and you—what will happen to you, the Judas of the plot, eh? You do not think that you will enjoy your blood-money in peace, do you?"

"What do you mean?" asked Philip, nervously; her wild way frightened him.

"Mean! why, that you are the sorriest knave of all. This man was at least led on to crime by passion; Bellamy entered into it to work out a secret revenge, poor fool; I acted because I could not help myself at first, and then for the sake of the game itself, for, when I take a thing in my hand, I *will* succeed. But you, Philip Caresfoot, you sold your own flesh and blood for money or money's worth, and you are the worst of all—worse than George, for even a brutal love is a nobler thing than avarice like yours. Well, as the sin is, so will the punishment be."

"It is a lie! I thought that he was dead."

"You thought that Arthur Heigham was dead! Then I read your thoughts very wrongly when we met upon the road on Christmas Day. You wished to think that he was dead, but you did not think it. Even now your conscience is making a coward of you, and, as you said just now, for you the silence of the dead is more terrible than the accusations of the living. I know a little about you, Philip. Do you not see shadows on your walls, and do not departed voices come to haunt you in your sleep? I know you do, and I will tell you this—the *Things* which you have suffered from at times shall henceforth be your continual companions. If you can pray, pray with all your strength that your daughter may not die; for, if she does, her shadow will always be there to haunt you with the rest. Why do you tremble so at the mere mention of a spirit? Stand still, and I will show you one. I can if I like."

Philip could stand it no longer. With a curse he burst out of the room. Presently she followed him, and found him standing in front of the house, wiping the cold perspiration from his forehead.

"You accursed woman," he said, "go, and never come near this house again!"

"I never shall come to this house again," she answered. "Ah, here is my carriage. Good-by, Philip Caresfoot. You are a very wealthy man now—worth I do not know how many thousands a year. You have been singularly fortunate—you have accomplished your ends. Few people can do that. May the accomplishment bring happiness with it! If you wish it to do so, stifle your conscience, and do not let your superstitions affect you. But, by the way, you know French, do you not? Then here is a maxim that, in parting, I recommend to your attention—it has some truth in it: Il y a une page effrayante dans le livre des destinées humaines: on y lit en tête ces mots 'les desirs accomplis.'" And she was gone.

"I owed him a debt for tempting George on in that business," thought Lady Bellamy to herself, as she rolled swiftly down the avenue of giant walnuts; "but I think that I have repaid it. The thorn I have planted will fester in his flesh till he dies of the sore. Superstition run wild in his weak mind will make the world a hell for him, and that is what I wish."

Presently she stopped the carriage, and walked to the top of a little knoll commanding what had been Isleworth Hall, but was now a black smoking blot on the landscape. The white front of the house was still standing, though riven from top to bottom, and through its empty window-places the westering sun poured great streams of fire which looked like flame shining through the eye-sockets of a gigantic skull.

"I did that well," she said; "and yet how blind I was! I should have known that he spoke the truth when he said the letters were not there. My skill failed me—it always does fail at need. I thought the fire would reach them somehow."

When she arrived at Rewtham House, she found that Sir John had left, taking luggage with him, and stating that he was going to put up at an inn at Roxham. On the hall-table, too, lay a summons to attend the inquest on the body of George Caresfoot, which was to take place on the morrow. She tore it across. Then she went up and dressed herself for dinner with such splendor that her maid thought it necessary to remind her that there was no company coming.

"No," she said, with a strange smile; "but I am going out to-night. Give me my sapphire necklace."

She sat through dinner, and afterwards went into the drawing-room, and, opening a despatch-box, read and burnt a great number of papers.

"There go the keys to my knowledge," she said aloud, as they flickered and fell into ashes. "No one shall reap the fruits of my labors; and yet it is a pity—I was on the right track, and, though I could never have succeeded, another might. I had the key, though I could not find the lock. I must go through with it now. I cannot live, deprived both of success and of my secret power, and I could never begin and climb that stair again."

Then, from a secret drawer in the despatch-box, she extracted a little phial, tightly stoppered and sealing-waxed. She examined it closely, and looked at the liquid in it against the light.

"My medicine has taken no harm during this twenty years," she thought. "It still looks what it is—strong enough to kill a giant, and subtle enough to leave little trace upon a child." Then she shut up the despatch-box and put it away, and, going to the open window, looked up at the stars, and then down at the shadows flung by the clouds as they swept across the moon.

"Shadows," she mused, "below, and gleams of light between the shadows—that is like our life. Light above—pure, clear, eternal—that is like the wider life. And between the two, the night; and above them both, the stars.

"In the immensity, where shall I find my place? Oh, that I might sleep eternally! Yes, that would be best of all—to sink into sleep never ending, unbroken, and unbreakable, to be absorbed into the cool vastness of the night, and lie in her great arms for ever. O Night! whom I have ever loved, you bring your sleep to wearied millions—bring *me* sleep eternal. But no, the stars are above the night, and above the stars is—what? Yes; the hour I dread like every other mortal with my body, and yet dare to long for with my spirit, has come. I am about to cast off Time, and pass into Eternity, to spring from the giddy heights of Space into the uncertain arms of the Infinite. Yet a few minutes, and my essence, my vital part, will start upon its endless course, and, passing far above those stars, will find the fount of that knowledge of which it has already sipped, and drink and drink till it grows like a God, and can look upon the truth and not be blinded. Such are my high hopes. And yet—if there be a hell! My life has been evil, my sins many. What if there be an avenging Power waiting, as some think, to grind me into powder, and then endow each crushed particle with individual sense of endless misery! What if there be a hell! In a few minutes, or what will seem but a few minutes—for surely, to the disembodied spirit, time cannot exist; though it sleep a billion years, it will be as a breath—I shall have solved the problem. I shall know what all the panic-stricken millions madly ask, and ask in vain! Yes, I shall know if *there is a hell!* Well, if there be, then I shall rule there, for power is native to my soul. Let me hesitate no longer, but go and solve the problem before I grow afraid. Afraid? I am not afraid. 'I have immortal longings in me.' Who was it said that? Oh, Cleopatra! Was Cleopatra more beautiful than I am, I wonder? I am sure that she was not so great; for, had I been she, Antony should have driven Cæsar out of Egypt. Oh! if I could have loved with a pure and perfect love as other women may, and intertwined my destiny with that of some *great* man—some being of a nature kindred to my own—I should have been good and happy, and he should have ruled this country. But Fate and Fortune, grown afraid of what I should do, linked my life to a soulless brute! and, alas! like him I have fallen—fallen irretrievably!"

She closed the window, and, coming into the room, rang the bell.

"Bring me some wine," she said to the servant. "I do not feel well."

"What wine, my lady?"

"Champagne."

The wine was brought, and stood, uncorked, upon the table.

"That will do," she said. "Tell my maid not to sit up for me: it will be late before I go to bed to-night."

The man bowed and went, and she poured out some of the sparkling wine, and then, taking the little phial, opened it with difficulty, and emptied its contents into the glass. The wine boiled up furiously, turned milk-white, and then cleared again; but the poison had destroyed its sparkle—it was dead as ditch-water.

"That is strange," she said; "I never saw that effect before." Next she took the phial and powdered it into a pinch of tiny dust with a whale's tooth that lay upon the table. The dust she took to the window and threw out, a little at a time. Lady Bellamy wished to die as she had lived, a mystery. Then she came and stood over the deadly draught she had compounded, and thought sometimes aloud and sometimes to herself.

"I have heard it said that suicides are cowards; let those who say it stand, as I stand to-night, with death lying in the little circle of a glass before them, and they will know whether they are cowards, or if they are spirits of a braver sort than those who can bear to drudge to the bitter end of life. It is not yet too late. I can throw that stuff away. I can leave this place and begin life anew in some other country; my jewels will give me the means, and, for the matter of that, I can always win as much money as I want. But no; then I must begin again, and for that I have not the patience or the time. Besides, I long to *know*, to solve the mystery. Come, let me make an end; I will chance it. Spirits like my own wear their life only while it does not gall them; if it begins to fret, they cast it from them like a half-worn dress, scorning to wrap it round them till it drops away in rags."

She raised the glass.

"How lonely this place is, and how still! and yet it may well be that there are millions round me watching what I do. Why does he come into my mind now, that good man, and the child I bore him? Shall I see them presently? Will they crush me with reproaches? And—have my nerves broken down?—is it fancy, or does that girl's pale face, with warning in her eyes, float between me and the wall? Well, I will drink to her, for her mind could even overtop my own. She was, at least, my equal, and I have driven her mad! Let me taste this stuff."

Lifting the glass to her lips, she drank a little, and set it down. The effect was almost magical. Her eyes blazed, a new beauty bloomed upon her cheek, her whole grand presence seemed to gain in majesty. The quick drug for a moment burnt away the curtain between the seen and the unseen, and yet left her living.

"Ah," she cried, in the silence of the room, "how it runs along my veins; I hear the rushing of the stars, I see strange worlds, my soul leaps through infinite spaces, the white light of immortality strikes upon my eyes and blinds me. Come, life unending, I have conquered death."

Seizing the poison, she swallowed what remained of it, and dashed the glass down beside her. Then she fell heavily on her face; once she struggled to her knees, then fell again, and lay still.

CHAPTER LXI.

After throwing George Caresfoot into the bramble-bush, Arthur walked steadily back to the inn, where he arrived, quite composed in manner, at about half-past seven. Old Sam, the ostler, was in the yard, washing a trap. He went up to him, and asked when the next train started for London.

"There is one as leaves Roxham at nine o'clock, sir, and an uncommon fast one, I'm told. But you bean't a-going yet, be you, sir?"

"Yes; have the gig ready in time to catch the train."

"Very good, sir. Been to the fire, I suppose, sir?" he went on, dimly perceiving that Arthur's clothes were torn. "It wore a fine place, it wore, and it did blaze right beautiful."

"No; what fire?"

"Bless me, sir, didn't you see it last night?—why, Isleworth Hall, to be sure. It wore burnt right out, and all as was in it."

"Oh! How did it come to get burnt?"

"Can't say, sir; but I did hear say how as Lady Bellamy was a-dining there last night along with the squire; the squire he went out somewhere, my lady she goes home, and the footman he goes to put out the lamp and finds the drawing-room a roaring fiery furnace, like as parson tells us on. But I don't know how that can be, for I heard how as the squire was a-dying, so 'taint likely that he was a-going out. But, Lord, sir, folks in these parts do lie that uncommon, 'taint as it used to be when I was a boy. As like as no, he's no more dying than you are. Anyhow, sir, it all burned like tinder, and the only thing, so I'm told, as was saved was a naked stone statty of a girl with a chain round her wrists, as Jim Blakes, our constable, being in liquor, brought out in his arms, thinking how as it was alive, and tried to rewive it with cold water."

At that moment Sam's story was interrupted by the arrival of a farmer's cart.

"How be you, Sam?"

"Well, I thank yer, for seventy-two; that is, not particlar ill."

"Have you a gentleman of the name of Heigham staying here?"

"I am he," said Arthur. "Do you want me?"

"No, sir, only the station-master at Roxham asked me to drop this here; as it was marked 'Immediate,'" and he handed Arthur a box.

Arthur thanked him, and, taking it, went up to his room, leaving old Sam delighted to find a new listener to his story of the fire.

It was from the florist, and contained the bouquet he had meant to give Angela on her wedding-day. It had cost him a great deal of thought, that bouquet, to say nothing of five guineas of the coin of the realm, and he felt a certain curiosity to look at it, though to do so gave him something of the same sensation that we experience in reading a letter written by some loved hand which we know grew cold before the lines it traced could reach us. He took the box to his room and opened it. The bouquet was a lovely thing, and did credit even to Covent Garden, and the masses of stephanotis and orange-bloom, relieved here and there by rising sprays of lilies-of-the-valley, filled the whole room with fragrance.

He drew it from the zinc-well in which it was packed in moss and cotton-wool, and wondered what he should do with it. He could not leave such a thing about, nor would he take it away. Suddenly an idea struck him, and he repacked it in its case as carefully as he could in the original moss and cotton-wool, and then looked about for the sheet of tissue-paper that should complete the covering. He had destroyed it, and had to search for a substitute. In so doing his eye fell upon a long envelope on his dressing-table, and he smiled. It contained his marriage-license, and he bethought him that it was a very fair substitute for tissue-paper, and quite as worthless. He extracted it, and, placing it over the flowers, closed up the box. Then he carefully directed it to "Mrs. George Caresfoot, Abbey House," and, ringing the bell, desired the boots to find a messenger to take it over.

When he had done all this, he sat down and wondered what could have come to him that he could take pleasure in doing a cruel action only worthy of a jealous woman.

Perhaps of all the bitter cups which are held to our lips in this sad world, there is none more bitter than that which it was his lot to drink of now. To begin with, the blow fell in youth, when we love or hate, or act, with an ardor and an entire devotion that we give to nothing in after-life. It is then that the heart puts forth its most tender and yet its most lusty shoots, and if they are crushed the whole plant suffers, and sometimes bleeds to death. Arthur had, to an extent quite unrealized by himself until he lost her, centred all his life in this woman, and it was no exaggeration to say, as he had said to her, that she had murdered his heart, and withered up all that was best in it. She had done more: she had inflicted the most cruel injury upon him that a woman can inflict upon a man. She had shaken his belief in her sex at large.

He felt, sitting there in his desolation, that, now he had lost Angela, he could never be the same man he would otherwise have been. Her cruel desertion had shattered the tinted glass through which youth looks at the world, and he now, before his day, saw it as it is, grim and hard, and full of coarse realities, and did not yet know that time would again soften down the sharpest of the rough outlines, and throw a garment of its own over the nakedness of life. He was a generous-hearted man and not a vain one, and had he thought that Angela had ceased to care for him and loved this other man better than himself, whatever suffering it might have caused him, he could have found it in his heart to forgive her, and even to sympathize with her; but he could not think this. Something told him that it was not so. She had contracted herself into a shameful, loveless marriage, and, to gain ends quite foreign to all love, had raised a barrier between them which had no right to exist, and yet one that in this world could, he thought, never be removed.

Misfortunes rain upon us from every quarter of the sky; but so long as they come from the sky we can bear them, for they are beyond the control of our own volition, and must be accepted, as we accept the gale or the lightning. It is the troubles which spring from our own folly and weakness, or from that of those with whom our lives are intertwined, which really crush us. Now Arthur knew enough of the world to be aware that there is no folly to equal that of a woman who, of her own free will, truly loving one man whom she can marry if she wills it, deliberately gives herself to another. It is not only a folly, it is a crime, and, like most crimes, for this life, an irretrievable mistake.

Long before he got back to London, the first unwholesome exaltation of mind that always follows a great misfortune, and which may perhaps be compared with the excitement that for a while covers the shameful sense of defeat in an army, had evaporated, and he began to realize the crushing awfulness of the blow which had fallen on him, and to fear lest it should drive him mad. He looked round his little horizon for some straw of comfort at which to catch, and could find none; nothing but dreadful thoughts and sickening visions.

And then suddenly, just as he was sinking into the dulness of despair, there came, like the first gleam of light in chaotic darkness, the memory of Mildred Carr. Truly she had spoken prophetically. His idol had been utterly cast down and crushed to powder by a hand stronger than his own. He would go to her in his suffering; perhaps she could find means to comfort him.

When he reached town he took a hansom and went to look for some rooms; he would not return to those he had left on the previous afternoon, for the sympathetic landlord had helped him to pack up the wedding clothes and had admired the wedding gift. Arthur felt that he could not face him again. He found some to suit him in Duke Street, St. James, and left his things there. Thence he drove to Fenchurch Street and took a passage to Madeira

The clerk, the same one who had given him his ticket about a year before, remembered him perfectly, and asked him how he got on with Mrs. Carr. But when his passage was taken he was disgusted to find that the mail did not sail for another five days. He looked at his watch: it was only half-past one o'clock. He could scarcely believe that what had happened had only occurred that morning, only seven hours ago. It seemed to him that he had stood face to face with Angela, not that morning, but years ago, and miles away, on some desolate shore which lay on the other side of a dead ocean of pain. And yet it was only seven hours! If the hours went with such heavy wings, how would the days pass, and the months, and the years?

What should he do with himself? In his condition perpetual activity was as necessary to him as air; he must do something to dull the sharp edge of his suffering, or the sword of madness which hung over him by such a slender thread would fall. Suddenly he bethought him of a man whom he had known slightly up at Cambridge, a man of wealth and evil reputation. This man would, he felt, be able to put him in a way of getting through his time. He knew his address, and thither he drove.

Four days later, a figure, shrunk, shaky, and looking prematurely old, with the glaze of intoxication scarcely faded from his eye, walked into Mr. Borley's office. That respectable gentleman looked and looked again.

"Good Heavens!" he said at length; "it isn't Arthur Heigham?"

"Yes, it is, though," said an unequal voice; "I've come for some money. I've got none left, and I am going to Madeira to-morrow."

"My dear boy, what has happened to you? You look so very strange. I have been expecting to see your marriage in the paper. Why, it's only a few days ago that you left to be married."

"A few days! A few years, you mean. I've been jilted, that's all; nothing to speak of, you know, but I had rather not talk about it, if you don't mind. I'm like a nag with a flayed back, don't like the sight of the saddle at present;" and poor Arthur, mentally and physically exhausted, put his head down on his arm and gulped.

The old lawyer took in the situation at a glance.

"Hard hit," he said to himself, "and gone on the burst;" and then aloud, "Well, well, that has happened to many a man; in fact, you mightn't believe it, but it once happened to me, and I don't look much the worse, do I? But we won't talk about it. The less said of a bad business the better, that's my maxim. And so you are going abroad again. Have you got any friends at Madeira?"

Arthur nodded.

"And you want some more money. Let me see: I sent you two hundred pounds last week."

"That was for my wedding tour. I've spent it now. You can

guess how I have spent it. Pleasant contrast, isn't it? Gives rise to moral reflections."

"Come, come, Heigham, you must not give way like that. These things happen to most men in the course of their lives, and if they are wise it teaches them that gingerbread isn't all gilt, and to set down women at their proper value, and appreciate a good one if it pleases Providence to give them one in course of time. Don't you go making a fool of yourself over this girl's pretty face. Handsome is as handsome does. These things are hard to bear, I know, but you don't make them any better by pitching your own reputation after a girl's want of stability."

"I know that you are quite right, and I am much obliged to you for your kind advice; but we won't say anything more about it. I suppose that you can let me have some money?"

"Oh, yes, if you want it, though I think we shall have to over-draw. What do you want? Two hundred? Here is the check."

"I am anxious about that young fellow," said Mr. Borley to himself, in the pause between Arthur's departure and the entry of the next client. "I hope his disappointment won't send him to the dogs. He is not of the sort who take it easy, like I did, for instance. Dear me, that is a long while ago now. I wonder what the details of his little affair were, and who the girl married. Captain Shuffle! yes, show him in."

CHAPTER LXII.

NEXT morning Arthur cashed his check, and started on his travels. He had no very clear idea why he was going back to Madeira, or what he meant to do when he got there; but then, at this painful stage of his existence, none of his ideas could be called clear. Though he did not realize it, what he was searching for was sympathy—female sympathy, of course; for in trouble members of either sex gravitate instinctively to the other for comfort. Perhaps they do not quite trust their own, or perhaps they are afraid of being laughed at.

Arthur's was not one of those natures that can lock their griefs within the bosom and let them lie there till in process of time they shrivel away. Except among members of the peerage as pictured in current literature, these stern, proud creatures are not common. Man, whether he figures in the world as a peer or a hedge-carpenter, is, as a matter of fact, mentally as well as physically, gregarious, and adverse to loneliness either in his joys or sorrows.

Decidedly, too, the homœopathic system must be founded on great natural facts, and there is philosophy, born of the observation of human nature, in the somewhat vulgar proverb that recommends a "hair of the dog that bit you." Otherwise, nine men out of every ten who have been badly treated, or think that they have been badly treated, by a woman, would not at once rush headlong for refuge to another, a proceeding which also, in nine cases out of ten, ends in making confusion worse confounded.

Arthur, though he was not aware of it, was exemplifying a natural law that has not yet been properly explained. But, even if he had known it, it is doubtful if the knowledge would have made him any happier; for it is irritating to reflect that we are the slaves of natural laws, that our action is not the outcome of our own volition, but of a vague force working silently as the Gulf Stream—since such knowledge makes a man measure his weakness, and so strikes at his tenderest point, his vanity.

But whilst we have been reflecting together, my reader and I, Arthur was making his way to Madeira, so we may as well all come to a halt off Funchal.

Very shortly after the vessel had dropped her anchor, Arthur was greeted by his friend, the manager of "Miles's Hotel."

"Glad to see you, sir, though I can't say that you look well. I scarcely expected to find anybody for us at this time of year. Business is very slack in the summer."

"Yes, I suppose that Madeira is pretty empty."

"There is nobody here at all, sir."

"Is Mrs. Carr gone, then?" asked Arthur, in some alarm.

"No; she is still here. She has not been away this year. But she has been very quiet; no parties or anything, which makes people think that she has lost money."

By this time the boat was rising on the roll of the last billow, to be caught next moment by a dozen hands, and dragged up the shingle. It was evening, or, rather, verging that way, and from under the magnolia-trees below the cathedral there came the sound of the band summoning the inhabitants of Funchal to congregate, chatter, and flirt.

"I think," said Arthur, "that I will ask you to take my things up to the hotel. I will come by and by. I should like the same room I had before, if it is empty."

"Very good, Mr. Heigham. You will have the place nearly all to yourself now."

Having seen his baggage depart, Arthur turned, and resisting the importunities of beggars, guides, and parrot sellers, who had not yet recognized him as an old hand, made his way towards the Quinta Carr. How well he knew the streets and houses, even to the withered faces of the women who sat by the doors! and yet he seemed to have grown old since he had seen them. Ten minutes of sharp walking brought him to the gates of the Quinta, and he paused before them, and thought how, a few months ago, he had quitted them, miserable at the grief of another, now to re-enter them utterly crushed by his own.

He walked on through the beautiful gardens to the house. The hall-door stood open. He did not wait to ring, but, driven by some impulse, entered. After the glare of the sun, which at that time of the year was powerful even in its decline, the carefully-shaded hall seemed quite dark. But by degrees his eyes adapted themselves to the altered light, and began to distinguish the familiar outline of the furniture. Next they travelled to the door of the drawing-room, where another sight awaited them. For there, herself a perfect picture, standing in the doorway for a frame, her hands outstretched in welcome, and a loving smile upon her lips, was Mildred.

"I was waiting for you," she said, gently. "I thought that you would come."

"Mildred, my idol has been cast down, and, as you told me to do, I have come back to you."

"Dear," she answered, "you are very welcome."

And then came Miss Terry, pleased with all her honest heart to see him, and utterly ignorant of the fierce currents that swept under the smooth surface of their little social sea. Miss Terry was not by nature a keen observer.

"Dear me, Mr. Heigham! who would have thought of seeing you again so soon? You *are* brave to cross the bay so often" (her thoughts ran a great deal on the Bay of Biscay); "but I don't think you look quite well, you have such black lines under your eyes, and, I declare, there's a gray hair!"

"Oh, I assure you your favorite bay was enough to turn anybody's hair gray, Miss Terry."

And so, talking cheerfully, they went in to the pleasant little dinner, Mildred leaning ever so slightly on his arm, and gazing into his sad face with full and happy eyes. After all that he had gone through, it seemed to Arthur as though he had dropped into a haven of rest.

"See here," said Mildred, when they rose from table, "a wonder has come to pass since you deserted us. Look, sceptic that you are!" and she led him to the window, and, lifting a glass shade which protected a flower-pot, showed him a green spike peeping from the soil.

"What is that?"

"What is it? Why, it is the mummy hyacinth which you declared that we should never see blossom in this world. It has budded; whether or not it will blossom, who can say?"

"It is an omen," he said, with a little laugh; and for the first time that evening their eyes met.

"Come into the garden, and you can smoke on the museum veranda; it is pleasant there these hot nights."

"It is dangerous, your garden."

She laughed softly. "You have proved yourself superior to danger."

Then they passed out together. The evening was still and very sultry. Not a breath stirred the silence of the night. The magnolia, the moon-flower, and a thousand other blooms poured out their fragrance upon the surrounding air, where it lay in rich patches, like perfume thrown on water. A thin mist veiled the sea, and the little wavelets struck with a sorrowful sound against the rock below.

"Tell me all about it, Arthur."

She had settled herself upon a long low chair, and as she leant back the starlight glanced white upon her arms and bosom.

"There is not much to tell. It is a common story—at least, I believe so. She threw me over, and the day before I should have married her, married another man."

"Well?"

"Well, I saw her the morning following her marriage. I do not remember what I said, but I believe I spoke what was in my mind. She fainted, and I left her."

"Ah, you spoke harshly, perhaps."

"Spoke harshly! Now that I have had time to think of it, I wish that I could have had ten imaginations to shape my thoughts, and ten tongues to speak them with! Do you understand what this woman has done? She has sold herself to a brute—oh, Mildred, such a brute—she has deserted me for a man who is not even a gentleman."

"Perhaps she was forced into it."

"Forced!—nonsense; we are not in the Middle Ages. A good woman should have been forced to drown herself before she consented to commit such a sacrilege against herself as to marry a man she hated. But she, 'my love, my dove, my undefiled'—she whom I thought whiter than the snow—she could do this, and do it deliberately. I had rather have seen her dead, and myself dead with her."

"Don't you take a rather exaggerated view, Arthur? Don't you think, perhaps, that some of the fault lies with you for overrating women? Believe me, so far as my experience goes, and I have seen a good many, the majority of them do not possess the exalted purity of mind you and many very young men attribute to them. They are, on the contrary, for the most part quite ready to exercise a wise discretion in the matter of marriage, even when the feeble tendencies which represent their affections point another way. A little pressure goes a long way with them; they are always glad to make the most of it; it is the dust they throw up to hide their retreat. Your Angela, for instance, was no doubt, and probably still is, very fond of you. You are a charming young man, with nice eyes and a taking way with women, and she would very much have liked to marry you; but then she also liked her cousin's estates. She could not have both, and, being forced to choose, she chose the latter. You should take a common-sense view of the matter; you are not the first who has suffered. Women, especially young women, who do not understand the value of affection, must be very much in love before they submit to the self-sacrifice that is supposed to be characteristic of them, and what men talk of as stains upon them they do not consider as such. They know, if they know nothing else, that a good income and an establishment will make them perfectly clean in the opinion of their own small world

—a little world of shams and forms that cares nothing for the spirit of the moral law, provided the letter is acted up to. It is by this that they mark their standard of personal virtues, not by the high rule you men imagine for them. There is no social fuller's soap so effectual as money and position."

"You speak like a book, and give your own sex a high character. Tell me, then, would you do such a thing?"

"I, Arthur? How can you ask me? I had rather be torn to pieces by wild horses. I spoke of the majority of the women, not of them all."

"Ah, and yet she could do it, and I thought her better than you."

"I do not think that you should speak bitterly of her, Arthur; I think that you should be sorry for her."

"Sorry for her? Why?"

"Because, from what I have gathered about her, she is not quite an ordinary young woman: however badly she may have treated you, she is a person of refined feelings and susceptibilities. Is it not so?"

"Without a doubt."

"Well, then, you should pity her, because she will bitterly expiate her mistake. For myself, I do not pity her much, because I will not waste my sympathy on a fool; for, to my mind, the woman who could do what she has done, and deliberately throw away everything that can make life really worth living to us women, is a most contemptible fool. But you love her, and, therefore, you should be sorry for her."

"But why?"

"Because she is a woman who at one-and-twenty has buried all the higher part of life, who has, of her own act, for ever deprived herself of joys that nothing else can bring her. Love, true love, is almost the only expression of which we women are capable of all the nobler instincts and vague yearnings after what is higher and better than the things we see and feel around us. When we love most, and love happily, then we are at our topmost bent, and soar farther above the earth than anything else can carry us. Consequently, when a woman is faithless to her love, which is the purest and most honorable part of her, the very best thing to which she can attain, she clips her wings, and can fly no more, but must be tossed, like a crippled gull, hither and thither upon the stormy surface of her little sea. Of course I speak of women of the higher stamp. Many, perhaps most, will feel nothing of all this. In a little while they will grow content with their dull round and the alien nature which they have mated with, and in their children, and their petty cares and dissipations, will forget that they possess a higher part, if indeed they do possess it. Like everything else in the world, they find their level. But with women like your Angela it is another thing. For them time only serves to increasingly unveil the Medusa-headed truth, till at last they see it as it is, and their hearts turn to stone. Racked with a sick longing to see a face that is gone from them, they become lost spirits, wandering everlastingly in the emptiness they have chosen, and finding no rest. Even her children will not console her."

Arthur uttered a smothered exclamation.

"Don't start, Arthur; you *must* accustom yourself to the fact that that woman has passed away from you, and is as completely the personal property of another man as that chair is mine. But, there, the subject is a painful one to you; shall we change it?"

"It is one that you seem to have studied pretty deeply."

"Yes, because I have realized its importance to a woman. For some years I have longed to be able to fall in love, and when at last I did so, Arthur," and here her voice grew very soft, "it was with a man who could care nothing for me. Such has been my unlucky chance. That a woman, herself beloving and herself worthily beloved, could throw her blessed opportunity away is to me a thing inconceivable, and that, Arthur, is what your Angela has done."

CHAPTER LXIII.

"THEN you will not marry now, Mildred?" said Arthur, after a pause.

"No, Arthur."

"No one?"

"No one, Arthur."

He rose, and, leaning over the railing of the veranda, looked at the sea. The mist that hid it was drifting and eddying hither and thither before little puffs of wind, and the clear sky was clouding up.

"There is going to be a storm," he said, presently.

"Yes, I think so; the air feels like it."

He hesitated a while, and looked down at her. She seemed very lovely in the half-lights, as indeed she was. She, too, looked up at him inquiringly. At last he spoke.

"Mildred, you said just now that you would not marry anybody. Will you make an exception?—will you marry me?"

It was her turn to pause now.

"You are very good," she murmured.

"No, I am not at all good. You know how the case stands. You know that I still love Angela, and that I shall in all probability always love her. I cannot help that. But if you will have me, Mildred, I will try to be a good husband to you, and to make you happy. Will you marry me, dear?"

"No, Arthur."

"Why not? Have you, then, ceased to care for me?"

"No, dear. I love you more than ever. You cannot dream how much I do love you."

"Then why will you not marry me? Is it because of this business?"

"No," and raising herself in the low chair, she looked at him with intense earnestness, "that is not the reason. I will not marry you because I have become a better woman since you went away, because I do not wish to ruin your life. You ask me to do so now in all sincerity, but you do not know what you ask. You come from the scene of as bitter a disappointment as can befall a man, and you are a little touched by the contrasting warmth of your reception here, a little moved by my evident interest, and perhaps a little influenced by my good looks, though *they* are nothing much. Supposing that I consented; supposing I said, 'Arthur, I will put my hand in yours and be your wife,' and that we were married to-morrow: do you think, when the freshness of the thing had worn off, that you would be happy with me? I do not. You would soon get horribly tired of me, Arthur, for the little leaven that leavens the whole lump is wanting. You do not love me; and the redundance of my affection would weary you, and, for my part, I should find it difficult to continually struggle against an impalpable rival, though, indeed, I should be very willing to put up with that."

"I am sorry you think so."

"Yes, Arthur, I do think so; but you do not know what it costs me to say it. I am deliberately shutting the door which bars me from my heaven; I am throwing away the chance I strove so hard to win. That will tell you how much I think it. Do you know, I must be a strange contradiction. When I knew you were engaged to another woman, I strained my every nerve to win you from her. While the object was still to be gained, I felt no compunction; I was fettered by no scruples. I wanted to steal you from her and marry you myself. But now that all this is changed, and that you of your own free will come and offer to make me your wife, I for the first time feel how wrong it would be of me to take advantage of you in a moment of pique and disappointment, and bind you for life to a nature which you do not really understand, to a violent and a jealous woman. Too late, when your life was hampered and your future spoiled, you would discover that you hated me. Arthur dear, I will not consent to bind you to me by any tie that cannot be broken."

"Hush, Mildred! you should not say such things about yourself. If you are as violent and jealous as you say, you are also a very noble-hearted woman, for none other would so sacrifice herself. Perhaps you are right; I do not know. But, whether you are right or wrong, I cannot tell you how you have made me respect you."

"Dear, those are the most comfortable words I have ever heard; after what has passed between us, I scarcely thought to win your respect."

"Then you will not marry me, Mildred?"

"No, dear."

"That is your fixed determination?"

"It is."

"Ah, well!" he sighed, "I suppose that I had better 'top my boom' again."

"Do what?"

"I mean I had better leave Madeira."

"Why should you leave Madeira?"

He hesitated a little before replying.

"Well, because if I do not marry you, and still come here, people will talk. They did before, you know."

"Are you afraid of being talked about, then!"

"I? Oh dear! no. What can it matter to me now?"

"And supposing I were to tell you that what 'people' say, with or without foundation, is as much a matter of indifference to me as the blowing of next summer's breezes, would you still consider it necessary to leave Madeira?"

"I don't know."

He again rose and leant over the veranda rail.

"It is going to be a wild night," he said, presently.

"Yes; the wind will spoil all the magnolias. Pick me that bud; it is too good to be wasted."

He obeyed, and, just as he stepped back on the veranda, a fierce rush of wind came up from the sea and went howling away behind them.

"I love a storm," she murmured, as he brought the flower to her. "It makes me feel so strong," and she stretched out her perfect arms as though to catch the wind.

"What am I to do with this magnolia?"

"Give it to me. I will pin it in my dress—no, do you fasten it for me."

The chair in which she was lounging was so low that, to do as she bade him, Arthur was forced to kneel beside her. Kneeling thus, the sweet, upturned face was but just beneath his own; the breath from the curved lips played amongst his hair, and again there crept over him that feeling of fascination, of utter helplessness, that he had once before resisted. But this time he did not attempt to resist, and no vision came to save him. Slowly drawn by the beauty of her tender eyes, he yielded to the spell, and soon her lips were pressed upon his own, and the white arms had closed around his neck, whilst the crushed magnolia bloom shed its perfume round them.

Fiercer swept the storm, the lightning flashed, and the gale catching the crests of the rising waves dashed them in spray to where they sat.

"Dear," he said, presently, "you must not stop here, the spray is wetting you."

"I wish that it would drown me," she answered, almost fiercely; "I shall never be so happy again. You think that you love me now; I should like to die before you learn to hate me. Come, let us go in!"

CHAPTER LXIV.

When Mildred received Lady Bellamy's telegram, she was so sure that it would prove the forerunner of Arthur's arrival at Madeira that she had at once set about making arrangements for his amusement.

It so happened that there was at the time a very beautiful sea-going steam-yacht of about two hundred and fifty tons burden lying in the roadstead. She belonged to a nobleman who was suddenly recalled to England by mail steamer, and, through a series of chances, Mildred was enabled to buy her at a bargain. The crew of the departed nobleman also continued in her service.

The morning after the storm broke sweet and clear, and, except that the flowers were somewhat shattered, all Nature looked the fresher for its violent visitation. Arthur, who had come up early to the Quinta, Mildred, and Miss Terry were all seated at breakfast in a room that looked out to the sea, which, although the wind had died away, still ran rather high. They made a pretty picture as they sat round the English-looking breakfast-table with the light pouring in upon them from the open windows, Miss Terry, with her usual expression of good-humored solemnity, pouring out the tea, and Mildred and Arthur, who sat exactly opposite to each other, drinking it. Never had the former looked more lovely than she did that morning.

"My dear," said Agatha to her, "what have you done to yourself? You look beautiful."

"Do I, dear? Then it is because I am happy."

Agatha was quite right, thought Arthur; she did look beautiful, there was such depth and rest in her clear eyes, such a wealth of happy triumph written on her features. She might have sat that morning as a study of the "Venus Victrix." Her talk, too, was as bright as herself. She laughed and shone and sparkled like the rain-drops on the bamboo sprays that rocked in the sunshine, and whenever she addressed herself to Arthur, which was often enough, every sentence seemed wrapped in tender meaning. Her whole life went out towards him, a palpable thing; she waited on his words and basked in his smile. Mildred Carr did nothing by halves.

Arthur was the least cheerful of the three, though at times he tried his best to join in Mildred's merriment. Any one who knew him well could have told that he was suffering from one of his fits of constitutional melancholy, and a physiognomist, looking at the somewhat dreamy eyes and pensive face, would probably have added that he neither was nor ever would be an entirely happy man.

By degrees, however, he seemed to get the better of his thoughts, whatever they might be.

"Now, Arthur, if you are quite awake," began, or rather went on, Mildred, "perhaps you will come to the window. I have something to show you."

"Here I am at your service; what may it be?"

"Good. Now look: do you see that little vessel in the bay beneath there to the right of Leeuw Rock?"

"Yes, and uncommonly pretty she is; what of her?"

"What of her? Why, she is my yacht."

"Your yacht! Goodness gracious, Mildred! you don't mean to say that you've been buying a yacht and told me nothing about it? Just think! Well, I call that sly."

"Yes, my dear Agatha, I have; a yacht and a ready-made crew, and the very prettiest saloon in the world, and sleeping-cabins that you will think it an honor to be sea-sick in, and a cook's galley with bright copper fittings, and a cook with a white cap, and steam steering-gear if you care to use it, and—"

"For goodness' sake, don't overwhelm us; and what are you going to do with your white elephant, now that you have got it?"

"Do with it? Why, ride on it, of course. 'Ladies and gentlemen,' or rather, 'Lady and gentleman.' Attention! You will both be in marching, or rather in sailing, order by four this afternoon, for at five we start for the Canaries. Now, no remarks; I'm a skipper, and I expect to be obeyed, or I'll put you in irons."

"You've done that already," said Arthur, *sotto voce.*

"Mildred, I won't go, and that's flat."

"My dear, you mean that you are afraid of being flat. But, Agatha, seriously, you must come; nobody is sick in those semi-tropical waters, and, if you won't, I suppose it would not be quite the thing for Arthur and I to go alone. And then, my dear, just think what a splendid place the Canaries must be for insects."

"Why?" asked Agatha, solemnly.

"Because of all the little birds it has to support."

"But I thought they lived on hemp-seed."

"Oh, no—not in their native land."

"Well, I suppose I must go; but I really believe that you will kill me with your mania for sea-voyages, Mildred. I suppose you will take to ballooning next."

"That is by no means a bad idea; I should like to see you in a balloon, Agatha."

"Mildred, I know where to draw the line. Into a balloon I will never go. I have been into a Madeira sledge, and that is quite enough for me. I always dream about it twice a week."

"Well, my dear, I promise never to ask you when I want to go ballooning; Arthur and I will go by ourselves. It would be a grand opportunity for a *tête-à-tête.* And now go and see about getting the things ready—there's a dear; and, Arthur, do you send John down to Miles's for your portmanteau."

"Hadn't I better go and see about it myself?"

"Certainly not; I want you to help me, and come down and talk to the skipper, for he will be under your orders, you know. He is such a delightful sailor-man, perfect down to his quid, and always says, 'Ay, ay,' in the orthodox fashion. Certainly you must not go; I will not trust you out of my sight—you might run away and leave me alone, and then what should I do?"

Arthur laughed and acquiesced. Sitting down, he wrote a note asking the manager of the hotel to send his things up to the Quinta Carr, together with his account, as he was leaving Madeira for the present.

The rest of the morning was spent by everybody in busy preparation. Boxes were packed and provisions shipped sufficient to victual an arctic expedition. At last everything was ready, and at a little after three they went down the steps leading to the tiny bay, and, embarking on the smart boat that was waiting for them, were conveyed in safety to the *Evening Star*, for such was the yacht's name. Arthur suggested that it should be changed to the *Mildred Carr*, and got snubbed for his pains.

The *Evening Star* was a beautiful craft, built on fine lines, but for all that a wonderful boat in a heavy sea. She was a three-masted schooner, square-rigged forward, of large beam. Her fittings below were perfect down to the painted panels after Watteau in the saloon and the electric bells, and she was rigged either to sail or steam as might be most convenient. On the present occasion, as there was not the slightest hurry and no danger of a lee-shore, it was determined that they should not avail themselves of the steam-power, so the propeller was hoisted up and everything got ready for that most delightful thing, a long cruise under canvas.

Arthur was perfectly charmed with everything he saw, and so was Agatha Terry, until they got under way, when she discovered that a mail-steamer was a joke compared with the yacht in the matter of motion. In short, the unfortunate Agatha was soon reduced to her normal condition of torpor. Mildred always declared that she hibernated on board ship like a dormouse or a bear. She was not very sea-sick, she simply lay and slept, eating very little and thinking not at all.

"By the way," said Arthur, as they sailed out of the bay, "I never gave any directions about my letters."

"Oh! that will not matter," answered Mildred, carelessly, for they were leaning over the taffrail together; "they will keep them for you at 'Miles's Hotel.' But, my dear boy, do you know what time it is? Ten minutes to seven; that dreadful bell will be going in a minute, and the soup will be spoiled. Run and get ready, do."

CHAPTER LXV.

When dinner was over—Miss Terry would have none—they went and sat upon the moonlit deck. The little vessel was under all her canvas, for the breeze was light, and skimmed over the water like a gull with its wings spread. In the low light Madeira was nothing but a blot on the sky-line. The crew were forward, with the solitary exception of the man steering the vessel from his elevated position on the bridge; and sitting as they were, abaft the deck-cabin, the two were utterly alone between the great silences of the stars and of the sea. She looked into his face, and it was tender towards her—that night was made for lovers—and tears of happiness stood in her eyes. She took his hand in hers, and her head nestled upon his breast.

"I should like to sail on for ever so, quite alone with you. I never again wish to see the land or the sun, or any other sea than this, or any other eyes than yours, to hear any more of the things that I have known, to learn to know any fresh things. If I could choose, I would ask that I might now glide gently from your arms into those of eternal sleep. Oh! Arthur, I am so happy now—so happy that I scarcely dare to speak, for fear lest I should break the spell, and I feel so good—so much nearer heaven. When I think of all my past life, it seems like a stupid dream full of little nothings, of which I cannot recall any memory except that they were empty and without meaning. But the future is worse than the past, because it locks fair, and snakes always hide in flowers. It makes me afraid. How do I know what the future will bring? I wish that the present—the pleasant, certain present that I hold with my hand—could last for ever."

"Who does know, Mildred? If the human race could see the pleasant surprises in store for it individually, I believe that it would drown itself *en masse*. Who has not sometimes caught at the skirt of to-day and cried, 'Stay a little—do not let to-morrow come yet!' You know the lines—

> "'O temps suspends ton vol, et vous heures propices
> Suspendez votre cours,
> Laissez nous savourer les rapides délices
> Des plus beaux de nos jours.'

Lamartine only crystallized a universal aspiration when he wrote that."

"Oh! Arthur, I tell you of love and happiness wide as the great sea round us, and you talk of 'universal aspirations.' It is the first cold breath from that gray-skied future that I fear. Oh! dear, I wonder—you do not know how I wonder—if, should you ask me again, I shall ever with a clear conscience be able to say, 'Arthur, I will marry you.'"

"My dear, I asked you to be my wife last night, and what I said then I say again now. In any case, until you dismiss me, I consider myself bound to you; but I tell you frankly that I should myself prefer that you would marry me for both our sakes."

"How cold and correct you are, how clearly you realize the position in which I am likely to be put, and in what a gentleman-like way you assure me that your honor will always keep you bound to me! That is a weak thread, Arthur, in matters of the heart. Let Angela reappear as my rival—would honor keep you to my side? Honor, forsooth! it is like a nurse's bogey in the cupboard—it is a shibboleth men use to frighten naughty women with, which for themselves is almost devoid of meaning. Even in this light I can see your face flush at her name. What chance shall I ever have against her?"

"Do not speak of her, Mildred; let her memory be dead between us. She who belonged to me before God, and whom I believed in as I believe in my God, she offered me the most deadly insult that a woman can offer to a man she loves—she sold herself. What do I care what the price was, whether it were money, or position, or convenience, or the approbation of her surroundings? The result is the same. Never mention her name to me again; I tell you that I hate her."

"What a tirade! There is warmth enough about you now. I shall be careful how I touch on the subject again; but your very energy shows that you are deceiving yourself. I wish I could hear you speak of me like that, because then I should know you loved me. Oh! if she only knew it—she has her revenge for all your bitter words. You are lashed to her chariot-wheels, Arthur. You do *not* hate her; on the contrary, you still long to see her face; it is still your secret and most cherished hope that you will meet her again either in this or another world. You love her as much as ever. If she were dead, you could bear it; but the sharpest sting of your suffering lies in the humiliating sense that you are forced to worship a god you know to be false, and to give your own pure love to a woman whom you see debased."

He put his hands to his face and groaned aloud.

"You are right," he said. "I would rather have known her dead than know her as she is. But there is no reason why I should bore you with all this."

"Arthur, you are nothing if not considerate, and I do not pretend that this is a very pleasant conversation for me; but I began it, so I suppose I must endure to see you groaning for another woman. You say," she went on, with a sudden flash of passion, "that you should like to see her dead. I say that I should like to kill her, for she has struck me a double blow—she has injured you whom I love, and she has beggared me of your affection. Oh! Arthur," she continued, changing her voice and throwing a caressing arm about his neck, "have you no heart left to give *me?* is there no lingering spark that *I* can cherish and blow to flame? I will never treat you so, dear. Learn to love me, and I will marry you and make you happy, make you forget this faithless woman with the angel face. I will—" here her voice broke down in sobs, and in the starlight the great tears glistened upon her coral-tinted face like dewdrops on a pomegranate's blushing rind.

"There, there, dear, I will try to forget; don't cry," and he touched her on the forehead with his lips.

She stopped, and then said, with just the faintest tinge of bitterness in her voice: "If it had been Angela who cried, you would not be so cold, you would have kissed away her tears."

Who can say what hidden chord of feeling those words touched, or what memories they awoke? but their effect upon Arthur was striking. He sprang up upon the deck, his eyes blazing, and his face white with anger.

"How often," he said, "must I forbid you to mention the name of that woman to me?" Do you take a pleasure in torturing me? Curse her! may she eat out her empty heart in solitude, and find no living thing to comfort her! May she suffer as she makes me suffer, till her life becomes a hell—"

"Be quiet, Arthur; it is shameful to say such things."

He stopped, and after the sharp ring of his voice, that echoed like the cry wrung from a person in intense pain, the loneliness and quiet of the night were very deep. And then an answer came to his mad, unmanly imprecations. For suddenly the air round them was filled with the sound of his own name uttered in such wild, despairing accents as, once heard, were not likely to be forgotten—accents which seemed to be around them and over them, and heard in their own brains, and yet to come travelling from immeasurable distances across the waste of waters.

"*Arthur! Arthur!*"

The sound that had sprung from nothing died away into nothingness again, and the moonlight glanced, and the waters heaved, and gave no sign of the place of its birth. It had come and gone, awful, untraceable, and in place of its solemnity reigned silence absolute.

They looked at each other with scared eyes.

"*As I am a living man, that voice was Angela's!*"

This was all he said.

CHAPTER LXVI.

Dr. Williamson was a rising young practitioner at Roxham, and, what is more, a gentleman and a doctor of real ability.

On the night that Lady Bellamy took the poison he sat up very late, till the dawn, in fact, working up his books of reference with a view to making himself as much the master as possible of the symptoms and most approved treatment in such cases of insanity as appeared to resemble Angela Caresfoot's. He had been called in to see her by Mr. Fraser, and had come away intensely interested from a medical point of view, and very much puzzled.

At length he shut up his books with a sigh—for, like most books, though full of generalities, they did not tell him much—and went to bed. Before he had been asleep very long, however, the surgery bell was violently rung, and, having dressed himself with the rapidity characteristic of doctors and schoolboys, he descended to find a frightened footman waiting outside, from whom he gathered that something dreadful had happened to Lady Bellamy, who had been found lying apparently dead upon the floor of her drawing-room. Providing himself with some powerful restoratives and a portable electric battery, he drove rapidly over to Rewtham House.

Here he found the patient laid upon a sofa in the room where she had been found, and surrounded by a mob of terrified and half-dressed servants. At first he thought life was quite extinct, but presently he fancied that he could detect a faint tremor of the heart. He applied the most powerful of his restoratives and administered a sharp current from the battery, and, after a considerable time, was rewarded by seeing the patient open her eyes—but only to shut them again immediately. Directing his assistant to continue the treatment, he tried to elicit some information from the servants as to what had happened, but all he could gather was that the maid had received a message not to sit up. This made him suspicious of an attempt at suicide, and just then his eye fell upon a wineglass that lay upon the floor, broken at the shank. He took it up; in the bowl there was still a drop or two of liquid. He smelt it, then dipped his finger in and tasted it, with the result that his tongue was burnt and became rough and numb. Then his suspicions were confirmed.

Presently Lady Bellamy opened her eyes again, and this time there was intelligence in them. She gazed round her with a wondering air. Next she spoke.

"Where am I?"

"In your own drawing-room, Lady Bellamy. Be quiet now; you will be better presently."

She tried first to move her head, then her arm, then her lower limbs, but they would not stir. By this time her faculties were wide awake.

"Are you the doctor?" she said.

"Yes, Lady Bellamy."

"Then tell me why cannot I move my arms."

He lifted her hand; it fell again like a lump of lead—and Dr. Williamson looked very grave. Then he applied a current of electricity.

"Do you feel that?" he asked.

She shook her head.

"Why cannot I move? Do not trifle with me; tell me quick."

Dr. Williamson was a young man, and had not quite conquered

nervousness. In his confusion he muttered something about "paralysis."

"How is it that I am not dead?"

"I have brought you back to life; but pray do not talk."

"You fool, why could you not let me die? You mean that you have brought my mind to life, and left my body dead. I feel now that I am quite paralyzed."

He could not answer her; what she said was only too true, and his look told her so. She gazed steadily at him for a moment as he bent over her, and realized all the horrors of her position, and for the first time in her life her proud spirit absolutely gave way. For a few seconds she was silent, and then, without any change coming over the expression of her features—for the wild gaze with which she had faced eternity was forever frozen there—she broke out into a succession of the most heart-rending shrieks that it had ever been his lot to listen to. At last she stopped exhausted.

"Kill me!" she whispered, hoarsely, "kill me!"

It was a dreadful scene.

As the doctors afterwards concluded, rightly or wrongly, a very curious thing had happened to Lady Bellamy. Either the poison she had taken—and they were never able to discover what its exact nature was, nor would she enlighten them—had grown less deadly during all the years that she had kept it, or she had partially defeated her object by taking an overdose, or, as seemed more probable, there was some acid in the wine in which it had been mixed that had had the strange effect of rendering it to a certain degree innocuous. Its result, however, was, as she guessed, to render her a hopeless paralytic for life.

At length the patient sank into the coma of exhaustion, and Dr. Williamson was able to leave her in the care of a brother-practitioner whom he had sent for, and in that of his assistant. Sir John had been sent for, but had not arrived. It was then eleven o'clock, and at one the doctor was summoned as a witness to attend the inquest on George Caresfoot. He had, therefore, two hours at his disposal, and these he determined to utilize by driving round to see Angela, who was still lying at Mr. Fraser's vicarage.

Mr. Fraser heard him coming, and met him in the little drive. He briefly told him what he had just seen, and what, in his opinion, Lady Bellamy's fate must be—one of living death. The clergyman's remark was characteristic.

"And yet," he said, "there are people in the world who say that there is no God."

"How is Mrs. Caresfoot?" asked the doctor.

"She had a dreadful fit of raving this morning, and we had to tie her down in bed. She is quieter now, poor dear. There, listen!"

At that moment, through the open window of the bedroom, they heard a sweet though untrained voice beginning to sing. It was Angela's, and she was singing snatches of an old-fashioned sailor-song, one of several which Arthur had taught her:

"Fare ye well, and adieu to all you Spanish ladies,
Fare ye well, and adieu to ye, ladies of Spain,
For we've received orders to return to Old England,
But we hope in a short time to see you again.

* * * * * * * *

"We hove our ship to with the wind at sou'-west, my boys;
We hove our ship to for to strike soundings clear;
It was forty-five fathom and a gray sandy bottom;
Then we filled our maintopsail, and up channel did steer.

* * * * * * * *

"The signal was made for the grand fleet to anchor,
All in the Downs that night for to meet;
So cast off your shank-painter, let go your cat's-topper,
Haul up your clew-garnets, let fly tack and sheet."

Without waiting to hear any more, they went up the stairs and entered the bedroom. The first person they saw was Pigott, who had been sent for to nurse Angela, standing by the side of the bed, and a trained nurse at a little table at the foot mixing some medicine. On the bed itself lay Angela, shorn of all her beautiful hair, her face flushed as with fever, except where a blue weal bore witness to the blow from her husband's cruel whip, her head thrown back, and a strange light in her wild eyes. She was tied down in the bed, with a broad horse-girth stretched across her breast, but she had wrenched one arm free, and with it was beating time to her song on the bed-clothes. She caught sight of Mr. Fraser at once, and seemed to recognize him, for she stopped her singing and laughed.

"That's a pretty old song, isn't it?" she said. "Somebody taught it me—who was it? Somebody—a long while ago. But I know another—I know another. You'll like it; you are a clergyman, you know." And she began again·

"Says the parson one day as I cursed a Jew,
Now do you not know that that is a sin?
Of you sailors I fear there are but a few
That St. Peter to heaven will ever let in.

"Says I, Mr. Parson, to tell you my mind,
Few sailors to knock were ever yet seen;
Those who travel by land may steer against wind,
But we shape a course for Fiddler's Green."

Suddenly she stopped, and her mind wandered off to the scene of two days previous with Arthur by the lake, and she began to quote the words wrung from the bitterness of his heart.

"'You miserable woman, do you know what you are? Shame upon you! Were you not married yesterday?' It is quite true, Arthur—oh yes, quite true! Say what you like of me, Arthur—I deserve it all; but oh! Arthur, I love you so. Don't be hard upon me—I love you so, dear! Kill me if you like, dear, but don't talk to me so. I shall go mad—I shall go mad!" and she broke into a flood of weeping.

"Poor dear, she has been going on like that, off and on, all night.

another man, or some such romantic nonsense, deserved all she got. Gone mad, had she?—well, it was a warning! And these aristocratic matrons sniffed and turned up their noses. They felt that Angela, by going mad and creating a public excitement, had entered a mute protest against the recognized rules of marriage sale-and-barter as practised in this country—and Zululand. Having daughters to dispose of, they resented this, and poor Angela was for years afterwards spoken of among them as that "immoral girl."

But the lower and more human strata of society did not sympathize with this feeling. On the contrary, they were all for Angela and the dog Aleck who was supposed to have choked that "carroty warmint," George.

The inquest on George's body was held at Roxham, and was the object of the greatest possible interest. Indeed, the public excitement was so great that the coroner was, perhaps insensibly, influenced by it, and allowed the inquiry to travel a little beyond its professed object of ascertaining the actual cause of death, with the result that many of the details of the wicked plot from which Angela had been the principal sufferer became public property. Needless to say that they did not soothe the feelings of an excited crowd. When Philip, after spending one of the worst half-hours of his life in the witness-box, at length escaped with such shreds of reputation as he had hitherto possessed altogether torn off his back, his greeting from the mob outside the court may fairly be described as a warm one. As the witnesses' door closed behind him, he found himself at one end of a long lane, that was hedged on both sides by faces not without a touch of ferocity about them, and with difficulty kept clear by the available force of the five Roxham policemen.

"Who sold his daughter?" shouted a great fellow in his ear.

"Let me come, there's a dear man, and have a look at Judas," said a skinny little woman with a squint, to an individual who blocked her view.

The crowd caught at the word. "Judas!" it shouted, "go and hang yourself! Judas! Judas!"

How Philip got out of that he never quite knew, but he did get out somehow.

Meanwhile, Sir John Bellamy was being examined in court, and, notwithstanding the almost aggressive innocence of his appearance, he was not having a very good time. It chanced that he had fallen into the hands of a rival lawyer, who hated him like poison, and had good reason to hate him. It is wonderful, by the way, how enemies do spring up round a man in trouble like dogs who bite a wounded companion to death, and on the same principle. He is defenceless. This gentleman would insist on conducting the witnesses' examination on the basis that he knew all about the fraud practised with reference to the supposed death of Arthur Heigham. Now, it will be remembered that Sir John, in his last interview with Lady Bellamy, had declared that there was no tittle of evidence against him, and that it would be impossible to implicate him in the exposure that must overtake her. To a certain extent he was right, but on one point he had overshot himself, for at that very inquest Mr. Fraser stated on oath that he (Mr. Fraser) had spoken of Arthur Heigham's death in the presence of Sir John Bellamy, and had not been contradicted.

In vain did Sir John protest that Mr. Fraser must be mistaken. Both the jury and the public looked at the probabilities of the matter, and, though his protestations were accepted in silence, when he left the witness-box there was not a man in court but was morally certain that he had been privy to the plot, and, so far as reputation was concerned, he was a ruined man. And yet legally there was not a jot of evidence against him. But public opinion required that a scapegoat should be found, and it was now his lot to figure as that unlucky animal.

By the time he reached the exit into the street, the impression that he had had a hand in the business had, in some mysterious way, communicated itself to the mob outside, many a member of which had some old grudge to settle with "Lawyer Bellamy," if only chance put an opportunity in their way. As he stepped through the door, utterly ignorant of the greeting which awaited him, his ears were assailed by an awful yell, followed by a storm of hoots and hisses.

Sir John turned pale, and looked for a means of escape; but the policeman who had let him out had locked the door behind him, and all round him was the angry mob.

"Here comes the —— that started the swim," roared a voice, as soon as there was a momentary lull.

"Gentlemen—" piped Sir John, all the pippin hue gone from his cheeks, and rubbing his white hands together nervously.

"Yah! he poisoned his own poor wife!" shouted a woman with a baby.

"Ladies—" went on Sir John, in agonized tones.

"Pelt him!" yelled a sweet little boy of ten or so, suiting the action to the word, and planting a rotten egg full upon Sir John's imposing brow.

"No, no," said the woman who had nicknamed Philip "Judas." "Why don't you drop him in the pond? There's only two feet of water, and it's soft falling on the mud. You can pelt him *afterwards.*"

The idea was received with acclamation, and notwithstanding his own efforts to the contrary, backed as they were by those of the five policemen, before he knew where he was, Sir John found himself being hustled by a lot of sturdy fellows towards the filthy duck-pond, like an aristocrat to the guillotine. They soon arrived, and then followed the most painful experience of all his life, one of which the very thought would ever afterwards move him most profoundly. Two strong men, utterly heedless of his yells and lamentations, took him by the heels, and two yet stronger than they caught him by his plump and tender wrists, and then, under the directions of the woman with the squint, they began to swing him from side to side. As soon as the lady directress considered that the impetus was sufficient, she said, "Now!" and away he went like a swallow, only to land, when his flying powers were exhausted, plump in the middle of the duck-pond.

Some ten seconds afterwards, a pillar of slimy mud arose and staggered towards the bank, where a crowd of little boys, each holding something offensive in his right hand, were eagerly awaiting its arrival. The squint-eyed woman contemplated the figure with the most intense satisfaction.

"He sold me up once," she murmured; "but we're quits now. That's it, lads; let him have it."

But we will drop a veil over this too-painful scene. Sir John Bellamy was unwell for some days afterwards; when he recovered he shook the dust of Roxham off his shoes for ever.

CHAPTER LXVIII.

A FORTNIGHT or so afterwards, when the public excitement occasioned by the Caresfoot tragedy had been partially eclipsed by a particularly thrilling child-murder and suicide, a change for the better took place in Angela's condition. One night, after an unusually violent fit of raving, she suddenly went to sleep about twelve o'clock, and slept all that night and all the next day. About half-past nine on the following evening, the watchers in her room—namely, Pigott, Mr. Fraser, and Dr. Williamson, who was trying to make out what this deep sleep meant—were suddenly astonished at seeing her sit up in her bed in a listening attitude, as though she could hear something that interested her intensely, for the webbing that tied her down had been temporarily removed, and then cry, in a tone of the most living anguish, and yet with a world of passionate remonstrance in her voice,

"*Arthur, Arthur!*"

Then she sank down again for a few minutes. It was the same night that Mildred and Arthur sat together on the deck of the *Evening Star*. Presently she opened her eyes, and the doctor saw that there was no longer any madness in them, only great trouble. Her glance first fell upon Pigott.

"Run," she said, "run and stop him ; he cannot have gone far Bring him back to me; quick, or he will be gone."

"Who do you mean, dear?"

"Arthur, of course—Arthur."

"Hush, Angela!" said Mr. Fraser, "he has been gone a long time; you have been very ill."

She did not say anything, but turned her face to the pillow and wept, apparently as much from exhaustion as from any other cause, and then dropped off to sleep again.

"Her reason is saved," said Dr. Williamson, as soon as they were outside the door.

"Thanks be to Providence and you, doctor."

"Thanks to Providence alone. It is a case in which I could do little or nothing. It is a most merciful deliverance. All that you have to do now is to keep her perfectly quiet, and, above all, do not let her father come near her at present. I will call in and tell him. Lady Bellamy? Oh! about the same. She is a strange woman; she never complains, and rarely speaks—though twice I have heard her break out shockingly. There will never be any alteration in her case till the last alteration. Good-by; I will look round to-morrow."

After this, Angela's recovery was, comparatively speaking, rapid, though of course the effects of so severe a shock to the nervous system could not be shaken off in a day. Though she was no longer mad, she was still in a disturbed state of mind, and subject to strange dreams or visions. One in particular that visited her several nights in succession made a great impression upon her.

First, it would seem to her that she was wide awake in the middle of the night, and there would creep over her a sense of unmeasured space, infinite silence, and intense solitude. She would think that she was standing on a daïs at the end of a vast hall, down which ran endless rows of pillars supporting an inky sky which was the roof. There was no light in the hall, yet she could clearly see; there was no sound, but she could hear the silence. Only a soft radiance shone from her eyes and brow. She was not afraid, though lonely, but she felt that something would presently come to make an end of solitude. And so she stood for many years or ages—she could not tell which—trying to fathom the mystery of that great place, and watching the light that streamed from her forehead strike upon the marble floor and pillars, or thread the darkness like a shooting star, only to reveal new depths of blackness beyond those it pierced. At length there came, softly falling from the sky-roof which never stirred to any passing breeze, a flake of snow larger than a dove's wing; but it was blood-red, and in its centre shone a wonderful light that made its passage through the darkness a track of glory. As it passed gently downwards without sound, she thought that it threw the shadow of a human face. It lit upon the marble floor, and the red snow melted there and turned to blood, but the light that had been its heart shone on pure and steady.

Looking up again, she saw that the vault above her was thick with thousands upon thousands of these flakes, each glowing like a crimson lamp, and each throwing its own shadow. One of the shadows was like George, and she shuddered as it passed. And ever as they touched the marble pavement, the flakes melted and became blood, and some of the lights went out, but the most part burnt on, till at length there was no longer any floor, but a dead-sea of blood on which floated a myriad points of fire.

And then it all grew clear to her, for a voice in her mind spoke and said that this was one of God's storehouses for human souls; that the light was the soul, and the red in the snow which turned to blood was the sin that had, during its earthly passage, stained its first purity. The sea of blood before her was the sum of the scarlet wickedness of her age; from every soul there came some to swell its awful waters.

At length the red snow ceased to fall, and a sound that was not a voice, but yet spoke, pealed through the silence, asking if all were ready. The voice that had spoken in her mind answered, "No, he has not come who is to see." Then, looking upwards, she saw, miles on miles away, a bright being with half-shut wings flashing fast towards her, and she knew that it was Arthur, and the loneliness left her. He lit, a breathing radiance, by her side, and again the great sound pealed, "Let in the living waters, and cleanse away the sins of this generation."

It echoed and died away, and there followed a tumult like the flow of an angry sea. A mighty wind swept past her, and after it an ocean of molten crystal came rushing through the illimitable hall. The sea and the wind purged away the blood and put out the lamps, leaving behind them a glow of light like that upon her brow, and where the lamps had been stood myriads of seraphic beings, whilst from ten thousand tongues rang forth a pæan of celestial song.

Then everything vanished, and deep gloom, that was not, how ever, dark to her, settled round them. Taking Arthur by the hand, she spread her white wings and circled upwards. Far, far they sailed till they reached a giant peak that split space in twain. Here they alighted, and watched the masses of cloud tearing through the gulfs on either side of them, and, looking beyond and below, gazed upon the shining worlds that peopled space beneath them.

From the cloud-drifts to the right and left came a noise as of the soughing of many wings; but they did not know what caused it, till presently the vapors lifted, and they saw that alongside of and beneath them two separate streams of souls were passing on outstretched pinion: one stream, that to their left, proceeding to their earthly homes, and one, that to the right, returning from them. Those who went wore grief upon their shadowy faces, and had sad-colored wings; but those who returned seemed for the most part happy, and their wings were tipped with splendor.

The never-ending stream that came flowed from a far-off glory, and that which returned, having passed the dividing cliff on which they stood, was changed into a multitude of the red snow-flakes with the glowing hearts, and dropped gently downwards.

So they stood, in happy peace, never tiring, from millennium to millennium. They watched new worlds collecting out of chaos, they saw them speed upon their high aërial course till, grown hoary, their foundation-rocks crumbling with age, they wasted away into the vastness whence they had gathered, to be replaced by fresh creations that in their turn took form, teemed with life, waxed, waned, and vanished.

At length there came an end, and the soughing of wings was silent forever; no more souls went downwards, and none came up from the earth. Then the distant glory from which the souls had come moved towards them with awful mutterings and robed in lightning, and space was filled with spirits, one of whom, sweeping past them, cried with a loud voice, "Children, Time is dead; now is the beginning of knowledge." And she turned to Arthur, who had grown more radiant than the star which gleamed upon his forehead, and kissed him. Then she would wake.

Time passed on, and gradually health and strength came back to Angela, till at last she was as powerful in mind, and—if that were possible—except that she was shorn of her lovely hair, more beautiful in body than she had been before her troubles overwhelmed her. Of Arthur she thought a great deal—indeed, she thought of little else; but it was with a sort of hopelessness that precluded action. Nobody had mentioned his name to her, as it was thought wiser not to do so, though Pigott and Mr. Fraser had, in as gentle terms as they could command, told her of the details of the plot against her, and of the consequences to the principal actors in it. Nor had she spoken of him. It seemed to her that she had lost him for good; that he could never come back to her after what had passed; that he must hate her too much. She supposed that, in acting as he did, he was aware of all the circumstance of her marriage, and could find no excuses for her. She did not even know where he was, and, in her ignorance of the uses of private detectives and advertisements, had no idea how to find out. And so she suffered in silence, and only saw him in her dreams.

She still stopped at the vicarage with Pigott; nor had there as yet been any talk of her returning to the Abbey House. Indeed she had not seen her father since the day of her marriage. But, now that she had recovered, she felt that something must be done about it. Wondering what it should be, she one afternoon walked to the churchyard, where she had not been since her illness, and, once there, made her way naturally to her mother's grave. She was moving very quietly, and had almost reached the tree under which Hilda Caresfoot lay, when she became aware that there was already somebody kneeling by the grave, with his head rested against the marble cross.

It was her father. Her shadow falling upon him, he turned and saw her, and they stood looking at each other. She was shocked at the dreadful alteration in his face. It was now that of an old man, nearly worn out with suffering. He put his hand before his eyes and said,

"Angela, how can I face you, least of all here?"

For the moment the memory of her bitter wrongs swelled in her heart, for she now to a great extent understood what her father's part in the plot had been, and she regarded him in silence.

"Father," she said, presently, "I have been in the hands of God, and not in yours, and though you have helped to ruin my life, and have very nearly driven me into a madhouse, I can still say, let the past be the past. But why do you look so wretched? You should look happy; you have got the land—my price, you know," and she laughed, a little bitterly.

"Why do I look wretched? Because I am given over to a curse that you cannot understand, and I am not alone. Where are those who plotted against you? George dead, Bellamy gone, Lady Bellamy paralyzed hand and foot, and myself—although I did not plot, I only let them be—accursed. But, if you can forget the past, why do you not come back to my house? Of course I cannot force you; you are free and rich, and can suit yourself."

"I will come for a time if you wish—if I can bring Pigott with me."

"You may bring twenty Pigotts, for all I care—so long as you will pay for their board," he added, with a touch of his old miserliness. "But what do you mean by 'for a time'?"

"I do not think I shall stop here long; I think that I am going into a sisterhood."

"Oh! well, you are your own mistress, and must do as you choose."

"Then I will come to-morrow," and they parted.

CHAPTER LXIX.

AND so on the following day Angela and Pigott returned to the Abbey House, but they both felt that it was a sad home-coming. Indeed, if there had been no other cause for melancholy, the sight of Philip's face was enough to excite it in the most happy-minded person. Not that Angela saw much of him, however, for they still kept to their old habit of not living together. All day her father was shut up in his room transacting business that had reference to his accession of property and the settlement of George's affairs; for his cousin had died intestate, so he took his personalty and wound up the estate as heir-at-law. At night, however, he would go out and walk for miles, and in all weathers—he seemed to dread spending the dark hours at home.

When Angela had been back about a month in the old place, she accidentally got a curious insight into her father's mental sufferings.

It so happened that one night, finding it impossible to sleep, and being much oppressed by sorrowful thoughts, she thought that she would read the hours away. But the particular book she wanted to find was downstairs, and it was two o'clock in the morning, and chilly in the passages. However, anything is better than sleeplessness, and the tyranny of sad thoughts and empty longings; so, throwing on her dressing-gown, she took a candle, and set off,

It clean breaks my heart to see it, and that's the holy truth," and Pigott looked very much as though she were going to cry herself.

By this time Angela had ceased weeping, and was brooding sullenly, with her face buried in the pillow.

"There is absolutely nothing to be done," said the doctor. "We can only trust to her fine constitution and youth to pull her through. She has received a series of dreadful mental shocks, and it is very doubtful if she will ever get over them. It is a pity to think that such a splendid creature may become permanently insane, is it not? You must be very careful, Pigott, that she does not do herself an injury; she is just in the state that she may throw herself out of the window or cut her throat. And now I must be going; I will call in again to-night."

Mr. Fraser accompanied him down to the gate, where he had left his trap. Before they got out of the front door, Angela had roused herself again, and they could hear her beginning to quote Homer, and then breaking out into snatches of her sailor-songs.

"'High aloft amongst the rigging
Sings the loud exulting gale.'

That's like me. I sing too," and then followed peal upon peal of mad laughter.

"A very sad case! She has a poor chance, I fear."

Mr. Fraser was too much affected to answer him.

CHAPTER LXVII.

PUBLIC feeling in Marlshire was much excited about the Caresfoot tragedy, and when it became known that Lady Bellamy had attempted to commit suicide the excitement was trebled. It is not often that the dullest and most highly respectable part of an eminently dull and respectable county gets such a chance of cheerful and interesting conversation as these two events gave rise to. We may be sure that the godsend was duly appreciated; indeed, the whole story is up to this hour a favorite subject of conversation in those parts.

Of course the members of the polite society of the neighborhood of Roxham were divided into two camps. The men all thought that Angela had been shamefully treated; the elder and most intensely respectable ladies for the most part inclined to the other side of the question. It not being their habit to look at matters from the same point of view in which they present themselves to a man's nicer sense of honor, they could see no great harm in George Caresfoot's stratagems. A man so rich, they argued, was perfectly entitled to buy his wife. The marriage had been arranged, like their own, on the soundest property basis, and the woman who rose in rebellion against a husband merely because she loved thinking, as she went, how she had in this same guise fled before her husband.

She got her book, and was returning, when she saw that there was still a light in her father's study, and that the door was ajar. At that moment it so happened than an unusually sharp draught, coming down one of the passages of the rambling old house, caught her candle and extinguished it. Making her way to the study-door, she pushed it open to see if anybody was there previous to asking for a light. At first she could see nobody. On the table, which was covered with papers, there stood two candles, a brandy-bottle, and a glass. She was just moving to the candle to get a light, when her eye fell on what she at first believed to be a heap of clothes huddled together on the floor in the corner of the room. Further examination showed her that it was a man—she could distinctly see the backs of his hands. Her first idea was that she had surprised a thief, and she stopped, feeling frightened and not knowing what to do. Just then the bundle straightened itself a little and dropped its hands, revealing to her wondering gaze her own father's face, which wore the same awful look of abject fear which she had seen upon it when he passed through the hall beneath her just before Isleworth broke into flame on the night of her marriage. The eyes appeared to be starting from the sockets in an effort to clearly realize an undefinable horror, the hair, now daily growing grayer, was partially erect, and the pallid lips half-opened, as though to speak words that would not come. He saw her too, but did not seem surprised at her presence. Covering up his eyes again with one hand, he shrank farther back into his corner, and with the other pointed to a large leather arm-chair in which Pigott had told her her grandfather had died.

"Look there!" he whispered, hoarsely.

"Where, father? I see nothing."

"There, girl, in the chair—look how it glares at me!"

Angela stood aghast. She was alarmed, in defiance of her own reason, and began to catch the contagion of superstition.

"This is dreadful," she said; "for heaven's sake tell me what is the matter!"

Philip's ghastly gaze again fixed itself on the chair, and his teeth began to chatter.

"*Great God*," he said, "*it is coming!*"

And, uttering a smothered cry, he fell on his face in a half-faint. The necessity for action brought Angela to herself. Seizing the water-bottle, she splashed some water into her father's face. He came to himself almost instantly.

"Where am I?" he said. "Ah! I remember; I have not been quite well. You must not think anything of that. What are you doing here at this time of night? Pass me that bottle," and he took nearly half a tumbler of raw brandy. "There, I am quite right again now; I had a bad attack of indigestion, that is all. Good-night."

Angela went without a word. She understood now what her

father had meant when he said that he was "accursed;" but she could not help wondering whether the brandy had anything to do with his "indigestion."

On the following day the doctor came to see her. It struck Angela that he came oftener than was necessary, the fact being that he would gladly have attended her gratis all the year round. A doctor does not often get the chance of visiting such a patient.

"You do not look quite so well to-day," he said.

"No," she answered, with a little smile; "I had bad dreams last night."

"Ah! I thought so. You should try to avoid that sort of thing; you are far too imaginative already."

"One cannot run away from one's dreams. Murder will out in sleep."

"Well, I have a message for you."

"Who from?"

"Lady Bellamy. You know that she is paralyzed?"

"Yes."

"Well, she wants you to go and see her. Shall you go?"

Angela thought a little, and answered,

"Yes, I think so."

"You must be prepared to hear some bitter language if she speaks at all. Very likely she will beg you to get her some poison to kill herself with. I have been obliged to take the greatest precautions to prevent her from obtaining any. I am not very sensitive, but once or twice she has positively made me shiver with the things she says."

"She can never say anything more dreadful to me than she has said already, Dr. Williamson."

"Perhaps not. Go if you like. If you were revengeful—which I am sure you are not—you would have good reason to be satisfied at what you will see. Medically speaking, it is a sad case."

Accordingly, that very afternoon, Angela, accompanied by Pigott, started off for Rewtham House, where Lady Bellamy still lived, or rather existed. It was her first outing since the inquest on George Caresfoot had caused her and her history to become publicly notorious, and as she walked along, she was surprised to find that she was the object of popular sympathy. Every man she met touched or took off his hat, according to his degree, and, as soon as she had passed, turned round and stared at her. Some fine folks whom she did not know—indeed, she knew no one, though it had been the fashion to send and "inquire" during her illness—drove past in an open carriage and pair, and she saw a gentleman on the front seat whisper something to the ladies, bringing round their heads towards her as simultaneously as though they both worked on a single wire. Even the children coming out of the village school set up a cheer as she passed.

"Good gracious, Pigott, what is it all about?" she asked, at last.

"Well, you see, miss, they talk of you in the papers as the 'Abbey House heroine'—and heroines is rare in these parts."

Overwhelmed with so much attention, Angela was thankful when at last they reached Rewtham House.

Pigott went into the housekeeper's room, and Angela was at once shown up into the drawing-room. The servant announced her name to a black-robed figure lying on a sofa, and closed the door.

"Come here, Angela Caresfoot," said a well-known voice, "and see how Fate has repaid the woman who tried to ruin you."

She advanced and looked at the deathly face, still as darkly beautiful as ever, on which was fixed that strange look of wild expectancy that it had worn when its owner took the poison.

"Yes, look at me; think what I was, and then what I am, and learn how the Spirit of evil pays those who serve him. I thought to kill myself, but death was denied me, and now I live as you see me. I am an outcast from the society of my kind—not that I ever cared for that, except to rule it. I cannot stir hand or foot, I cannot write, I can scarcely read, I cannot even die. My only resource is the bitter sea of thought that seethes eternally in this stricken frame like fire pent in the womb of a volcano. Yes, Angela Caresfoot, and like the fire, too, sometimes it overflows, and then I can blaspheme and rave aloud till my voice fails. That is the only power which is left to me."

Angela uttered an exclamation of pity.

"Pity—do not pity me; I will not be pitied by you. Mock me if you will; it is your turn now. You prophesied that it would come; now it is here."

"At any rate, you are still comfortable in your own house," said Angela, nervously, anxious to turn the subject, and not knowing what to say.

"Oh! yes, I have money enough, if that is what you mean. My husband threatened to leave me destitute, but fear of public opinion—and I hear that he has run away, and is not well thought of now—or perhaps of myself, cripple as I am, caused him to change his mind. But do not let us talk of that poor creature. I sent for you here for a purpose. Where is your lover?"

Angela turned pale and trembled.

"What, do you not know, or are you tired of him?"

"Tired of him! I shall never be tired of him; but he has gone."

"Shall I tell you where to find him?"

"You would not if you could; you would deceive me again."

"No, oddly enough, I shall not. I have no longer any object in doing so. When I was bent upon marrying you to George Caresfoot, I lashed myself into hating you; now I hate you no longer, I respect you—indeed, I have done so all along."

"Then, why did you work me such a bitter wrong?"

"Because I was forced to. Believe me or not as you will, I am not going to tell you the story—at any rate, not now. I can only repeat that I was forced to."

"Where is Arthur?"

"In Madeira. Do you remember once telling me that you had only to lift your hand—so—ah! I forgot, I cannot lift mine—to draw him back to you, that no other woman in the world could keep him from you if you chose to bid him come?"

"Yes, I remember."

"Then, if you wish to get him back, you had better exercise your power, for he has gone to another woman."

"Who is she? What is she like?"

"She is a young widow—a Mrs. Carr. She is desperately in love with him—very beautiful and very rich."

"Beautiful! How do you mean? Tell me exactly what she is like."

"She has brown eyes, brown hair, a lovely complexion, and a perfect figure."

Angela glanced rapidly at her own reflection in the glass and sighed.

"Then I fear that I shall have no chance against her—none!"

"You are a fool! If you were alone in the same room with her, nobody would see her for looking at you."

Angela sighed again, this time from relief.

"But there is worse than that; very possibly he has married her."

"Ah; then it is all over!"

"Why? If he loves you as much as you think, you can bring him back to you, married or unmarried."

"Perhaps. Yes, I think I could; but I would not."

"Why? If he loves you and you love him, you have a right to him. Among all the shams and fictions that we call laws, there is only one true—the law of Nature, by virtue of which you belong to each other."

"No, there is a higher law—the law of duty, by means of which we try to curb the impulses of Nature. The woman who has won him has a right to consideration."

"Then, to gratify a foolish prejudice, you are prepared to lose him for ever?"

"No, Lady Bellamy; if I thought that I was to lose him for ever, I might be tempted to do what is wrong in order to be with him for a time; but I do not think that. I only lose him for a time that I may gain him for ever. In this world he is separated from me; in the worlds to come my rights will assert themselves, and we shall be together and never part any more."

Lady Bellamy looked at her wonderingly, for her eyes could still express her emotions.

"You are a fine creature," she said, "and, if you believe that, perhaps it will be true for you, since Faith must be the measure of realization. But, after all, he may not have married her. That will be for you to find out."

"How can I find out?"

"By writing to him, of course—to the care of Mrs. Carr, Madeira. That is sure to find him."

"Thank you. How can I thank you enough?"

"It seems to me that you owe me few thanks. You are always

foolish about what tends to secure your own happiness, or you would have thought of this before."

There was a pause, and then Angela rose to go.

"Are you going? Yes, go. I am not fit company for such as you. Perhaps we shall not meet again; but, in thinking of all the injury that I have done you, remember that my punishment is proportionate to my sin. They tell me that I may live for years."

Angela gazed at the splendid wreck beneath her, and an infinite pity swelled in her gentle heart. Stooping, she kissed her on the forehead. A wild astonishment filled Lady Bellamy's great dark eyes.

"Child, child, what are you doing? you do not know what I am or you would not kiss me!"

"Yes, Lady Bellamy," she said, quietly, "I do; that is, I know what you have been; but I want to forget that. Perhaps you will one day be able to forget it too. I do not wish to preach, but perhaps, after all, this terrible misfortune may lead you to something better. Thank God, there is forgiveness for us all."

Her words touched some forgotten chord in the stricken woman's heart, and two big tears rolled down the frozen cheeks. They were the first Anne Bellamy had wept for many a day.

"Your voice," she said, "has a music that awakes the echoes from a time when I was good and pure like you, but that time has gone forever."

"Surely, Lady Bellamy, the heart that can remember it can also strive to reach another like it. If you have descended the cliff whence those echoes spring, into a valley however deep, there is still another cliff before you that you may climb."

"It is easy to descend, but we need wings to climb. Look at me, Angela; my body is not more crippled and shorn of power than my dark spirit is of wings. How can *I* climb?"

Angela bent low beside her and whispered a few words in her ear, then rose with a shy blush upon her face. Lady Bellamy shut her eyes. Presently she opened them again.

"Do not speak any more of this to me now," she said. "I must have time. The instinct of years cannot be brushed away in a day. If you knew all the sins I have committed, perhaps you would think too that for such as I am there is no forgiveness and no hope."

"Whilst there is life there is hope, and, as I once heard Mr. Fraser say, the real key to forgiveness is the desire to be forgiven."

Again Lady Bellamy shut her eyes and thought, and when she drew up their heavy lids Angela saw that there was something of a peaceful look about them.

"Stand so," she said to Angela, "there where the light falls upon your face. That will do; now shall I tell you what I read there? On your forehead sit resolute power to grasp, and almost measureless capacity to imagine; in your eyes there is a sympathy not to be guessed by beings of a coarser fibre; those eyes could look at Heaven and not be dazzled. Your whole face speaks of a purity and single-mindedness which I can read but cannot understand. Your mind rejects the glittering bubbles that men follow, and seeks the solid truth. Your spirit is in tune with things of light and air; it can float to the extremest heights of our mental atmosphere, and thence can almost gaze into the infinite beyond. Pure, but not cold, thirsting for a wider knowledge, and at times breathing the air of a higher world; resolute, but patient; proud, and yet humble to learn; holy, but aspiring; conscious of gifts you do not know how to use, girl, you rise as near to what is divine as a mortal may. I have always thought so, now I am sure of it."

"Lady Bellamy!"

"Hush! I have a reason for what I say. I do not ask you to waste time by listening to senseless panegyrics. Listen: I will tell you what I have never told to a living soul before. For years I have been a student of a lore almost forgotten in this country—a lore which once fully acquired will put the powers that lie hid in Nature at the command of its possessor, that will even enable him to look beyond Nature, and perhaps, so far as the duration of existence is concerned, for a while to triumph over it. That lore you can learn, though it baffled me. My intellect and determination enabled me to find the cues to it, and to stumble on some of its secrets, but I could not follow them; too late I learnt that only the good and pure can do that. Much of the result of years of toil I destroyed the other night, but I still know enough to empower you to reconstruct what I annihilated; you can learn more in one year than I learnt in ten. I am grateful to you, and, if you wish it, I will show you the way."

Angela listened, open-eyed. Lady Bellamy was right: she was greedy of knowledge and the power that springs from knowledge.

"But would it not be wrong?" she said.

"There can be nothing wrong in what the ruling Wisdom allows us to acquire without the help of what is evil. But do not be deceived; such knowledge and power as this is not a thing to be trifled with. To obtain a mastery over it, you must devote your life to it; you must give it

"'Allegiance whole, not strained to suit desire.'

No earthly passion must come to trouble the fixed serenity of your aspirations; that was one, but only one, of the reasons of my failure. You must leave your Arthur to Mrs. Carr, and henceforward put him as much out of your mind as possible; and this that you may be able to separate yourself from earthly bonds and hopes and fears. Troubled waters reflect a broken image."

"I must, then, choose between this knowledge and my love?"

"Yes; and you will do well if you choose the knowledge; for, before you die—if, indeed, you do not in the end, for a certain period, overcome even death—you will be more of an angel than a woman. On the one hand, then, this proud and dizzy destiny awaits you; on the other, every-day joys and sorrows shared by all and find out how things stand, and I almost think that she is right."

"Certainly," answered Mr. Fraser, rising and looking out of the window. "You have a great deal at stake."

"You do not think that it would be immodest?"

"My dear Angela, when in such a case as this a woman goes to seek the man she loves, and whom she believes loves her, I do not myself see where there is room for immodesty."

"No, nor do I, and I do love him so very dearly; he is all my life to me."

Mr. Fraser winced visibly.

"What is the matter? have you got a headache?"

"Nothing, only a twinge here," and he pointed to his heart.

Angela looked alarmed; she took a womanly interest in anybody's ailments.

"I know what it is," she said. "Widow James suffers from it. You must take it in hand at once, or it will become chronic after meals, as hers is."

Mr. Fraser smiled grimly as he answered:

"I am afraid that I have neglected it too long—it has become chronic already. But about Madeira; have you, then, made up your mind to go?"

"Yes, I think that I shall go. If he—is married, you know—I can always come back again, and perhaps Pigott is right; the letter might miscarry, and there is so much at stake."

"When shall you go, then?"

"By the next steamer, I suppose. They go every week, I think. I will tell my father that I am going to-morrow."

"Ah! you will want money, I suppose."

"No, I believe that I have plenty of money of my own now."

"Oh! yes, under your marriage settlement, no doubt. Well, my dear, I am sure I hope that your journey will not be in vain. Did I tell you I have also written to Mr. Heigham by this mail, and told him all I knew about the matter?"

"That is very kind and thoughtful of you; it is just like you," answered Angela, gently.

"Not at all, not at all; but you have never told me how you got on with Lady Bellamy—that is, except what she told you about Mr. Heigham."

"Oh! it was a strange interview. What do you think she wanted to teach me?"

"I have not the faintest idea."

"Magic."

"Nonsense!"

"Yes, she did; she told me that she could read all sorts of things in my face, and offered, if I would give myself up to it, to make me more than human."

"Pshaw! it was a bit of charlatanism; she wanted to frighten you."

"No, I think she believed what she said, and I think that she the world, and an ordinary attachment to a man against whom I have, indeed, nothing to say, but who is not your equal, and who is, at the best, full of weaknesses that you should despise."

"But, Lady Bellamy, his weaknesses are a part of himself, and I love him all, just as he is; weakness needs love more than what is strong."

"Perhaps; but, in return for your love, I offer you no empty cup. I do not ask you to follow fantastic theories—of that I will soon convince you. Shall I show you the semblance of your Arthur and Mrs. Carr as they are at this moment?"

"No, Lady Bellamy, no; I have chosen. You offer, after years of devotion, to make me *almost like an angel*. The temptation is very great, and it fascinates me. But I hope, if I can succeed in living a good life, to become altogether an angel when I die. Why, then, should I attempt to filch fragments of a knowledge that will one day be all my own?—if, indeed, it is right to do so. Whilst I am here, Arthur's love is more to me than such knowledge can ever be. If he is married, I may learn to think differently, and try to soothe my mind by forcing it to run in these hidden grooves. Till then, I choose Arthur and my petty hopes and fears; for, after all, they are the natural heritage of my humanity."

Lady Bellamy thought for a while, and answered:

"I begin to think that the Great Power who made us has mixed even His most perfect works with an element of weakness, lest they should soar too high and see too far. The prick of a pin will bring a balloon to earth, and an earthly passion, Angela, will prevent you from soaring to the clouds. So be it. You have had your chance. It is only one more disappointment."

CHAPTER LXX

ANGELA went home very thoughtful. The next three days she spent in writing. First, she wrote a clear and methodical account of all the events that had happened since Arthur's first departure, more than a year ago, and attached to it copies of the various documents that had passed between herself and George, including one of the undertaking that her husband had signed before the marriage. This account was in the form of a statement which she signed, and, taking it to Mr. Fraser, read it to him, and got him to sign it too. It took her two whole days to write, and, when it was done, she labelled it "to be read first." On the third day she wrote the following letter to go with the statement:

"For the first time in my life, Arthur, I take up my pen to write to you, and in truth the difficulty of the task before me, as well as my own want of skill, tends to bewilder me, and, though I have much upon my mind to say, I scarcely know if it will reach you—

if, indeed, this letter is ever destined to lie open in your hands—in an intelligible form.

"The statement that I enclose, however, will—in case you do not already know them—tell you all the details of what has happened since you left me more than a year ago. From it you will learn how cruelly I was deceived into marrying George Caresfoot, believing you dead. Oh, through all eternity, never shall I forget that fearful night, nor cease to thank God for my merciful escape from the fiend whom I had married. And then came the morning, and brought you—the dead—alive before my eyes. And whilst I stood in the first tumult of my amaze—forgetful of everything but that it was you, my own, my beloved Arthur, no spirit, but you in flesh and blood—whilst I yet stood thus, stricken to silence by the shock of an unutterable joy—you broke upon me with those dreadful words, so that I choked, feeling how just they must seem to you, and could not answer.

"And yet it sometimes fills me with wonder and indignation to think of them; wonder that you could believe me so mad as to throw away the love of my life, and indignation that you could deem me so lost as to dishonor it. They drove me mad, those words, and from that moment forward I remember nothing but a chaos of the mind heaving endlessly like the sea. But all this has passed, and I am thankful to say that I am quite well again now.

"Still, I should not have written to you, Arthur; I did not even know where you were, and I never thought of recovering you. After what has passed, I looked upon you as altogether lost to me for this world. But a few days ago I went at her own request to see Lady Bellamy. All she said to me I will not now repeat, lest I should render this letter too wearisome to read, though a great deal of it was strange enough to be well worth repetition. In the upshot, however, she said that I had better write to you, and told me where to write. And so I write to you, dear. There was also another thing that she told me of sad import for myself, but which I must not shrink to face. She said that there lived at Madeira, where you are, a lady who is in love with you, and is herself both beautiful and wealthy, to whom you would have gone for comfort in your trouble and in all probability have married.

"Now, Arthur, I do not know if this is the case, but, if so, I hasten to say that I do not blame you. You smarted under what must have seemed to you an intolerable wrong, and you went for consolation to her who had it to offer. In a man that is perhaps natural, though it is not a woman's way. If it be so, I say from my heart, be as happy as you can. But remember what I told you long ago, and do not fall into any delusions on the matter; do not imagine because circumstances have shaped themselves thus, therefore I am to be put out of your mind and forgotten, for this is not so. I cannot be forgotten, though for a while I may be justly discarded; it is possible that for this world you have passed out of my reach, but in the next I shall claim you as my own.

"Yes, Arthur, I have made up my mind to lose you for this life as a fitting reward for my folly. But do not think that I do so without a pang, for, believe me, since my mind emerged stronger and clearer from the storms through which it has passed, bringing back to me the full life and strength of my womanhood, I have longed for you with an ever-increasing longing. I am not ashamed to own that I would give worlds to feel your arms about me and your kiss upon my lips. Why should I be? Am I not yours, body and soul?

"But, dear, it has been given to me, perhaps as a compensation for all I have undergone and that is still left for me to undergo, to grasp a more enduring end than that of earthly ecstasy: for I can look forward with a confident assurance to the day when we shall embrace upon the threshold of the Infinite. Do not call this foolish imagination, or call it imagination, if you will—for what is imagination? Is it not the connecting link between us and our former and future state, the scent of heaven yet clinging to our souls, and recalling memories of our home. Imagination, what would our higher life be without it? It is what the mind is to the body, it is the soul's *thought*.

"So in my imagination—since I know no better term—I foresee that heavenly hour, and I am not jealous for the earthly moment. Nor, indeed, have I altogether lost you, for at times, in the stillness of the night, when the earthly part is plunged in sleep and my spirit is released from the thraldom of the senses, it, at indefinite periods, has the power to summon your beloved form to its presence, and in this communion Nature vindicates her faithfulness. Thus, through the long night rest comes upon me with your presence.

"And at last there will come a greater rest; at last—having lived misunderstood—we shall die, alone, and then the real life or lives will begin. Of this, dear Arthur, reason and religion alike assure me. Indeed, were it not so, it would be better to be a drop of dew sparkling for an hour, and then vanish into ether, rather than a human soul, conscious, languishing, suffering year by year, only to evaporate at last into some undefined ocean of being that must be full of sorrow, if it be the direct consequence of life. But death is not the end of our individual and conscious existence. For, if nothing remained but the ashes from the burnt taper, or a formless essence that soars away and mingles with the elements—if our glowing hopes, our lofty aspirations, our consciousness of capacities for knowledge and happiness which have but just begun to expand, were all cut off by death and buried in the grave, then indeed we should be the greatest enigma in the universe. If that is so, compared with the possibilities of our nature, we are as a morning cloud fading into space—as a tale that is told only to be forgotten.

"But if, as I *know* they must be, our budding hopes, and consciousness of dawning desires which no earthly good can fill, are but the swelling germs of faculties that will blossom hereafter and bear immortal fruit—if we leave in the grave only the swaddling clothes of our spiritual infancy, and rise as from a sleep in human form made perfect, with all our memory and our certainty of individual being, to enter upon an endless career in which hope is changed into fruition and aspirations into attainment—then death is the grandest step of life. It solves all its enigmas; it is the fulfilment of which this existence is the prophecy, and to the wise and pure it throws wide the shining portals of an endless day.

"Oh! Arthur, even now I long for the purer air and flashing sympathies of that vast Hereafter, when the strong sense of knowledge shall scarcely find a limit ere it overleaps it; when visible power shall radiate from our being, and, living on together through countless Existences, Periods, and Spheres, we shall progress from majesty to ever-growing majesty! Oh for the day when you and I, messengers from the Seat of Power, shall sail high above these darkling worlds, and, seeing into each other's souls, shall learn what love's communion is!

"Do not think me foolish, dear, for writing to you thus. I do not wish to make you the victim of an outburst of thought that you may think hysterical. But perhaps I may never be able to write to you again in this way; your wife, if you are married, may be jealous, or other things may occur to prevent it. I feel it, therefore, necessary to tell you my inmost thoughts now whilst I can, so that you may always remember them during the long coming years, and especially when you draw near to the end of the journey. I hope, dearest Arthur, that nothing will ever make you forget them, and also that, for the sake of the pure love you will for ever bear me, you will always live up to your noblest and your best, for in this way our meeting will be made more perfect.

"Of course it is possible that you may still be free, and, after you know that I am not quite so much to blame as you may have thought, still willing to give your name to me. It is a blessed hope, but I scarcely dare to dwell upon it.

"The other day I was reading a book Mr. Fraser lent me, which took my fancy very much, it was so full of contradictions. The unexpected always happened in it, and there was both grief and laughter in its pages. It did not end quite well or quite badly, or, rather, it had *no* end, and deep down underneath the plotless story, only peeping up now and again when the actors were troubled, there ran a vein of real sorrow and sad, unchanging love. There was a hero in this odd book which was so like life—who, by the way, was no hero at all, but a curious, restless creature who seemed to have missed his mark in life, and went along looking for old truths and new ideas with his eyes so fixed upon the stars that he was always stumbling over the pebbles in his path, and thinking that they were rocks. He was a sensitive man, too, and as weak as he was sensitive, and often fell into pitfalls and did what he should not, and yet, for all that, he had a quaint and gentle mind, and there was something to like in him—at least so thought the women in that book. There was a heroine, too, who was all that a heroine should be, very sweet and very beautiful, and she really had a heart, only she would not let it beat. And of course the hero and heroine loved each other: of course, too, they both behaved badly, and things went wrong, or there would have been no book.

"But I tell you this story because once, in a rather touching scene, this hero who made such a mess of things set forth one of the ideas that he had found and thought new, but which was really so very old. He told the heroine that he had read in the stars that happiness has only one key, and that its name is 'Love;' that, amidst all the mutabilities and disillusions of our life, the pure love of a man and woman alone stands firm and beautiful, alone defies change and disappointment; that it is the heaven-sent salve for all our troubles, the remedy for our mistakes, the magic glass reflecting only what is true and good. But in the end her facts overcame his theories, and he might have spared himself the trouble of telling. And, for all his star-gazing, this hero had no real philosophy, but in his grief and unresting pain went and threw himself into the biggest pitfalls that he could find, and would have perished there, had not a good angel come and dragged him out again and brushed the mud off his clothes, and, taking him by the hand, led him along a safer path. And so for a while he drops out of the story, which says that, when he is not thinking of the lost heroine, he is perhaps happier than he deserves to be.

"Now, Arthur, I think that this foolish hero was right, and the sensible heroine he worshipped so blindly, wrong.

"If you are still unmarried, and still care to put his theories to the test, I believe that we also can make as beautiful a thing of our lives as he thought that he and his heroine could, and, ourselves supremely happy in each other's perfect love, may perhaps be able to add to the happiness of some of our fellow-travellers. That is, I think, as noble an end as a man and woman can set before themselves.

"But if, on the other hand, you are tied to this other woman who loves you by ties that cannot be broken, or that honor will not let you break; or if you are unforgiving, and no longer wish to marry me as I wish to marry you, then till that bright hour of immortal hope—farewell. Yes, Arthur, farewell till the gate of Time has closed for us—till, in the presence of God our Father, I shall forever call you mine.

"Alas! I am so weak that my tears fall as I write the word. Perhaps I may never speak or write to you again, so once more, my dearest, my beloved, my earthly treasure and my heavenly hope, farewell. May the blessing of God be as constantly around you as my thoughts, and may He teach you that these are not foolish words, but rather the faint shadow of an undying light!

"I send back the ring that was used to trick me with. Perhaps, whatever happens, you will wear it for my sake. It is, you know, a symbol of Eternity.

"ANGELA CARESFOOT."

CHAPTER LXXI.

JUST as Angela was engaged in finishing her long letter to Arthur—surely one of the strangest ever written by a girl to the man she loved—Mr. Fraser was reading an epistle which had reached him by that afternoon's post. We will look over his shoulder, and see what was in it.

It was a letter dated from the vicarage of one of the poorest parishes in the great Dock district in the east of London. It began—

"DEAR SIR,

"I shall be only too thankful to entertain your proposal for an exchange of livings, more especially as, at first sight, it would seem that all the advantage is on my side. The fact is, that the incessant strain of work here has at last broken down my health to such a degree that the doctors tell me plainly I must choose between the comparative rest of a country parish and the certainty of passing to a completer quiet before my time. Also, now that my children are growing up, I am very anxious to remove them from the sights and sounds and tainted moral atmosphere of this poverty-stricken and degraded quarter.

"But, however that may be, I should not be doing my duty to you if I did not warn you that this is no parish for a man of your age to undertake, unless for strong reasons (for I see by the Clergy List that you are a year or so older than myself). The work is positively ceaseless, and often of a most shocking and thankless character; and there are almost no respectable inhabitants; for nobody lives in the parish except those who are too poor to live elsewhere. The stipend, too, is, as you are aware, not large. However, if, in face of these disadvantages, you still entertain the idea of an exchange, perhaps we had better meet. . . . ."

The letter then entered into details.

"I think that will suit me very well," said Mr. Fraser, aloud to himself, as he put it down. "It will not greatly matter if my health does break down; and I ought to have gone long ago. 'Positively ceaseless,' he says the work is. Well, ceaseless work is the only thing that can stifle thought. And yet it will be hard, coming up by the roots after all these years. Ah me! this is a queer world, and a sad one for some of us! I will write to the bishop at once."

From which it will be gathered that things had not been going well with Mr. Fraser.

Meanwhile, Angela put her statement and the accompanying letter into a large envelope. Then she took the queer emerald ring off her finger, and, as there was nobody looking, she kissed it and wrapped it up in a piece of cotton-wool, and stowed it away in the letter, and sealed it up. Next she addressed it, in her clear miniature handwriting, to

"*Arthur P. Heigham, Esq.*,
"*Care of Mrs. Carr*,
"*Madeira*,"

as Lady Bellamy had told her; and, calling to Pigott to come with her, started off to the post-office to register and post her precious packet, for the Madeira mail left Southampton on the morrow.

She had just time to reach the office, affix the three shillings' worth of stamps that the letter took, and register it, when the postman came up, and she saw it stamped and bundled into his bag with the others, just as though it were nothing, instead of her whole life depending on it; and away it went on its journey, as much beyond recall as yesterday's sins.

"And so you have been a-writing to him, Miss?" said Pigott, as soon as they were out of the office.

"Yes, Pigott," and she told her what Lady Bellamy had said. She listened attentively, with a shrewd twinkle in her eyes.

"I'm thinking, dearie, that it's a pity you didn't post yourself, that's the best letter; it can't make no mistakes, nor fall into the hands of them it isn't meant for."

"What can you mean?"

"I'm thinking, miss, that change of air is a wonderful good thing after sickness, especially sea-air," answered Pigott, oracularly.

"I don't in the least understand you. Really, Pigott, you drive me wild with your parables."

"Lord, dear, for all you're so clever you never could see half an inch into a brick wall, and that with my meaning as clear as a haystack in a thunderstorm."

This last definition quite finished Angela. Why, she wondered, should a haystack be clearer in a thunderstorm than at any other time. She looked at her companion helplessly, and was silent.

"Bless me, what I have been telling, as plain as plain can be, is, why don't you go to this Mad—Mad—what's the name?—I never can think of them foreign names. I'm like Jakes and the flowers: he says the smaller and 'footier' they are, the longer the name they sticks on to them, just to puzzle a body who—"

"Madeira," suggested Angela, with the calmness of despair.

"Yes, that's it—Madeiry. Well, why don't you go to Madeiry along with your letter to look after Mr. Arthur? Like enough he is in a bit of a mess there. So far as I know anything about their ways, young men always are, in a general sort of a way, for everlasting a-caterwauling after some one or other, for all the world like a tom on the tiles, more especial if they are in love with somebody else. But, dear me, a sensible woman don't bother her head about that. She just goes and hooks them out of it, and then she knows where they are, and keeps them there."

"Oh, Pigott, never mind all these reflections, though I'm sure I don't know how you can think of such things. The idea of comparing poor dear Arthur with a tom-cat! But tell me, how can I go to Madeira? Supposing that he is married?"

"Well, then, you would learn all about it for yourself, and no gammoning; and there'd be an end to it, one way or the other."

"But would it be quite modest, to run after him like that?"

"Modest, indeed! And why shouldn't a young lady travel for her health? I have heard say that this Madeiry is a wonderful place for the stomach."

"The lungs, Pigott—the lungs."

"Well, then, the lungs. But it don't matter; they ain't far off each other."

"But, Pigott, who could I go with? I could not go alone."

"Go with? Why, me, of course."

"I can hardly fancy you at sea, Pigott."

"And why not, miss? I dare say I shall do as well as other folks there; and if I do go to the bottom, as seems likely, there's plenty of room for a respectable person there, I should hope. Look here, dear. You'll never be happy unless you marry Mr. Arthur; so don't you go and throw away a chance, just out of foolishness, and for fear of what folks say. That's how dozens of women make a mess of it. Folks say one thing to-day and another to-morrow, but you'll remain you for all that. Maybe he's married; and, if so, it's a bad business, and there's an end of it; but maybe, too, he isn't. As for that letter, as likely as not the other one will put it in the fire. I should, I doubt, if I were in her shoes. So don't you lose any time, for, if he isn't married, it's like enough he soon will be."

Angela felt that there was sense in what her old nurse said, though the idea was a new one to her, and it made her thoughtful.

"I'll think about it," she said, presently. "I wonder what Mr. Fraser would say about it."

"Perhaps one thing, and perhaps another. He's good and kind, but he hasn't got much head for these sort of things, he's always thinking of something else. Just look what a fool Squire George (may he twist and turn in his grave) made of him. You ask him, if you like; but you be guided by yourself, dearie. Your head is worth six Reverend Frasers' when you bring it to a thing. But I must be off, and count the linen."

That evening, after tea, Angela went down to Mr. Fraser's. He was directing an envelope to the Lord Bishop of his diocese when she entered; but he hurriedly put it away in the blotting-paper.

"Well, Angela, did you get your letter off?"

"Yes, Mr. Fraser, it was just in time to catch the mail to-morrow. But, do you know, that is what I want to speak to you about. Pigott thinks that, under all the circumstances"—here Angela hesitated a little—"she and I had better go to Madeira

has some sort of power. She seemed disappointed when I refused, and, do you know, if it had not been for Arthur, I do not think that I should have refused. I love power, or rather knowledge; but then I love Arthur more."

"And why is he incompatible with knowledge?"

"I do not know; but she said that, to triumph over the mysteries she wished to teach me, I must free myself from earthly love and cares. I told her that, if Arthur is married, I would think of it."

"Well, Angela, to be frank, I do not believe in Lady Bellamy's magic, and if its practice brings people to what she is, I think it is best left alone; indeed, I expect that the whole thing is a delusion arising from her condition. But I think she is right when she told you that to become a mistress of her art—or, indeed, of any noble art—you must separate yourself from earthly passions. I owe your Arthur a grudge as well as Lady Bellamy. I hoped, Angela, to see you rise like a star upon this age of insolence and infidelity. I wanted you to be a great woman; but that dream is all over now."

"Why, Mr. Fraser?"

"Because, my dear, both history and observation teach us that great gifts like yours partake of the character of an accident in a woman; they are not natural to her, and she does not wear such jewels easily—they put her outside of her sex. It is something as though a man were born into the world with wings. At first he would be very proud of them, and go sailing about in the sky to the admiration of the crowds beneath him; but by and by he would grow tired of flying alone, and, after all, it is not necessary to fly to transact the ordinary business of the world. And perhaps at last he would learn to love somebody without wings, somebody who could not fly, and he would always want to be with her down on the homely earth, and not alone up in the heavenly heights. If a woman had all the genius of Plato or all the learning of Solomon, it would be forgotten at the touch of a baby's fingers.

"Well, well, we cannot fight against human nature, and I dare say that in a few years you will forget that you can read Greek as well as you can English, and were very near finding out a perfect way of squaring the circle. Perhaps it is best so. Lady Bellamy may have read a great many fine things in your face. Shall I tell you what I read there? I read that you will marry your Arthur, and become a happy wife and a happier mother; that your life will be one long story of unassuming kindness, and that, when at last you die, you will become a sacred memory in many hearts. That is what I read. The only magic you will ever wield, Angela, will be the magic of your goodness."

"Who knows? We cannot read the future," she answered.

"And so you are going to Madeira next week. Then this will be the last time we shall meet—before you go, I mean—for I am off to London to-morrow, for a while, on some business. When next we meet, if we do meet again, Angela, you will be a married woman. Do not start, dear; there is nothing shocking about that. But perhaps we shall not meet any more."

"Oh, Mr. Fraser! why do you say such dreadful things?"

"There is nothing dreadful about it, Angela. I am getting on in life, and am not so strong as I was; and you are both young and strong, and must in the ordinary course of things outlive me for many years. But, whatever happens, my dear, I know that you always keep a warm corner in your memory for your old master; and as for me, I can honestly say that to have known and taught you has been the greatest privilege of a rather lonely life."

Here Angela began to cry.

"Don't cry, my dear. There is, thank God, another meeting-place than this, and, if I reach the shore of that great future before you, I shall—but, there, my dear, it is time for you to be going home. You must not stop here to listen to this melancholy talk. Go home, Angela, and think about your lover. I am busy to-night. Give me a kiss, dear, and go."

Presently, she was gone, and he heard the front-door close behind her. He went to the window, and watched the tall form gradually growing fainter in the gloaming, till it vanished altogether.

Then he came back, and, sitting down at his writing-table, rested his grizzled head upon his hand and thought. Presently he raised it, and there was a sad smile flickering round the wrinkles of the nervous mouth.

"And now for 'hard labor at the London docks,'" he said, aloud.

CHAPTER LXXII.

NOTHING occurred to mar the prosperity of the voyage of the *Evening Star*. That beautiful little vessel declined to simplify the course of this history by going to the bottom with Mildred and Arthur, as the imaginative reader may have perhaps expected. She did not even get into a terrific storm, in order to give Arthur the opportunity of performing heroic feats, and the writer of this history the chance of displaying a profound knowledge of the names of ropes and spars. On the contrary, she glided on upon a sea so still that even Miss Terry was persuaded to arouse herself from her torpor, and come upon deck, till at last, one morning, the giant peak of Teneriffe, soaring high above its circling clouds, broke upon the view of her passengers.

Here they stopped for a week or so, enjoying themselves very much in their new surroundings, till at length Arthur grew tired of the islands, which was of course the signal for their departure. So they returned, reaching Madeira after an absence of close upon a month. As they dropped anchor in the little bay, Mildred came up to Arthur, and, touching him with that gentle deference which she always showed towards him, asked if he was not glad to be home again.

"Home!" he said. "I have no home."

"Oh, Arthur!" she answered, "why do you try to pain me? Is not my home yours also?"

So soon as they landed, he started off down to "Miles' Hotel," to see if any letters had come for him during his absence, and returned, looking very much put out.

"What is the matter, Arthur?" asked Miss Terry, once again happy at feeling her feet upon solid soil.

"Why, those idiots at the hotel have returned a letter sent to me by my lawyer. They thought that I had left Madeira for good, and the letter was marked, 'If left, return to Messrs. Borley and Son,' with the address. And the mail went out this afternoon into the bargain, so it will be a month before I can get it back again."

Had Arthur known that this letter contained clippings of the newspaper reports of the inquest on George Caresfoot, of whose death even he was in total ignorance, he would have had good reason to be put out.

"Never mind, Arthur," said Mildred's clear voice at his elbow—she was rarely much further from him than his shadow; "lawyers' letters are not, as a rule, very interesting. I never yet had one that would not keep. Come and see if your pavilion—isn't that a grand name?—is arranged to your liking, and then let us go to dinner, for Agatha here is dying of hunger—she has to make up for her abstinence at sea."

"I was always told," broke in that lady, "that yachting was charming, but I tell you frankly I have never been more miserable in my life than I was on board your *Evening Star*."

"Never mind, dear, you shall have a nice long rest before we start for the coast of Spain."

And so Arthur soon settled down again into the easy tenor of Madeira life. He now scarcely made a pretence of living at the hotel, since, during their cruise, Mildred had had a pavilion which stood in the garden luxuriously fitted up for his occupation. Here he was happy enough in a dull, numb way, and, as the days went on, something of the old light came back to his eyes, and his footfall again grew quick and strong, as when it used to fall in the corridors of the Abbey House. Of the past he never spoke, nor did Mildred ever allude to Angela after that conversation at sea which had ended so strangely. She contented herself with attempting to supplant her, and to a certain extent she was successful. No man could have for very long remained obdurate to such beauty and such patient devotion, and it is not wonderful that he grew in a way to love her.

But there was this peculiarity about the affair—namely, that the affection which he bore her was born more of her stronger will than of his own feelings, as was shown by the fact that, so long as he was actually with her and within the circle of her influence, her power over him was predominant; but, the moment that he was out of her sight, his thoughts would fall back into their original channels, and the old sores would begin to run. However much, too, he might be successful in getting the mastery of his troubles by day, at night they would assert themselves, and from the constant and tormenting dreams which they inspired he could find no means of escape.

For at least four nights out of every seven, from the moment that he closed his eyes till he opened them again in the morning, it would seem to him that he had been in the company of Angela, under every possible variety of circumstance, talking to her, walking with her, meeting her suddenly or unexpectedly in crowded places or at dinner-parties—always her, and no one else—till at last poor Arthur began to wonder if his spirit took leave of his body in sleep and went to seek her, and, what is more, found her. Or was it nothing but a fantasy? He could not tell; but, at any rate, it was a fact, and it would have been hard to say if it distressed or rejoiced him most.

Occasionally, too, he would fall into a fit of brooding melancholy that would last him for a day or two, and which Mildred would find it quite impossible to dispel. Indeed, when he got in that way, she soon discovered that the only thing to do was to leave him alone. He was suffering acutely, there was no doubt about that, and when any animal suffers, including man, it is best left in solitude. A sick or wounded beast always turns out of the herd to recover or die.

When Mildred saw him in this state of mental desolation, she would shake her head and sigh, for it told her that she was as far as ever from the golden gate of her Eldorado. As has been said, hers was the strongest will, and, even if he had not willed it, she could have married him any day she wished; but, odd as it may seem, she was too conscientious. She had determined that she would not marry him unless she was certain that he loved her, and to this resolution, as yet, she firmly held. Whatever her faults may have been, Mildred Carr had all the noble unselfishness that is so common in her sex. For herself and her own reputation she cared, comparatively speaking, nothing; whilst for Arthur's ultimate happiness she was very solicitous.

One evening—it was one of Arthur's black days, when he had got a fit of what Mildred called "Angela fever"—they were walking together in the garden, Arthur in silence, with his hands in his pockets and his pipe in his mouth, and Mildred humming a little tune by way of amusing herself, when they came to the wall that edged the precipice. Arthur leant over it and gazed at the depths below.

"Don't, dear, you will tumble over," said Mildred, in some alarm.

"I think it would be a good thing if I did," he answered, moodily.

"Are you, then, so tired of the world—and me?"

"No, dear, I am not tired of you; forgive me, Mildred, but I am dreadfully miserable. I know that it is very ungracious and ungrateful of me, but it is the fact."

"You are thinking of *her* again, Arthur?"

"Yes, I have got a fit of it. I suppose that she has not been out of my mind for an hour together during the last forty-eight hours. Talk of being haunted by a dead person, it is infinitely worse being haunted by a living one."

"I am very sorry for you, dear."

"Do you suppose, Mildred, that this will go on for all my life, that I shall always be at the mercy of these bitter memories and thoughts?"

"I don't know, Arthur. I hope not."

"I wish I were dead—I wish I were dead," he broke out, passionately. "She has destroyed my life, all that was happy in me is dead, only my body lives on. I am sure I don't know, Mildred, how you can care for anything so worthless."

She kissed him, and answered:

"Dearest, I had rather love you as you are than any other man alive. Time does wonders; perhaps in time you will get over it. Oh! Arthur, when I think of what she has made you, and what you might have been if you had never known her, I long to tell that woman all my mind. But you must be a man, dear; it is weak to give way to a mad passion, such as this is now. Try to think of something else; work at something."

"I have no heart for it, Mildred; I don't feel as though I could work; and, if you cannot make me forget, I am sure I do not know what will."

Mildred sighed and did not answer. Though she spoke hopefully about it to him, she had little faith in his getting over his passion for Angela now. Either she must marry him as he was, or else let him go altogether; but which? The struggle between her affection and her idea of duty was very sore, and as yet she could come to no conclusion.

One thing there was that troubled her considerably, and this was that, though Madeira was almost empty, there were enough people in it to get up a good deal of gossip about herself and Arthur. Now, it would have been difficult to find anybody more entirely careless of the judgments of society than Mildred, more especially as her great wealth and general popularity protected her from slights. But, for all her oddities, she was a thorough woman of the world; and she knew, none better, that, in pursuance of an almost invariable natural law, there is nothing that lowers a woman so much in the estimation of a man as the knowledge that she is talked about, even though he himself is the cause of the talk. This may be both illogical and unjust, but it is, none the less, true.

But, if Mildred still hesitated, Arthur did not. He was very anxious that they should be married; indeed, he almost insisted on it. The position was one that was far from being agreeable to him, for all such intimacies must, from their very nature, necessitate a certain amount of false swearing. They are throughout an acted lie; and, when the lie is acted, it must sometimes be spoken. Now, this is a state of affairs that is repugnant to an honorable man and one that not unfrequently becomes perfectly intolerable. Many is the love-affair that comes to a sudden end because the man finds it impossible to permanently constitute himself a peregrinating falsehood. But, oddly enough, it has been found difficult to persuade the other contracting party of the validity of the excuse, and, however unjust it may be, one has known of men who have seen their defection energetically set down to more vulgar causes.

Arthur was no exception to this rule. He found himself in a false position, and he hated it. Indeed, he determined before long he would place it before Mildred in the light of an alternative, that he should either marry her or that an end should be put to their existing relations.

CHAPTER LXXIII.

As the autumn came on, a great south-west gale burst over Madeira, and went sweeping away up the Bay of Biscay. It blew for threw days and nights, and was one of the heaviest on record. When it first began, the English mail was due; but when it passed there were still no signs of her, and prophets of evil were not wanting who went to and fro shaking their heads, and suggesting that she had probably foundered in the Bay.

Two more days went by, and there were still no signs of her, though the telegraph told them that she had left Southampton Docks at the appointed time and date. By this time, people in Madeira could talk of nothing else.

"Well, Arthur, no signs of the *Roman?*" said Mildred, on the fifth day.

"No; the *Garth Castle* is due to-day. Perhaps she may have heard something of her."

"Yes," said Miss Terry, absently; "she may have fallen in with some of the wreckage."

"I must say that is a cheerful suggestion," answered Arthur. "She is an awful old tub, and, I daresay, ran before the gale for Vigo, that is all."

"Let us hope so," said Mildred, doubtfully. "What is it, John?"

"The housemaid wishes to speak to you, please, ma'am."

"Very good; I will come."

It has been hinted that Agatha Terry was looking absent on the morning in question. There was a reason for it. For some time past there had been growing up in the bosom of this excellent lady a consciousness that things were not altogether as they should be. Miss Terry was not very clever, indeed it may be said that she was dense; but still she could not but see that there was something odd in the relations between Arthur and Mildred. For instance, it struck her as unusual that two persons who were not married, nor even, so far as she knew, engaged, should habitually call each other "dear," and even sometimes "dearest."

But on the previous evening, when engaged in a search after that species of beetles that loves the night, she chanced to come upon the pair standing together on the museum veranda, and, to her horror, she saw, even in that light, that Mildred's arm was round Arthur's neck, and her head was resting on his heart. Standing aghast, she saw more; for presently Mildred raised her hand, and, drawing Arthur's head down to the level of her own, kissed him upon the face.

There was no doubt about it, it was a most deliberate kiss—a kiss without any extenuating circumstances. He was not even going away, and Agatha could only come to one conclusion, that they were either going to be married—or "they ought to be."

She sought no more beetles that evening, but on the following morning, when Mildred departed to see the housemaid, leaving Arthur and herself together on the veranda, she thought it was her "duty" to seek a little information.

"Arthur," she said, with a beating heart, "I want to ask you something. Are you engaged to Mildred?"

He hesitated, and then answered,

"No, I suppose not, Miss Terry."

"Nor married to her?"

"No; why do you ask?"

"Because I think you ought to be."

"I quite agree with you. I suppose that you have noticed something?"

"Yes, I have. I saw her kissing you, Arthur."

He blushed like a girl.

"Oh, Arthur," she went on, bursting into tears, "don't let this sort of thing go on, or poor Mildred will lose her reputation; and you must know what a dreadful thing that is for any woman. Why don't you marry her?"

"Because she refused to marry me."

"And yet—and yet she kisses you—like that!" added Miss Terry, as the peculiar fervor of the embrace in question came back to her recollection. "Ah! I don't know what to think."

"Best not think about it at all, Miss Terry. It won't bear reflection."

"Oh, Arthur, how could you?"

He looked very uncomfortable as he answered:

"I know that I must seem a dreadful brute to you. I dare say I am; but, Miss Terry, it would, under all the circumstances, be much more to the point if you insisted on Mildred's marrying me."

"I dare not. You do not know Mildred. She would never submit to it from me."

"Then I must; and, what is more, I will do it now."

"Thank you, Arthur, thank you. I cannot tell you how grateful I am to you."

"There is no need to be grateful to the author of the mischief."

"And supposing she refuses—what will you do then?"

"Then I think that I shall go away at once. Hush! here she comes."

"Well, Arthur, what are you and Agatha plotting together? You both look serious enough."

"Nothing, Mildred—that is, only another sea-voyage."

Mildred glanced at him uneasily. She did not like the tone in his voice.

"I have a bit of bad news for you, Arthur. That fool, that idiot, Jane"—and she stamped her little foot upon the pavement—"has upset the mummy hyacinth-pot and broken the flower off just as it was coming into bloom. I have given her a quarter's wages and her passage back to England, and packed her off."

"Why, Mildred," remonstrated Miss Terry, "what a fuss to make about a flower!"

She turned on her almost fiercely.

"I had rather have broken my arm, or anything short of my neck, than that she should have broken that flower. Arthur planted it, and now the clumsy girl has destroyed it," and Mildred looked as though she were going to cry.

As there was nothing more to be said, Miss Terry went away. As soon as she was gone, Mildred turned to Arthur and said,

"You were right, Arthur; we shall never see it bloom in this world."

"Never mind about the flower, dear; it cannot be helped. I want to speak to you of something more important. Miss Terry saw you kiss me last night, and she not unnaturally is anxious to know what it all means."

"And did you tell her?"

"Yes."

It was Mildred's turn to blush now.

"Mildred, you must listen to me. This cannot go on any more; either you must marry me, or—"

"Or what?"

"Or I must go away. At present our whole life is a lie."

"Do you really wish me to marry you, Arthur?"

"I not only wish it, I think it necessary."

"Have you nothing more to say than that?"

"Yes, I have to say that I will do my best to make you a good and faithful husband, and that I am sure you will make me a good wife."

She dropped her face upon her hands and thought.

Just then Miss Terry came hurrying up.

"Oh, Arthur!" she said, "just think: the *Roman* is in, after all, but all her boats are gone, and they say that half of her passengers and crew are washed overboard; do go down and see about it."

He hesitated a little.

"Go, dear," whispered Mildred. "I want time to think. I will give you my answer this afternoon."

Mildred sat still on the veranda thinking, but she had not been there many minutes before a servant came with her English letters that had been brought by the unfortunate *Roman*, and at the same time informed her that the *Garth Castle* had been sighted, and would anchor in a few hours. Mildred reflected that it was not often they got two English mails in one day. She began idly turning over the packet before her. Of late letters had lost much of their interest for Mildred.

Presently, however, her hand made a movement of almost electric swiftness, and the color left her face, as she seized a stout envelope directed in a hand of peculiar delicacy to "Arthur Heigham, Esq., care of Mrs. Carr, Madeira." Mildred knew the handwriting; she had seen it in Arthur's pocket-book. It was Angela Caresfoot's. Next to it there was another letter addressed to Arthur in a hand that she did not know, but bearing the same postmarks, "Bratham" and "Roxham." She put them both aside, and then took up the thick letter and examined it. It had two peculiarities — first, it was open, having come unsealed in transit and been somewhat roughly tied up with a piece of twine; and secondly, it contained some article of jewelery—at least, Mildred judged that it was jewelry. Indeed, by dint of a little pressing on the outside paper, she was able to form a pretty accurate opinion as to what it was. It was a ring. If she had turned pale before when she saw the letter, she was paler still now.

"Heavens!" she thought, "why does she send him a ring? Has anything happened to her husband? If she is a free woman, I am lost."

Mildred looked at the letter lying open before her, and a terrible temptation took possession of her. She took it up and put it down again, and then again she took it up, wiping the cold perspiration from her forehead.

"My whole life is at stake," she thought.

Then she hesitated no longer, but, taking the letter, slipped off the piece of twine, and drew its contents from the envelope. The first thing to fall out, wrapped in a little cotton-wool, was the ring. She looked at it, and recognized it as Arthur's engagement-ring, the same that Lady Bellamy had taken with her. Then putting aside the statement, she deliberately unfolded the letter, and read it.

Do not think too hardly of her, my reader. The temptation was very sore. But when one yields to temptation, retribution is not unfrequently hard upon its track, and it would only have been necessary to watch Mildred's face to see that, if she had sinned, the sin went hand in hand with punishment. In turn it took an expression of astonishment, grief, awe, despair. She read the letter to the last word; then she took the statement, and glanced through it, smiling once or twice as she read. Next she replace everything in the envelope, and, taking it, together with the other letter addressed to Arthur, unbuttoned the top of her loose-bodied white dress, and placed them in her bosom.

"It is over," she said to herself. "I can never marry him now. That woman is as far above me as the stars, and sooner or later he would find it all out. He must go, ah, God! he must go to marry *her*. Why should I not destroy these letters, and marry him to-morrow? bind him to me by a tie that no letters can ever break? What! purchase his presence at the price of his daily scorn? Oh, such water is too bitter for me to drink! I have sinned against you, Arthur, but I will sin on more. Good-by, my dear, good-by."

And she laid her throbbing head upon the rail of the verandad, and wept bitterly.

CHAPTER LXXIV.

About three o'clock that afternoon Arthur returned to the Quinta, having lunched on board the *Roman*. He found Mildred sitting in her favorite place on the museum veranda. She was very pale, and if he had watched her he would have seen that she was trembling all over; but he did not observe her particularly.

"Well," he said, "it is all nonsense about half the crew being drowned; only one man was killed, by the fall of a spar, poor chap. They ran into Vigo, as I thought. The other mail is just coming in—but what is the matter, Mildred? You look pale."

"Nothing, dear; I have a good deal to think of, that is all."

"Ah yes! Well, my love, have you made up your mind?"

"Why did I refuse to marry you before—for your sake or mine, Arthur?"

"You said—absurdly, I thought—for mine."

"And what I said I meant, and what I meant I mean. Look me in the face, dear, and tell me, upon your honor as a gentleman, that you love me, really love me, and I will marry you to-morrow."

"I rm very fond of you, Mildred, and will make you a good and true husband."

"Precisely; that is what I expected; but it is *not* enough for me. There was a time when I thought that I could be well satisfied if you would only look kindly upon me, but I suppose that *l'appêtit vient en mangeant*, for, now you do that, I am not satisfied. I long to reign alone. But that is not all. I will not consent to tie you, who do not love me, to my apron-strings for life. Believe me, the time is very near when you would curse me, if I did. You say"—and she rose and stretched out her arms—"that you will either marry me or go. I have made my choice. I will not beat out my heart against a stone. I will *not* marry you. Go, Arthur, go!"

A great anxiety came into his face.

"Do you fully understand what you are saying, Mildred? Such ties as exist between us cannot be lightly broken."

"But I will break them, and my own heart with them, before they become chains so heavy that you cannot bear them. Arthur"—and she came up to him, and put her hands upon his shoulders, looking, with wild and sorrowful eyes, straight into his face—"tell me now, dear—do not palter, or put me off with any courteous falsehood—tell me as truly as you will speak on the judgment-day, do you still love Angela Caresfoot as much as ever?"

"Mildred, you should not ask me such painful questions; it is not right of you."

"It is right; and you will soon know that it is. Answer me."

"Then if you must have it, *I do.*"

Her face became quite hard. Slowly she took her hands from his shoulders.

"And you have the effrontery to ask me to marry you with one breath, and to tell me this with the next! Arthur, you had better go. Do not consider yourself under any false obligation to me. Go, and go quickly."

"For God's sake, think what you are doing, Mildred!"

"Oh! I have thought—I have thought too much. There is nothing left but to say good-by. Yes, it is a very cruel word. Do you know that you have passed over my life like a hurricane, and wrenched it up by the roots?"

"Really, Mildred, you mystify me. I don't understand you. What can be the meaning of all this?"

She looked at him for a few seconds, and then answered, in a quiet, matter-of-fact voice:

"I forgot, Arthur; here are your English letters;" and she drew them from her bosom and gave them to him. "Perhaps they will explain things a little. Meanwhile, I will tell you something. Angela Caresfoot's husband is dead; indeed, she was never *really* married to him." And then she turned, and slowly walked towards the entrance of the museum. In the boudoir, however, her strength seemed to fail her, and she sank on a chair.

Arthur took the letter, written by the woman he loved, and warm from the breast of the woman he was about to leave, and stood speechless. His heart stopped for a moment, and then sent the blood bounding through his veins like a flood of joy. The shock was so great that for a second or two he staggered, and nearly fell. Presently, however, he recovered himself, and another and very different thought overtook him.

Putting the letters into his pocket, he followed Mildred into the boudoir. She was sitting, looking very faint, upon a chair, her arms hanging down helplessly by her side.

"Mildred," he said, hoarsely.

She looked up with a faint air of surprise.

"What, are you not gone?"

"Mildred, beyond what you have just said I know nothing of the contents of these letters; but whatever they may be, here and now, before I read them, I again offer to marry you. I owe it to you and to my own sense of what is right that I should marry you."

He spoke calmly, and with evident sincerity.

"Do you know that I read your letter just now, and had half a mind to burn it; that I am little better than a thief?"

"I guessed that you had read it."

"And do you understand that your Angela is unmarried, that she was never really married at all—and that she asks nothing better than to marry you?"

"I understand."

"And you still offer to make me your wife?"

"I do. What do you say?"

A flood of light filled Mildred's eyes as she rose and confronted him.

"I say, Arthur, that you are a very noble gentleman, and, that though from this day I must be a miserable woman, I shall always be proud to have loved you. Listen, my dear. When I read that letter, I felt that your Angela towered over me like the Alps, her snowy purity stained only by the reflected lights of heaven. I felt that I could not compete with such a woman as this, that I could never hope to hold you from one so calmly faithful, so dreadfully serene, and I knew that she had conquered, robbing me for Time, and, as I fear, leaving me beggared for Eternity. In the magnificence of her undying power, in the calm certainty of her command, she flings me your life as though it were nothing. 'Take it,' she says; 'he will never love you—he is mine; but I can afford to wait. I shall claim him before the throne of God.' But now, look you, Arthur, if you can behave like the generous-hearted gentleman you are, I will show you that I am not behind you in generosity. I will *not* marry you. I have done with you; or, to be more correct," and she gave a hard little laugh, "you have done with me. Go back to Angela, the beautiful woman with inscrutable gray eyes, who waits for you, clothed in her eternal calm, like a mountain in its snows. I shall send her that tiara as a wedding-present; it will become her well. Go back, Arthur; but sometimes, when you are cloyed with unearthly virtue and perfection, remember that a *woman* loved you. There, I have made you quite a speech; you will always think of me in connection with fine words. Why don't you go?"

Arthur stood utterly confused.

"And what will you do, Mildred?"

"I!" she answered, with the same hard laugh. "Oh, don't trouble yourself about me. I shall be a happy woman yet. I mean to see life now—go in for pleasure, power, ritualism, whatever comes first. Perhaps, when we meet again, I shall be Lady Minster, or some other great lady, and shall be able to tell you that I am very, very happy. A woman always likes to tell her old lover that, you know, though she would not like him to believe it. Perhaps, too"—and here her eyes grew soft, and her voice broke into a sob—"I shall have a consolation you know nothing of."

He did not know what she meant; indeed, he was half distracted with grief and doubt.

For a moment more they stood facing each other in silence, and then suddenly she flung her arms above her head, and uttering a low cry of grief, turned, and ran swiftly down the stone passage into the museum. Arthur hesitated for a while, and then followed her.

A painful sight waited him in that silent chamber; for there—stretched on the ground before the statue of Osiris, like some hopeless sinner before an inexorable justice, with her brown hair touched to gold by a ray of sunlight from the roof—lay Mildred, as still as though she were dead. He went to her, and tried to raise her, but she wrenched herself loose, and, in an abandonment of misery, flung herself upon the ground again.

"I thought it was over," she said, "and that you were gone. Go, dear, or this will drive me mad. Perhaps sometimes you will write to me."

He knelt beside her and kissed her, and then he rose and went.

But for many a year was he haunted by that scene of human misery enacted in the weird chamber of the dead. Never could he forget the sight of Mildred lying in the sunlight, with the marble face of mocking calm looking down upon her, and the mortal frames of those who, in their day, had suffered as she suffered, and ages since had found the rest that she in time would reach, scattered all around—fit emblems of the fragile vanity of passion, which suck their strength from earth alone.

CHAPTER LXXV.

When Arthur got out of the gates of the Quinta Carr, he hurried to the hotel, with the intention of reading the letters Mildred had given him, and, passing through the dining-room, seated himself upon the "stoep" which overlooked the garden in order to do so. At this time of the year it was, generally speaking, a quiet place enough; but on this particular day scarcely had Arthur taken the letter from his pocket, and—having placed the ring that it contained upon his trembling finger, and repudiating the statement, marked "to be read first," on account of its business-like appearance—glanced at the two first lines of Angela's own letter, when the sound of hurrying feet and many chattering voices reminded him that he could expect no peace anywhere in the neighborhood of the hotel. The second English mail was in, and all the crowd of passengers, who were at this time pouring out to the Cape to escape the English winter, had come, rejoicing, ashore, to eat, drink, be merry, and buy parrots and wicker chairs while the vessel coaled.

He groaned, and fled, in his hurry leaving the statement on the bench on which he was seated.

Some half-mile or so away, to the left of the town, where the sea had encroached a little upon the shore of the island, there was a nook of peculiar loveliness. Here the giant hand of Nature had cleft a ravine in the mountains that make Madeira, down which a crystal streamlet trickled to the patch of yellow sand that edged the sea. Its banks sloped like a natural terrace, and were clothed with masses of maidenhair fern interwoven with feathery grasses, whilst up above among the rocks grew aloes and every sort of flowering shrub.

Behind, clothed in forest, lay the mass of mountains, varied by the rich green of the vine-clad valleys, and in front heaved the endless ocean, broken only by one lonely rock that stood grimly out against the purpling glories of the evening sky. This spot Arthur had discovered in the course of his rambles with Mildred, and it was here that he bent his steps to be alone to read his letters. Scarcely had he reached the place, however, when he discovered, to his intense vexation, that he had left the enclosure in Angela's letter upon the veranda at the hotel. But, luckily, it chanced that, within a few yards of the spot where he had seated himself, there was a native boy cutting walking-sticks from the scrub. He called to him in Portuguese, of which he had learned a little, and, writing something on a card, told him to take it to the manager of the hotel, and to bring back what he would give him. Delighted at the chance of earning sixpence, the boy started at a run, and at last he was able to begin to read his letter.

Had Arthur not been in quite such a hurry to leave the hotel, he might have seen something which would have interested him, namely, a very lovely woman—so lovely, indeed, that everybody turned their heads to look at her as she passed, accompanied by another woman clad in a stiff black gown, not at all lovely, and rather ancient, but, for all that, well-favored and pleasant to look on, being duly convoyed to their room in the hotel by his friend the manager.

"Well, thank my stars, here we be at last," said the elderly stout person, with a gasp, as the door of the room closed upon the pair; "and it's my opinion that here I shall stop till my dying day, for, as for getting on board one of those beastly ships again, I couldn't do it, and that's flat. Now look here, dearie, don't you sit there and look frightened, but just set to and clean yourself up a bit. I'm off downstairs to see if I can find out about things; everybody's sure to know everybody else's business in a place like this, because, you see, the gossip can't get out of a bit of an island, it must travel round and round till it ewaporates. I shall soon know if he is married or not, and if he is, why, what's done can't be undone, and it's no use crying over spilt milk, and we'll be off home, though I doubt I sha'n't live to get there, and if he isn't why so much the better."

"Oh! nurse, do stop talking, and go quickly; can't you see that I am in an agony of suspense? I must get it over one way or the other."

"Hurry no man's cattle, my dear, or I shall make a mess of it. Now, Miss Angela, just you keep cool; it ain't no manner of use flying into a state. I'll be back presently."

But, as soon as she was gone, poor Angela flew into a considerable state; for, flinging herself upon her knees by the bed, she broke into hysterical prayers to her Maker that Arthur might not be taken from her. Poor girl! alternately racked by sick fears and wild hopes, hers was not a very enviable position during the apparently endless ten minutes that followed.

Meanwhile, Pigott had descended to the cool hall, round which were arranged rows of hammocks, and was looking out for some one with whom to enter into conversation. A Portuguese waiter approached her, but she majestically waved him away, under the impression that he could not speak English, though as a matter of fact his English was purer than her own.

Presently a pretty little woman, leading a baby by the hand, came up to her.

"Pray, do you want anything? I am the wife of the manager."

"Yes, ma'am, I want a little information—at least, there's another that does. Did you ever happen to hear of a Mr. Heigham?"

"Mr. Heigham? Indeed, yes; I know him well. He was here a few minutes since."

"Then perhaps, ma'am, you can tell me if he is married to a Mrs. Carr that lives on this island?"

"Not that I know of," she answered, with a little smile; "but there is a good deal of talk about them—people say that, though they are not married, they ought to be, you know."

"That's the best bit of news I have heard for many a day. As for the talk, I don't pay no manner of heed to that. If he ain't married to her, he won't marry her now, I'll go bail. Thank you kindly, ma'am."

At that moment they were interrupted by the entrance of a little ragged boy into the hall, who timidly held out a card to the lady to whom Pigott was talking.

"Do you want to find Mr. Heigham?" she said. "Because, if so, this boy will show you where he is. He has sent here for a paper that he left. I found it on the veranda just now, and wondered what it was. Perhaps you would take it to him if you go. I don't like trusting this boy—as likely as not he will lose it."

"That will just suit. Just you tell the boy to wait while I fetch my young lady, and we will go with him. Is this the paper? And in her writing, too! Well, I never! There, I'll be back in no time."

Pigott went upstairs far too rapidly for a person of her size and years, with the result that when she reached their room, where Angela was waiting half dead with suspense, she could only gasp.

"Well," said Angela, "be quick and tell me."

"Oh, Lord! them stairs!" gasped Pigott.

"For pity's sake, tell me the worst!"

"Now, miss, *do* give a body time, and don't be a fool—begging pardon for—"

"Oh, Pigott, you are torturing me!"

"Well, miss, you muddle me so—but I am coming to it. I went down them dratted stairs, and there I see a wonderful nice-looking party with a baby.".

"For God's sake tell me—*is Arthur married?*"

"Why, no, dearie—of course not. I was just a-going to say—"

But whatever valuable remark Pigott was going to make was lost to the world forever, for Angela flung her arms round her neck and began kissing her.

"Oh, oh! thank God—thank God! Oh, oh, oh!"

Whereupon Pigott, being a very sensible person, took her by the shoulders and tried to shake her, but it was no joke shaking a person of her height. Angela stood firm, and Pigott oscillated—that was the only visible result.

"Now, then, miss," she said, giving up the shaking as a bad job, "no highstrikes, *if* you please. Just you put on your hat and come for a bit of a walk in this queer place with me. I haven't brought you up by hand this two-and-twenty year or thereabouts, to see you go off in highstrikes, like a housemaid as has seen a ghost.

Angela stopped, and did as she was bid.

CHAPTER LXXVI.

ARTHUR read his letter, and his heart burned with passionate love of the true woman he had dared to doubt. Then he flung himself upon the grass and looked at the ocean that sparkled and heaved before him, and tried to think; but as yet he could not. The engines of his mind were reversed full speed, whilst his mind itself, with quick shudders and confusion, still forged ahead upon its former course. He rose, and cast upon the scene around him that long look we give to the place where a great happiness has found us.

The sun was sinking fast behind the mountains, turning their slabbed sides and soaring pinnacles to giant shields and spears of fire. Beneath their mass, shadows—forerunners of the night—crept over the forests and the crested rollers, whilst farther from him the ocean heaved in a rosy glow. Above, the ever-changing vault of heaven was of a beauty that no brush could paint. On a groundwork of burning red were piled, height upon height, deep ridges of purples and of crimsons. Nearer the horizon the colors brightened to a dazzling gold, till at length they narrowed to the white intensity of the half-hidden eye of the sun vanishing behind the mountains; whilst underlying the steady splendor of the upper skies flushed soft and melting shades of rose and lilac. Blue space above him was broken up by fantastic clouds that floated all on fire, and glowed like molten metal, The reflection, too, of all these massed and varied lights in the azure of the eastern skies was full of sharp contrasts and soft surprises, and a travelling eagle, sailing through space before them, seemed to gather all their tints upon his vivid wings, and, as he passed away, to leave a rainbow track of broken light.

But such a glory was too bright to last. The sun sank swiftly, the celestial fires paled, the purples grew faint and died, and, where they had been, night trailed her sombre plumes across the sea and sky.

But still the quiet glow of evening lingered, and presently a line of light was shot athwart it, cutting a track of glory across the shadowed sea, so weird and sudden, that it might well have been the first ray of a resurrection morn breaking in upon the twilight of the dead.

He gazed almost in awe, till the majestic sight stilled the tumult of his heart, and his thoughts went up in thanks to the Creator for the pure love he had found again, and which had not betrayed him. Then he looked up, and there, stately and radiant, standing out clear against the shadows, her face illumined by that soft yet vivid light, her trembling arms outstretched to clasp him—was his lost Angela.

He saw her questioning glances fall upon him, and the red blood waver on her cheek; he saw the love-lights gather in her eyes; and then he saw no more, for she was in his arms, murmuring sweet broken words.

Happy are those who thus shall find their Angela, whether it be here or—on the farther shore of yonder solemn sea.

And Mildred? She lay there before the stone symbol of inexorable judgement, and sobbed till the darkness covered her, and her heart broke in the silence.